CW00498003

THE HANGED WOMAN

MICHAEL BRADY BOOK 6

MARK RICHARDS

E S RICHARDS

AUTHORS NOTE

Mark Richards sadly passed away in September 2023, before his work on Michael Brady could be completed.

This book was picked up by his daughter, Elle, who completed the planning, writing and editing of what will be the final book in the Brady series.

Every effort has been made to ensure the book not only feels like it was written in one voice, but that it honours the work of Mark Richards and the legacy he has left behind through the Brady series.

Like all the Brady books, *The Hanged Woman* is set in and around Whitby, on the North Yorkshire Coast. British English has been used and the dialogue is realistic for the characters, which means they occasionally swear.

As this is a work of fiction, names, characters, organisations, some places, events and incidents are either products of the authors' imaginations, or used fictionally. All the characters in this book are fictitious. Any resemblance to actual persons, living or dead, is purely coincidental.

www.markrichards.co.uk

www.esrichards.com

ABOUT THE AUTHOR

I have always known I wanted to be a writer. I used to write my own bedtime stories as a child and give them to my parents to read to me. I would disappear up to my bedroom for hours at a time and come out with binders filled with stories. I've always known I could write, and both my mum and my dad encouraged me every step of the way.

After graduating from Sheffield University with a degree in Journalism and a masters in Marketing – I moved to Leeds and spent a couple of months searching for my first job. I didn't want to spend my days doing nothing, so I wrote.

Within a year I'd written and self-published my first dystopian trilogy: The Generation Series. The next time I was home for Christmas, my dad gifted me my website, which he'd had designed and built for me. This was just one of the many ways he always supported me and helped me to understand how much belief he had in my writing.

I then signed to an American indie publishing house and over a period of two years I wrote three rapid-release six book series: Solar Crash, Escaping Darkness & Wipeout.

However, this took its toll and after the publication of my 18th book with that publisher, I decided to take a break from writing until I could be inspired again.

That inspiration has now hit – but unfortunately, it's happened in the worst of circumstances. Losing my dad has helped me to get back into writing. It's been an incredibly difficult process finishing Brady 6 so quickly after his passing, but more than anything I've wanted to make him proud through my writing. And I really hope I've achieved that.

THE CLEVELAND WAY: APRIL 2017

She pulled the towel round herself.

As if pulling could make it bigger.

A faded, worn beach towel. Veteran of a hundred trips to the sea.

Pink, cream, yellow, pale blue stripes. Irregular white tassels at both ends.

Worn thin, a couple of holes.

Barely big enough to cover her.

She stared at him.

He stared back. His voice cold. Flat. Dispassionate.

"Your choice," he said. "They're the only clothes you're getting. And it's a long drive. Twenty miles. Long enough if you're naked. The towel doesn't cover much."

"And then you're going to kill me."

She'd known from the moment she saw him.

"Yes. You know that."

"Why?"

"You know that as well. You're not stupid."

"When?"

"Tonight. If the rain holds off. Wouldn't want to leave any footprints, would we?"

He turned to go. Stopped. Turned back to her.

"You're disappointed, aren't you? You're wondering why you're so calm. You thought you'd be angry. Fighting back. Swearing."

She carried on staring at him. Didn't speak.

"Don't be. That's how it is on Death Row. Screaming, wailing, crying like a baby, begging for mercy. That's Hollywood. B-movies. Real life is different." He gestured at the bare room. "This is real life."

He shook his head. "No-one tries to be heroic. Or funny. Or memorable. No famous last lines. They wait patiently. Wait for their turn to die. And now it's your turn." He shrugged. "Like I said, it's a long drive. I'd get dressed. But it's your choice."

"You should let me see someone. A priest. A vicar."

He laughed. "Say a prayer if you like. I'm sure you know some."

"How?" she said. "How are you going to kill me?"

"You'll find out soon enough." He smiled. "I like it though. It's apt. Fitting. Get dressed."

He turned. Walked out of the door.

She heard the lock click.

Let the beach towel fall to the floor. Crossed over to the bed. Picked up the top. Looked at the label.

Shook her head.

"Primark. Fuck me, I'm going to die in Primark."

Looked around the room for the thousandth time.

No carpet. No curtains.

Nothing sharp. No mirror she could break. Not even a light bulb.

"The window it is then."

She walked across the bare floorboards.

Looked at the old catch.

Wondered if she could do it.

Knew she had no choice.

That and the beach towel...

1

———

Michael Brady stood on the cliff edge. Looked out to sea. Felt the wind. Still closer to winter than summer.

Turned, bent down, ruffled the top of his Springer Spaniel's head.

"Two years today, Archie," he said. "Two years since I scattered her ashes."

Two years since I watched that red and white fishing boat. Two years since I watched the cloud of ash float away. Tried to see her face in it. Two years since I thought there'd never be enough time to heal...

Am I healed now?

Part of me.

But only part of me...

'*I need to know who killed her, Dad. Who took her from me. From both of us. Because... Out there. Somewhere out there. Is the person who killed her. And if I don't know... Well, I don't know if I can cope with that. And I don't know how you'll cope with that. Forever.*'

Brady pushed his daughter's words out of his head. Tried to pretend that he didn't already know she was right.

"Come on, mate. Time to get back. I need some breakfast. We can walk back along the beach. Watch the sun rise. Get to Dave's just as he's opening. First customer of the day, Archie. That's probably worth *two* sausages."

BRADY CLIPPED Archie's lead on. Walked up the slipway off Whitby beach. Past the bandstand.

Sitting there with Patrick. Gerry Donoghue.

Memories. One bad. One good...

Glanced across the harbour – dominated by the bright yellow hull of the dredger – to his house. Walked another 50 yards past the amusement arcades on Pier Road and stopped. Waited patiently while Dave served two hopeful-looking fishermen.

"Madness, Dave. Bloody madness."

"See someone's climbed out of bed on the wrong side. What's madness?"

"April. Frost on the beach. Easter a week away and there's frost on the beach. I'll come to Spain with you next winter."

"High pressure though isn't it? Frost on the beach is the price you pay for a beautiful day. An' it can stay like this for Easter n' all. Then six months' hard labour through to September. Any road, apart from frost on the beach, what's up?"

Brady laughed. "Nothing's up, Dave. Contrary to appearances I'm happy. Nothing to worry about except the weather. Whitby's behaving itself. I'm even up to date with Kershaw's e-mails."

"An' what about that girlfriend of yours? When's she back?"

"Tonight. I haven't seen her for three weeks."

Dave raised his eyebrows. "You'll have a bit of catching up to do then. I'll forget the bacon shall I? Double portion of oysters, Mr Brady? Bit o' lead in your gentleman's pencil?"

"You're fine. She says she's exhausted. Sixteen hour days getting the music for the film finished. Music for a wet Dublin street she says."

"Any good?"

"Very. What I've heard. Haunting. Atmospheric. But she's only sent me clips. Besides, what do I know about music? Less than zero."

"Here." Dave passed him a bacon sandwich over the counter. Looked down. Laughed as Archie stared up at him expectantly.

Shook his head.

"All my profits go on your dog, Mike. Sausage a day, it all mounts up. Then again if Siobhan's back I'll not see yous for a week. Romantic breakfasts in bed..."

"Dave, you know it and I know it. You can't have a romantic breakfast in bed if you own a Springer. He's either whining at the door or trying to climb in with you."

"So what's on the agenda today?"

"I am," Brady said.

"You are? I don't follow – "

"School. Last year – when Ash was having a few problems – I told the headmaster – "

"Head teacher these days, Mike. Even an old bugger like me knows that."

"I stand corrected. Anyway, I told him I'd happily give a talk. And he's called my bluff. Last day of term. They're having a careers day. So ten o'clock and I'm talking to Ash's year. Ash, her friends, her boyfriend. Obviously I've had my instructions."

"Don't embarrass her?"

"*Don't* embarrass me, Dad. *Don't* try and be funny. *Don't* wear an orange tie with a red shirt – "

"Green an' yellow stripes then?"

"Got it in one, Dave. That's the problem with young people. No sense of style. But they can tell the time. Or their phones can, so I'd best be off. Give her a lift to school."

"Then back home and find your red shirt?"

"Exactly. You're famous for your fashion sense, Dave. What do you think? Maybe the lime green tie…"

2

———

Michael Brady walked back along Pier Road. Past the Magpie, past Gypsy Sara's.

Still holding the secrets of all our futures. Still consulted by the rich and famous...

"Facts, Archie," Brady said out loud. "Facts and evidence. That's all we need, old son."

Crossed the swing bridge and turned left into Church Street.

Five minutes later took one last look across the harbour and put his key in the lock. Paused.

Two weeks and it's Ash's birthday. Two more years and she's old enough to drive. Another year and she's eighteen. Then she's off to uni.

So make the most of it...

SIGHED. Pushed the door open. Shouted upstairs. "Are you ready, Ash? Give me two minutes to find my orange tie and I'll be – "

Heard his phone ring. Unclipped Archie's lead. Pulled the phone out of his back pocket. Saw it was the station.

"Morning, Sue, what can I do for you?"

"Probably nothing, boss. There's been a report of a missing person out at Roxby – "

"Roxby? I should know where that is – "

"It's about two miles from Staithes, boss. On the road to Scaling Dam."

"Scaling Dam? That's more or less the Arctic Circle. Is it in our patch?"

"By about five miles. Five miles of Moors and sheep before you get to Cleveland."

"Sorry, Sue, I'm feeling unusually flippant this morning. A missing person..."

"Sarah Trueman. Used to be a teacher. Just coming up to fifty. Apparently she wasn't at church on Sunday. The vicar went round last night. And again this morning. And he says she's been away before, but she always lets someone know. Gets them to go in and feed her cats. Not this time. So he thought we ought to know."

"OK, who's in this morning?"

"Frankie's not in until later. She's got a doctor's appointment. Dan Keillor just walked in."

Brady laughed. "Dressed? Or is he committing indecent exposure in his cycling shorts again?"

"The latter, boss."

"Right. Tell him to get changed and take a drive out there. What'll it take him? Twenty minutes?"

"About that."

"OK. Phone the vicar, Sue. Tell him someone's on his way. And tell Dan I'll see him when he gets back. I've got to go. I'm late for school."

3

———

Brady had been talking for forty minutes. Twenty minutes from his notes: twenty minutes answering questions.

Was being a real policeman like being a policeman on TV?

No, there's never any paperwork on TV.

If you weren't in the police what would you be?

In a perfect world, manager of Middlesbrough.

Do you need to be intelligent to be a detective?

I'll leave you to be the judge of that...

"Just time for one more question before break."

Ash's boyfriend put his hand up.

"Spencer?"

Still looking like a young Clark Kent. How long now? Four months?

"Mr Brady, what's the worst thing about your job?"

Lying, Spence. Lying to people I love. Telling my daughter I'm going out for a walk when I know I'll come face-to-face with a killer. Getting tasered. Lying helpless on the edge of the cliff. Jimmy Gorse on the end of the pier...

"Unpredictability," Brady said. "But in many ways it's the worst thing – and the best. The worst because it means there are times when you make promises and can't keep them. When you let down people you care about. The best because... I never know what's going to happen. I'm never bored."

"So not like being a teacher?"

"Thank you, Darren."

The class comedian. There's always one.

"...And that's all we've got time for. I'm sure you'd all like to thank Mr Brady for giving up his valuable time."

Brady watched his daughter self-consciously applauding. Realised how much he'd enjoyed it. That he'd happily have answered questions for another 40 minutes. Shook hands with the head teacher. Said, yes, he'd be more than willing to do it again next year.

Drove back to the station.

Wondered what Dan Keillor had found at Roxby.

4

———

"Morning, Frankie. All OK?"

"That's your concerned voice, boss. I'm fine."

"Sue said you'd been to the doctor's."

Frankie nodded. Turned away from Brady. "Yes. Nine o'clock, in theory. But I'm fine, boss. Thank you for asking."

She's clearly not. But that's as much as she's going to tell me. And it's none of my business...

"I've sent Dan out to Roxby."

"Roxby? That's – "

"A couple of miles from Staithes. Population not very many. The vicar rang. Reported someone missing. A retired teacher called Sarah Trueman. So I've sent Dan to have a look." Brady looked at her. "You're sure you're OK, Frankie?"

She nodded. Wouldn't look him in the eye. "Never better, boss. Apart from paperwork, obviously."

"WHAT HAVE you got for me, Dan?"

Dan Keillor shook his head. "Nothing, boss. An empty

cottage. A nice one – bit isolated for me – but essentially an empty cottage."

"You meet the vicar there?"

"I did. The Reverend Croft. He was wearing jeans and a cricket jumper. I was – "

Brady laughed. "You were expecting one of Agatha Christie's vicars? Dog collar and amateur sleuth? I think the Church of England has moved on, Dan. I'm not even sure it's about God anymore. 'More relevant' or something."

The same attitude Kershaw has. Arresting criminals is fourth or fifth on his list...

"I don't know, boss. The vicar seemed a bit worried. Met me at the cottage. It's just across from the church. She'll need earplugs when the bells are ringing."

"OK, campanology aside, what did you see?"

Dan reached for his notebook. "Like I said, boss, it's a nice cottage. But it was empty. So all I can tell you is what I saw peering in through the windows. It's tidy. Neat – "

"Does she live alone?"

"The vicar said she did."

"What did your eyes tell you, Dan? If a woman lives on her own the house is neat. Tidy. Everything's put away. A man's the opposite. When I lived on my own I didn't see the point of cupboards. Tins of beans lined up on the worktop. I was going to eat them in two days. What was the point of putting them in the cupboard? All changed when Grace moved in, obviously."

Dan Keillor shook his head. "You're wrong, boss. 'Only dull women live in tidy houses.' That's what my mum used to say."

"Really? Does that extend to bedrooms? In which case my daughter is the most interesting person on the planet. So was there any sign of anyone else? Scratches on the door? Any sign of someone trying to break in?"

Keillor shook his head. "Nothing, boss. Just that it was really tidy. *Really* tidy."

"OK. What did Father Brown have to say?"

"Boss?"

Brady sighed. "Father Brown, Dan. G K Chesterton. Part priest, part detective. Developed a deep understanding of human wickedness by listening to confessions. Let's hope the Reverend Croft was similarly insightful."

"Maybe. She came to the village three or four years ago. The cottage belonged to her mother. The old lady died six months later. She re-decorated – the vicar said the place needed modernising – and carried on living there."

"Did he give you a description?"

Dan Keillor looked at his notebook. "Blonde hair. Down to her shoulders. Loosely permed. 'Sort of ringlets' were his exact words. Blue eyes. A few pounds overweight."

Brady nodded. "What did she do? She's what? Fifty?"

"Nearly. Croft said she'd taken early retirement from teaching. Ill-health he thought. And she'd travelled a bit before she came to Roxby."

"Where?"

"He said South America."

Brady raised his eyebrows. "That's a stretch. Rio to Roxby. Then again Middlesbrough signed a player from Sao Paulo, so anything's possible. Go on..."

"There's not much more to tell. Said she went to church most Sunday mornings. Got involved in a few events. Made apple chutney for the fundraisers. Other than that, lived fairly quietly."

"Friends?"

"No-one he mentioned specifically."

"So that was that? Retired teacher living on her own? That sounds... I don't know, she's not much older than me. She didn't do anything else?"

Dan Keillor shook his head. "The vicar didn't say anything. Except there was one other thing, boss."

"What's that?"

"Cats. There was a grey one mooching about. Didn't look over-friendly. And she'd left food out for them. Judging by the number of bowls the grey one had company."

"Did you ask the vicar about that?"

"I did. He said she usually asked someone to call in and feed them. If she was away for the weekend or anything."

"Not this time?"

"Not as far as he knew. It didn't look like it to me. I counted nine bowls. If someone's coming in they'd just use one bowl wouldn't they?"

"Two maybe, Dan. One for food, one for water. Did you ask the vicar how many she had?"

Dan Keillor shook his head. "Sorry, boss..."

Nine bowls. That has to be more than one. Two cats? Two days? Three days at the most. So if you went on Saturday you're due back today, Ms Trueman.

Or I'm going to start worrying about you...

5

"You had a cat, didn't you?" Michael Brady said to his sister.

"Max? You're going back a bit, but yes."

"What did you do if you went away?"

"On holiday you mean? He went to the cattery. Why? Are you – "

"Thinking of getting one? No. I've more than enough with Archie. Supposing you were just away overnight?"

Kate pursed her lips. "I'm not sure we ever were. Once, maybe, when Bill's sister got married. So we left his food out and asked Alison next door to keep an eye on him."

"So two bowls? Food and water?"

Kate nodded. "I thought you'd called in for a cup of tea, Mike? Is this the latest crime wave sweeping Whitby? People not leaving enough cat food out?"

"No. It's nothing. Something Dan Keillor said to me. A woman missing out at Roxby. Nothing important."

"Right. So drink your tea and tell me about my niece. Is she still seeing... What did you call him? Clark Kent junior?"

"I did. I was probably being unkind."

"How long now?"

"Four months. That's all. But…"

"But what?"

"I'm starting to worry."

"Worry. What have you got to worry about?"

"Supposing she's having sex with him, Kate?"

"*Is* she having sex with him?"

"How the hell do I know? Her room's at the top of the house. And I'm out. Walking Archie on the beach. I don't *think* so. But like I say…"

"Look, Mike, Ash is an attractive girl. More than attractive. She obviously gets it from her mother – "

"Thanks, Kate."

" – But she's sensible as well. And let me tell you, as the mother of two teenage girls, that a steady boyfriend – one you've met, who *talks* to you – is a far better bet than someone you've never met. Someone you don't know, who she sneaks out to meet. You're her dad. You're going to imagine things. You can't help that. But far better you imagine them in Ash's bedroom – in your house – than in a back alley down by the harbour. Anyway, do you like Spencer?"

Brady nodded. "I do. To tell you the truth, Kate, the more I see of him the more I like him. And he doesn't see that much of his dad. Ash says his parents split up about five years ago."

"So you're a father figure?"

Brady shook his head. "I don't know. That sounds… presumptuous, I guess. But I'm there if he wants to talk."

"What does he want to do?"

Brady laughed. "What are his prospects? Not sure we're at the *Pride and Prejudice* stage just yet."

"You know what I mean."

"Some sort of software engineer? For computer games? To be honest, Kate, he did explain but I wasn't bright enough to understand. But I can't help worrying. I worry that she's too young."

Kate shook her head. "Better the right boy at 15 than the wrong boy at 16 – and 17. Look at that one you had to rescue Maddie from. Tattooed bloody Ty. Dear God, I still wake up in a hot sweat in the middle of the night."

"I thought – "

"No, Mike. I can tell the difference between the menopause and a boyfriend I don't like. Anyway, I've something to tell you."

She's smiling. The girls? No, it's personal –

"Doug's asked me to marry him."

Brady stepped forward. Took her in his arms. Squeezed her. "Ah, Kate. That's lovely. I'm so pleased for you."

She pushed him away. Looked up at him. "I said 'no.' Or at least 'not yet.'"

"I – Why?"

"You don't know what to say? No, I'm not sure I do. He makes me laugh. He's got clean fingernails. All his own teeth. What more does a woman need? But it's too soon, Mike. It *feels* too soon. It's not much more than a year since Bill died. Lucy has her exams coming up." She shook her head. "I'm not ready. Not yet."

"How did he take it?"

Kate pursed her lips. Nodded. "He understood. Said he understood. Quite well, I think. He's booked flights for us to go to Italy. Bologna. The food capital of Italy. Says if I don't come back half a stone heavier he'll have failed."

"So he *does* understand?"

She nodded. "I hope so. He's been divorced for six years. Bill died... Well, you know when Bill died. And it takes time.

Part of me still thinks I'm Mrs Calvert. I like Doug. More than like him. I look forward to him coming round – "

"But you look forward to him going as well?"

"Yes. No, that sounds harsh. I look forward to having the house to myself. To being me. Doing what I want to do. Now I sound selfish."

Brady shook his head. "No. I understand. I'm the same. There are nights... Nights when I just want to sit on the balcony and think. Sometimes Siobhan's everything I want. Everything I need. But other times..."

Kate poured him some more tea. Nodded. "There are nights when you want to sit and think."

"Right. Watch Middlesbrough without feeling guilty."

"Wallow in depression."

"I didn't know you watched illegal football streams, Kate..."

"As if..." Kate sipped her tea. Looked at Brady over the rim of her cup. "Body clock," she said.

Brady laughed. "Which is my sister's not-very-subtle way of asking if my girlfriend wants children."

"She's past thirty, Mike..."

"The answer is 'no,' Kate. At least I think it is. Right now all her energy's going into this film. Finishing the music. I'm... I suppose 'impressed' is the word. She's driven. Focused."

"So she reminds you of yourself?"

"Does she? I hadn't looked at it that way. But if her body clock's ticking it's ticking very quietly. So quietly I can't hear it. But..."

"But what?"

"If you want me to be honest with you, I'm more worried about someone else's body clock."

"Whose?"

"Frankie's."

"Frankie? I saw her the other day. Bumped into her in the middle of the swing bridge."

"She had a doctor's appointment. When I asked her about it she didn't answer. Wouldn't look at me. And – "

"Mike, women are allowed to have a doctor's appointment without telling their boss what it's about."

"She was eating jelly babies. I've never seen her eat jelly babies."

Kate laughed out loud. Shook her head. "Christ, Mike, I nearly snorted Yorkshire Tea down my nose. So on the basis of a doctor's appointment and a packet of jelly babies, Mike Brady, ace detective, has concluded that Frankie is pregnant? I think I'll turn to crime..."

Brady shook his head, tapped the side of his nose. "The jelly babies are evidence, Kate. And there's previous. When Grace was pregnant she wanted pineapple with everything. A bacon sandwich with bloody pineapple."

"You'll need more than that, Mike. Go on with you. I need to go and collect Lucy. And you clearly need to arrest someone."

Brady stood up. Nodded at the worktop. "That container, Kate. Are those chocolate brownies in it?"

"They are. Baked by my own fair hand."

"Can I take one with me?"

"Why? Have you gone off bacon sandwiches?"

Brady shook his head. "It was Sue's birthday last month. She brought some brownies in." He winked at his sister. Reached for the brownies. "Frankie didn't have one. Said they were too sweet for her. So you're absolutely right. Mike Brady, ace detective. If Frankie has a brownie with her morning coffee I'll know, won't I?"

Kate laughed. "Here. Take two. Coffee and lunch. Then you'll be doubly sure, won't you?"

Brady smiled. Took the brownies from his sister. Heard his phone ring.

Glanced at the number. Sighed. Mouthed 'the station' at Kate.

"What's up, Sue?"

Listened. Didn't speak. Frowned.

Finally spoke.

"Where's Frankie? OK, ask her to collect me. I'm at Kate's. Is someone on their way? Jake? Fine. Thank you."

Looked at his sister. Didn't need to speak.

"What's happened?"

"Someone's found a body. Somewhere between May Beck and Falling Foss."

"The woman from Roxby?"

Brady shook his head. "I don't know. But the brownies will have to wait. Whoever she is she's hanging from a tree."

6

"What did Sue say?"

"There's a body. A woman's body. Hanging from a tree. Between May Beck and Falling Foss."

"Falling Foss? We used to go there as kids."

Brady nodded. Dropped down a gear and overtook a caravan. "Same. And I remember taking Ash. She must have been three or four. That age when they're young enough to demand daddy carries them back up the hill. And old enough to be bloody heavy."

"That's it? Hanging?"

"That's what Sue said."

"It could be suicide."

"You're right. In which case we've wasted a morning. But Sue said she listened to the tape. The people that found her. 'Something about their tone of voice, boss.'"

"On a sunny April morning as well."

Brady drove past the entrance to the potash mine. Shook his head. "There's a bloody blight on the landscape if there ever was one." Realised he was getting more and more protective of the Moors.

Braked. Indicated. Turned sharp left towards May Beck. Crossed the cattle grid. Braked again. Stopped the car and laughed.

"North Yorkshire, Frankie. A woman's hanging from a tree and we can't get there because there a bloody sheep in the middle of the road."

"Patience, boss. It's moving – "

"Bloody reluctantly. Sheep or no sheep I love this time of year."

"You lightening the mood?"

"Not deliberately. But I do. The gorse coming – "

"Despite the name?"

"Despite the bloody name. That's what I thought when I scattered Grace's ashes. Every spring the gorse comes into bloom. Bright yellow. Then the cherry blossom. Not on the cliff top I grant you. Ash's birthday around the corner."

"Favourite time of year?"

"Absolutely my favourite time of the year. Anything ever happens to me, Frankie, don't bother with a police funeral. I don't want all that bollocks. Just plant a gorse bush and a cherry tree."

"That's a bit morbid for a sunny morning, boss."

"Maybe." Another sheep. Brady drove up onto the grass verge. "I've got a bad feeling about this. Between May Beck and Falling Foss? It's about a mile isn't it? So someone's walked half a mile to commit suicide? I don't think so."

"May Beck's on the Coast to Coast isn't it?"

"You think some poor bloody walker couldn't face the last five miles to Robin Hood's Bay? A hundred and ninety miles and they'd had enough? I'll settle for that, Frankie.

Maggie Stokes last year. Getting tasered. That bloody madman at Christmas. Whitby's had enough for one year."

"We're hardly downtown LA, boss."

Brady passed the entrance to the caravan park. The road started to drop downhill. Bent right and then immediately left round an isolated farmhouse.

"May Beck," he said. "It must be quieter than the car park at Falling Foss. Are the cavalry on their way?"

Frankie nodded. "Anya for sure."

"Phone Paul will you, Frankie? Like I said, I've got a bad feeling about this."

"I thought you didn't do feelings, boss? Cold, hard evidence."

"Maybe I'm getting old."

Ferns on the left, the road dropping away to the valley on their right. Brady reached the bottom of the hill. Turned right across the bridge. Right again into the car park.

A police car. Two camper vans. Brady nodded through the windscreen. "A VW Camper. I used to want one of those. When I was about eighteen."

"Orange and white? It's a van that needs a surfboard on top."

"Surfboard or not you've got to love each other."

Frankie laughed. "You've got to love each other?"

"Bloody right. Two people in a van that size? Probably throw in a dog as well? It wouldn't work for me. Or maybe it's more evidence of old age. Wanting my space."

Brady climbed out of the car. Saw Jake Cartwright fastening crime scene tape to one of the trees. Start to stretch it across the car park.

"Morning, Jake," Brady said. Smiled. Nodded at the PC's face. "It's coming on then."

Jake Cartwright laughed. "The beard, boss? Girlfriend's idea. I'm too fair. But what can you do?"

"Cordon it all off will you, Jake? The whole car park. Put something across the road as well. Make sure no-one comes anywhere near. Where's Dan?"

"Falling Foss, boss. Doing the same at the other end."

Brady nodded. "Bang on the door of the camper vans. Find out which one phoned it in. And run a check on the reg numbers as well. Then tell them to stay put until Frankie and I get back."

Brady turned to her. Black leather jacket. Black jeans. "You ready, Frankie? Let's do this."

7

———

They crossed back over the bridge. Turned left along the footpath. More ferns on the right. Trees between them and the beck.

"How deep is it?"

"The beck. Not deep enough, boss. If you're wondering if she could have drowned herself."

"You know me too well, Frankie."

The occasional gorse bushes in among the ferns. The flowers a paler yellow than on top of the hill. Faded, as though someone had adjusted the settings. Opened the control panel. Turned the brightness down.

The trees on their left cleared. Gave them a view of the beck, running over the stones.

"Bring the kids," Brady said. "Have a picnic. Play Pooh sticks on the bridge."

"While the weather's good? How long since it rained? A week? Two? So much for April showers."

Brady nodded. Stepped onto the grass to avoid some stones in the middle of the path. Wondered how much further they'd have to walk.

'Not much' was the answer.

THE PATH BENT slightly to the right. Opened out into a clearing. Stone steps at the far end.

One tree standing alone in the centre.

The trunk was split at the base.

Lightning? Two trees in one...

A branch was coming off the left hand trunk. Eight, maybe nine feet from the ground. Growing at a 45 degree angle before bending abruptly, running parallel to the ground. Another ten feet before a few desultory leaves on the end.

A woman's body hanging from the branch.

Upside down.

Swaying gently in the breeze.

Tied by her right ankle. The rope going up and over the branch.

Diagonally down to a much smaller tree at the side of the beck. Wound round and round the trunk.

Neither of them spoke.

Stood.

Stared.

Red jeans. Blue jacket.

What do I call that? Cornflower blue?

Frankie finally spoke. "We can rule out suicide."

Brady nodded. Forced himself to speak. "Blonde hair. Sort of ringlets. A few pounds overweight."

"So it's Sarah Trueman."

"Bloody hell. I thought Billy and Sandra was bad enough. This... She must have been able to see it, Frankie."

"The rope?"

"Wanted to reach out and untie it. Except..."

Her hands were fastened behind her back. Her blonde hair falling straight to the ground.

Brady shook his head. Was silent again. Stared up at the body.

Shivered.

Pulled his coat round him.

Turned. Looked at Frankie.

"Her left leg..."

Her left leg was bent. Her foot behind her right leg, just above the knee.

A number four. That's what she is.

An upside down number four.

"What is it?" Brady said.

"The tree? Birch? Elm? I don't know. It doesn't make any bloody difference to her."

Sarah Trueman.

Still swaying gently in the early morning breeze...

Frankie took a step forward. Careful not to trip over the tree roots.

Tilted her head to look up at the body.

"We're in trouble here, boss."

Brady didn't speak. Stepped forward and stood next to Frankie.

Blonde hair. Sort of ringlets. Blue eyes.

Blue eyes that are bulging. Blue eyes that want to go on living...

"Homework," Brady said. "He did his homework. Made plans. Went to a lot of trouble."

Frankie nodded. "All that and more. He sure as hell isn't going to hand himself in."

Brady took another pace forward. Could have reached up and touched her face.

'Did his homework. Made plans. Went to a lot of trouble.'

You did.

Michael Brady nodded to himself.

Challenge accepted, you bastard.

8

B rady reached for his phone. Opened contacts. Rang Geoff Oldroyd.

"Geoff? We're at May Beck. Five minutes along the path from the car park. Sarah Trueman. The woman from Roxby who went missing. I'm certain it's her. She's hanging from a tree. No, I don't want to say any more. I want you to see her. I want your first impressions. No, Geoff. Whatever Mr Victory died of he'll have to wait. Put him back in the fridge. And Geoff? If you've got any brandy down there in the underworld you might want to bring it with you."

GEOFF OLDROYD – blunt, bluff Yorkshireman – stood and stared at the body.

Carried on staring. Spoke to Brady without turning round.

"Cause of death's not a problem then, Mike."

"I'm guessing it's suffocation?"

"Maybe. But a madman, Mike. A fucking madman is the

cause of death. But you know that. You want the medical details? They'll have to wait 'til we've cut the poor lass down. You're probably right with suffocation. There's a couple of other options though. But that's your cause of death. A fucking madman hung her upside down from a birch tree."

"Birch? Frankie and I weren't sure."

"Birch, ash, oak, giant bloody redwood. It's irrelevant isn't it?" Geoff shook his head. Looked back at the body. "Bloody hell, Mike, some work went into this."

"How did he get her here, Geoff? Carried her? Five minutes from the car park?"

Geoff pursed his lips. "Maybe. He'd need to be a big, strong lad. Then again he'd need to be bloody strong to haul her up there." Geoff paused. "Don't like to say it but he might have drugged her. Date rape drug. So she could walk."

Brady nodded. Tried to push the image out of his head.

Sarah Trueman. Staggering along the path. The killer steering her by the elbow. 'Not long now, love. Just round this corner...'

"Mike?"

"Sorry, Geoff. I was trying to picture it."

Trying not to picture it...

"I was saying this is serious, Mike. Meticulous. Planned. It's your job to catch him. I don't envy you."

"Meticulous is right, Geoff. Hung like that, though. Upside down. Was she certain to die? Absolutely certain?"

"It's likely, Mike. *Almost* certain. But you want certainty you shoot someone. You don't leave them hanging upside down and go home for your tea."

Bloody hell. Are we back with Diane Macdonald? Maggie Stokes? 'I let the fates decide.'

"He wouldn't do that," Frankie said. "He can't hang her up and leave. Supposing someone comes?"

"Courting couple, Frankie? Some sad bugger out for a walk on his own – "

"Turning a murder case over and over in his head? You've got your balcony for that, boss."

Geoff shook his head. "He's probably safe. What time's that café at Falling Foss close at this time of year? Four? And it's April. Sunset at eight o'clock. The dog walkers are long gone."

"And it's a school day. No families."

"He's still taking a risk. A calculated risk."

"What are we saying, boss? He stayed there until it got dark? Watching her?"

"Or watching for other people, Frankie. Prepared to make sure no-one disturbed his handiwork."

"He's prepared for collateral damage? Casualties of war?"

"I don't know. Another question for you. The vicar said she wasn't in church on Sunday. So she goes missing on Saturday. Today's Wednesday. Where's she been held? *Why* has she been held for three days?"

"Like I said, Mike. It's your job to catch him. I don't envy you."

"We need to get back," Brady said. "Talk to the people who found her. You alright, Geoff? Anya and Paul are on their way. Alan Swinbank will be back in a minute."

"I'm good, Mike. I'll have a long, hard look at her. Have a word with Anya."

Brady nodded. "I'll send Dan Keillor as well. What did you say, Geoff? 'A big, strong lad?' That's Dan. And some poor sod's got to lift her down."

9

"What did I say, Frankie? Half an hour ago? Bring the kids? Have a picnic? Play Pooh sticks? Seeing her there... I'm numb. Emotionally bloody numb."

Do I say this? Should I say this?

"I'm starting to take it personally, Frankie. Billy and Sandra. Diane Macdonald. More and more I'm taking it personally."

"I thought you were dispassionate, boss? Cold, hard evidence?"

"How the hell can you be dispassionate? She's someone's daughter. Someone's sister. Maybe she's got a partner. A boyfriend."

"So we have to find the killer."

"We *will* find the killer, Frankie."

Yes, I do say this...

"You know what I thought back there? When we were standing looking at her? Not speaking?"

"What, boss?"

"Four words. 'Challenge accepted, you bastard.'"

"How long do you think he stayed?"

"Is that you changing the subject, Frankie? Watching the
_ "

Brady suddenly stumbled. Hopped on one foot. Winced. Swore.

"Ouch! Shit!"

"What've you done?"

"Turned my ankle on a bloody tree-root. Not looking at the path."

"Ice."

"Not before we talk to whoever found the body. Jesus that hurts. How long do I think he stayed? Like Geoff said, long enough. Long enough to make sure no-one came along the path."

"We're back," Frankie said. "The bridge. The car park. The people who found the body. You ready for this?"

Brady nodded. "Always ready. You think they've got a kettle in the camper van? I could do with a cup of tea. And a couple of paracetamol."

Brady looked at the faded camper van. Wasn't optimistic.

10

A white van, badly in need of a respray.

The dashboard littered with a collection of coffee cups and screwed-up sandwich bags a builder would have envied.

Faded blue waves along the side. A dent above one of the wheel arches, rust spreading ominously. 'Myrtle' stencilled on the door.

Camper van? Mobile home? Somewhere between the two. And Myrtle's seen better days. Much better days...

Brady glanced at Frankie. Raised his eyebrows. "Sign of the times," he said. "Finding a body? Dog walkers are out. Camper vans are in."

Knocked on the door.

How many times have I done this? The poor buggers who found her...

Brady looked up at the woman who opened the door.

Cropped blonde hair. A pinched face. Uneven teeth. A dressing gown over a pink jumper.

"Mrs Lindsay? Detective Chief Inspector Michael Brady. Detective Sergeant Thomson."

She nodded. "Carol."

Brady held his hand out. Carol Lindsay raised a hand that was holding a chipped blue and white mug.

'Sorry. Can't shake hands. I'm drinking tea.'

Fair enough...

"We've obviously come to talk about... Well, what you found this morning."

She nodded. Turned her head. Shouted into the van. Didn't have to project her voice very far. "Rob, coppers are here. Warm your tea up an' come an' talk."

She stepped forward onto the first of the two steps. Forced Brady and Frankie to step back.

"You don't want to talk inside?"

"Not enough room is there? Two person van. One person really. Like my dad said. 'You're marrying t'runt of t'litter, lass.' Handy in a small van though."

Rob Lindsay emerged, another blue and white mug clasped in his hand. Stood slightly behind his wife, a good six inches shorter than she was. Jeans, a washed-out grey hoodie. A man who'd accepted his position in the marital pecking order.

"You were out early..." Brady prompted.

"Mushrooms," Carol Lindsay said. She nodded her head at her husband. "He'd seen something on telly. Some bugger foraging. Knew what he was foraging for, didn't he? I said to him, 'Course I'm coming with you, before you pick bloody toadstools an' kill us both.'"

"This is early? Just after sunrise?"

"Just after first cuppa of the day. Stupid o'bloody clock. But neither of us could sleep. Bloody birds starting up."

Mrs Lindsay, why park your camper van at May Beck if you don't like hearing birds in the morning...

"You're walking along the path..."

"That bit where it goes uphill. 'Keep up,' I said to him. He's only got little legs. And then we round the corner an' there she is. Hanging up like a pheasant outside a butcher's shop. 'Fresh local game birds.' That's what me uncle used to write on his sign. Exactly what I thought of. Done up like a pheasant."

"Is that how you remember it, Mr Lindsay?"

'What my wife says.' I already know the answer before –

Rob Lindsay shook his head. "It was the stillness," he said. "We're walking. You can hear noise. The birds. Then we turn the corner. And she's hanging. Just hanging. And no noise. Like suddenly the birds are paying their respects."

– Which tells me how much I know about human nature...

"You didn't touch her?"

Rob had been allowed his thirty seconds of fame. "We watch telly, don't we?" his wife said. "Know a crime scene when we see one."

"You didn't take photos?"

She shook her head. "Didn't even think about it. Would've been a good 'un though. Light filtering through the trees."

Which means you did...

"Besides, we're not ghouls. Not like some people. That café at Falling Foss, they'll do alright from it. Once you've caught him. Spread a rumour the woods are haunted. That's what I'd do. That'll bring 'em in."

Twenty years of interviewing witnesses to murder. The first one who sees it as a business opportunity...

"You didn't see anyone? Anything that looked out of place?"

Another shake of the head. "Step-ladder. Think we'd have noticed. Weren't really looking though. 'Cos once you've seen her you forget everything else don't you?"

"Mr Lindsay?"

"What she said. Just her hanging there. And the silence."

"What about last night? Did you see anything? A car? A van like yours?"

Carol Lindsay shook her head. "Had a flat tyre didn't we? Spent an hour in that car park. Hole of Horcum is it?"

It is. Where Jimmy Gorse and I had a 'wee chat...'

"So we didn't get here 'til nine. Didn't see anything."

Was he still in the woods? Did he see the lights of the camper van coming down the hill...

Carol Lindsay looked at Brady. "Cut the poor lass down have you?"

Brady nodded. "We will do. So we can do the post-mortem." He reached into his pocket. Handed her a business card. "If you think of anything else. Both my numbers are on there."

She took the business card. Looked at it suspiciously. Put it in the pocket of her dressing gown.

"We'll need your contact details," Brady said. "There's a good chance we'll need to talk to you again. Sergeant Thomson will jot them down."

Brady didn't offer to shake hands. Didn't want to lose out to a mug of tea a second time. "One more thing," he said. "I know you didn't take photos. And you look like sensible people. But please don't speak to the press. This is a murder investigation. And I don't want it hampering. By anyone."

Carol Lindsay nodded. Pulled Brady's business card out of her pocket. Squinted at it.

"How much?" she said.

What? How much for not speaking to the press –

"How much do we get?"

"I'm not sure I follow you, Mrs Lindsay. There are no rewards for finding a body."

"Compo. Compensation. We're victims of crime, aren't we? Traumatised. Look at him, you can see he's traumatised."

If your husband's traumatised it's not by finding Sarah Trueman...

"We'll likely have nightmares. So how much?"

Brady shook his head. "Compensation is paid to relatives, Mrs Lindsay. No-one else. Thank you for your help this morning. I really appreciate it. But unless you were related to the victim... I'm sorry."

"What about counselling then? We'll need that an' all. *And* we came straight back. Didn't find no mushrooms."

Brady shook his head. Walked away. Left Frankie to get their details.

Sitting on my balcony at three in the morning. Seeing Sarah Trueman hanging in front of me. What's the compo for that?

Catching the bloody killer...

11

―――――――――

"What did you make of that?"

"What they said? Their thwarted search for mushrooms? Or the demands for compensation? Compo, sorry."

"What they said. If we start talking about compensation I'll start ranting. I mean seriously, Frankie, what is wrong with people? Sarah bloody Trueman hanging upside down, clearly murdered and that bloody woman wants to phone Murder-Victims-For-U. Like all that matters is what impact it has on her.

"*Traumatised*? She wants to talk about being traumatised? I'd say living in a camper van that's the size of a sardine tin with a woman like her is being traumatised. Poor bugger might only have – what did she say? – short little legs but he needs to use them to run away as fast as he can. Why can people not accept that sometimes shit happens? That sometimes they're unlucky? Just in the wrong place at the wrong time? That accidents happen. That not everything is somebody's fault. That – "

"Boss?"

"What Frankie?"

"You're ranting."

Brady shook his head. "I'm sorry. You're supposed to get more tolerant as you get older. I'm going the other way. And I've waved the white flag. Finally accepted I need reading glasses. I'm at the opticians on Saturday morning."

Frankie nodded. "Only a matter of time before Ash is phoning the chair lift people..."

"I can't wait. Sorry. My personal feelings on Mrs Lindsay are irrelevant. Was she telling the truth? Yes. Did she have anything useful to say? No."

"Nice analogy..."

"Pheasants hanging up outside the butcher's shop? Right. So how much compo are we entitled to for that, Frankie? Can't go to the butcher's any more? What about tomorrow morning when Geoff tells us how she died? What – "

"Boss. Ranting..."

"Sorry. Two choices, Frankie. He parked at May Beck or he parked at Falling Foss. He's closer to May Beck so that's the obvious conclusion."

"There's a third choice."

"What's that?"

Frankie nodded at the road. "Just up the hill. There's a passing place. Supposing he's pulled in there?"

"Made her walk down the hill?"

"Why not? If someone sees the car what are they going to think? A couple of teenagers..."

"And the Lindsay's probably aren't going to notice. They've changed a wheel. They're tired – "

"Arguing."

"Right. Car park or just up the hill, Frankie. That theory

of Geoff's – he made her walk." Brady nodded. "It makes sense."

"Rohypnol? The date rape drug?"

Brady nodded. "One of my many worries with Ash. I'm worried she's having sex with Spencer. I'm worried when she goes to a party with her friends. I was reading about it the other day. Geoff's right. Rohypnol would work. She could walk. Anyone sees them – "

"They just think she's drunk. And even if by some chance she survives she can't remember."

"What about the three days he kept her? Unless he's had her drugged up from Saturday to Tuesday?"

Frankie shook her head. "No. Her clothes. They looked new. I don't think she was mistreated."

"Just murdered? I think that counts as being mistreated..."

12

_____

"We need to get back, Frankie. I have to tell the vicar. He reported her missing."

"So he gets to identify the body?"

Brady nodded. "Someone has to. And right now he's the only volunteer."

"Reverend Croft. My name is Michael Brady. Detective Chief Inspector Michael Brady."

There was no reply.

Then Brady heard a sigh.

"Good morning, Inspector. And very clearly it isn't a good morning. You're phoning to tell me you've found Sarah Trueman."

A hint of a Lancashire accent. An upmarket Fred Dibnah. Burnley? No, Bolton.

And a statement, not a question.

But he reported her missing. Why else would I phone him?

"I am," Brady said. "And you're right. It's not a good morning."

As far from a good morning as you can get...

"Ms Trueman was found this morning at May Beck – "

"May Beck? That's – "

"South of Whitby. Sixteen or seventeen miles from Roxby."

And you know what comes next...

"I'm very sorry to tell you that she's dead. And to use the well-worn police cliché, we suspect foul play."

Hung upside down. Hands tied behind her back. About as foul as foul play can get...

"I... I don't know what to say. My first parish. Rochdale." His voice was faltering. On the point of breaking. "We had... Someone... What you're going to tell me..."

Murder. He can't say the word...

"Reverend Croft. I am truly sorry to tell you the news. And I can only apologise again. I have something else to ask you."

And there's no gentle way to do it...

"I'm led to believe Sarah Trueman lived alone. You reported her missing. You clearly knew her reasonably well. We need someone to formally identify the body."

"In Whitby?"

"Yes, in Whitby."

"It will take me twenty minutes. Half an hour."

A different tone of voice. Gone onto auto-pilot. A defence mechanism. And not a good idea to drive.

"There's no rush. I know this has come as a massive shock to you. Perhaps wait a while? If there's someone who can drive you?"

"There's a coffee morning. At the church hall. One of the ladies – "

"That sounds like a good idea..."

Brady ended the call as gently as he could. Looked up at Frankie. "The vicar's coming. The badly shaken vicar."

"A small parish, boss. He's bound to be shaken. What is it, the Parable of the Lost Sheep? The shepherd's got a flock of a hundred? He leaves the ninety-nine and goes looking for the one lost sheep? That must be about the population of Roxby."

Brady nodded. "A hundred and twenty, I checked. Even so…"

"Everyone's going to know her."

"They will." Brady sighed. Tapped his middle finger on the desk. "Logic says the answer will be in the village. I'm tempted to do the house-to-house myself, Frankie. Take you out there. We could do it in a day."

"Except you can't. *We* can't."

"Right. Because if I don't delegate how do Dan and Jake ever learn anything?"

"When's the vicar coming?"

"When the ladies have finished drinking coffee and eating lemon drizzle cake. I told him not to drive. So around lunchtime is my guess."

lightly taller than Brady. Balding, wire-rimmed glasses, pale blue eyes, an angular face.

'He was wearing jeans and a cricket jumper, boss.'

Not for identifying a body.

A dark suit, black clerical shirt, a white dog collar. A simple, wooden crucifix hanging low round his neck.

Brady shook hands.

"You didn't drive?"

"I took your advice. Mrs Archer is waiting in the car."

A voice that sounds even more educated than it did on the phone.

The posh part of Bolton then...

The vicar looked at Brady. "No time like the present, I suppose?"

Brady nodded. "As I said, I'm very sorry to ask this. But as she lives alone – "

"And doesn't have any family."

Doesn't she? Thank you for that...

"Yes. You obviously know her well. I'm sorry, I should

introduce you. Geoff Oldroyd, our pathologist. Geoff will be doing the post-mortem."

Reverend Croft nodded. "A necessary evil."

"A very necessary evil. Geoff will lift the sheet back, Reverend. All you need to do is say yes or no."

Geoff reached his hand out to move the sheet covering the body. Croft stepped forward. Held Geoff's wrist.

"Before you do that. Whether it's Sarah... Whoever it is. Let me pray for her."

Brady glanced at Geoff. Nodded. Realised he didn't know what to do. Self-consciously clasped his hands in front of him. Bowed his head.

I'm back in the school assembly.

My father's funeral. Bill's funeral.

"May Christ who was crucified for you bring you freedom and peace. May Christ who died for you admit you into the garden of paradise. May Christ, the true Shepherd, acknowledge you as one of his flock. May He forgive all our sins, and set you among those He has chosen. Amen."

Brady took a step forward. The vicar turned. Held his hand up. Turned back to Sarah Trueman's body.

He must know it's her...

"Saints of God come to her aid. Hasten to meet her, angels of the Lord. With God there is mercy and fullness of redemption."

He paused. Leaned forward slightly. Put his hand on her shoulder.

"Lord God, we have sinned against you; we have done evil in your sight. We are sorry and repent. Have mercy on us according to your love. Wash away our wrongdoings and cleanse us from our sin. Renew a right spirit within us and restore us to the joy of your salvation. Through Jesus Christ our Lord. Amen."

"Amen," Brady and Geoff self-consciously said in unison.

Brady stepped forward. For the second time Steven Croft shook his head.

Now what?

"Now let us pray as Jesus taught us. Our Father..."

Brady mumbled his way through the Lord's Prayer. Waited ten seconds after 'Amen.' Glanced at Steven Croft. Saw him nod at Geoff.

Saw him lift the pale green sheet back. Saw Steven Croft look down at the body. Show no reaction. No emotion.

Then suddenly sway.

Retch.

Rush for the door.

14

———

"That's a first, Mike. Prayers over the body."

"You think it was for himself as much as for her? His way of steeling himself to look at the body?"

"I thought we were going to lose him for a minute."

Brady nodded. "He was OK. Sue got him a glass of water. I talked to him outside."

"The handkerchief in her mouth?"

"I think so. I didn't notice it at May Beck. Too busy looking at the ropes. The angle of her leg. Wondering if he had a degree in engineering."

"Me too. Not 'til we got her down. Completely filled her mouth."

"So no chance of screaming? Calling for help?"

Geoff shook his head. "None at all. None whatsoever. You'll be face-to-face with the bastard one day, Mike. I don't envy you."

"I'm looking forward to it, Geoff. And there'll be none of that second prayer nonsense."

Geoff laughed. "Wash away our wrongdoings? I thought that when he said it."

Brady shook his head. "Not a bloody chance. We'll catch him. Listen to the satisfying click of the handcuffs. Let the courts deal with the wrongdoings. Sarah Trueman hanging there? Twisting in the wind? That's going to stay with me for a bloody long time – "

"Stay with all of us, Mike."

Brady nodded. "Sorry, Geoff, I was being selfish."

"Where do you go from here?"

"Right now? Upstairs. Talk to Anya. Then organise the troops. The house-to-house." Brady shook his head. "I was talking to Frankie. Told her I was tempted to do it myself. Well, me and Frankie."

"But you can't."

"I can't, Geoff. Because if Jim Fitzpatrick hadn't trusted me... That's management isn't it? Giving them the freedom to make mistakes. Between you and me, Geoff, I'm getting worse at delegating as I get older, not better."

"Or maybe you want it clearing up."

Brady shook his head. "Long haul this one, Geoff. Right now I can think of a hundred questions."

"How many answers have you got?"

"Two. And both of them are probably wrong."

Brady walked over to the table. Lifted the green sheet back. Looked down at Sarah Trueman. Tried not to see the handkerchief in her mouth.

Slowly shook his head. Sighed.

"I'll leave you to it, Geoff. No chance of getting her finished today?"

"Not a hope. Today and a bloody good chunk of tomorrow."

"So what you're saying is I'll owe you a pint of Doom by tomorrow night?"

Geoff shook his head. "Long post-mortem? Suspected drug use? The wife away at her sister's? Could be more than one, Mike. And a bag of pork scratchings..."

15

"There's a boot print, boss."

Brady looked up. "Seriously?"

Anya nodded.

"Brilliant. Bloody brilliant. It's a Tibetan marching boot, right? Hand-made for the Dalai Lama and his personal bodyguard. Only six made every year and individually numbered on the sole. Tell me I'm right."

"Mountain Warehouse, boss. Their most popular range. Yours for fifty-nine ninety-nine. Ideal for walking the dog."

Brady nodded. "Or for walking along the path by May Beck and leaving a totally useless footprint."

He's done his homework. Knows he can't avoid leaving some trace. So he's left the most obvious trace he can.

"How many pairs of those boots do you think they've sold in the last year?"

Anya shrugged. "Thousands. Tens of thousands."

Brady nodded. "And then some. And if he's paid cash – which he will have – there's no trace."

"Nothing else, boss. No cigarette ends, no ripped clothing hanging from a bush."

"No distinctive tyre tracks in the car park?"

Anya shook her head. "Nothing, boss."

"We were wondering how he got her there. The simplest solution is always the most likely. We think she walked. Or staggered. Geoff's bet me a pint of Doom he's going to find traces of a date rape drug in her system."

"Rohypnol?" Anya shook her head.

Blinked away a tear?

"That happened to a friend of mine at uni. She's... I was going to say she's never been the same. A slightly irrelevant comment where Sarah Trueman's concerned. The worst thing... The worst thing is that someone could have seen her. And they wouldn't have done anything."

Brady nodded. "'You alright, mate?' 'Yeah, wife's not feeling too good. She'll be fine.'"

"He did it in the union bar. Walked out with her. Maybe a hundred people saw them together. No-one did anything."

"Did he get convicted?"

Anya shook her head. "The case collapsed. Lack of evidence. The police lost it. His father was well-connected in Glasgow. It won't be the last time."

"So Sarah Trueman walked into the woods with her killer. Maybe she was seen. I doubt it. You know what the poem says. 'The woods are lovely, dark and deep.' Or words to that effect."

"You can see the marks on the ground," Anya said. "Maybe you and Frankie didn't. No disrespect, boss – "

Brady laughed. "Don't worry. But you can see them if you know what you're looking for?"

She nodded, "He laid her on her back. Tied her by her ankle. Threw the rope over a branch. Pulled her up. Swept her along the floor for two or three feet. Like you said, if you know what you're looking for. And the back of her jacket. Very clearly pulled along the ground."

Brady nodded. Didn't speak. Looked out of his window. Saw the tree. Saw Sarah Trueman lying on the ground.

Did she know what was happening? See the rope go over the branch?

Or was she drugged?

Two or three tugs to make sure it was secure. Then he pulls her up. Except...

"What about her hands?" Brady said. "They were tied behind her back."

Anya shook her head. "Almost certainly after she was off the ground. More than almost certainly. Definitely. Her hands were clean. No traces of dirt. Nothing. I don't think Geoff will find anything under her fingernails. He might find that they were tied twice though. Once in front of her so he could pull her up. Then behind her back like we found her. That's my best guess."

"So she's hanging there. Upside down. He's pulled her up high enough so she can't scrape the floor. Can't grab for the rope."

Anya nodded. "If she's been drugged she wouldn't think about it, boss. My friend. That's what destroyed her. Feeling that she let it happen. Didn't fight."

"So then he unties and reties her hands – "

Why was it so important they were tied behind her back?

"He used cable ties. A fiver on Amazon. Or any garden centre. My dad uses them to fasten his tomatoes to a stake."

" – And does the same with her left leg?"

"A knot this time. But the sort of rope you can buy anywhere."

"What about the rope he used to hang her?"

"The same. Buy it anywhere. We could walk down to the harbour and find it on a dozen boats."

Brady nodded. Looked at her. "What about you, Anya? Are you alright?"

She nodded. "Geoff stayed with me. Dan Keillor was there. Paul and his camera."

Brady smiled. "Right. Wherever you are Paul can't be far behind."

"So yeah, I'm OK. It just reminded me of that friend of mine."

"Any time you want to talk. Me. Frankie. We're always here. Don't bottle it up."

"I won't, boss."

Brady nodded. "I need to brief the troops. Get the house-to-house organised. You want to sit in? Or do you want to write your notes up?"

She shook her head. Not for the first time surprised Brady with her resilience. "I'll sit in, boss, if that's alright. We need to catch him quickly, don't we? That's what you always say."

I do. But this time I have my doubts...

16

Brady perched on the corner of a desk in the main office. "We few," he said. "We happy few. We band of brothers. And sisters. You've heard me say it before. We're a small team. York, Scarborough. Whitby's always at the back of the queue when it comes to resources. So it's just us. David and Goliath. Or in this case, David and the bloody madman who murdered Sarah Trueman."

He looked round the room. Frankie, Dan Keillor, Jake Cartwright and Anya.

'We happy few,' is right. In Manchester I had two football teams. Here I've barely got enough for a five-a-side...

"I'll draft in as much extra help as we need," he said. "But right now it's us. And it's Brady's Rules. Nothing's off limits. No idea is too stupid. You say something, it sparks an idea from someone else. So let's go – "

And that's where I win. Because I don't have a room full of jaded, cynical, seen-it-all-before coppers. I don't have half a dozen too-terrified-to-speak new recruits. I've a tight-knit team...

" – let's try and establish some sort of timeline. She

leaves her house on Saturday or Sunday. Dan, you're absolutely sure on the bowls for the cats?"

Dan Keillor nodded. "Nine, boss. I counted, there were so many."

"So nine bowls. Two cats? Three cats?"

"She can't be gone long, boss. The food will go off."

"Water," Anya said. "She'd have left water for them as well."

"Good point. So what are we saying? A day? Day and a half? Either way she's going to be away overnight. Which suggests she's meeting someone?"

"Not necessarily a man, boss. Friends. Away day at a spa? Something like that."

"Saturday night? Is Saturday a normal day for that? I thought that was more a mid-week thing?"

What the hell do I know? I could live to a hundred and not go to an away day at a spa...

"Did she *always* go to church, boss?"

"The vicar said most Sundays, Dan. Often enough for him to be surprised when he doesn't see her. Enough for him to walk round on Monday night. Vicarage to the church. I'm guessing that's not far?"

"Two hundred yards. At the most."

Frankie shook her head. "It doesn't make sense, boss? If she's meeting someone he picks her up. Any woman, she's going on a date, the guy picks her up. He doesn't say, 'walk to the end of the road and I'll collect you there.'"

"Not this time," Dan said. "There's a path from her house to the road, Frankie. Twenty, thirty yards."

"So he's waiting for her in the car," Brady said. "Early morning? Late at night? Someone in the village must have seen something."

"Suppose there's two people involved, boss? It's unlikely,

but suppose she goes off with one guy? Somehow ends up with the killer?"

"Thoughts on that anyone? Jake? Dan? Anya, what do you think?"

Anya shook her head. "Like Frankie says, boss, it's unlikely. What have you just said to me? The simplest solution is always the most likely."

"So one killer, not two?" Brady looked at his small team. Saw two or three shake their head. "No, neither do I. I don't think we're going to find anyone else. I think there's only one person involved. I think it's personal."

"You think the answer's in the village, boss?"

"She lived in the village. She disappeared in the village. Logic says the answer is in the village. Like Anya said, the simplest solution. So the house-to-house is crucial. Dan and Jake, first thing tomorrow morning. Ask your questions. And *look*. Really look. Anything that seems out of place? Anyone unwilling to answer your questions?"

Brady paused. Realised his back was aching.

I'm getting too old to perch on a desk...

"Village life has moved on from Miss Marple, but they can still be tight-knit communities. Someone must know something. So our job's simple. Ask the right questions. And find out everything we can about Sarah Trueman. Frankie, life story? I can leave that to you?"

Brady turned, picked up his plastic cup of water, took a sip. "OK. Open house. Theories. And like I said, nothing is off-limits."

"Blackmail?"

Brady pursed his lips. Looked doubtful. "Single woman, Dan? According to the vicar she doesn't have a family. Inherited the cottage from her mother."

"Dark past, boss?"

"Maybe. Let's see what the house-to-house throws up. And all Frankie's background checks."

"Some sort of pre-arranged meeting? You know, your first boyfriend. I'll meet you on the top of the Eiffel Tower on New Year's Day twenty-twenty."

Brady laughed. "I did that, Anya. One of my girlfriends. I think I'm about five years late. Besides, Sarah Trueman's nearly fifty. Bit old for dreams of her first boyfriend."

"Why hang her like that?" Frankie said. "That's what I can't get my head round. This isn't a date that went wrong, boss. Bloody hell, we've all had arguments. But we don't all have thirty yards of heavy-duty rope lying around."

"Which is why the house-to-house is so important... Jake, you've not said anything. Any ideas? Thoughts while you were at May Beck? Jake? You with us?"

"Sorry, boss. I was thinking. No. Nothing. Like you say, house-to-house."

"Right," Brady said. "It's late. You probably have homes to go to. Thank you. House-to-house tomorrow morning. Frankie and I will go to Sarah Trueman's cottage. Let's see what day two brings. Let's see what the village gossip has to tell us. Hopefully about the man she was meeting."

Brady stood up, stretched. Put both hands in the small of his back. Stretched again. Told Frankie he'd see her in the morning. Glanced at his watch.

There's just time.

Home. Shower. Make dinner.

See Siobhan for the first time in three weeks...

17

"**I** missed you," Brady said.

I did. More than I thought I'd miss you...

She leaned forward. Kissed him. Kissed him a second time. "I missed you too, Michael Brady."

"I thought you were too busy to miss me?"

"I was. I *was* busy. But... You know. In my lonely bed at night. I did think of you. Once or twice..."

"What do you want to do?" Brady gestured at Archie. "I don't seem to be the only one who's missed you."

Siobhan laughed. "That's because he sees me and thinks 'walk.' Then 'biscuit.' Feed me first. Talk to me. Bring me up to date. Then maybe we'll walk Archie. Assuming you don't lead me astray..."

"You made a mistake," Siobhan said half an hour later as the rain swept in off the sea. "You should have put a roof on the balcony. We could have sat outside. Talked. Sipped a romantic hot chocolate. Watched the rain."

"I thought of it," Brady said. "Ash talked me out of it."

"What did she say?"

"Two things. She didn't want to look out of her bedroom window and see a roof covered in seagull shit. And how was I going to clean it?"

Siobhan laughed. "Top cop plunges to death cleaning seagull shit. Not how you want to be remembered, my love."

"Tell me about the film."

"Come outside."

"It's raining."

She nodded. Took hold of his hand. "That's the whole point of the exercise. Come and stand on your balcony with me."

This is important to her. Really important. She's changed...

She opened the balcony doors. Pulled him out into the rain.

"Am I allowed to put my hood up?"

"I thought I was dating a real man. Of course you can put your hood up. But look. What do you see?"

"Rain. The harbour. Not much through the rain."

"Go on..."

"You want me to describe the scene?"

"Yes. Tell me what you see. Everything. Imagine you're a camera. Pan around."

"Pan around? Into the rain?"

"Dating a real man, remember..."

Brady turned. Felt the rain against his face. Wiped it out of his eyes. "The beach to begin with. *Some* beach. It's low tide. But not as low as it can be. Then the piers. East Pier. West Pier. The red and green lights on the end of them – "

There's no need to see Jimmy Gorse...

"The harbour again. Shops. Cafés. A few people. One man walking his dog. Trying to keep himself dry. Then down here... Henrietta Street. My car-that-needs-replacing across the road. The pavement. Lights in some of the houses. More rain."

Brady turned towards her. "And you," he said. "And you've asked me to describe the opening shot of your film."

She nodded. "Except it's Whitby not Dublin. But yes, I have. And you've told me the story."

"There isn't any commentary in the opening scene of a film."

Her eyes are shining. Sparkling. Like they were the first time I watched her play. When she stepped onstage...

"Now imagine Henrietta Street is in Dublin," Siobhan said. "It's raining, just like it is now. The cobbles are wet, reflecting the light. There's a girl walking up the street. Slowly coming towards the camera. Sinead. How old is she? Twenty? Maybe a little older? She's home at last. Her parents took her to America when she was ten. But they're both dead now. And New York wasn't kind to her. So she's spent all her money. A one-way ticket home. She's got family. Her mother's sister. But as she gets closer – as the rain eases – you see she's carrying something. Cradling a child. *Her* child. An unmarried mother coming home to a Catholic country. It's not going to be easy..."

"And that's the story the film's telling."

Siobhan nodded. Smiled. Held his eyes. "That's the story *I'm* telling. *We're* telling – Helen and I – as the film opens. And we're telling it with music. *Our* music. And it's... I don't know, Mike. I thought nothing would ever come close to being on stage. But we had a screening. A hundred people. I sat in a cinema. In the dark. Watched the film start. Watched Sinead walking through the rain. Watched the audience. Heard the music. *Our* music..."

"And it was magical?"

"It was beyond magical, Mike. It was... It was *me*, Mike. It was my soul. What I was put on this earth to do. Tell stories. Tell stories with my music."

Brady rolled over in bed. Reached for his phone. Looked at the time.

2:47

Close enough to three...

Rolled gently out of bed. Did his best not to wake Siobhan. Reached for his dressing gown. Closed the bedroom door as quietly as he could.

Bent down and ruffled the top of Archie's head. Gave him a biscuit. Eased the balcony doors open. Wiped the wet chair with a towel. Changed his mind. Remained standing.

Looked from the beach to the pier to the harbour to Henrietta Street. Saw Sinead walking towards him.

'As the rain eases you see she's carrying her child. And that's the story we're telling with our music. It's what I was put on this earth to do, Mike.'

And I was put on this earth to stand in a wood, Siobhan. Stand in a wood and look at Sarah Trueman. Hanging by her right ankle. I missed you. Really missed you.

But one day we'll be travelling in different directions. Not now. Not next month. Maybe.

One day.

Sooner or later...

18

Michael Brady gave Dan Keillor and Jake Cartwright their final instructions. Fought back one last urge to do the house-to-house himself.

Walked along the path to Sarah Trueman's cottage. Glanced at the church. Pushed the garden gate open. Spoke to the locksmith.

"You're alright with the door, Joe?"

"No problem, boss. New lock, new keys. Here." The locksmith handed Brady two keys. "There's only one person going in and that's you. And anyone you give the key to."

Brady nodded. "Thanks. Appreciate you doing it so quickly. Give my best to Mrs Joe when you see her."

Brady walked across to the scene of crime van. "Anya, give us twenty minutes will you? I want to look round with Frankie. Get a feel for the place. And for Sarah Trueman."

See her living there.

Get to know her...

. . .

FRANKIE SHOOK HER HEAD. "Red and black diamond tiles. Bloody hell. How did she cope with a hangover?"

Brady laughed. Looked around the kitchen. White units, pale cream tiles behind them. Two pictures – white sand beaches – on the walls. Yellow and white check blinds on the windows. A view of a neat, orderly garden, fruit trees at the bottom.

"I've got sink envy," Brady said. "Is there such a thing?"

Frankie laughed. "It's like the one we had in the farm kitchen. Carved out of a single piece of stone. Mum decided to modernise. And grow herbs in the sink. It took two of the farm labourers to carry it out into the garden. I saw one of them the other day. Threatened to sue me for his hernia."

"Dan Keillor was right," Brady said. "It's tidy. Obsessively tidy."

"You're a man, boss. That means there's no washing up..."

"Everything, Frankie. The cookbooks, the jars. Even those three pots of herbs on the windowsill. All neatly lined up. Turned so the herbs grow in the same direction for God's sake." Brady shook his head ruefully. "As far from my kitchen as you can get."

Frankie nodded at the floor. "The cat bowls."

"Dan Keillor said someone came up to him. Said she was taking care of the cats. So that's one out of two boxes ticked."

Frankie pulled a pair of gloves on. Opened the fridge. Lifted the milk out, looked at the date. "Best before today," she said. "So she bought it, what? A week ago?"

"Good. There'll be some CCTV somewhere. Tesco or Sainsbury's."

"Neither, boss. It's North Yorkshire Dairy. A local supplier. Garages. Corner shops."

"A corner shop with no CCTV? Brilliant."

Brady reached for his phone. "Sue? Mike Brady. Do something for me, will you? North Yorkshire Dairy. Give them a ring. I need a list of every shop they supply in the area. Twenty mile radius of Roxby. So down to Whitby, up to Middlesbrough. And halfway to Denmark..."

Frankie raised her eyes. "A tour of North Yorkshire's corner shops? That's going to be an exciting job..."

Brady laughed. "Part of the learning curve, Frankie. We've all been there. Let's see what else there is. Assuming there are no more clues in the fridge?"

"Coleslaw. Half a cheesecake. A *lot* of orange juice. She kept her fruit in the fridge. Not much else."

Frankie systematically went through the kitchen drawers. Looked up at Brady. "If you've got sink envy, boss, I've got casserole envy. They're all Le Creuset. A posh bread making machine. She didn't do things by halves."

"Let's have a look in the lounge," Brady said. "See if it's as OCD as the kitchen."

FRANKIE STOOD IN THE DOORWAY. "Stick 'country cottage' into Google. This is what you get. The estate agents will be salivating."

"We've a killer to catch first. And if we have to take it apart brick-by-brick we will do. But I take your point."

Nine wooden beams ran the length of the ceiling. One, much thicker beam ran floor-to-ceiling.

"Remind you of anything?" Brady said.

"Billy and Sandra Garrity?"

"In one. Billy and Sandra. Tied to the fireplace. There's an image we'll never get out of our heads."

"Except it's not carved. Not a witch post. It's just a simple wooden beam, boss. Holding the bedrooms up."

"How old do you think it is?"

Frankie shook her head. "The cottage? Lochie would date it to the exact week. Tell you what the builder had for his lunch. Eighteen-fifties? Around then. Did you say it was modernised when her mother died?"

"According to the vicar."

Frankie walked across to the cream sofa, touched one of the cushions. "This is neat as well. This is someone-coming-to-look-at-your-house neat. When you're trying to sell it. Something's not right here, boss. This isn't the house of someone who put food out for the cats and was coming back a day later."

"What are you saying?"

"Let me ask you a question. What's missing?"

"What's missing? I don't know. The local paper? Fruit in the fruit bowl – "

"Fridge, remember?"

Brady shook his head. "Tell me – no, don't. There are no books. Cookbooks in the kitchen but – "

"Books and photos," Frankie said. "How much have you and I learned from books and photos over the years? Something else though."

"What?"

"A list."

"A list?"

"Yes. You're going away, even overnight. You make a list. What you need to take with you. What you need to pack. And it's always on the worktop."

"Or on your phone, Frankie. They've got a *Notes* app now you know."

"At her age boss? Come on. She's writing things down.

It's in her hand as she walks around the house, checks things off. Then it's back on the worktop. So what's the first thing you see when you get back?"

"Your list."

"Bingo. And there isn't one. We need to look at the other rooms, boss. But right now I think Sarah Trueman left the house on Saturday. And I think someone came in later and tidied it."

BRADY STARTED UP THE STAIRS. "It's tasteful, I'll give her that. What are these called? Dado rails? I thought about having them in the house. Ash talked me out of it."

"She said they'd need dusting?"

"Right. I gave in after ten seconds."

Frankie nodded at the pictures on the walls. "More beaches, boss."

Brady nodded. "More beaches I don't recognise. If she likes the beach so much why is she in Roxby? Why not sell the house when her mother dies? Go two miles down the road to Staithes?"

"I don't know. But if someone's putting it up for sale I could move in. Two bedrooms, quiet country village. I'll make an offer."

"I thought you liked living in Whitby?"

"Maybe. Being out at Hutton-le-Hole with Lochie has made me appreciate the countryside. Being woken up by a bird outside the window. Not lorry loads of cod and haddock rumbling past at five in the morning..."

Brady pushed the door of the main bedroom open. A double bed with a heavy wooden frame. A white quilt, a pale blue throw folded neatly at the bottom, the cord of an electric blanket snaking across to the plug. Pale yellow walls, more beams, an old-fashioned, free-standing wardrobe diagonally across the far corner of the room.

"Curiouser and curiouser," Frankie said. "Or in this case, neater and neater."

Brady walked over to the corner of the room. Looked down. "All the bins have been emptied. You're – "

"I thought you said bins were *never* empty?"

"Sorry. They're not. Not once Anya gets to work. But you're right. Someone's been in. And one other thing."

"What's that?"

"Remember Gina Foster? What we said the first time we were in the house? No pictures. This is the same. A hundred and one pictures of a beach. No pictures of Sarah Trueman. Friends, family. Nothing."

"Maybe she didn't like her own photo? She wouldn't be the first woman."

"Her parents? When she was younger? Go through all the drawers, Frankie. I'll go downstairs and do the same. There must be something."

There wasn't. Brady was back ten minutes later. Shaking his head in frustration. Getting the same answer from Frankie.

"One last room," he said. "Let's see what the spare bedroom has to tell us."

"...THAT she didn't have people to stay," Frankie said.

The room was long and narrow. A window looking out onto the church. The same pale yellow paint, another dado rail, grey and white striped wallpaper underneath. But a bedroom without a bed.

A mahogany card table instead. Green baize on the top.

A single, Victorian-period dining chair at one side, two identical chairs facing it.

Cards laid out on the top.

"Playing cards," Brady said. "You think she was running Roxby's illicit casino?"

"Not playing cards, boss. Tarot cards."

THE CARDS WERE FANNED out across the table in the shape of a crescent moon. Face down, a blue/grey criss-cross pattern on the back. Three cards had been turned over.

"A tarot reading?" Brady said.

Frankie nodded at the chairs. "For herself? Or for a client?"

"Plenty of fingerprints then. You think this is how she supported herself, Frankie? Reading tarot cards? There can't have been much demand in Roxby. The vicar didn't say anything either."

"He wouldn't, would he, boss? The Church of England and tarot cards. They're hardly natural bedfellows."

Brady looked down at the three cards that had been turned over. Read the words at the bottom. "The Tower. The Lovers. And this one. Two people with wine goblets."

"The Two of Cups," Frankie said. "Suits. Like hearts, diamonds, spades, clubs. There are cups, swords, wands. And one more I can't remember."

"Do you believe in this nonsense, Frankie?"

She laughed. "I've got a Maths degree, boss. I believe in long, complicated equations. And sexy Greek symbols."

"And proof." Brady shook his head dismissively. "Tarot and Ouija boards. The preserve of teenage girls and the gullible."

Frankie stood next to him. Looked down at the cards.

"The Lovers," she said. "Two naked people in front of what looks like a volcano. How many active volcanoes are there in Whitby?"

"But she *was* going to meet someone. We're sure of that. And this other one – the Two of Cups – looks like two people who've just got married."

"The marriage doesn't last long," Frankie said. "The last card. The Tower. People falling out of a burning building?"

"Two of the cards are upside down."

Frankie shrugged. "Not if you're on the other side of the table. But if you want answers they're over there." She pointed at the far end of the room. "No books downstairs. Plenty upstairs. Tarot reading room and library."

Brady walked across to the bookcase. What looked like reclaimed wood running the length of the far wall. Irregular shelves, the books arranged haphazardly. Some laid flat, some upright. Novels, travel guides, more cookbooks. A dozen books on the tarot.

"The Ancient Wisdom of Tarot," Brady said. "Tarot of the Old Path."

"The killer," Frankie said. "The person who tidied up. He knew her. Well."

Brady looked at her. "What makes you suddenly say that?"

"Because the rest of the house is tidy. OCD tidy. But he's left the bookcase. Knows it's more than his life's worth to tidy her books."

"*His* life's worth? He was going to kill her Frankie. Hang her up by her right ankle. Besides, tidying this bookcase is a day's work. He'd have run out of time. Simpler explanation. He had a key. Joe said there were no marks on the door. No signs of forced entry."

"He's kidnapped her? He's planning to kill her? He's not

going to get an extra life sentence for taking the key out of her handbag?"

"Exactly."

Frankie shook her head. "I still think he knew her. And I think he knew her well."

Brady gestured at the cards. "So he was her lover? Standing in front of a volcano with her? Or throwing her out of a burning building? It doesn't make sense, Frankie. Like I said, teenage girls and the gullible. Come on, Anya will be chomping at the bit."

Brady moved towards the door. Stopped. Reached for his phone. Photographed the bookcase. Photographed the cards on the table.

"Paul will do that for you."

"I know. But Paul's photos will be at the station."

"Not on your balcony at three in the morning?"

"Exactly..."

BRADY AND FRANKIE stood outside in the garden. Watched Anya and Paul go into the house. Brady shook his head. "Paul's got a new camera every time I see him."

"And Anya's got more equipment. *That's* where the police budget goes, boss."

Brady walked across to the green bin. Lifted the lid. "Empty," he said.

"You'd be surprised if it wasn't empty, boss. It's Friday. Even if we were here at six in the morning there's an eighty percent chance it's been emptied."

"So that proves nothing. Walk down the garden with me, Frankie."

"Are you getting wistful, boss?"

Brady laughed. "Wishing I had a garden? All that salt off

the sea? I'd be lucky if I could grow nettles."

The lawn gave way to raised beds. Two compost bins half-screened behind some makeshift fencing. Then the fruit trees.

"She's organised," Frankie said. "I have the vague feeling you're supposed to have two compost bins."

"So she made her own compost, grew her own veg. They're not motives for murder. Come on, Frankie, let's get back. Geoff will have finished the post-mortem. I want to talk to him before Dan and Jake report on the house-to-house."

19

Geoff Oldroyd shook his head. Looked down at Sarah Trueman's body, covered by the green sheet. Turned to Brady and Frankie.

"No sign now," he said. "She looks peaceful doesn't she? Could have died in one of a hundred ways. Slipped away in her sleep."

"Except she wouldn't be lying on your table, Geoff."

Geoff sighed. "She wouldn't, Mike. And we wouldn't be having this conversation. I'm getting too old for this. I've got grandchildren. I should be on the beach with them. Buying ice creams..."

Brady didn't speak. Glanced at Frankie. Waited for Geoff to compose himself.

"She was hung upside down," he said. "Hung upside down with her left leg bent at an angle and tied behind her right leg. Just above the knee. Hands tied behind her back. A rope slung across the branch. Then he hauled her up. But you know all that."

I do. We all do. And we'll never stop seeing it...

"The cause of death was a brain haemorrhage. Time of

death? My best guess is around two in the morning. But it could easily be an hour either way."

So three. When I'm sitting on the balcony...

"But it's a lot more complicated than that," Geoff said. Shook his head a second time. "Let me explain."

"Our bodies are designed to stand upright. So we're designed to stop blood pooling in our feet. The blood vessels in our legs have... 'valves' in them, for want of a better word. Constrict the blood vessels when we're standing upright. So you can stand on your feet all day – teaching, serving fish and chips – "

"Directing traffic if we don't find the killer."

"Whatever you're doing, Mike, you can stand on your feet and the blood won't pool."

"But it's different when we're turned upside down?"

"Very, very different. There's nothing to stop blood pooling in our heads if we're upside down. Your brain doesn't have what your legs have. Nothing to constrict the blood vessels. So you get brain swelling and – in Sarah's case – haemorrhage. But – poor bloody woman – it's even more complicated than that."

"Didn't the Romans crucify people upside down?"

Geoff nodded. "They did, Frankie. And it led to death in any number of ways. Let me come back to that."

"So the killer was certain she was going to die? He just didn't know *how* she was going to die?"

"Did he *care* how she died, Mike? Look at it from the killer's point of view. He's done a bloody good job. She's conscious enough to know she's going to die. Conscious enough to feel her own urine trickling down her body. How would you like that?"

Brady shook his head. "Just when you thought you'd seen it all."

"Fitness is a big problem for her, Mike. Who's that American guy that does the stunts?"

Brady shook his head. "Search me. Harry Houdini?"

"He was born in Hungary, boss. And he died a hundred years ago. You're thinking of David Blaine, Geoff."

"Right. Thanks, Frankie. He did one where he was standing on a pole. A hundred feet up, thirty-five hours. Something like that. He doesn't just wake up one morning and think, 'Nothing to do today, I'll stand on a pole.' He's trained, practised. And he's fit. You bet your life that if he announced he was going to hang upside down for twenty-four hours he'd know every single thing that could go wrong. And he'd have trained. Trained for a year."

"And Sarah Trueman hadn't."

Geoff shook his head. "Sarah Trueman's forty-seven. Five foot four, eleven stone. So slightly overweight – "

"A completely normal woman?"

"Right. Muscle tone's OK. It's not great. I'd say she went for a few walks in the country. She definitely *wasn't* training for a marathon. So in short she's a bloody long way from David Blaine. Hanging upside down is going to kill her. And the killer knew that."

"Can I take you back to time of death, Geoff? You said two in the morning."

"It's a very rough estimate, Mike. It was cold that night. She's found the next morning. We spent a long time looking at her. It's all imprecise. But there was an American guy – "

"Not someone else on a pole?"

"A caver. Montana. Utah, maybe. Somehow he got trapped upside down. They think he survived for ten or twelve hours. But he was in his twenties. Fit. A lot fitter than Sarah Trueman."

"Didn't it happen in West Yorkshire as well?" Frankie

said. "Someone climbed one of those old mill chimneys? Was going to jump off but he slipped? Hanging by his ankle in the middle of January?"

"So the killer doesn't need specialist knowledge. All he needs is a search engine."

"Right. Google. 'Will you die if you're hung upside down?' And there's all the information he needs. Like you said, Frankie. Right back to the Romans. Saint Peter, is that the one? But whoever you are the effects are the same. The muscles she needs for breathing become exhausted. Her body weight is working against them. So's gravity. Sooner or later respiration simply fails."

"If the brain haemorrhage doesn't get her she suffocates?"

"She does. And if he hangs her there at eight at night... Body temperature. General fitness. I'd say she dies at one in the morning. But it's the same as the tree. Birch, oak, ash. One o'clock. Two o'clock. Totally bloody irrelevant."

"And she can't cry out."

"She can't cry out because he's stuffed a white handkerchief into her mouth. Bog standard, fourteen inches square white handkerchief. Your Auntie Marjorie. One year it's socks, the next year it's hankies. If she does cry out no-one hears her. And the more she tries to cry out the more she gags on the handkerchief. The weaker she becomes... You don't need me to spell it out."

"You think she was conscious, Geoff?"

"I've sent the blood off for analysis, Mike. With a bloody great 'urgent' on the envelope. I'm still betting on a date rape drug. But either way she'd have drifted in and out of consciousness. And if there's a God... Well, if there is he'll have made sure she was out a lot more than she was in."

20

None of them spoke.

Drifting in and out of consciousness. Until the end comes...

Geoff broke the silence. "You said you owed me a pint of Doom tonight, Mike. Make that two. There's something else."

"Now what, Geoff? You're looking... More serious if that's possible."

Geoff Oldroyd nodded. "You need to catch this bastard, Mike."

"We need to catch them all, Geoff."

The pathologist shook his head. "This one more than most. Here. Look. And this is something you might not want to share."

Geoff walked across to a table in the corner of the mortuary. Carefully picked up an evidence bag. Handed it to Brady.

"It's..."

Brady stared at the object. A small pewter-coloured locking nut, maybe half an inch across.

"I've seen one of these before. It's – "

"It's to fasten a sash window," Frankie said. "An old-fashioned sash window. A small one. My Grandma's house had them. You closed the window, pulled the catch across, then screwed that onto it. Job done. You'd locked the window."

Brady looked up at Geoff. "She swallowed it? Or was it somewhere else?"

Geoff nodded. "I'm coming to somewhere else in a minute. Yes, she swallowed it. Which is a very brave – and desperate – thing to do."

Brady stared at the evidence bag again. "Is that even possible, Geoff? It's the size of... I don't know – if it was cheese I'd cut it in half."

"Most things are possible if we're determined enough, Mike."

Frankie reached across. Took the bag from Brady. "You're saying this is where she was held, Geoff? A house with old-fashioned sash windows?"

"I'm not saying it, Frankie. Sarah Trueman's saying it. Sending us a message. 'This is where I was held.'"

Brady shook his head. "So she swallowed it? Hoping the acid in her stomach doesn't dissolve it?"

"There's no way stomach acid would have dissolved that, Mike. In the normal course of events her body would have got rid of it. By the conventional route."

Brady winced. "Ouch."

"More than 'ouch,' boss. If that was her way of telling us something – it was her *only* way."

"...Meaning everything else – mirrors, lights – had been removed."

Brady shook his head. "This bastard goes up in my estimation with every hour that passes."

"Not everything else," Geoff said. "I told you I'd get to 'somewhere else.' Here."

He picked up a second evidence bag. Opened it. Reached inside with a pair of tweezers. Brought a strip of material out.

Raised his eyebrows. "In her vagina," he said. "A long way in."

Brady nodded. "Determined to tell us something."

"Determined to tell us where she was held, boss. So we can prove it when we catch him."

"Match the window catch. Match the material. Don't worry, Frankie, we will. This would have dissolved in her stomach, Geoff?"

"In time. Probably not as quickly as she thought."

"But she doesn't know how long it is until she's found."

"What do we think it is? It's too thick for string. Too thin for rope."

Frankie reached across. Took the tweezers from Geoff. Lifted them. "It's a tassel," she said.

"Off a curtain? The ties you use to hold them back?"

She shook her head. "Too big for that. Maybe tied in her hair? That's possible. But it's a tassel. Definitely."

"Geoff?"

"Frankie's right. They're on hats aren't they? Those Nordic bonnets the kids wear in the winter."

"So we need to find a house with sash windows. And somewhere in that house we'll find a hat – or a curtain – missing a tassel. Maybe..."

Brady looked at the tassel again. "Both of these. They're for afterwards. To secure a conviction. So we need someone to convict."

"Which starts with the house-to-house."

"It does. Let's see what Dan and Jake have to say."

Brady paused. Picked up the evidence bag with the locking nut in it. Stared at it.

"Don't, boss..."

"I'm not going to be able to resist, Frankie. Go home, cut a piece of cheese that size. If I'm not in tomorrow morning... Break the door down will you?"

"Mike..."

"What, Geoff? You look worried."

"You owe me two pints of Doom. If you're planning to choke to death, do it after the Black Horse will you?"

21

"**D**an, Jake, what've you got to tell me?"

Dan Keillor – still far too good-looking to be a copper in Brady's view – sucked his breath in. Did a passable impression of a garage mechanic delivering bad news. "Not much, boss. Nowhere near as much as you'd have wanted."

Brady nodded. "Let's go through it. See what we've got."

"First things first, boss. Plenty of the houses were empty."

"Holiday homes?"

"Holiday homes or Airbnb. Two or three with those key holders by the front door. You know, put the security code in, get the key out."

Brady sighed. "Another village fighting a losing battle? Tell me about the ones that were in. What did they have to say about her?"

Dan flipped through his notebook. "There's a common theme. She was quiet. Polite. Didn't have any particular friends. Or didn't seem to. Most people saw her in church on a Sunday. A feeling that she went to church to meet people rather than for religious reasons. No-one mentioned any family. One person said one of her cats spent too much time in their garden. They'd got a pond."

"Should be grateful. Probably keeping the local heron away. Anyone you think I should talk to?"

"Two," Dan said. "Mrs Hornby. Mrs Archer. You need to talk to both of them, boss."

"Why?"

"One, Mrs Hornby seemed to know her better than anyone else. Said Sarah Trueman had been round for coffee a couple of times. And she'd had a tarot reading."

Brady raised his eyebrows. "She'd been to Sarah for a reading? She's the only one who said that?"

"Maybe the only one who'd admit it, boss."

"What did she say?"

"Said she was good." Dan glanced down at his notebook. "'Scarily good' were her exact words. Said she was a bit frightened at how accurate it was."

"What about the other one? Mrs Archer?"

"She'd been in to feed her cats a few times. Said – "

"Did she have a key?"

Dan nodded. "She did. She said Sarah went away maybe once a month. She was... She struck me as the village gossip, boss."

Brady tapped his finger on the desk.

Have I always done that when I'm thinking? If not when did I start?

"Once a month, Dan. That sounds like a regular commitment. Meeting someone. Going to see someone. Jake, what's your take on that?"

Jake Cartwright didn't reply. Carried on staring out of the window.

Staring but not seeing. The other day in the briefing...

"Jake? Are you with us?"

Jake turned his attention back to Brady. Shook his head. "Sorry, boss. You were saying?"

Brady narrowed his eyes. Looked at him. "Are you alright, Jake? Is something bothering you?"

Jake shook his head. "No, nothing. Sorry, boss. Not been feeling too good. We had crab last night. Might've been a bit off."

Brady nodded. Wasn't remotely convinced. Let it pass. "Have you got anything to add to what Dan has said? Any impressions? Thoughts, observations..."

"No, boss. Dan has covered it all. Pretty much word for word."

If you've heard any of it, Jake...

"So that's your conclusion, Dan?"

Dan Keillor shook his head. "It's hard to come to a conclusion, boss. No-one had a bad word to say about her. But no-one had a really *good* word either. Mrs Archer said she made the best apple chutney she'd ever tasted if that helps."

Brady laughed. "Remind me to get a jar from the church. So just those two, Dan? Thank you. I'll see them tomorrow. Leave me their numbers, will you? And Jake, if you're not feeling well get yourself home."

Because, PC Cartwright, you're not focused on what you're doing. And if you're going to make a mistake I'd rather you did it at home...

22

"I need to pay my debts, Frankie."

"Geoff?"

"Who else? You want a large gin to end the day? Or are you driving out to Hutton-le-Hole?"

Frankie shook her head. "Yes and no. In that order. Gin then fish and chips. The Whitby diet."

"Bloody hell, Frankie. You've cracked it. The Whitby Diet! Brilliant. All we need is a celebrity endorsement and we've an instant bestseller."

Brady stood up. Stretched. "The Black Horse? While we wait for fame and fortune..."

"Give me ten minutes will you, boss? I need to descend into the underworld. There's something I forgot to ask Geoff this morning."

"OK. Ten minutes. And drag Geoff away. Tell him the reports will wait until the morning."

. . .

BRADY SAT ON HIS OWN. Messaged Ash. Messaged Siobhan. Checked the football news. Did everything he could to push Sarah Trueman out of his head.

Failed.

Looked up as Frankie walked in on her own. Raised his eyebrows.

Frankie shook her head. "He insists. Says if he leaves it 'til morning he'll forget what he's writing."

Brady laughed. "Right. Tell me about it. I sent myself an e-mail the other day. Gin? Bombay Sapphire?"

Another shake of her head. "Just Perrier thanks, boss. Or whatever mineral water they've got."

"I thought it was gin then fish and chips?"

"Sorry, boss. The Whitby Diet falls at the first hurdle..."

Brady walked across to the bar. Came back with Frankie's drink.

"What do you want to talk about, Detective Chief Inspector? Football? Will Middlesbrough win tomorrow?"

"Why don't you tell me how the countryside gardens are looking, Detective Sergeant? The cherry blossom must be out?"

"The cherry blossom *is* coming out. It looks lovely. And he definitely knew her, boss. *Definitely*."

Brady looked at her. "You're suddenly very certain..."

"I'm *absolutely* certain."

"Why?"

"Her clothes. The labels in her clothes. I looked in her wardrobe. One example. Her jeans. N – Y – D – J."

Brady shook his head. "You've got me. New York Denim Jeans."

"Not Your Daughter's Jeans. A hundred and fifty pounds. Maybe a hundred if she bought them in the sale."

"That's not possible, Frankie. Jeans are thirty quid. Forty tops."

Frankie laughed. "You're right, boss. Assuming you fell asleep in nineteen-ninety. Ask Siobhan how much she pays for her jeans. Ask Ash how much she'd *like* to pay. But it's not just her jeans. *All* her clothes. The same in the kitchen. The pans, the casserole dishes. They're Le Creuset. How much is a Le Creuset casserole dish? Two hundred quid. She bought the best she could, boss. She didn't mind paying. But she died in Primark."

"What?"

"Her clothes. That's what I did just now. Went down to the mortuary. Looked at her clothes. Jeans, jacket, top. All from Primark. The blue jacket. Fifteen quid? Twenty?"

"And there was nothing else from Primark in her wardrobe?"

"Nothing at all. Nada. Zip. Zero. Wardrobe, underwear drawer. Nothing."

"So you're saying the clothes are significant."

"I'm saying the clothes are very bloody significant, boss. Someone bought them for her."

"Where's the nearest Primark?"

"Online."

Brady shook his head. "Online leaves a trace, Frankie. A footprint. Cash doesn't. So York? Middlesbrough?"

"Both."

"This doesn't make sense, Frankie. I kidnap you. I hold you for three days. OK, I'll keep you alive. But I'm not going to buy you clothes. Especially – "

"When you don't know what size I am?"

Brady nodded. "Exactly. Ten? Twelve? If I'm buying clothes for you I need to know what size you are."

"That's very kind of you, boss. But it's not my birthday for another six months."

"You see my point, Frankie. Grace was a ten. Sometimes she was a twelve. Sometimes she was ten on the top half and twelve on the bottom half. Or the other way round. I can't remember. You? Ten or twelve is my guess. Sue at the station? I see her every day. Fourteen? Sixteen? Bloody hell, I don't even know what size my own daughter is. So I'm not buying any of you clothes. But you're saying someone bought clothes for Sarah Trueman – in advance, presumably. And they fitted."

"Which means he knew her. Knew her well enough to know what size she was."

"What other explanation is there?"

Frankie shrugged. Spread her hands. "He bought a lot of clothes? No, you don't know what size I am. But you've been married, you can take a reasonable guess. So you buy a ten *and* a twelve. One of them is going to fit. This guy went to a lot of trouble. He's not going to stop at an extra pair of jeans. Especially from Primark."

"So where *are* the extra jeans? The ones she didn't wear?"

"We both know the answer to that. Where she was held."

Brady shook his head. "There's one other thing... I kidnap you. I hold you for three days. *Why* do I buy you clothes?"

"Because you know I'm going to be found. Because –"

Brady nodded. "Because I want to send a message. There's no other explanation."

"Who to though, boss? Us? The people who find her? Someone who hears about it?"

"This looks like a bloody serious conversation."

Brady looked up. Laughed. "It is, Geoff. Sorry. Frankie

and I were just discussing the cherry blossom. Apparently it's out early this year."

"Of course you were, Michael. And I'll have a lemonade shandy."

"Sit yourself down, Geoff. I'll get your drink. While you swap gardening tips with Frankie."

Brady walked to the bar. Bought Geoff's pint. Smiled.

"Here you are, Geoff. New glasses from the brewery. Look at that. Doom Bar written on the glass."

"To remind me? In case I'm going senile? Cheers, Mike."

Frankie stood up. "I'll leave you two to gossip. I'm sorry, boss. I have to go. I'll see you in the morning. Chapter and verse on Sarah Trueman." She stepped away from the table. Stopped. Turned. Put her hand on Brady's shoulder.

"One last thing, boss. While we're talking about clothes."

"What's that?"

"Your daughter. She's an eight. And last time I had coffee with her she needed some new tops. That shop in Church Street. There's one in the window. A sort of burnt orange..."

"That was a bit abrupt, wasn't it?"

Brady nodded. "It was. We were just talking, Geoff. No prizes for guessing what about."

Geoff nodded. "Not my business to say anything, Mike, but is Frankie alright? A couple of times lately..."

"Me too. A message from Lochie maybe? The short answer is I don't know."

"You don't think – "

"I *daren't* think, Geoff. The idea of losing Frankie? It makes my blood run cold. Talk to me about something happier."

"Sarah Trueman?"

"What else?"

Geoff drained half his glass. "I needed that. Long after-noon finishing off Mr Victory."

"Sorry he had to go back in the fridge."

Geoff shook his head. "There are priorities, Mike, even among the dead... I've got a question to ask you."

"Sarah Trueman? Add it to the list."

"You think the killer rehearsed it, Mike?"

Brady nodded. "I've been asking myself the same ques-tion. Siobhan said something to me. I didn't answer. You know why?"

"You were hanging someone from a tree?"

"I was, Geoff. 'How would I do it?' Have you read *Day of the Jackal*? Frederick Forsyth? He wants to shoot de Gaulle. Gets a melon, goes into the middle of a French forest. Cali-brates his rifle. Shoots the melon from five hundred yards. Re-calibrates..."

"That's what you'd do?"

"I would. Tying the knot, pulling her up, drugging her – "

"Assuming the tests come back positive."

"Which they will. We both know that. But I'd rehearse it all, Geoff. What time it gets dark. What time the café closes. I'd probably have a notebook."

Geoff finished his pint. Looked at Brady. "Unless this one is the rehearsal, Mike."

Brady shook his head. "What did I say to you the other day? A hundred questions and two answers? I'm beginning to think it's two hundred questions and no bloody answers."

23

Michael Brady ruffled the top of Archie's head. Walked into the kitchen. Reached for the dog biscuits.

"Come on, mate. Come and sit with me. Inside though. It's pouring down."

Brady sat on the floor. Leaned back against the sofa. Patted the carpet next to him. Archie flopped down. Rested his head on Brady's leg. Gazed up at him.

"Two," Brady said. "One biscuit at three in the morning. That's the rule. Absolutely unbreakable. But I've a question. So an extra biscuit when you've answered it."

Because you've as much chance of answering it as I have, Arch...

"I'm missing something, pal. Something obvious. What is it?"

Brady rested his hand on Archie's side. Felt him breathing. Felt his heart beating. Remembered how close he'd come to losing him.

Shivered.

"Something about the murder scene, Arch. Hanging

there. *Don't* think about biscuits, Arch. Concentrate. Otherwise you'll be like me. Can't sleep."

"Dad?"

Brady looked up. Saw Ash standing in the doorway. Grey/blue pyjamas, half-asleep.

"You alright, sweetheart?"

"I came down for a drink. How long have you been awake?"

"Not long. I'm discussing the case with Archie."

"He's stringing you along, Dad. Knows you'll give him extra biscuits."

Ash disappeared into the kitchen. Came back with a glass of water. "Don't stay up too long, Dad. It's not healthy. Read a book if you can't sleep. And not crime either."

"You hear that, Archie? Read a book. Instead of talking. You've been a big help, pal. Here's your extra biscuit. I've been ordered back to bed."

Brady pushed himself stiffly to his feet.

'Read a book if you can't sleep. And not crime.'

"Maybe she's right, Arch..."

Reached for his phone. Opened Amazon.

Found what he wanted.

Ordered it.

—————

24

'*That was a bit abrupt, wasn't it? Is Frankie alright? A couple of times lately...*'

Do I say anything? There's clearly something wrong.

No. She'll tell me when she's ready...

"Sarah Frances Trueman," Frankie said. "Born on Midsummer's Day, Nineteen-seventy. A conventional childhood in the leafy outskirts of Bradford. Nothing to report at school – "

"Brothers? Sisters?"

"An only child. Her mother was in her late thirties when Sarah was born. Probably decided that once was enough. Southampton University, a degree in Chemistry. Various teaching jobs, gradually working her way back up north, probably as her parents got older. Finally ending up at Lady Anne Clifford's."

"Lady Anne Clifford's? I've heard of that – "

"A very exclusive, *very* expensive boarding school high up in the Dales. That part of North Yorkshire where you're wondering if you've strayed into the Lake District. Thirty grand a year. Plus stabling if Cordelia wants to bring her horse. Sarah's the head of Chemistry. Was the head of Chemistry."

"So far motives for murder are thin on the ground, Frankie."

"So far motives for murder are non-existent, boss."

"Her parents are still in Bradford?"

"Parent. By the time she's at Lady Anne's her father is dead. Mother? Yes, still in the village where Sarah grew up."

"And Sarah's what? An hour away?"

Frankie shook her head. "Sixty miles. But given half of it is on country lanes through the Dales, closer to two."

"So it's a compromise between career and caring? Then her mother suddenly ups sticks and moves to Roxby?"

"Not until Sarah has left Lady Anne's. Five years ago. At which point Her Majesty's Passport Office takes up the story."

"The vicar said she travelled. Is this where those pictures of the beaches come in?"

"South America. Colombia, Peru, Paraguay – "

"Not working? How's she paying for it?"

"Her last job before Lady Anne's was in Cheshire. Sold her house there, so she's not short of money. No children. Did you buy that top for Ash?"

"It's eight in the morning, Frankie. Give me chance. But I looked in the shop window. So thank you. Back to Sarah. She's having a mid-life crisis in South America."

Frankie tutted. "Everyday sexism, boss. A woman's entitled to a mid-life crisis just as much as a man. Probably felt she'd gone straight from uni into teaching. Never seen the world. Was determined to do it before she was too old."

Is that what's bothering Frankie? Does she feel the same? Or has her body clock ticked? Struck twelve...

"And then she comes back. Apparently to look after her mother."

"It's a hell of a leap, Frankie. Rio to Roxby."

Frankie shrugged. "We'll never know the reason, boss. We sure as hell can't ask Sarah Trueman. Or her mother..."

"When did she die? Six months after Sarah moved in? Which suggests her health was failing. That's what the vicar said." Brady paused. Decided it was worth asking the question. "Chemistry teacher, Frankie. Her mum dies. She inherits the cottage..."

"You've watched too many episodes of *Breaking Bad*, boss. Besides – "

"Mum was duly cremated. So we'll never know. Where do you think tarot cards come into all this, Frankie?"

"You're asking me when she started? I've no idea. You want me to speculate? Maybe she realised there was more to life than Chemistry and staffroom politics. Maybe she'd always had an interest. Very clearly she was doing it professionally. And judging by the labels in her clothes, successfully."

"We need her laptop, Frankie."

Half an hour's work for Mozart to give me a list of her clients...

"Except it's presumably at the bottom of the harbour. Having been hit several times with a hammer."

Brady nodded. "Not in the house, so she took it with her. And if the killer's going to tidy the house – "

"He's going to make sure her laptop is never seen again. You want to walk down to Dave's, boss?"

Brady nodded. "Get your coat, Frankie. I thought you'd never ask. What about her phone? Bank account?"

Frankie shook her head. "Her phone's presumably with

her laptop. And the bank's the same. If it's all on her laptop..."

"We'd have to try every bloody bank in the world. Come on, let's have breakfast. And there's something I need to talk to you about on the way."

"What's that?"

"Cheese."

"I LOVE it at this time of year."

"Whitby?"

Brady nodded. "It's sort of fresh. New. Clean after the winter."

"That's a bit philosophical for you, boss."

"You know what I mean, Frankie. And you can feel the first hint of summer. Plus it's quiet. Doesn't take ten minutes to walk across the swing bridge."

"Cheese," Frankie said. "You were going to talk about cheese. Which can only mean one thing. You tried it."

Brady laughed. "I did. We had some Edam in the fridge. Completely tasteless if you ask me but Ash likes it. So I cut a chunk – "

"Told Archie it wasn't for him."

"Right. About three times. So I cut it, the same size as that nut off the window. And I try and swallow it."

"Could you?"

Brady shook his head. "No. Because it's cheese. Food. Basic instinct takes over. You can't help chewing it."

"But if you were desperate? And if it *wasn't* food?"

"Then the answer's yes. It wouldn't be easy. And it'd be bloody painful. But if I was Sarah Trueman. If I knew what was going to happen to me. Then yes."

Frankie stopped opposite Trencher's, her back to the

harbour. "We're going to walk down to Dave's. Supposing we go in the opposite direction, boss? Bagdale. Walk up Prospect Hill? Every other house will have sash windows."

"With locking nuts."

Frankie nodded. "And not just Prospect Hill. Half the houses in Whitby. Half the *old* houses in Whitby."

"Is that what we're saying, Frankie? She was held in Whitby?"

"Maybe the killer's taking the piss, boss. Holding her on Skinner Street. Two minutes' walk from the station."

Brady sighed. "How wide do we want to draw the circle?"

"Semi-circle, boss. Draw a circle round Whitby and half of it is the North Sea."

"OK. Semi-circle. Up to Saltburn? Down to Scarborough? Hell's bells, Frankie, she lived in Roxby. That's almost as close to Middlesbrough as it is to Whitby."

"Plenty of sash windows..."

"A million bloody sash windows. What are we supposed to do? Visit every house? We'd have more chance dressing Dan Keillor as Prince Charming and giving him a glass slipper."

25

___

'I'm going back to Roxby, Frankie. Speak to Dan Keillor's widows. Mrs Archer and Mrs Hornby. I'll be back this afternoon. Talk to all the schools, will you? Anything they can tell you about Sarah Trueman. And do your best to keep Jake focused...'*

Grey hair swept to one side, a face that had laughed a lot. A grandma that said, 'Chocolate? No, no. None at all.' Then winked at her granddaughter when mummy wasn't looking.

"You went in and looked after her cats?"

Molly Archer nodded enthusiastically. "That's what I told your young man. Dan, was it? He's a charmer. You can send him back to question me. The other one didn't have much to say for himself. But that's what I told them."

She finished filling the kettle. "You'll have tea, Mr Brady. And I made a new batch of flapjacks yesterday."

An instruction, not a question...

"Where was I? So yes, I went in to feed the cats."

"How often did you do that, Mrs Archer?"

She poured water into the kettle from a filter jug. "Yorkshire Tea alright for you is it, Mr Brady? And I'd say once a month. Sometimes more, sometimes less. Since the old lady passed over."

"Sarah Trueman's mother?"

'Chemistry teacher, Frankie. Her mum dies. She inherits the cottage...'

'You've watched too many episodes of Breaking Bad, boss.'

"She didn't look well at the end. I saw her once." Molly laughed. "But then we don't do we? If we looked well we wouldn't be knocking on the Pearly Gates. I just hope it's quick when my time comes. 'Let me get the flapjack out, Lord,' I'll say. 'Then I'll be ready.'" She shook her head. "Where was I?"

Brady laughed. "Going in to see the cats. Every month or so..."

And you're fine, Molly. Absolutely fine. Go at your own pace...

"Malkin, 'e were a bugger. Three dinners he'd have if you let him. 'No' I told him. 'One cat, one dinner, Malkin.' Fancie, he bullied her. Had to put her food up on the top, I did."

"Malkin and Fancie? That's..."

"Malkin, Fancie and Jeb. The cats in the Pendle witch trials. Not names I'd have chosen, but each to their own. I've lost track again. Fancie. That's right. She needed looking after."

Brady nodded. Assumed Jeb must have been able to fend for himself. "And Sarah gave you a key?"

She nodded again. "She did. On a special fob. You know, when you used to stay in a hotel? In the old days? And they gave you a proper, old-fashioned key to your room? Not the silly credit card thing they give you nowadays. *And* it doesn't work half the time."

"You let yourself in?"

A third nod. "I used to go for my walk in the morning. Every morning, rain or shine. 'You go for your walk, Molly.' That's what the doctor told me. And I do, and then I'd call in as I was coming back."

"There wasn't an alarm?"

She shook her head. "Not in Roxby."

Brady nodded. "Sorry to interrupt. You went in the morning..."

"Eight o'clock more or less. And in the afternoon I went round after *Countdown*. I got the conundrum yesterday. Reluctant."

Brady smiled. "A nine letter anagram? That's impressive."

"I usually can't get it. Well, they don't give you very long do they? But reluctant. It popped straight into my head."

"Can I ask a question, Mrs Archer? I'd value your opinion."

She smiled. Lowered her head. Looked coyly up at Brady.

Bloody hell, is she flirting with me? She's seventy if she's a day.

Another smile. "Of course you can, Mr Brady."

She is. I don't think I'll tell Frankie. Or Ash...

"Two questions, if you don't mind."

"Not at all. How's your flapjack, Mr Brady?"

Brady nodded. Chewed furiously so he could answer. "Lovely, Mrs Archer. The best I've ever tasted." Swallowed the last mouthful. "The last time you went round. Four weeks ago? Five? Did you notice anything unusual? Out of the ordinary?"

She shook her head. "I didn't. I'm not what you'd call observant. And *definitely* not nosy. Live and let live is what I say. But no. I went in, fed the cats and came out. Oh, there was a bit of post. I picked that up and put it on the side. One letter I noticed. Lovely handwriting. Italic? Is that what you call it? You don't see handwriting very often do you? Only at Christmas."

"Nothing else?"

She shook her head.

"And when you went round to feed the cats... This will sound an odd question. Was the house tidy?"

Molly Archer took her time replying. "I'd say this, Mr Brady. 'Tidy' is a relative term. If you'd asked my husband – God rest his soul – he'd have said it was spotless. Except men don't know what the word means, do they – "

Brady laughed. "But I know what you mean..."

"Me? I'd say it was a normal house. I mean the sink wasn't overflowing but it wasn't what you'd call spotless. Not like what my mother meant when she said 'spotless.' My grandma? Now she was a tartar. A proper tartar. All done by hand as well – "

Brady tried to stop her as gently as he could. Didn't need her family tree delineated by standards of cleanliness.

"Thank you. That's really helpful."

"What's going to happen now, Mr Brady?"

"We'll carry on with the investigation, Mrs Archer. I – "

"No, not that. With the cats."

Bloody hell. Diane Macdonald dies and I have to re-home her dog. Now it's three cats. I'm in the wrong job...

Brady smiled. "Dan said you were looking after them?"

"Doing my best..."

"Could I leave it to you, Mrs Archer? I can tell you're an animal lover..."

She nodded. "You can, Mr Brady. And Fancie, I think I'll keep her myself. She needs some love does Fancie. An' I'll find someone for Jeb no bother. Mrs Gristwood down the road, she lost her cat the other week. Can't say I like her much so maybe I'll see if she wants Malkin. Serve her right to have a bad-tempered cat."

Brady stood up and shook hands. "You're a treasure, Mrs Archer. And thank you for everything you've told me. You've been very helpful. And the flapjack. Lovely. Like I said, just lovely."

Another coy glance. "You call in any time you want, Mr Brady. The kettle's always on for a good looking young man like you." She winked. "And if there's no flapjack I'm sure I could treat you to a ginger nut or two..."

Brady promised he would. Escaped to his car. Checked Denise Hornby's address.

Wondered if he'd led a sheltered life.

Wondered if 'ginger nut' was a euphemism he hadn't come across...

26

B rady parked outside Denise Hornby's cottage. Reached for his phone.

"Dan? Mike Brady. A simple question. The cat bowls. When you went to Sarah Trueman's – when she was reported missing. Where were the cat bowls? All of them? *Definitely* none on the worktop? No, that's it. Thanks, Dan."

So Fancie missed her dinner. But Molly Archer's telling the truth. Whoever went in, it wasn't her...

He climbed out of the car. Pushed the gate open. Walked up a garden path that needed weeding. Rang the bell. Wasn't certain it was working. Knocked as an insurance policy.

"Mrs Hornby? Detective Chief Inspector Brady."

Grey hair, glasses, a thin face. A worried frown.

The old lady out of the ad. The one who hasn't put enough away for her funeral.

"Come in, Inspector."

A South Yorkshire accent. Not so much Rio to Roxby as Rotherham to Roxby.

She led the way into the kitchen. Gestured for Brady to

sit at the table. Flicked the kettle on without asking. Reached for two mugs. Passed him a weak, milky tea.

"I won't keep you long, Mrs Hornby. There were just a couple of questions I wanted to ask you. A follow-up to when you saw DC Keillor."

"An' the other one. He didn't have much to say for himself."

Someone else. What's going on, Jake?

"DC Keillor said you'd had a tarot reading, Mrs Hornby."

She nodded. Looked suddenly pensive. "I did an' all. She came for coffee. It was Freddie's anniversary."

"Freddie?"

"My husband. October the first. Four years gone. An' my birthday on the second. The last thing he said to me in the hospice. 'Happy birthday, lass.' 'Happy birthday, lass' an' he were gone. So there you are. There's me sitting at the kitchen table with my lonely cup of tea, thinking back. An' there's a couple of other things I'm thinking about as well. Our Ros, things weren't right with her. An' there's a knock on the door. An' it's Sarah. So we get talking. An' she's a good listener, I'll give her that."

"Did she know?"

"Did she know it was his anniversary? I don't know. Maybe. October the first, it's not hard to remember is it? Maybe I'd mentioned it. I can't remember. She'd been somewhere. Middlesbrough, I think. Somewhere up there. Some shop for a new pack of cards – "

"Tarot cards?"

She nodded. "Lovely they were. Beautiful pictures."

Brady reached for his phone. Opened *photos*. Showed her the cards laid out on Sarah Trueman's table. "Those cards?"

"Well, I'm not an expert, am I? But they look the same."

"So she offered to do a reading for you?"

"Not so much offered as said she could see something was troubling me. 'Why don't you let the cards guide you, Denise?' she said. An' I said I'd always been suspicious of things like that. 'Specially with going to church an' all. But she said, not to worry. 'The Lord moves in mysterious ways,' she said."

Brady nodded. Stayed silent.

Let her tell you the story in her own time...

"So she got this new pack of cards out. Like she's eager to see what they can do. Reminded me of Freddie. When he bought a new car he always took me out for a drive. 'See what she can do, lass.' She were the same wi' her new cards. But I'm worrying that she wants some money 'cos I'm a widow now and I don't have much. But she could sense that an' all and she said, 'No, I was a friend and she could see I was troubled.' An' she winked an' said 'I'll add a bit on to some rich fella from Leeds.'"

"Can I ask what she told you? DC Keillor said you were impressed."

She nodded. "I was. She said I had to think of a question. A specific question. An' I thought about Rosaline. An' the first card she turns up is the Devil. Revenge, she said. Violence. And that's him – "

"That's..."

"Kenny. The bloke she's with at the time. Father of her bairns worse luck but they seem to take after their mum. At least for now. Then the next one is the Ten of Cups. An' she says that means there'll be a happy ending. An' two weeks later your lads pick him up. Well – "

"Kenny?"

"The very same. Not *your* lads, but over in Liverpool where they live. Two weeks! I don't drink, Mr Brady but I raised a glass. Fraud. An' the bugger gets ten years. Felt like I'd won the lottery." She shook her head. "I told her. 'Don't marry him,' I said. But you know how it is with some women. They can't resist a bad boy."

Brady nodded. Let her tell the story.

"So that's the tale, Mr Brady. An' now your tea's gone cold. Let me make you a fresh one. 'Cos you'll want to know more than what happened to Kenny."

"I'm fine, Mrs Hornby. Really. I've been drinking tea all morning."

And eating flapjack...

"I said to her. 'It hurts right now,' I said. 'But you're better off without him.' An' she's seeing a lovely bloke now. Treats her right."

She brightened. Gave Brady his cue.

"How well did you know Sarah, Mrs Hornby?"

She shrugged. "Not that well. But like I said, she were a good listener. An' a teacher. I know that. That posh school up in the Dales. Lady Anne's something or other."

"Did you ever ask her why she left?"

"Well, I'm not nosy – "

No, of course not...

" – But she said something came up. She didn't say what but I got the feeling it was a disagreement. She went travelling, did you know that? South America? On her own. Brave woman. I wouldn't do that. Even when I was younger. You hear stories don't you? Freddie, bless him, he could be a bit annoying but if I wanted to get away I went down the garden. Didn't need to go to South America that's for sure."

"And she didn't have any enemies? As far as you know? No-one held a grudge against her?"

She shook her head. "Like me. Kept herself to herself.

Besides, you've already talked to the village magpie. If anyone – "

"The village – "

"Molly Archer. Not many secrets that one doesn't know."

"You know I can't comment, Mrs Hornby." Brady stood up. Held his hand out. "Thank you. You've been very helpful. Now I need to get back to Whitby."

"There's something else," she said. "Before you go."

"Something about Sarah?"

She shook her head. "That morning your lads came. I had thirty pounds under the biscuit tin. Money for the gardener. He comes once a month 'cos I can't do the hedge now. An' it were gone."

"I'm sorry. I don't – "

"The money for the gardener. I always put it in the same place. An' it were gone."

Is she accusing Dan and Jake?

"Neither DC Keillor nor PC Cartwright mentioned anything, Mrs Hornby."

She shook her head again. A very clear it's-not-right expression. "It was under the biscuit tin. Where I always put it. And then it wasn't there. That's all I'm saying."

"Maybe the gardener..."

She shook her head. "No. 'Cos I always give him it when I make him a cup of tea. Cup of tea an' a biscuit he has when he's finished. Not before or he gets nowt done. An' the money wasn't there 'cos I had to go upstairs an' find some more."

She is accusing Dan and Jake...

I need to speak to them. And I need to change the subject.

"I'm sorry about the confusion, Mrs Hornby. Why don't you leave it with me? And I might need to speak to you again about Sarah."

"You do that, Mr Brady. I'm not going anywhere."

Brady walked back down the path. Thought that if Mrs Hornby had escaped Freddie by going into the garden it hadn't been to do the weeding.

Knew he needed to speak to Dan Keillor...

27

Brady's phone rang as he was driving through Lythe. "Make it quick, Frankie. I'm just about to go down Lythe Bank."

"You've answered my question, boss."

"Am I on my way back? I am. I need to see Dan Keillor, so don't let him cycle off into the sunset."

"I'll tell him. I – "

"I thought you were off to Scotland this weekend? Lochie's dad's birthday or something?"

"We are. But I've told him we're going to be late. I need to see you before I go. Specifically, I need to take you to May Beck."

"OK. I do need to speak to Dan though. Five minutes with him. No more."

Brady braked as he started down Lythe Bank.

'I need to take you to May Beck.' What for? Something new? A breakthrough...

Turned right at the bottom of the hill. Drove through Sandsend lost in thought. Didn't even glance at Siobhan's front door as he drove past...

. . .

PARKED OUTSIDE THE STATION. Switched the engine off.

How do I want to play this...

Reached for his phone. "Dan? Mike Brady. I need a word with you. Walk downstairs will you? I'm in the car outside."

Sit in the car? Stand outside?

Brady climbed out of the car. Saw the door of the police station open. Dan Keillor come out. Blond, a shade over six foot. Navy shirt, grey chinos.

"Walk up the road with me, Dan. I've a question for you."

Dan Keillor looked puzzled.

"I'm getting old, Dan. Humour me. It's unofficial. But important."

They started walking up Spring Hill, occasional glimpses of the harbour to their left, a patch of open ground on their right.

"I was in Roxby this morning, Dan. Mrs Archer and – more pertinently – Mrs Hornby. Did she make you a cup of tea?"

Dan Keillor laughed. "No, she didn't. That's not your question is it, boss?"

"No. And if you escaped the tea count yourself lucky. She said something to me, Dan. There's no simple way for me to say it, so I'll just come straight out with it. She told me she'd put thirty quid out for the gardener. 'Under the biscuit tin, Mr Brady.' And it was there before you and Jake arrived. And wasn't there when you'd gone."

Dan Keillor stopped in his tracks. Stared at Brady. "She's accusing Jake and me of taking it?"

Brady nodded. "Not in those exact words. But that was the implication. Did you see the money, Dan?"

He shook his head. "No. I was focused on asking the questions. Taking notes."

"How long where you there?"

"Ten minutes? Fifteen maybe."

"And that's all that happened? Knock on the door, introduce yourselves, ask your questions, leave?"

"That's all, boss."

Brady nodded. "Which is why you didn't mention it. Thanks, Dan. She's obviously mistaken. Come on, let's get back. Frankie needs to see me."

They turned. Started walking back along Spring Hill.

Dan Keillor suddenly stopped. "There was one thing, boss..."

"What's that?"

"Probably nothing. But she had a delivery. A big bag of flour. She asked me if I could help her with it. Carry it from the front door into her utility room. She bakes her own bread. Said her neighbour usually moves it for her but he was away for the day."

"A bag of flour?"

"One of those bloody enormous ones bakers use. She must bake bread for the whole village."

Brady slowed down. "The bag of flour, Dan. You didn't notice how much it weighed did you?"

"Yeah, I did. I do weights at the gym twice a week so I looked. Twenty-five KG."

Twenty-five kilogrammes. About a third of Sarah Trueman...

"The neighbour, Dan. Check him out will you? Take a drive out there if you have to."

"With Jake?"

Brady shook his head. "No, it's not a two-man job. You do it, Dan."

28

'I had thirty pounds under the biscuit tin. Money for the gardener. I always put it in the same place. An' it were gone.'

'She's accusing Jake and me of taking it?'

'That was the implication, Dan...'

Do I say anything to Frankie? No. Because there's no need. Because Mrs Hornby's made a mistake.

FRANKIE TURNED. Looked at the rain beating against the window. Shook her head. "I was going to take you to May Beck, boss..."

"Is it something we can do in the office, Frankie? Soaked to the skin. Not quite how I planned to end the week. And you've got to drive to Scotland."

And you should be halfway up the A1 by now. So what's so important...

She sighed. "Tell me about it. Friday night. Half an hour to crawl past the Metro Centre. Can't see a bloody thing on the A1 because of the spray. The last sixty miles in the dark.

And then a scolding from Lochie's mother when we get there. 'I was expecting you earlier, dear.' Said in the tone of voice that – " She stopped. Shook her head. "I'm being unkind. Theory not practice then, boss. You'll need to use your imagination."

"Before you do that," Brady said. "The schools. Lady Anne's in particular. What did they have to say? I'll trade you the schools for Dan Keillor's widows."

"You'll be disappointed. Nothing. Almost nothing."

"How come?"

"Staff turnover, mostly. The schools she was at before Lady Anne's. Nearly all the staff had changed. I spoke to one person who'd worked with her. 'Good teacher. Popular among her colleagues. The kids liked her.' Nothing you couldn't have guessed."

"Tarot? Any clues on that?"

"I asked that question. 'What did she do outside school?' 'Well, Detective Sergeant, I didn't know her *that* well. She walked. Played badminton, I think. Kept herself fit.'"

"Relationships?"

"Nothing significant that anyone mentioned. One of the schools – the one in Cheshire. I spoke to the school secretary. She said she thought Sarah had been involved with one of the other teachers. And no, before your eyes light up, he doesn't live in Staithes. He emigrated. He's teaching in Christchurch now."

"Hampshire or New Zealand?"

"New Zealand. You can't emigrate to the south, boss."

"We're from Whitby, Frankie. Of course we can. Anywhere south of Doncaster."

Brady nodded at the window. "And it's getting heavier. The steps up to St Mary's will be a waterfall. What did Lady Anne's have to say?"

"Absolutely nothing, boss. 'It is not our policy to discuss previous members of staff. It is not our policy to give information over the telephone.' The blankest of blank walls."

"You think they've something to hide?"

"No, boss. I think they're so far up their own arse they've completely disappeared."

Brady smiled. "So I get a trip to the Dales. Fair enough. Dan Keillor's widows. And first things first. If you get a choice, interview Mrs Archer."

"Better biscuits?"

"Home-made flapjack. She went in and fed the cats once a month. I'm certain she's telling the truth. But next time we're in the house we need to look for a 'proper, old-fashioned key.' On a proper, old-fashioned fob, presumably."

"We're going back then?"

Brady nodded. "We are. Because I've missed something. And it's tapping me on the shoulder."

"Annoyingly out of reach? That makes two of us."

"I asked Mrs Archer if it was tidy when she went in. 'Normal,' she said. 'Not spotless.' So you're right, Frankie. Someone went in. Three other things. She mentioned a handwritten letter. 'With lovely handwriting. Italic.'"

"Except if she went in a month ago the letter will be long gone."

"Unless it's in a drawer. Handwritten letters. They're the ones people keep. And she said Sarah Trueman's mother wasn't looking well."

"Possibly why she died, boss? I told you. *Breaking Bad*. You said three things. What about the other one?"

"The cats. Malkin, Fancie and Jeb. Named after the cats in the Pendle witch trials apparently."

"Do I think that's significant? Is that what you're saying? Tarot cards? Witch trials?" Frankie shook her head. "No. You get cats at the same time, you give them names that are linked. Batman and Robin. Homer and Marge – "

"Thelma and Louise?"

"Let's hope it has a happier ending, boss. What about your second widow. Mrs Hornby?"

"*Don't* drink her tea. But she was impressed by her tarot reading. Sarah Trueman told her about her son-in-law. The Devil, no less."

"Literally?"

"I don't think anything in the tarot is literal, Frankie. She said it meant revenge and violence. Her son-in-law apparently. But it's followed by the Ten of Cups. A happy ending. And two weeks later the son-in-law is arrested for fraud. Ten years."

"We can check that?"

Brady nodded. "I've only got his first name but one of the guys in Merseyside was in Manchester with me. I'll phone him."

"Did she say anything about Sarah?"

"She had the impression she left the school because of a disagreement. And then went travelling in South America."

"Taking photos of beaches."

Brady nodded. "What were you going to tell me about May Beck? Rain or no rain you'll want to be on your way."

Or maybe not, judging by your expression...

"I was going to give you a Maths lesson, boss." Frankie held her hand up, forefinger extended. "But one more thing..."

"Good news?"

"Maybe. Geoff got the bloods back. He was right. Rohypnol. Like we thought, the date rape drug."

"So she walked. He helps her out of the car and she walks to her execution." Brady shook his head. "What did I say the other day, Frankie? 'I'm starting to admire this guy?' Something like that. Yes, he did his homework but bloody hell, he's a cold bastard."

"Or they are, boss."

Brady looked at her. "*They* are? You're suggesting there's more than one person involved?"

"Possibly."

"Possibly? So yes or no?"

Frankie smiled. "Possibly."

"You're not as certain as someone buying her clothes?"

"I am. But it's complicated. And it's Maths."

Brady nodded. "You're going to explain. Do I need a coffee?"

"The machine's broken."

"Bloody hell. Has someone called the engineer? Or shall we impound a kettle and giant tin of Nescafé off some luckless B&B?" Brady shook his head in frustration. "Before you start, how's Jake been today?"

"What I've seen of him, OK. We got a call about some domestic violence. Littlebeck. He's been out there with Alan Swinbank. You're worried about him, aren't you?"

Brady nodded. "I am, Frankie."

'I had thirty pounds under the biscuit tin. An' it were gone.'

"Why don't you speak to him?"

"What will he say? 'Everything's fine, boss.' Let's see what develops. Teach me some maths, Frankie. What did Geoff say? 'Cause of death a madman.' How many madmen, Frankie? One? Two? Or a football team?"

"SOMETHING TAPPING you on the shoulder, boss. In my case it was Maths. So imagine you're at May Beck. You're staring up at the body. How much do you think she weighs?"

"We know that. Eleven stone. Just over."

"Right. Let's do it in kilogrammes. That'll make the maths easier. And eleven stone is seventy kilos, give or take an extra portion of chips. You OK with this?"

"So far. I can understand seventy kilos."

And an extra portion of chips...

"Go on..."

"So the gravitational force is ten Newtons. Nine point eight really but ten for the sake of – "

"What's a Newton?"

Frankie shook her head. "Sadly Michael spent much of his time in Mathematics staring out of the window. It's a unit of force, boss. Equal to the force that would give a mass of one kilogramme an acceleration of one metre per second per second. Equivalent to a hundred thousand dynes." Frankie smiled. "Maybe you were ill for that lesson?"

"I must have been..."

"Where was I? Keeping it simple. So the gravitational force is ten Newtons. That means the killer needs to exert a force of seven hundred Newtons – ten times seventy – to lift the body. More because of the friction on the tree branch. It's a pulley, but a very inefficient one. She's three feet off the ground. So seven hundred Newtons for three feet. That do you, boss?"

Brady didn't speak. Looked at Frankie. Narrowed his eyes. "Are you trying to outwit me, Detective Sergeant? Or proving you're far too bright to be a copper? Was it one person or two, Frankie? With or without Isaac Newton's help?"

"You just wanted a simple answer, boss?"

"If there is a simple answer..."

"One. *Providing* he's strong. And I mean really strong. No disrespect, boss, but you probably couldn't do it. He's in a standing position, only using his arms. So seriously strong. And fit."

"Like who?"

"That we know? Dan Keillor maybe?"

'A big bag of flour. Twenty-five kilogrammes. Said her neighbour usually moves it for her but he was away for the day.'

"But even then I wouldn't put money on it. Dave? But thirty years ago – in his rugby playing days."

"So two people is more likely?"

Frankie nodded. "Much more likely. Two people pull her up. One holds her in place while the other ties the rope round that branch. Except…"

"Except what?"

"He might have jumped."

"Jumped? I thought you said he was standing still?"

"He was. But why *that* tree, boss? Out of all the trees in the wood? Remember the steps at the side of it?"

Brady nodded.

"Supposing he held the rope, walked up the steps and jumped? I went out there this morning. Just after sunrise. It's doable."

Brady didn't speak.

Saw the killer holding the rope.

Walking up the steps…

"He's using his own body weight," Frankie said. "Gravity pulls him down."

"He goes down. Sarah Trueman goes up?"

Frankie nodded. "How many trees are there in that wood, boss?"

"I don't know. A thousand. Ten thousand."

"Right. How many have a convenient set of steps next to them?"

"And you and I don't believe in coincidence…"

Frankie shook her head. "We don't. Coincidences don't catch killers. Facts do."

"Facts and evidence. Except – "

"Except what?"

"Suppose he's playing with us, Frankie? Suppose there *are* two people – "

"And he wants us to think it's one?"

"The bastard did his homework. *Really* did his home-work. Something else as well."

"What?"

"He enjoyed it."

Because I can see you. Standing on those bloody steps. Congratulating yourself on finding them. Congratulating yourself on being so bloody clever.

Don't spend too long feeling smug, you bastard. I'm coming for you...

beautiful morning. The sun rising out of the sea. The light sparkling and dancing across the water. The first hint of summer.

Michael Brady threw Archie's ball.

Looked up and saw Sarah Trueman's body.

Red jeans, cornflower blue jacket. Hanging by her right ankle. Swaying gently in the wind.

Heard snatches of conversation.

'*He did his homework, Frankie. Made plans. Went to a lot of trouble.*'

'*The locking nut. Could you swallow it, boss?*'

'*Yes. It wouldn't be easy. And it'd be bloody painful. But if I was Sarah Trueman. If I knew what was going to happen to me. Then yes.*'

'*So yes or no, Frankie? One person or two?*'

Stop it. Just bloody well stop it. Saturday. You're on the beach. It's a perfect morning. The beach is deserted.

What's Ash say? 'Be happy in the moment.' So do it.

Archie was back. Panting. Dropping the ball at Brady's feet.

"You've covered it in gob again, Arch. You're going to make me admit to middle age. Buy one of those whippy sticks. Here."

Brady kicked the ball. Watched it hit the remains of a sandcastle. Stop dead.

"Sorry, Arch. Hit the post. One more, OK? Then we need to go and see Dave. Get some breakfast. Last one. *Don't* cover it in gob and you've earned a biscuit."

A drop-kick this time. Brady watched Archie scamper after the ball. Skid to a halt. Grab the ball in his mouth. Trot back.

Brady rummaged in his pocket. Found the last dog biscuit. Held it between two fingers.

"Pay attention, Arch. I'm going to throw this biscuit up in the air. This biscuit you're staring at. And Frankie says gravity is going to bring it back to earth. Or the beach in our case. And you can eat it. They're called Newton's, Arch. According to Frankie. Acceleration. I'm not sure if it applies to dog biscuits but we'll soon find out."

Brady tossed the biscuit into the air. Watched Archie jump. Twist. Catch it in mid-air.

"Hell's bells, Archie. You're not supposed to leap up like some salmon-on-steroids. Catch it halfway. Take your time. Admire the physics. Learn something."

"Good morning. Lovely day."

Brady turned. Saw an elderly man with an even more elderly Labrador. Mumbled an embarrassed 'good morning.'

He clipped Archie's lead on. Started walking back towards the slipway. Glanced up at the houses on West Cliff.

Plenty with sash windows.

'Maybe the killer's taking the piss, boss. Holding her on Skinner Street. Two minutes' walk from the station.'

Maybe he was, Frankie. Or on West Cliff. Maybe the condemned cell had a sea view...

"Good walk, Mike?"

"Lovely, Dave. Sun shining, beach more or less deserted. And I gave Archie a physics lesson."

Dave paused. Looked at Brady over his shoulder. "You gave Archie a physics lesson?"

"I did. Newtons. The way gravity acts on a dog biscuit."

Dave flipped the bacon over on the griddle. Turned. Nodded. "Two things, Mike. The stress might be getting to you."

"What's the second?"

"Archie. Make sure he swots up for the exam."

Brady laughed. "Can I ask you a question, Dave?"

"Course you can. So long as it's not about physics. I was sat next to Barbara Fraser in science. Other things on my mind."

"Rugby, Dave. Your playing days. Did you do that thing where you lifted someone in the lineout?"

Dave shook his head. "Illegal in my day, Mike. So yes, we did it all the time."

"It must have taken a hell of an effort."

"Aye, it did. That's why two of us did it. Eighteen stone lock forward? Can't do it on your own, can you?"

"So two of you?"

Dave nodded. "Here's your bacon butty. Hope you've plenty on today. Stuck you an' extra rasher in. An' yeah, two of us. Go home an' look at a YouTube video. One catcher. Two guys to lift him. One by his knees, the other one more or less grabs his arse."

Brady nodded. "But a woman. Someone much lighter..."

"Could you do it on your own? Is that what you're asking? In theory. You'd still need to be a big, strong lad though."

'Was it one person or two, Frankie?'

'One. Providing he's strong. And I mean really strong. You couldn't do it, boss. He's in a standing position, only using his arms.'

Like a rugby player...

"Mike?"

"Sorry, Dave, I was miles away."

Dave shook his head. "Your own worst enemy, Mr Brady. Take the day off. Take your daughter shopping. Or is that pretty girlfriend of yours coming round?"

"Tonight. She's been away for a couple of days. So yeah, I need to call at the butcher's. Get something for dinner."

Dave winked at him. "Chocolate, Mike. Dark chocolate and chillies. Not from the butcher's, obviously."

Brady laughed. "Aphrodisiac, Dave? The only aphrodisiac she needs is a boyfriend that listens when she speaks."

A boyfriend that's not in a wood. Staring at a tree...

"I'll leave you to it. Have a good weekend. See yous Monday morning. Frankie n' all?"

"Hopefully. She's up in Scotland for the weekend. Driving back tomorrow night."

"Bloody long way for a weekend."

Do I say anything? Who else do I talk to?

"Between you and me, Dave, I get the feeling Frankie might be thinking that. Like you say. A bloody long way. Especially in the dark."

Brady bent down. Ruffled the top of Archie's head. "Come on, mate, we need to get home. Time to do some – "

"*Not* work, Mike. Remember what I said."

"Reading, Dave. Amazon delivery. Need to get home before the delivery guy decides the East Pier is close enough."

30

———

"What are you reading, Dad?"

Brady braced himself for the derision. Held the book up.

Ash looked. Turned away. Looked again. Did an exaggerated double-take any cartoon character would have been proud of.

"*Tarot for Beginners*? Detective Chief Inspector Cold Hard Evidence is reading *Tarot for Beginners*? That was your Amazon delivery?"

"That was my Amazon delivery. I'm..."

What the hell am I doing?

"...I'm trying to understand. Get some background. Teach myself."

"Because of this case?"

Brady nodded. "Yes. Because of this case."

"What's next, Dad? A Ouija board? You, Frankie and an upturned glass? That would make the job a lot simpler. Contact the victim, ask her who did it."

Brady laughed. "It would, I'll grant you that. And..."

"What, Dad?"

Do I want to have this discussion with her? Why not?

"It's happened. In the police."

"What? You've used a Ouija board? When?"

"Not me. There was a case in the eighties or nineties. A ten year old girl had disappeared. Surrey, Middlesex. Somewhere down that way. This guy in his thirties is working on a building site. He's been brought up in a spiritualist family. And he's got a guide – "

"A guide?"

"A spirit guide. A Native American who died in the Battle of the Little Big Horn."

"Why is a Native American working on a building site?"

"Don't be cynical, Ash. This guy gets a message that the spirit guide knows about the little girl. He goes to see the police, convinces them he's genuine – "

"How?"

"What is this, cross-examination? I think he invited them to a séance. Anyway, he convinces them he's genuine, gives them information. They find the girl's body, and arrest the guy she's spent her life calling 'uncle.' She used to walk his dog on a Saturday morning."

"And he did it?"

Brady nodded. "Pleaded not guilty I think. But he got about twelve years."

"So why don't you use someone like that this time? Why don't you use them *every* time?"

"Because ninety-nine per cent of people who volunteer to help the police are cranks or frauds. Because I'm convinced the answer is closer to home."

Because I can do without Kershaw's withering sarcasm.

And the newspaper headlines. 'Desperate Detective begs Spirit Guide for Help...'

"But just in case you're reading a book on the tarot?"

Brady laughed. "There you are. Just in case."

"So which one are you, Dad?"

"Which one – "

"Which card? The King of Swords? The Knight of Wands?"

"I haven't got that far yet. I'm on 'framing the question.' Apparently you need to have a specific question in mind."

"Like 'what's for lunch?' I'm starving."

"I think maybe a touch more subtle than that Ash? Anyway, how come you know so much?"

"There's a new girl at school. Leanne. She's into all that sort of stuff. She had a pack at school."

Brady laughed. "Right. I'll tell Gypsy Sara to watch out shall I? Talk to me about something more practical. How's work going? Schoolwork?"

Ash shrugged. "Yeah. Good. Law's interesting this term."

"What are you doing?"

"Different legal systems? You know, around the world. Some of them are... Even you wouldn't approve, Dad."

"Crime and punishment, Ash."

"Crime and *some* punishments. Dad. Not all of them."

Change the subject. Before she wins the argument...

"I bought you something," Brady said. He nodded at a carrier bag in the corner of the room. "You've been so busy interrogating me you didn't notice."

Ash turned, saw the bag. "The Studio? You've been into The Studio?"

Brady nodded. "I have. Open it."

Ash opened the bag. A blouse, halfway between yellow and burnt orange. A black and white feather print.

"I love it, Dad! Love it. Thank you."

She walked across to Brady. Hugged him. Hugged him again.

"Like my favourite shirt. Half-placket."

"Popover, Dad, that's what you call it."

"Batwing sleeves?"

"Careful, Dad. Knowing too much about fashion is dangerous at your age. But I love it. Thank you."

Ash narrowed her eyes. Looked at him. "Batwing sleeves? You've been talking to someone, haven't you? Frankie. She told you."

Brady laughed. "Ten out of ten, detective. But you've been working hard. You deserve it."

"Thanks, Dad. And say thank you to your informant. I clearly owe her coffee. I'm going to put that pizza in the oven, you want some?"

"Maybe. A couple of slices. You eat the rest. Ash, one thing..."

A question I shouldn't ask...

"Pepperoni, Dad."

"I know it's pepperoni. I bought it. Frankie, Ash. Is she alright?"

Can I mention doctor's appointments? No.

"She's... I don't know. I get the impression there's something on her mind."

Ash nodded. "Maybe. Maybe not."

"And if there was you wouldn't tell me?"

"Maybe – "

So there is something. Ash knows. And Frankie's asked her not to say anything...

"OK. Understood. I won't ask you to break a confidence."

"Thanks, Dad. I'm sure she'll tell you when the time's right. Just two slices? You're sure?"

"Maybe three then. You twisted my arm."

. . .

BRADY GOT OFF THE SOFA. Made a coffee. Told Archie the afternoon walk was still two hours away. Went back to the book. Was beginning to think it was a waste of time. Started skipping pages. Jumped to the tarot cards.

The Fool. That's me. Innocence. A leap of faith. You need to be clearer. Damn right I need to be clearer. Clearer about who killed Sarah Trueman.

"And if it's upside down, Arch, recklessness and risk-taking. Judging by those black clouds that's what we'll be doing this afternoon, mate."

"You alright, Dad? I'm going to tidy the kitchen then Spence is coming round."

"No problem. And I'm fine, Ash. Just telling Archie his fortune."

Brady went back to the book. Glanced at the clouds. Decided that the sooner he went out with Archie the better.

Flipped the page over.

Saw the picture.

Felt the breath leave his body.

The Hanged Man.

A black and white picture. A man hanging upside down.

Hung by his right foot. His left leg crossed behind his right knee.

Sarah Trueman. Sarah bloody Trueman.

Exactly like that...

Reached for his phone. Tapped it into Safari.

Knew what he'd find.

Red trousers. A cornflower blue jacket.

What's it say? Sacrifice. Letting go. Accept the pause... Accept something new. Embrace the stillness. The poor bloody woman has all eternity to embrace the stillness. Reversed... Fear of change. Missed opportunities. Don't stay in your comfort zone.

Right now what it says is irrelevant...

Brady didn't think. Dialled her number.

Three rings. Then the answerphone.

"Shit. Frankie. Sorry. For swearing. Frankie, ring me will you? As soon as you get the message. And go on Google. The tarot card. The Hanged Man. It's her, Frankie. Sarah Trueman."

"Dad... Dad!"

"What is it, Ash? I'm on the phone."

"There's someone at the door. Someone for you."

"There can't be. Sorry, Frankie. Ash was talking to me. Ring me. When you get the message. What is it, Ash? There can't be anything for me, I haven't ordered anything else."

"Not Amazon, Dad. A real person. Without a parcel. She's young. Good-looking. Have I got a secret half-sister?"

"Don't – "

"I'm teasing. She says her name is Claire."

31

She was in her early-twenties. Brown eyes, long dark hair, visibly nervous. A denim jacket over a white T-shirt. Jeans.

She brought her right hand up, brushed her hair back. Looked at him.

"Mr Brady?"

Hesitantly held her hand out.

"I'm Claire. Claire Gardner."

"I'm sorry. I – "

"We haven't met. I'm Jake's girlfriend."

Brady's mind was still on The Hanged Man. "Jake? Cartwright? PC Cartwright?"

Yes. Jake. Your Jake. And this can only mean one thing. There's a problem...

She nodded again. "More than his girlfriend. We're engaged. I – "

"How did you find me? I can't believe Jake gave you the address."

She shook her head. "I'm sorry. I followed you home. The other night. Waited for you to leave the station. Jake had said you lived close-by. I'm sorry…"

Brady smiled. "Good job you're not a Russian spy. And you clearly need to talk to me. Obviously about Jake. And I'm guessing Jake doesn't know about this? Or you'd have come into the station."

"Yes. Exactly that." She tried to laugh. "He said you were a good detective." Reached for a tissue instead. Blew her nose. Made a visible effort not to cry.

Invite her in? Listen what she has to say? Then I'm going behind Jake's back. But it's clearly important to her. Important enough for her to wait outside the station. And follow me…

"Come in, Claire. You clearly need to talk to me."

Brady led the way into the lounge. Introduced her to Ash. His daughter made a tactical retreat to her bedroom. Said she'd meet Spencer in town.

"You want a coffee or anything? A cold drink?"

Claire shook her head. "I'm too nervous."

That important…

"Claire, this puts me in a slightly difficult position. Obviously I'm Jake's boss. And I don't like going behind people's back. But – "

She nodded. "I understand that. I've been awake all night. That was one of the things I worked out. But…" She reached for another tissue. Blew her nose a second time. "… I'm his girlfriend. *I* don't like going behind his back either. But he needs help, Mr Brady. You must have noticed."

Ten out of ten for courage. I'll give you that…

Brady nodded. "Yes, I have. We're obviously busy. More than busy. But you're right. I'd be lying if I said I hadn't noticed something. Tell me the problem. Start from the beginning. And if you want a drink, just say."

She nodded. Started hesitantly. "Jake and me – we've been together eighteen months. Bonfire night. His best mate was at school with my sister. She introduced us. We started talking about plans. You know, *serious* plans, maybe around Christmas time. So we're not really engaged. But – "

"But close enough?" Brady smiled. Willed her to relax. "Take as much time as you want, Claire."

Realised how to help her relax. "Hang on, Claire. One minute…"

Brady stood up. Walked into the kitchen. Came back with two dog biscuits. Handed them to Claire. "Here. Make friends. I promised him a walk – "

"I'm sorry. He's beautiful. What's he called?"

"Archie. And there you go. You're friends. And he understands. Tell me what you do, Claire."

"I'm a midwife. Training to be a midwife. At Scarborough. Not much fun driving there in the winter. But I like it. More than like it."

"So what's the problem?" Brady said as gently as he could.

She sniffed. Reached for her tissue. "I need to talk to someone. And you're the only person I could think of. I can't talk to my mum and dad. They're not… I don't think they're very keen on Jake. Think I should come home with a doctor."

Brady nodded. Smiled. "My wife's parents felt the same. Thought she could do better than a lowly copper. Go on, I'm listening…"

"There was a mum, a week ago. She'd just had her baby. It was two o'clock in the morning. I was trying to help her feed. A little girl. Smashing little lass. But she won't latch on. She's crying, saying she's going to be a bad mother. I'm telling her it's normal. And we just got talking. The middle of the night. I made a cup of tea. She said to me, 'He's not the father. I should have said something. But it's too late now. I don't love him. And now I'm stuck with him.'"

"And she's the one who persuaded you to talk to me?"

Claire looked surprised. Nodded. "Not directly. But she's the one..." She sighed. Shook her head. "She's the one that made me see I had to do something. How did you know?"

"Because that's how it happens. Because someone says something. You don't notice it at the time. Afterwards, you realise it was significant."

"That's it exactly. 'Cos I do love Jake. He's not perfect, but..."

She looked up. Looked Brady in the eye. "I don't want it to be too late."

"So tell me the problem..."

She took a deep breath. Said it so quietly that Brady had to lean forward to hear her. "Jake's addicted to gambling, Mr Brady. It's destroying him. It's destroying *us*. And I can't do anything. I don't know *what* to do. And that's why I'm here."

'I had thirty pounds under the biscuit tin. Money for the gardener. I always put it in the same place. An' it were gone.'

'She's accusing Jake and me of taking it?'

Shit...

"You want to tell me how it started, Claire? As much as you know?"

She shook her head. "I've been stupid. Really stupid. I should have seen it earlier."

"We don't, Claire. The people closest to us. Sometimes we don't see it."

"Other lads his age go on their PlayStation. Jake goes online. And when he's not online he's watching football – "

"And the ads come on at half-time? Or his team's sponsored by a bookie?"

"Right. But it's not just football. You remember – you

probably don't. You'd have more important things to do – a month or so ago. Jake didn't come in. I phoned in for him. Lied to protect him. Said he'd been up all night being sick. We'd eaten some crab or something." She shook her head. "It wasn't that. He'd been gambling all night. Until three, maybe four in the morning."

"And losing money?"

She nodded. "Everything he had on his card. Not that much 'cos he was near the limit. But enough. The deposit for our holiday."

And that can't be doing your relationship any good...

"And then it all fell into place. Times when he said he was too tired to go out. When he didn't want to phone for a takeaway."

"Because he had no money?"

She nodded. Another deep breath.

Halfway between a sigh and a sob.

She's not that much older than Ash. Six years. Seven...

"I'm embarrassed. It was our first anniversary. He wouldn't come to bed."

"Because he'd got some bets on the football?"

She nodded. "I can't help thinking back to that girl in hospital. I kept saying it to myself. 'She should have done something.' Even if it was hard. Maybe even if it meant getting rid of the baby. Talked to her mum and dad. But she should have done *something*."

"And that's what you're doing."

"I hope so. Before it's too late. Because I love him. Because I don't want him to throw it all away."

And you don't know how close he's come to doing that. All for thirty quid...

"I mean, he's in debt – "

"Do you know how much?"

She shook her head. "He won't discuss it with me. Just tells me to mind my own business. Or says he can handle it. He'll sort it out. And then he won't talk to me. Just shuts himself off. An' I know what he's doing. Like gambling has caused all his problems and he thinks the only way he can forget them is more gambling. He's in denial, Mr Brady. He doesn't see – he *won't* see – what it's doing to him. What it's doing to *us*. He's completely addicted. And I just don't know what to do."

So you came to see me. And you've answered a simple question for me. And asked about a dozen more. And you've no idea about the thirty quid. Or you'd have mentioned it.

"Claire. Right now you're feeling guilty. You've gone behind Jake's back. *I'm* feeling guilty because I've done the same. But you've done the right thing. I'll be honest with you, gambling… This is a first for me."

A fiver on the Middlesborough game every now and then sure. Maybe a couple of quid when Root comes in to bat. But nothing like this.

"But I'll make sure Jake gets help. I'll absolutely make sure he gets help. Give me your mobile number. I'll get back to you."

"Will you have time? You've got – "

"We've got a murderer to catch? We have. And that's the priority. But Jake's one of the team. If I can't find time to help him what sort of boss am I?"

What sort of man am I?

"Leave it with me. I'll get back to you. And Claire – "

"Yes, Mr Brady?"

"Thank you. Thank you for being brave enough. Having the courage to knock on the door."

· · ·

"What did she want, Dad?"

"Problems, Ash. Problems, problems. She gave me an explanation. But essentially, problems."

"That you can't discuss?"

Brady nodded. Sighed. "And it'll be the same for you, Ash. Remember I told you? Last time we talked about it? There'll be someone you love, you won't be able to go to dinner with them. Why? Because you've got a client. 'What about the client?' they'll say. And you won't be able to tell them. That's how it is this time. Except it's one of the team, not someone outside. And there you go. Four words and I've told you too much."

"So you have to swear me to secrecy?"

"I do. Not that I need to ask."

"No, Dad. You don't. But..."

"What, love?"

"*You* need someone to talk to, Dad. I know you're old-fashioned. Don't like to talk about things. But you can't do it all on your own. And you don't need your tarot book to tell you that."

Is that an implied criticism? 'You need someone to talk to. And it's not Siobhan?'

But Jake's my responsibility.

My team, my responsibility.

And if I need someone to talk to I've got Archie.

Speaking of which...

Brady looked at the rain running down the window.

Sighed. Reached for the dog's lead...

32

Brady kissed his daughter. "Around twelve then? You think Fiona will have had enough of you all by then?"

"Very funny." Ash rolled her eyes. "Try not to burn Siobhan's Spaghetti Bolognese."

"Two things, sweetheart. You can't burn Spag Bol. And we're having steak. Steak, fat chips, peppercorn sauce."

"Save some for Archie."

"You have a lovely time. Make sure you say thank you to Fiona from me. And no. It's my favourite. You know that. This is emphatically one meal that's *not* going in Archie."

THE SAME PALE yellow jacket and skinny jeans she'd been wearing when he first met her. Green eyes, dark hair pinned up, overnight bag in her left hand.

Brady kissed her. Pulled her to him. "I've missed you."

Have I? I didn't even look at her front door when I drove through Sandsend. Does that mean something?

"I've missed you too, Michael Brady. And I saw the news. I'm sorry."

Brady nodded. "Tough, tough week. And it didn't get any easier this afternoon."

He took the bag from her. Put it on the stairs.

"What happened this afternoon?"

Shook his head. "I can't talk about it. And I don't want to talk about it, Siobhan. Come here. Three days? Is that all you were away? How's Helen? How are the plans for the film?"

"I *can* talk about it. But I don't want to. Can we have a night off? Both of us? Eat dinner. Watch a film? I haven't seen *The Revenant*. It must be on Sky by now."

"It's set on the Dakota frontier. It'll be bleak and cold."

"So it'll remind me of Whitby in winter. Besides, I've got you to keep me warm."

"You find it then. I'll start cooking. And before you ask, the answer's no."

She turned her mouth down. "No wine with the world's best Spag Bol?"

"No Spag Bol, my love..."

BRADY REACHED FOR THE GRIDDLE. Opened the packet of peppercorn sauce.

Next step. Learn to make it properly...

Glanced in the oven. Checked the chips. Poured Siobhan a glass of Shiraz. Took it through to the lounge.

Leaned forward. Kissed the top of her head. Breathed in her perfume.

Went back to the kitchen. Checked the temperature of the griddle. Laid the steak in it. Heard it sizzle. Realised he'd forgotten to put his apron on.

World's Best Chef. Thanks, Ash...

Turned the steak over.

Hanging by her right foot. Left leg crossed behind her right knee.

Red trousers. A cornflower blue jacket.

Fear of change. Missed opportunities. Don't stay in your comfort zone. Sacrifice...

Is that it? Did someone sacrifice Sarah Trueman?

HEARD HIS PHONE RING. Glanced at the display. *Frankie*

"Frankie. Thank you."

"Sorry, boss. We've been out on the hills. Your message has only just made it to Scotland."

"The Hanged Man, Frankie. Have you seen a picture?"

"I'm looking at one now. It's her, boss."

"It is, isn't it? But *why*, Frankie? Why the hell would someone do that?"

"I don't know. But it's an exact copy. Even down to the shoes."

"Shoes?"

"She was wearing yellow shoes, boss. Sneakers. I checked the clothes, remember?"

She's right. Too busy focusing on her jacket and jeans...

"I saw it in a book. I've been reading *Teach Yourself Tarot* or something. I need to see someone, Frankie. A tarot reader. Make sure I understand."

"We have to go back in the house, boss. Check the cards. Go through the whole house again."

"The vicar as well. He must know far more than he told us. And the school, I need to go there next week. When are you back, Frankie?"

"In a perfect world? In about half an hour. Tomorrow afternoon. Before it gets bloody dark."

"OK. This is what we need to do – "

"What's that noise, boss?"

Brady turned. Heard the beeps. Saw the smoke. Saw Siobhan standing in the doorway.

Saw the steak.

What was left of the steak.

"Fuck. Fuck, fuck, fuck. I've got to go, Frankie..."

"Turn the oven off, Siobhan. The chips – "

"Aren't quite as burned as the steak. Bloody hell, Michael."

"It's only smoke. Open the window. How the hell do I stop the alarm making that noise?"

"The pan's ruined."

"It's only a pan."

She stared at him. "That was Frankie."

Brady nodded. "You know it was Frankie. I needed to speak to her."

"It's Saturday night, Mike."

"I needed to speak to her, Siobhan."

"And what the hell can she do on a Saturday night? When she's two hundred miles away? All you can do is fuck up someone else's weekend."

"The weekend isn't fucked up."

"Mike, your kitchen looks like a war zone."

She shook her head. "You can't do this, Mike."

"Do what? I can soon tidy up."

"It's not tidying up, Mike. It's not the steak. It's..." She gestured at the kitchen. "It's... the whole bloody thing. You can't do it. Twenty-four seven. You owe it to yourself. You owe it to me. You owe it to *us*."

"Siobhan, a woman's been murdered."

"I know that. And I know it's bloody serious. But it's the effect it has on you. You know something, Mike?"

"What?"

"It's what turns you on."

"That's ridiculous."

"No, it's not ridiculous. It's you against him. It's an intellectual challenge. But it's more than that. He's come to Whitby. He's murdered someone and he thinks he can get away with it. And you take it personally. You're insulted. 'Fuck that, he's not doing that. Not on *my* patch.' You know what, Mike? Some men buy a Ferrari to prove how big their dick is. You catch a murderer."

"Siobhan, you're talking... You're talking complete crap. It's my job. And yes, you're right. I believe in crime and punishment. I think people who do bad things should be caught. And bad things don't come any badder – or worse, or whatever I'm bloody well supposed to say – than hanging Sarah Trueman by her right foot. So you're damn right I'm going to catch him."

"And you're going to do whatever it takes."

"Yes, of course I am. What am I supposed to do? Only go so far? Say, 'I'd quite like to catch the killer but I'm cooking steak and chips? I have to do whatever it takes, Siobhan. I don't want to sound like a pretentious arse. But I *have* to do it. Because the law demands it."

She shook her head. Made no attempt to hide the tears. "No, Mike. You have to do whatever it takes... Not because the law demands it. Because Michael Brady demands it."

She walked into the hall. Came back holding her bag.

"Where are you going?"

"I'm going home."

"That's ridiculous."

"No, it's not ridiculous."

"I've cooked the steak."

"Mike, you've burned the bloody steak. And the chips."

"There's the peppercorn sauce. And red wine. And there's chocolate cake in the fridge. I haven't burned the bloody chocolate cake."

"So you can drink red wine and eat chocolate cake."

"With you."

"No, Mike, without me. I'm going home. And you're going to do what you really want to do."

"What's that?"

"Sit on your balcony. Get your pad of paper out. Start making notes. Drawing diagrams. Question marks."

Arrows leading nowhere...

"What about the steak?"

"Give it to Archie."

BRADY ADMITTED DEFEAT. Phoned her a taxi. Watched its taillights disappear down Henrietta Street. Walked into the kitchen. Looked at the steak.

Laughed.

"Christ, Archie, it'd pass for a lump of coal in an ID parade."

Looked down.

"Anyway, mate, how do you like your steak? Well done or nuclear accident? 'Cos well done's off tonight."

Brady reached for the carving knife. Sawed the steak into small strips. Tried one. Winced.

Put them in Archie's bowl. Watched them disappear.

"Come and sit with me, Arch. We'll make some notes. Then we'll fall asleep in front of the football."

He poured himself a glass of wine. Reached for his pad. Wondered for a second whether he should be more upset about the argument. Realised that he wasn't. Found a pen. Walked through into the lounge.

"At least you've had a good day, Arch. Sausage from Dave for breakfast. Butcher's best steak for your dinner. And you had a physics lesson. What more does a dog need?"

33

"We've got the details back boss. From the house. Lots of fingerprints."

Brady put down his disappointing machine coffee.

"*Lots* of fingerprints Anya? I'm confused. I thought the place was scrubbed from top to bottom."

"It was boss. Just not her tarot room. It seems whoever did the cleaning didn't go in there. Maybe the cards forbade it."

Brady laughed. "Any matches?"

"A few partial. Nothing that looks worth following up though. Someone who was once picked up for car theft in York. Another with a drink driving record. No mass murderers though if that's what you're asking."

"Just our luck. Dan – check out the two matches anyway, will you? See if either of them were in the area recently and if they have an alibi for the time Sarah went missing."

"Will do boss."

"Anything else Anya?"

"Not really. There's only – one second boss. It's my mum. She never normally calls when she knows I'm at work. Do you mind?"

"Go ahead," Brady nodded as Anya put her phone to her ear and turned away from him.

It didn't sound like they were going to get much else from the house report anyway. Brady didn't have high hopes for the partial prints, though he was curious about a car thief letting tarot cards guide them.

He picked up his coffee. Immediately put it down again. A cold coffee – the perfect excuse for a walk to Dave's. Not that he ever needed an excuse.

"Boss?"

"Everything alright Anya?"

"Not really boss. It's my dad – he's had a fall. Mum's had to take him to hospital. They think he might have slipped a disc in his back. Do you mind if I – is it okay – "

"Go, Anya. Of course. Give him my best and report back when you're ready."

"Thank you." Anya smiled at him. "I'll leave the reports on your desk."

"WHERE WAS ANYA GOING?"

"Hospital. Her dad's had a fall."

Frankie shook her head. "Oh dear. I wonder what age it is where you stop falling over and instead you've *had a fall*. It feels like a real turning point."

"You're definitely still in the *she's fallen over* category, Frankie. Me on the other hand?"

"You're close boss, I think it might depend if it's cold out..."

Brady smiled. "Speaking of cold, fancy a trip to Dave's? I need a coffee and a bacon sandwich. And there's another of our colleagues I need to update you on."

34

"Gambling? That's not good. I'd noticed he'd been a little distant lately, but I thought maybe trouble with his girlfriend. Nothing like this. What are you going to do boss?"

"In the short term – just make sure he's okay. The long term can come afterwards. There's Mrs Hornby's thirty quid which I'll have to deal with. But I can't think about that now. The HR department will undoubtedly need to know. And I'll have a talk with him as soon as he comes in today. But after that? Your guess is as good as mine, Frankie."

"There's gambler's anonymous boss, just like the AA. There must be a meeting somewhere nearby?"

"Good idea. I'll look into that. Morning Dave – good job there's no bacon-sandwiches-anonymous or I'd be up the creek without a paddle."

"You'd be what now?"

Dave turned around and faced them. Tossed a rag over his left shoulder. Grinned.

"How was the book?"

"Confusing. But insightful. *Tarot for beginners.* Not something I ever thought I'd find on my bookshelf."

"Tarot?" Dave looked at Brady quizzically. "My sister had a reading once. Mystic Meg told her she was going to be blessed with riches or some rubbish. The next morning the neighbour hit her dog with their car. Only the vet that were blessed with riches that week."

Dave huffed and flipped over the bacon. Pressed it down firmly on the griddle.

"Still good luck to you. You always seem to catch 'em in the end."

At least Dave believes in me then.

"What happened? To your sister's dog I mean."

"Lucky bugger lived another twelve years. Bit of a limp mind, but that never stopped him on the beach."

"Just like Archie then," Frankie added, reaching across and taking the sandwiches from Dave. "Bandstand boss?"

"Right behind you Frankie."

"So what's the plan of action?"

"Pretty much as you've said. I'll find the nearest gamblers anonymous and see what advice they have. And I'll speak to Jake. Not necessarily in that order."

"And what about Sarah Trueman?"

"We've got the vicar this afternoon. The television appeal tomorrow morning – you know I love those – and then the school after that. Dan is looking into the two partial prints from the house."

"We got prints?"

"Oh – yeah. Before Anya left earlier, apparently our cleaner didn't scrub her tarot room quite as closely as the rest of the house. Or at all. Two positive IDs – a car thief from York and someone who was picked up for drink driving."

"Neither of those sound like our guy boss."

"That's exactly what I said. But we'll see. Leave no stone unturned Frankie. That's police work one-oh-one."

"Right boss. Or page unread by the sounds of things. You going to go and get your fortune told as well?"

Brady smiled. Dropped the last piece of his bacon sandwich into his mouth. Balled up the paper bag. Knew he'd miss if he tried to land it in the bin.

"How did you guess? I'm expecting a call back from one *Madame Elvina* later today."

"Christ. A vicar and a madame in one day. Who said police work was all paperwork?"

"Only a fool would say that, Frankie. Although we better get back. Anya said she'd leave her report on my desk."

35

Brady pushed the door of the police station open. Heard Sue say, "He's just walked in."

Pointed upstairs. Mouthed 'In the office.' Took the stairs two at a time. "Mr Brady?"

She sounded hesitant. Apologetic.

"Morning Claire. What can I do for you? I'm still waiting for Jake to come in."

"He won't be. Coming in, I mean. He's ill. Really ill."

'A month ago. Jake didn't come in. I phoned in for him. Lied to protect him. Said he'd been up all night being sick.'

"I need to see him, Claire."

"I know. And I know you think I'm lying. I understand that. I'm not. I promise."

Brady closed his office door. Sat down. Took a deep breath. "What happened, Claire? After you left me?"

"Nothing. Not on Saturday. Then on Sunday... I'm not a good liar, Mr Brady. Jake could tell there was something. I told him I'd been to see you."

"So you had a blazing row?"

"No, we didn't. I was expecting it but – "

"Let me guess. You told him on Sunday afternoon? When the football was on TV. When he'd had half-a-dozen bets?"

Or maybe 'half-a-dozen' is an understatement...

"I think so. He just sort of shrugged. And that was it. Until first thing this morning. He's lying in bed. Shaking. Sweating. Some sort of panic attack. Suddenly he can't breathe. His mum told me he had asthma when he was a child. I phoned 1-1-1."

"What did they say?"

"They said keep an eye on him. Phone an ambulance if it gets worse. I've had to take the day off."

"You want one of us to come round?"

"No. His mum's here. Making me feel a bit useless to tell you the truth."

Brady laughed. "That's what mums are for. Take good care of him, Claire. And thank you for letting me know."

Brady sighed. Put the phone down. Looked at his list.

If I can't speak to him, maybe I can at least find out how to help him.

He typed a few words into Google. Picked up the phone again. Had a lot more luck with the second call. Went to speak to Frankie.

"Well that's one conversation I won't be having today."

"Your madame let you down boss?"

"Not exactly. Claire's phoned me – "

"Jake's girlfriend?"

"Right. Our boy won't be in today."

"Why not?"

"He's ill. Asthma and a panic attack apparently. She phoned 1-1-1."

"Did she tell him? That she'd seen you?"

"She did. Sunday afternoon."

"How did he react?"

Brady shook his head. "He didn't. 'He just sort of shrugged.' My guess is that she told him while football was on. He probably had half a dozen bets on the Liverpool game."

"So when was the panic attack?"

"This morning. She said he was sweating, shaking, struggling to breathe."

Frankie nodded. "Psychosomatic. He's worried about seeing you – "

"Right. That's what I thought. But maybe there's a silver lining. I'm meeting someone tomorrow morning. Seven. A transport café in Middlesbrough."

Frankie raised her eyebrows. "You should have joined the Met, boss. Could have met your informers in the Park Lane Hilton."

"Five quid for a coffee? I'll stick with Middlesbrough. And he's not an informer. He runs a small haulage business. And the Middlesbrough branch of Gamblers Anonymous. Monday to Friday he has his breakfast in the same café. Says if I can get there for seven he'll talk to me."

"So we know what we're up against?"

"Right. So up at five. Walk Archie. Drive to Middlesbrough. And the same on Wednesday. Except into the Dales. Lady Anne Clifford's. At least Roxby isn't too far away today. Grab your coat. He said he had a meeting at eleven."

"Coast road or Moors road?" Brady said.

"What did we do last time? The coast road. And about a dozen caravans."

"Moors road it is then. And a dozen tractors..."

Brady slowed down and indicated. Turned right just before Scaling Dam. Took the road to Borrowby.

His phone rang.

"Bloody hell, Frankie. A miracle. A phone signal on the Moors..."

"Michael Brady."

"Mr Brady. My name's Elvina. You left me a message. I'm sorry, I missed most of it. My answerphone has seen better days."

Brady slowed down. Saw a run-off at the side of the road. Stopped while he still had a signal. Avoided looking at Frankie as she raised her eyebrows.

"Thank you for phoning me back. You want me to run through it again?"

"If you wouldn't mind..."

"My name's Michael Brady. I'm a Detective Chief Inspector with North Yorkshire Police. I'd like to see you. Ideally today. We're investigating a murder and there are some tarot cards we'd like interpreting. Whatever you normally charge... That's fine."

There was a long pause. So long Brady wondered if he'd lost the signal. Then, "I can't do today, Inspector. I have an appointment. The hospital, unfortunately. Tomorrow morning, perhaps? Eleven o'clock, say?"

"That's fine. Thank you... Elvina was it? I'll see you in the morning."

"The cards you want interpreting, Inspector. You have a photo of them?"

"I do, yes. The Tower. Two others..."

"Then we'll see what they have to tell us. You know where I am?"

"The Market Vaults. I found you online."

"I'll look forward to it."

The line went dead.

"The Lovers," Frankie said. "The Two of Cups."

"I didn't want to give her them over the phone. I don't want a quick answer while I'm sitting in a lay-by. I want to *understand*. The cards. What Sarah Trueman was thinking."

"Elvina. She sounds like something out of *Lord of the Rings*."

"It's an elf isn't it? And she's not the only one out of *Lord of the Rings*."

"What do you mean?"

Brady looked at her. Smiled. "You. That's exactly what I thought when I first saw you. First impressions. You reminded me of the girl in *Lord of the Rings*. The one who straps on armour and goes off to fight for her father."

"Éowyn. And she was the niece of the king. But thank you. I'll take that as a compliment."

Brady started the engine. Looked out onto the moors. Could almost see the dust being kicked up from a herd of wild horses galloping across them.

"Can you imagine it, Frankie? Turn the clock back four, five hundred years? We're riding across these hills on horseback? The wind in our hair – or yours at least – charging into battle?"

"*Lord of the Rings*? Horseback? You're unusually lyrical this morning, boss."

Brady shook his head. "Antidote to the weekend, I suppose. Jake's girlfriend. The shit hitting the fan with Siobhan. But Archie enjoyed his steak. And I sold the other one for carbon dating. Come on, we're nearly there. You do the house, I'll do the vicar."

"Once we've found a hitching post for the horses."

"Obviously..."

36

Brady hadn't known what to expect. Wasn't sure if he'd ever set foot in a vicarage.

He was shown into a lounge dominated by three bookcases. A landscape in a gilt frame above a wide fireplace, early morning mist rising off a Scottish loch. Old fashioned sash windows with pale, tartan blinds.

Two leather armchairs, one brown, one maroon, both at 45 degree angles to a well- worn footstool.

"First things first, Reverend Croft" Brady said. "Thank you again for identifying the body. That's not an easy thing to do. And it takes courage. So thank you."

Steven Croft nodded. "I won't say 'you're welcome.' It's... Well, you see people do it on TV – "

"But nothing prepares you? Nothing *can* prepare you. So as I say, thank you."

Brady glanced at the bookcases. "Philosophy and reli-gion," Steven Croft said. "Then History and Archaeology." He nodded at the smallest bookcase. "Cricket. And some of my wife's novels," he added in a tone of voice that suggested 'charity shop' would soon be on his to-do list.

"You mind if I look?" Brady said.

Because like Frankie says, books and pictures...

Brady stepped forward. Stopped. Realised he wasn't looking at the books, but at the way they were arranged. The 'philosophy and religion' bookcase divided into nine sections. Plants in the central sections. The books on the left arranged by height. Falling away to the plants. The books on the right rising up away from them.

Up and down like a valley. Or waves. Precise, ordered waves flowing across his bookcase...

Brady glanced to his right. 'History and Archaeology' was reversed, the waves flowing in the opposite direction. Only cricket and 'my wife's novels' had refused to cooperate.

"Sᴀʀᴀʜ Tʀᴜᴇᴍᴀɴ," Brady said. "Someone's been murdered, ninety-nine per cent of the time the answer is in their past. More than ninety-nine per cent."

"You want me to go right back to the beginning?"

"Before that if you can, Reverend Croft."

"Please. Call me Steven. Identifying a body. It's a reasonable introduction."

Brady laughed. "Thank you. And as much as you know. A case like this... Anything could be important."

Croft nodded. Gestured for Brady to sit down. Sat opposite him. Leaned forward. Made a minute adjustment to the footstool.

He nodded. "We'd heard stories. From Rose – "

"Her mother?"

"Talking about this mythical creature in South America. One day she arrived. By that time Rose wasn't in the best of health."

"That's why Sarah came home?"

He nodded. "I think so. It was the only logical explanation."

"Rose was a widow?"

Steven Croft shook his head. "She never married, Mr Brady. Sarah's father was American. A visiting professor, supposedly. Rose? She was here the day I turned left on the Moors and landed in Roxby."

He brought his hands together in front of him, only the fingertips touching.

A gesture of prayer. No. Not prayer. Reflection. 'Did I make the right decision?'

"Twelve years ago now. The day after Hurricane Katrina in the US. Almost the first thing I did was walk into the church and pray for the victims."

"Rose didn't go to church?"

Croft laughed. "Rose? No. She drank gin. Shouted at carol singers. Walked her dog – a little Jack Russell that was even more irritable than its owner. I'd see her occasionally – but only to say 'good morning.' The dog eventually died. Rose lost the will to live. Or so it seemed."

"She died six months after Sarah came to look after her?"

"Six, seven months. I'd need to check. Certainly within the year."

"How old was she?"

"From memory? Eighty-five? Again, I'd need to check."

Eighty-five. A decent whack. So why is a small voice whispering 'Check the death. Is it suspicious?'

"But you know – knew, sorry – Sarah much better?"

"I did. I saw her once or twice around the village. Then she came to church. Started helping with church events."

"Didn't you... I'm sorry, I can't think of a subtle way to phrase this. Didn't you find that difficult? She read tarot cards. The tarot and the Eucharist. They don't exactly go hand-in-hand."

Steven Croft laughed. "Thou shalt have no other gods before me? We're a slightly broader church these days, Mr Brady. Church of England attendances are like county cricket. Not what they were. We're not in a position to turn people down. Especially someone who makes apple chutney you'd cheerfully do penance for."

Brady smiled. "I saw. The cookbooks, the herbs."

"A lot of it picked up on her travels."

"You mentioned South America. Do you know much about that?"

Croft shook his head. "Almost nothing. It wasn't something she talked about."

Do I believe him? Do I talk about my gap year? Thailand's beaches? Not much. Not even to Siobhan...

"What about Sarah herself? We've reconciled the tarot and the Sunday morning service. What was she like as a person?"

Croft took his time replying. "She had empathy," he finally said. "She was kind. I shouldn't say this, but there are people who come to church and think that makes them a Christian. I'm in St Matthew's camp. 'By their deeds you will know them.' She ticked that box."

Brady nodded. "She clearly had a spiritual side."

Croft gestured at his 'philosophy and religion' books. "Like many of us, Inspector. I think she'd reached the age where the only thing she really knew was how much she *didn't* know."

Amen to that. Especially on this case...

"Did she talk about her time in teaching?"

"Lady Anne Clifford's? 'Excellence. Character. Example.' She was slightly sceptical on the school motto, I can tell you that. 'Excuses. Compromise. Expediency' was her version."

Brady laughed. "I know a few senior coppers who are signed up to that one. She taught Chemistry?"

He nodded. "She did. With even more scepticism. 'The English kids can't wait to drop it. The Russians want me to turn it into *Breaking Bad*. Only the Chinese are interested in passing the exam.' Cynical even. But like all cynicism, with a healthy dash of truth."

"Why did she leave?"

"Disagreement. The Head said her exam results were disappointing. She pointed out that she had a cohort more familiar with the Russian mafia than magnesium. But I got the feeling there was something else. An argument. A personality clash. She never said."

Michael Brady nodded. Stood up. Took one last look at the waves rippling across the bookcase. Held his hand out. "Thank you," he said. "I've enjoyed talking to you. You've been very helpful."

But not as helpful as you're going to be...

Steven Croft shook hands. Brady watched him walk over to the TV set. Adjust the remote controls on top of it.

"Do you mind going out of the back door, Inspector? The front door... It's not the weekend."

"No problem at all."

'We need to find a house with sash windows. And somewhere in that house we'll find a curtain missing a tassel.'

"Just before I do, Steven – could I look at your windows? I need to renovate one of the sashes in my house. I'm in Whitby's conservation area. So I have to get it right."

Brady didn't wait for an answer. Crossed quickly to the window.

The wrong type of locks. Bugger. And blinds. Not curtains...

"Thank you. That's helpful."

Not that I hadn't already ruled you out. At least as far as murder goes...

Steven Croft led the way through to the kitchen. Brady glanced at the wall. Eight kitchen knives on a magnetic wooden holder. A small peeling knife on the left, neatly rising to a long, elegant bread knife.

Reached a hand out for the door handle. Spoke with his back to Steven Croft.

"Why did you do it, Steven?"

37

Brady turned.

Steven Croft was staring at him. Eyes wide, mouth open.

Brady watched him make a conscious effort to speak.

"I didn't kill her."

"I know that."

Because her head wasn't exactly level with the lowest branch. The rope wasn't perfectly centred on the branch.

"But you *did* clean the house," Brady said. "After you reported her missing. So I think we need to go and sit down again, don't you?"

"Would... would you like a cup of tea."

Brady shook his head. "No. Thank you, but no."

Because you're in a state of shock. And I'm not going to waste it...

"You reported her missing on Monday morning," Brady said. "My guess is that some time on Monday afternoon you cleaned the house."

Steven Croft nodded. "Two o'clock."

"Which meant you had a key. Or you knew where the

key was. Which means you knew her well. 'Mythical creature,' Steven? We don't use words like that about casual
acquaintances. And we probably don't know their father
was American. So did you have a key?"

Croft's tongue flicked out. Wet his lips. "No. I knew
where the key was. Under the middle plant pot. I'd fed the
cats before."

"Not this time though? She didn't ask you?"

He shook his head.

So she was only planning to be away overnight...

"She didn't ask. But I put food down. Fancie, she – "

Brady held his hand up. Stopped him.

*Don't let him get sidetracked. Keep him focused. And
worried...*

"You know what gave you away?"

"My OCD, I suppose."

"The jars in the kitchen all perfectly lined up? The TV
remotes at a forty-five degree angle?" Brady nodded. "But
something else as well. Those three words. 'Excuses,
compromise, expediency.' That's not the sort of comment we
make to someone we see once a week. And I'm sorry. I've
some bad news for you..."

"What's that?"

"We'll need your fingerprints. If only to officially rule
you out."

He stared helplessly at Brady.

*A schoolboy who's been caught raiding the tuck shop. Asking
to be let off...*

"Fingerprints? That means – "

"It does. I'd like you to come into the station. Tomorrow
morning. Like I said, Steven, I don't think you killed her. If I
did we'd be having this conversation somewhere else. But
I'm a police officer. There are certain procedures."

He nodded. "Nine o'clock?"

"That's fine. The sooner the better. There'll be somebody waiting for you. Ask for DC Keillor."

Croft didn't reply. Brady let him imagine being fingerprinted... "Why?" Brady asked.

"Why? Why did I go to the house?"

Brady nodded. "I'm curious. Tell me."

"I went to feed the cats. I was worried about them. Then I saw that it needed tidying. My OCD. I couldn't help it – "

Brady smiled. Held his hand up a second time. "Don't Steven. This lying business – being economical with the truth – you're not good at it. And if your OCD is that bad you can come round to my house. Single dad, teenage daughter, Springer Spaniel? There's enough for an OCD conference. But you didn't tidy my house. You tidied Sarah's. Because you *knew* it needed tidying. How did you know that? Because you were there a lot. Why were you there a lot?"

"She was a friend. We talked – "

Brady shook his head. "She was a lot more than a friend, Steven. You were sleeping with her."

"How – "

"How did I know? Well, your wife's very evidently not here. And I'd guess she hasn't been here for some time. More than that, though. The prayer."

"The prayer?"

"'May Christ, the true Shepherd, acknowledge you as one of his flock. May He forgive all our sins.' I was struck by the words, Steven. I Googled it."

At three in the morning.

Wondering if someone would say a prayer for me one day...

"And it's not 'forgive all *our* sins' is it? It's 'forgive all *your* sins.'"

Steven Croft nodded. Didn't speak.

"'Lord God, we have sinned against you; we have done evil in your sight. Wash away our wrongdoings.' You were praying for yourself as much as for Sarah, weren't you?"

But don't be too hard on him...

"That's why I needed to apologise, Steven. ID-ing the body of someone you love..."

Croft nodded again. "You need me to tell you the full story?"

"You know I do."

He sighed. Looked out of the window. An expression that was easy to read.

It wasn't meant to be like this...

"I came here twelve years ago. I told you. Hurricane Katrina. My wife came a fortnight later. Finalising the sale of our house. For the first two years... It was good. We were trying for a baby." He shook his head. "Once we started the tests... My fault, I'm afraid. And gradually we seemed to go in different directions. 'I feel like I'm in prison,' she said one morning. 'Trapped.'"

Brady glanced out of the window. Saw the garden just coming into bloom, falling away to the fields, hills in the distance.

It's not quite Her Majesty's Prison Durham...

"I thought she was talking about Roxby."

"She wasn't though..."

"No. Her mother's health was failing. A convenient excuse to spend more and more time back in Lancashire. And eighteen months ago 'more and more' became all the time."

"But you're not divorced. And there's part of you still hopes she'll come back."

"Yes." The vicar stared at Brady. "Is there anything you can't work out?"

Brady laughed. Felt the tension in the room release. "My teenage daughter?" He gestured at the bookcase. "And maybe your books... Your wife's books. You can't bring yourself to send them to the charity shop. Because you still think – whatever happened with Sarah – you think there's a chance your wife might come back. And once you've taken the books to the charity shop..."

"It's over. You're right."

"But you're angry. Her books have no place in your... Pattern? Is that the word?"

Steven Croft laughed. "Obsession," he said. "OCD? I'm not even sure it's an obsession. It's who I am. I have brown hair, brown eyes, I'm a touch overweight, I have OCD. I can't do anything about any of them." He looked at Brady. "And I know she's not coming back. There's someone else."

"So you started seeing Sarah?"

He nodded. "I did. And you're going to ask me when. October. She was helping at the church. We had a wedding on the Saturday. There was a sudden downpour. Absolutely pouring down. And dark. I offered her a lift home."

"And one thing led to another?"

"Not that night. No. But there'd been... 'hints' I suppose. Suggestions. And we both knew a bridge had been crossed."

"That must have been hard for you?"

"I'm a Church of England vicar, Mr Brady. Part of my job involves saying the words 'those whom God has joined together.' And I'm more than familiar with the sixth commandment. But Sarah... She made me laugh. Deliberately re-arranged things. Made me laugh at myself. And you're right. The prayer was as much for me as it was for her. I'm not proud. But I was lonely. Matthew again. 'The spirit is willing but the flesh is weak.'" A rueful smile. "That's the problem with the bloody Bible. It has a quotation for everything."

Brady laughed. Found he liked this man who'd been abandoned by his wife. Who'd taken comfort in someone else's arms and wrestled with his conscience. Who'd felt compelled to clean her house. Who was hopeless at lying.

But you're a copper. So ask your questions...

"Steven, I need to find the killer. No, let me be honest with you. I *have* to find the killer. You have to re-arrange the TV remotes. I have to find the killer. There's no difference."

"Obsessive compulsive detection?"

"Exactly. So two questions. You cleaned the house. You couldn't stop yourself. Not the tarot room though. I'm guessing that part of Sarah's life clashed somewhat with your beliefs. But at the same time... You were removing any trace of yourself, weren't you? And you'd probably never been in there..."

Croft nodded. "Have you ever done something... You're ashamed of doing it? But you're powerless to stop doing it? Exactly how I felt about Sarah."

"You thought she was away overnight. So when you went round. You must have expected to see her?"

"Yes. But she'd done it once before. Gone off for three days. About a year ago, she said. Told me she was walking. Stayed at a pub."

"*Before* you started seeing her?"

"Yes. Not a year. Ten months. June, the summer solstice."

"Let me ask you again. Can you think of anyone who might want to harm her? Anything she's said? Hinted at?"

Now we know you lay in bed and talked about rather more than apple chutney...

"I've asked myself that. Every day I've asked myself that.

And the answer is always the same. No-one. Nothing. I'm sorry."

Brady nodded. Knew he'd gone as far as he could for one day. Stood up.

"I'll need to talk to you again, Steven. Maybe not tomorrow. But nine o'clock. Don't forget."

Croft nodded. "I won't." Glanced at the clock. "I'm late. Arrangements for a funeral."

Brady shook hands. Went out of the back door because it wasn't the weekend. Walked across to Sarah Trueman's house and Frankie.

What did I say to her? 'Find the cleaner. Find the killer.'

Maybe not...

38

"What did I say to you, Frankie? Find the cleaner? Find the killer?"

"Judging by your expression – a fifty-fifty blend of smugness and disappointment, boss – you've found the cleaner. But the Reverend Croft is not the killer."

"Got it in one. Not so much Reverend Croft in the woods with the rope as Reverend Croft in the kitchen with the rubber gloves and the Domestos."

"Why?"

"OCD. Or whatever comes after OCD." Brady nodded at the kitchen shelves. "Her storage jars. Arranged in ascending order. All the labels perfectly centred. The TV remotes all at the same angle. It's the same in his house. The vicarage. His bookcases are a shrink's wet dream. The poor bugger can't get out of his chair without adjusting the TV remotes. Christ, I'm happy if I can *find* mine. And there's more."

"You've waved the white flag. Invited him round for dinner."

"And then my phone rings? An urgent appointment? I

come back two hours later and the place is spotless? It didn't even cross my mind. He was sleeping with her, Frankie."

"The vicar? Sarah Trueman?"

Brady nodded. "For about six months. His wife had left him – "

"Driven mad by his OCD?"

"Driven mad by living in Roxby, I think. They're not divorced. Not yet – "

"Bloody hell, boss. The tabloids would be all over that one. Married vicar's raunchy romps with murder victim."

"Randy rev's raunchy romps, Frankie. You need to work on your alliteration. But they're not going to find out from me. And the morals of the Church of England aren't our concern."

"Are you sure, boss?"

"Am I sure he was having an affair with her? Or am I sure he's not the killer?"

"Both."

"Yes. 'There was a sudden downpour,' he said. 'It was dark. I offered her a lift home. We both knew a bridge had been crossed.'"

"How did you know?"

"About the affair? The prayer."

"The prayer?"

"The prayer he said when he identified the body. 'May He forgive all our sins.' One of my three-in-the-morning Google searches. It's not 'our sins,' it's 'your sins.' He was asking for forgiveness for himself as much as for her."

"He knew it was wrong but he couldn't stop?"

"Exactly."

"But he didn't kill her?"

Brady shook his head. "He didn't, Frankie. Definitely.

Some people cause events. Some people react to them. Steven Croft is in the second camp."

"Brilliant. I'm impressed, boss. Smug face fully justified. And that's good, because I've found the square root of nothing-at-all here. We didn't miss anything."

"You're sure?"

"Certain. He did a good job with the rubber gloves and Mr Sheen."

"Domestos."

"Sorry. I bow to your superior knowledge of cleaning products. When did she leave then, boss?"

"I'm sorry?"

Frankie stared at him. "Sarah Trueman, boss. When did she leave the house? The key question."

"I don't – "

"They were having an affair, boss. She was going away. She'd have told him. Texted him."

"I didn't ask..."

Because I was so busy congratulating myself on the OCD. Looking at waves on the bloody bookcases. Feeling smug about the prayer. The affair. So far up my own arse I didn't ask the obvious question...

"He said he was going out, Frankie. How fast can you run?"

39

Faster than Brady was the answer.

Frankie was standing at the bottom of the vicarage drive. A mystified Steven Croft was climbing out of a Nissan Qashqai.

"My apologies, Steven," Brady panted. "Meet Detective Sergeant Thomson. She's considerably more intelligent than me. And needs to ask you a question."

Because I'm out of breath...

"DCI Brady told me about your meeting, Reverend. But there's a question he forgot to ask."

Steven Croft shook his head. Continued to look mystified. "I told him everything."

"You did. Except for the one question Inspector Brady didn't ask."

Go ahead, Frankie. Twist the knife...

"When did Sarah leave her house?"

"When did – "

Brady saw Frankie's expression. Couldn't help smiling. *Two men. Both as useless as each other...*

"When did Sarah leave her house?"

"She – "

"You were having a relationship with her. She was going away. She didn't just pack her bag and leave. She told you when she was going. She sent you a text. Perhaps I could have a look at your phone?"

Croft nodded. Reached for his phone. Passed it to Frankie. "Twenty-nine eleven."

"The passcode?"

"Jeremiah. 'For I know the plans I have for you,' declares the Lord." He glanced at Brady. "I told you. A quote for everything."

Frankie looked at the phone. Didn't speak. Handed it to Brady.

Hope the wedding goes well. You don't need to adjust the groom's buttonhole. I'll miss you. Xx

Looked at the date and time.

"Bloody hell. Friday afternoon."

So much for Saturday or Sunday. Someone held Sarah Trueman for five nights. And then they murdered her...

"Five nights, Frankie."

"Why, boss? Why hold someone for four or five nights and then kill them?"

Brady shook his head. "Right now I don't know. A significant date? The full moon? It wasn't that. But five nights, Frankie. *Five.* Food, clothes, somewhere to hold her..."

"'An old friend.' That's who Croft said she was meeting."

"Another teacher? Someone she hadn't seen for a few years."

"Supposing an 'old friend' wasn't an old friend, boss? Suppose it was another man?"

"She'd been seeing Croft for six months. That's an affectionate message."

Frankie looked at the message again. Looked up at

Brady. "I was twenty-two," she said. "Still with my boyfriend from uni. I started seeing someone else behind his back. The archetypal 'bad boy.' A total shit. I'm still ashamed to this day. But he was exciting. Different. Exactly like Steven Croft. I knew it was wrong but I couldn't stop. Every woman has one man in her life like that."

"You're saying – "

"I'm saying that the more I saw this other guy the more affectionate I was with Phil. Felt guilty at Christmas, bought him far too much. Finally told the truth in January. That's exactly the sort of message I'd have sent him. So maybe Steven Croft wasn't the only man in Sarah Trueman's life. Maybe her 'old friend' was a lot more than an old friend."

"So what are we saying, Frankie? 'Find the cleaner, find the killer' didn't work."

"We got it wrong, boss. Maybe it's 'find the bad boy, find the killer.'

40

Brady eased his car into one of the few spaces left in the car park. Sighed. Stretched.

'Wouldn't it be easier for them to send a TV crew to Whitby, boss?'

'Can't do it until Friday, Frankie. But if I can drive to Leeds...'

Seventy bloody miles. And Middlesbrough tomorrow morning. Glanced at the clock.

Just time...

Tried her number again. The answerphone for the third time.

"Anya, hi it's Mike Brady. Hope everything with your dad is going well. Or as well as it can. Just to say there's no immediate need to rush back. We know who cleaned the house. The vicar. He was having an affair with her. You can confirm it all when you're back. Give my best to your dad. Take care."

Bloody hell. I feel guilty. Finding the cleaner. Doing her job for her...

Brady walked into reception at Yorkshire TV. Told them he needed help catching a murderer.

Surrendered himself to the make-up artist.

A round face. A ready smile. Blue eyes behind enormous black glasses. Pink hair fading to blonde. A cream sweater. Long black beads.

Yorkshire wit.

"You need to wear make-up, love. Just a touch. Stops your face being shiny. Face looks shiny you don't look like a man who can be trusted. Take my word for it, love. Good-looking bloke like you? You ever think about a career in television, did you? Better than that miserable sod who does the news. No wonder we're all reaching for the gin and phoning Just Eat. Where was I? Make-up. There you are, lovely, you're done. Just a dab, that's all it needed."

"Thank you. I – "

"That woman out at May Beck is it? Heard about that. Love Whitby, I do. Go there in the summer. Bacon sandwich and a cuppa to get us started. The café at Falling Foss. And then walk through the woods. 'Not any more' I told him. No, don't get up. There's a bit I've missed. Getting careless in my old age. Done this before, have you?"

"Yes, I – "

"You don't say much. Nervous are you? One word of advice. Confidence. My youngest, she's got it in buckets. Wants to be an influencer when she grows up. I said to her, 'Influencer? What sort of job is that?' 'Ten grand a week job,' she says. That's me put in my place. But like I say. Confidence. Cameras are funny things. They can sense it. Don't ask me how, but they can. Like dogs and horses I suppose. Know when you're confident, know when you're afraid."

"Thanks, I – "

"Anyway, they're signalling for you. Remember what I

said. And make sure you catch the bugger. Let me know when it's safe to walk through the woods again. Got your script have you, love?"

I have. And I've added five words. The vicar didn't do it...

41

Brady cleared his throat.

"Two days ago a woman was found murdered at May Beck. Sarah Trueman was a retired teacher who lived in Roxby.

"Let me first send my sincere condolences to all her friends in the village, and to any former pupils and colleagues who have heard of her death. Secondly I need to appeal to anyone watching this bulletin."

Look up. Straight into the camera...

"We need your help. Sarah Trueman left her house on Friday afternoon. She was found on Wednesday morning. So far we have no idea – "

Shit. I should have re-written that. 'Top cop admits he has no idea...'

"So if anybody saw – or thinks they might have seen – Sarah between Friday and Tuesday night please, get in touch with us. If she stayed at your B&B, checked into your hotel, if you think you saw her on the train, on the bus... Any sighting, any possible sighting, could be important. Could be crucial in finding the killer.

"Nothing is too inconsequential. Any detail, however small, might be important. So please, get in touch with us."

Brady wrapped it up, repeated the appeal for help. Relied on the producer to show Sarah's picture. Gave the phone number. Repeated the phone number. Wondered if they'd find the needle in the haystack of hoax calls.

Wasn't optimistic...

BRADY CLIMBED INTO THE CAR. Realised he was tired. And hungry.

Briefly considered stopping on the way home.

No. I haven't seen Ash. And Archie will need a walk...

Pointed the car at the Leeds ring road. Turned the radio on. Couldn't even remember what the Monday night football match was.

The phone rang just as he was crossing the A1.

"Dad?"

"Hi, sweetheart. What's up?"

"I wanted to phone you. But I thought I ought to wait. I didn't want to ring while you were driving out of Leeds. And we watched you on TV."

"We? That's nice. What did Archie think of my performance?"

"It was really funny. As soon as he heard your voice he looked up at the TV. But I didn't mean me and Archie. You've got a visitor – "

Claire. Again. More problems with Jake...

"Siobhan's here, Dad. She's cooking dinner for us. And I've taken Archie for a walk. Siobhan needs to know when you'll be home. So she can time everything."

"What's she cooking?"

"She says it's a surprise."

Not nuclear accident steak then...

"An hour, sweetheart. An hour and ten minutes, say. And can you put Siobhan on the phone?"

I think it's time to eat some humble pie. A large slice...

———————

42

Brady closed his front door behind him. Stood for a moment. Let the smell of Siobhan's cooking permeate his nostrils. It was sweet. Notes of basil. Something citrusy that he couldn't quite place.

"Dad? Is that you? Do you want wine?"

Brady walked into his kitchen to find his daughter holding a bottle of white wine. Sauvignon Blanc to be precise.

"I hope you don't mind," Siobhan said to him as she turned from the hob. "I said she could have a glass."

Brady looked at Ash. Saw the cheeky smile creeping onto her face.

"One won't hurt I suppose. Better with us than out on some street corner."

"Right dad. Because I'm always hanging around on street corners. I'm going to try and find a film."

Ash walked out of the kitchen leaving Brady and Siobhan. Two more glasses of white wine on the table.

"It's okay, isn't it? She asked and I didn't feel like I could say no. It's her house after all."

"Of course. She's sixteen next year. I'm sure she's already drank a lot more than a glass of wine without me knowing. Now what are you cooking? It smells incredible."

Brady closed the two paces between him and Siobhan quickly. Pulled her into him. Kissed her.

"And I'm sorry about the other night. I promise I'll try not to let it happen again."

"But you will. And it's okay. I understand that your job comes first."

"It's not that. It doesn't always. It's just this case. It's – "

"It's fine. Let's not go through it again. I missed you. And it's gnocchi. *Gnocchi con pesto di arancia e basilico.*"

"Well that puts my Spag Bol to shame."

Brady smiled. Wrapped his arms around Siobhan. Kissed her again.

Maybe this can work after all. Siobhan and Ash waiting for me when I get home. The three of us eating dinner together. Watching a film...

But she said it. Your job comes first. Blame the case as much as you want. There's always another one.

"We've had an update about the film." Siobhan turned back to the hob. Squeezed an orange into a saucepan. "I'm flying back out tomorrow."

"Is everything alright?"

"There are a couple of sections they want us to re-do. Nothing serious. It should only be a few days."

"So they're still happy with it then? *You're* still happy with it?"

Siobhan smiled. "Definitely. I didn't think anything could match up to performing on stage. But then I see the music and the film come together. It's incredible. I can't wait for you to see it."

"Me neither. I'm proud of you. Now – what can I do to

help?"

43

An early morning drive over the Moors. Still a hint of overnight frost. Mist hanging in the valleys.

Brady parked in a side street. Walked the hundred yards to the transport café. Pushed the door open. Was hit by the smell of frying bacon. Wondered if he could be unfaithful to Dave.

A man lifted his hand. Gestured for Brady to sit down.

Fading photos of England's World Cup winners on the walls. The glass sugar-pourers Brady had never been able to master. Tomato sauce in a huge plastic bottle.

"Thanks for seeing me. Especially this early in the morning."

Grizzled. Four or five days of a grey beard. A faded LA Dodgers baseball cap covering what you knew was a bald head. An even more faded T-shirt. A disappointingly-new leather jacket that would need at least five years to catch up with its colleagues.

But a ready smile. A firm handshake.

"Michael Brady."

"Ian Henshaw." He nodded. "That your real name? 'Cos I'm not fussed if it isn't."

Brady laughed. "No, it's my real name. Can I get you anything? Bacon sandwich?"

He shook his head. "Cholesterol. Two slices of toast do me in the morning. Can't give up butter though. Bloody low-fat spread. Might as well put water on your toast."

Brady laughed again. Walked to the counter. Ordered a coffee. Was surprised to discover some will-power.

"Thanks again. For seeing me so quickly. I appreciate it."

Ian shook his head. "No bother. Normally people just come along to the meetings. Takes a lot of courage though. Walk through that door. Sit down. 'My name's Ian. I'm a compulsive gambler. My last bet was half an hour ago.' Bloody brave thing to do. So this. Cup of tea, have a chat first. No problem."

He paused. Took a bite of toast. Reached for his blue and white mug. Smiled at Brady. "I'm not. A gambler, I mean. Never have been."

"So why – "

"Why am I involved? My brother. Twenty years coming up. Horses and dogs. Proper old school gambling. Killed himself three days before Christmas. Been saving up all year. Money for the Christmas presents. Wife. Two kids. Lost the lot at Sunderland dog track. Didn't even make it to the last race. Drove up the road to a place called Killing-worth. Unmanned crossing. Parked his car on the London to Edinburgh line. Sat and waited."

"I'm sorry – "

Ian shook his head. "Don't be. I miss him. Of course I miss him. Who wouldn't? But she's re-married. He's a good bloke. And the kids were young. They don't remember Rich.

But yeah, that's what got me involved. Do what I can. Touch wood we haven't had any more on the railway line."

Brady sipped his coffee. "You sure you don't want anything else to eat?"

"No, I'm good. Wife's doing dumplings tonight. We're all addicted to something, aren't we? Dumplings, me." He laughed. "Stew n' Dumplings Anonymous. I'd be there every week. What about you then? Like I say, brave thing to come to your first meeting. So chatting like this. No problem."

Brady shook his head. "No, not me. I've got a... a friend."

Ian laughed. Raised his eyebrows. "Bit old for that, aren't you? *Penthouse*? *Mayfair*? 'Not for me, mate. I'm buying it for a friend.' You're supposed to grow out of that when you're twenty. What do you do anyway? You don't look – "

Brady laughed. "Like someone who comes to your meetings? That's because – " Stopped himself. "I'm sorry, that's wrong. I'm being judgemental. I'm a copper. A detective."

Ian nodded. "Copper? You lads are usually drinkers aren't you? Along with the lawyers an' the journos. Now who's being judgemental? Like I say, twenty years with my finger in the dyke. Trying to hold back the tide. Tell me what your friend wants to know."

Brady finished his coffee. "I want to know what he needs to do. What he's up against. What we can do to help."

"First things first, come to the meetings. An' the sooner the better. Salvation Army, Admiral's Avenue. Monday. Seven-thirty. And what can you do to help? Be there. Just bloody well *be* there. 'Cos there's more bollocks talked about gambling than any subject under the sun."

Brady didn't know whether to laugh. "Maybe. Police work would run it close."

Ian shook his head. "You need to see it. I remember watching a game with Rich once. Newcastle – Liverpool.

Told me afterwards he had fifteen bets on the game. Fifteen, for fuck's sake. I could see, watching him, sitting there on the sofa trying to pretend everything's normal. Three-three it is. Then Fowler scores in the last minute. And he races into the kitchen. In the sink. Throwing up."

Brady nodded. Didn't speak.

"Twenty-two grand of debts when he died. Nothing really. There'll be footballers drop that in a day and not think twice. Him? It was what he earned in a year."

"How big's the problem?"

Ian shook his head. "How big? About ten times as big as the official figures. It pisses me off. I don't blame the industry. It's like asking a poacher to stop catching rabbits. Government could do something, easy as you like. Can't advertise fags but you can advertise gambling. We need legislation. But what can you do? The betting companies take the MPs to Royal Ascot. Get 'em pissed up. They stagger back to Parliament and decide the industry can regulate itself. Like hell it can."

"And the football teams," Brady said. "Half of them sponsored by bookmakers."

"Don't. I'm out of blood pressure tablets. And the profile's changing. More women. Younger people. When I first got involved it was older blokes and betting shops. An old man's problem. Like incontinence. Now? Bloody internet and mobile phones have changed everything. Slots, casinos, bingo. You name it, it's on your phone. And you'll lose money playing it."

"Why?" Brady said.

"Why do they gamble? You like your questions, don't you?"

"Like I said, I'm a detective."

"What do you want then? The medical explanation or

Henshaw's Law?"

"Both, if you've time. You want another tea?"

"Sure. I've had worse."

"Remind me to invite you to the police canteen."

Ian laughed. "Maybe not. The technical explanation." He sighed. Shook his head. "The technical explanation says that placing a bet releases dopamine. Feel-good factor."

Brady nodded. "I read that."

"Win or lose. It doesn't matter. It's the excitement of placing the bet. Read your Dostoevsky did you? *The Gambler*? All about his addiction to roulette. Had to write the book to pay off his gambling debts. And nothing's changed. Except it's on your phone. Old Fyodor finished the book with the help of his girlfriend. Lucky man. If you're an addict you need someone in your corner."

Claire. Coming to see me...

He narrowed his eyes. Looked at Brady. "You sure you're not asking for yourself?"

Brady shook his head. "Honestly. I've had a fiver on Middlesbrough to stay up."

"There's a fiver you'll not see again. And Middlesbrough? You'll know all about Merson then. Lost the deposit for his house betting on table tennis. Table fucking tennis for God's sake."

"My friend bets on football."

"Football, dogs, roulette, bingo, doesn't matter. Dopamine doesn't give a toss what you're betting on, only that you're having a bet."

"What's Henshaw's Law then?"

"Henshaw's Law says that addiction is a sneaky bastard. And you get lucky or unlucky."

"How?"

"It's simple. You get addicted to business, work sixteen

hours a day, make a fortune, everyone says you're a hero. 'Here you are, mate, slot on *Dragon's Den* for you.' But the fates flip the coin an' it lands the other way – your addictive personality settles on booze or gambling. Or just taking bloody risks."

"Taking risks?"

Ian nodded. "I've seen it. Having an affair usually. It isn't the other woman. It's the thrill of getting away with it. But gambling? Like booze, it destroys you. Twenty years. I've seen it all."

"How many? Over the years."

"Don't ask. I daren't count."

"Can I ask one more question?"

"Ask as many as you like."

"Lying," Brady said. "Your brother. Any of the people that come to the meetings. Do they lie about it?"

Ian laughed. "What do you think? All addicts lie. Gambling, booze, women, of course they lie. Lie to everyone. But most of all to themselves. 'I can control it.' 'I can stop.' Exactly what Rich said. It took the nine-forty from Durham to make him stop."

"I'm sorry. I didn't – "

"No. Don't worry. Like I said, twenty years ago."

"You think you can help him?"

"Your 'friend?' Honestly? I don't know. There's no guarantees. For every one that stays sober – so to speak – there's another one drops off the wagon. I wish I could, but there's no promises. No guarantees. But I'll do everything I can."

Brady stood up. Held his hand out. "Thanks, Ian, I appreciate your help. Really appreciate it. Next Monday. I'll make sure he's there."

"You do that, mate. Glad I could help. Thanks for the tea. And I'll see you Monday. Your friend, I mean. Sorry..."

44

"Boss, there's someone downstairs to see you."

"I'm supposed to be in Scarborough in an hour."

'Eleven o'clock, Mr Brady. See what the cards tell us.'

"Maybe not, boss. She's asking for 'the good-looking man I saw on TV last night.'"

Brady laughed. "I'll send Dan Keillor. Don't want to disappoint her."

"Sorry, boss, I was being tactful. 'The good-looking *older* man I saw on TV.'"

"Thanks, Sue. That's a stake hammered through my ego. Two minutes. And judging by your tone of voice it's important."

Or you're intrigued. The same tone of voice you used when Gerry Donoghue turned up...

"I do, boss. She doesn't look like a woman who wastes her time."

Now I'm intrigued...

Brady pushed Sarah Trueman's file to one side. Walked down to reception.

Was immediately struck by her height. Sitting down, long legs stretched out in front of her.

Late forties, Brady guessed. Maybe early fifties. The type of check jacket that always made him think of show jumping. A cream blouse, a pale blue scarf loosely round her neck. Thick auburn hair pulled back from her face. No rings on her fingers.

A face that's used to giving instructions. But listening as well. What is she? A schoolteacher? Headmistress?

She reached for a walking stick as Brady approached. Pushed herself painfully to her feet. Visibly winced.

Clearly in pain. But still looking confident. In control...

Extended her hand. A firm, no-nonsense grip. "Julie Stott," she said.

A trace of West Yorkshire in her accent.

"Michael Brady. And thank you for coming in." Brady gestured at the walking stick. "It clearly wasn't easy."

She shook her head. "It wasn't but... Here I am. And life has its compensations. I've parked on double yellow lines outside a police station."

Brady laughed. Glanced through the window. Saw a white Audi Q3. "I'll tell them not to tow you away. How can I help? Sue said you saw the appeal on TV."

She nodded. "I did."

"Did DC Keillor – "

And Jake. Poor bloody Jake...

" – talk to you on the house to house?"

She shook her head. "I don't live in Roxby. Staithes. Two miles up the road. The wind off the sea. The screech of seagulls..."

Brady gestured at the walking stick, the top shaped like a shepherd's crook. "Where would you like to talk? The chairs in the interview room aren't exactly forgiving."

The hard, plastic ones schools buy so they can torture the parents...

Julie Stott shook her head. "I've made it this far. And I've never been in a police interview room."

Brady smiled. "Another one ticked off the bucket list? Would you excuse me for two minutes? I need to make a phone call. I had an appointment. Sue will make you a cup of tea."

SHE SIPPED HER TEA. Looked at Brady over the rim of the cup.

"I've been awake all night. Hesitated about coming to see you. But... You're clearly not making much progress."

Not much? I'd take 'not much' over none...

Brady smiled. "Police work is very often 'not much.' Then we make a breakthrough. Someone parks on our double yellow lines..."

She nodded. Considered her next question. "How confidential is this, Mr Brady?"

"I'm not a journalist, Ms Stott. I'm a copper. Investigating a murder. A murder that... I work with some battle-hardened people. None of us are going to forget what we saw at May Beck."

"So I tell you my story and I take my chances?"

Brady raised his eyebrows. "Do you need to 'take your chances?' You don't look like a woman who's walked in here to confess."

She laughed. "Hobbled, you mean? I would assume that what happened to Sarah... That it would have required some physical prowess. Those days are behind me. And not coming back."

She wants to tell me her story. My job's simple. Listen.

Brady sat back. Picked up his cup of tea.

45

"As I said, I was awake all night. Battling with my conscience. But I have clearly crossed the Rubicon. Or the River Esk. So here I am."

Brady nodded. Didn't speak.

"I came to Staithes three years ago. Before that I lived in Harrogate."

"Escape to the country? Or the coast?"

"Harrogate is hardly Leeds or Bradford, but yes. I wanted a... simpler life. Quieter. More reflective."

"What did you do?"

"Ah, the sixty-four thousand dollar question. And maybe you'll understand why I wondered about coming forward. Why I've been wrestling with my conscience. Twenty years of professional ethics."

Professional ethics. What was she? An accountant? Solicitor?

"I was a dominatrix, Mr Brady."

Brady shook his head. "You were – "

"A dominatrix. Mistress Anastasia. Men came to me – " She saw Brady smiling. Laughed with him. "Julie Stott was a touch too Yorkshire, don't you think? Perhaps if I'd made award-winning black puddings? Sadly for the English breakfast I found I had other talents."

A face that's used to giving instructions. You got that one right, Michael Brady...

"And that's what you did in Harrogate?"

She nodded. "My story is by no means unique. I went to university. Worked as a trainee journalist. Married. Had a child. My husband walked out while I was in labour. I had to feed my daughter. Went back to journalism. Juggled child care and court reports. Became increasingly aware I didn't like the job. A new editor arrived. He wanted to make the paper more – 'edgy' was the word he used. He didn't mean to, but he changed my life. Sent me to do a story on a dungeon – "

"A dungeon?"

"This was Leeds, Mr Brady. Well over two million people in an hour's drive. Some of them a long way from vanilla. There I am asking questions, my reporter's notebook perched primly on my knee. I was tall. It seemed I had 'presence' – for want of a better word. They offered me a job. And two months later I resigned as a journalist."

"And moved to Harrogate?"

"After I'd spent two years learning the ropes." She smiled. "So to speak. I wanted to be my own boss. And what does daytime TV teach us? 'Location, location, location.' I was five minutes' walk from the conference centre."

"So why move over here? Staithes in particular? It's hardly – "

"Heavily populated? As I say, I wanted a simpler life. More reflective. Walks on the beach. And..." She shrugged. "As you can see, I am no longer in my twenties. We all have younger competitors..."

Brady forced himself not to laugh.

Exactly what Mozart said about hackers...

"...And gravity takes its inevitable toll on a woman's body. Plus what I did was physically demanding. Laying it on with a paddle for an hour, Mr Brady. It's a young woman's job. You know what they say in Yorkshire. 'Tha's med a few bob wi'out breaking sweat.' I did break sweat."

My grandma beating carpets in the spring. Doing it by hand. Complaining how tiring it was...

"So you retired?"

She shook her head. "Not quite. I told ten or twelve of my regulars what I was doing. That and my savings. The money I made downsizing from Harrogate."

"Harrogate to Staithes? What's that? Sixty miles? Seventy? It's a long way to drive."

She laughed. "Two points, Mr Brady. Number one, there is no limit to the distance a man will drive when he has an erection. Or needs to be a puppy. And punished when he's a naughty puppy. Number two, regular clients. I *listened*. They came for the cup of tea afterwards as much as my other services. You've no idea of the amount of marital advice I gave. And they enjoyed it. 'A bloody good spanking then fish and chips on the pier? A perfect day out, Mistress.'"

Brady laughed. "I can see it on the advertising posters. You met Sarah Trueman in Roxby? Or Staithes?"

"At church, I think. But they're small communities. You 'know' people before you've even been introduced. She came to church one Sunday morning. We started chatting after the service. And became... 'friends' may not be the right word. Comfortable in each other's company."

"Did she know what you do?"

"No. And it's 'did,' Mr Brady. Very much the past tense." She gestured at the stick. "I was parked. Admiring the view. Over the fields, out to sea. A tourist in a Range Rover drove into the back of me. Also admiring the view, but doing it at fifty. Whiplash. Damage to my neck. And you know how it is. Pain travels down the nerves. Retirement on the grounds of ill-health. I converted my dungeon into a sewing room."

"So what do you do now?"

"Live rather more frugally. Grow vegetables. Make soup. Take comfort in the word of Our Lord."

'She came to church one Sunday morning...'

"How well did you know Sarah?"

Julie took her time replying. "Reasonably well, I think. I saw her in church every week, various other social events. Were we friends? Maybe I was being unkind. If Facebook allows you to describe someone you've never met as a friend then maybe we were. We were women of a similar age. If nothing else we had hot flushes in common."

"How did she reconcile going to church with tarot readings? I thought the two – "

"Were at opposite ends of the spectrum? I doubt that fifty per cent of our very small congregation believe in God. But they believe in doing the right thing. They believe in helping each other. They see a freezing church and wearing thermals every Sunday until the end of April as a price worth paying."

"And the vicar... He didn't mind what Sarah did?"

She shook her head. "As I said, the word of Our Lord. 'He that is without sin among you, let him first cast a stone at her.' If my previous life taught me anything it was not to judge people. And Steven Croft? He's one of life's optimists. I'm sure he had Sarah filed under 'potential converts.'"

He had her filed under a lot more than 'potential converts...'

Brady nodded. "When you were working. You must have told people – "

"What I did? I tell them I'm a teacher who's taken early

retirement. At which point you say, 'but surely other teachers would realise..."' She shook her head. "I simply moan about what a shit the deputy head was. Every teacher I meet nods in agreement."

Brady laughed. "It's the same in every organisation. Especially the police."

Except maybe it's not the Deputy Head...

"So I understand why you're here. Thank you. Sarah Trueman... You clearly have some information."

She nodded. "As I say, I've thought long and hard. Prayed for guidance. I'm doing something I thought I'd never do. Break a confidence. Tell someone the name of one of my clients. But – "

"You've read the story?"

She nodded. "I've read the story. Seen you on TV. Been online. Read how she died. And I suspect you've kept some details to yourselves – "

You could say that...

" – But I know someone who was going to see her, Mr Brady. On Friday afternoon."

"Friday afternoon?"

Hope the wedding goes well. I'll miss you. Friday at 15:23

So did he arrive after she'd gone? Or is this the killer?

"I have a name for you."

"One of your clients?" Brady tried to keep his voice level. "I thought you'd retired?"

She nodded. "Very definitely retired. But he still had my number. And boundless optimism. He sent me a text."

She reached into her bag. Brought her phone out. Opened one of the apps. Passed the phone to Brady.

Small world! I'm going to be down the road from you on Friday. Seeing what the future holds. I could come early, Mistress. One last time for old time's sake? 200, same as it always was?

"You didn't see him?"

"No. I was in the church, arranging flowers. There was a wedding on the Saturday. So I politely declined. As you can see."

Sadly, no. As you know, Timmy, I've retired. But hopefully you still enjoy the fish and chips.

Brady read the message a second time.

"Timmy? That was the dog in *Famous Five* wasn't it?"

She smiled. "Different strokes, Mr Brady..."

She reached into her bag again. Passed Brady a piece of paper.

A6. Torn out of a notebook. Tim Carrick. A phone number. An address just north of Leeds...

Brady nodded. "Thank you. Thank you very much. We'll need to see Mr Carrick. I won't tell him how we know – "

She shook her head. "Tim Carrick's not an idiot, Mr Brady. None of my clients were idiots. Some were successful. Some *very* successful. But however much power we have... There are days when we all need someone else to take control. Tell us what to do."

"You think he definitely went to her house that day?"

"I'm certain. Tim Carrick didn't break appointments. Once, twice in fifteen years maybe? And you've read his message. That's the only interpretation there is."

"Fifteen years? You must have known him – "

"Better than his wife? Very possibly. And yes. Once a month for fifteen years. I should have named the house after him. I totted it up. He paid for the conservatory and the loft conversion."

"There's no-one else in the village he could have been going to see?"

She shook her head. "Roxby is hardly a village of fortune tellers and soothsayers is it? No, Mr Brady. If Tim Carrick was going to find out what the future held, Sarah Trueman was his only option."

"Did he kill her?"

"Blunt, if nothing else, Mr Brady. You're asking if I think he's *capable* of killing her. My initial reaction is no. But twenty years? Nothing men do – or want – surprises me."

46

B rady smiled. "I've just spent half an hour with a
dominatrix, Frankie."

She shook her head. "No thanks, boss. Too easy.
I don't need an open goal. I'm assuming it had something to
do with your starring role on TV?"

Brady nodded. "She's called Julie Stott. Mistress Anastasia in her working life. Which ended when someone ran
into the back of her car."

"So what's she do now?"

"Lives in Staithes. Lives a quieter life, she said. Goes to
church."

"So she's exchanged BDSM for the Bible?"

"Something like that. 'I take comfort in the word of Our
Lord.'"

"She knew Sarah?"

Brady shook his head. "More than that, Frankie. *Much*
more than that. She knew someone who was going to see
her. On Friday."

"Friday? That's – "

"Right. When she left the cottage."

"Who?"

Brady passed her the piece of paper. "Tim Carrick. Find out everything you can, will you? He's in Otley. North Leeds."

"You've phoned him?"

Brady nodded. "He's on his way back from a meeting in London as we speak. Give it an hour and we'll head over."

"You think she's reliable, boss?"

Brady nodded. "I do. Number one, she made a hell of an effort to get here. Two, she'd been agonising over breaking a client's confidence."

"I thought you said she'd retired?"

"She has. Trust me, Frankie. She looked in real pain. Walking with a stick."

"Walking with a stick doesn't mean she *needs* a stick, boss. And a dominatrix. Knots. Tying someone up. That's what they do."

'After I'd spent two years learning the ropes...'

Brady nodded. "Fair point. Julie Stott. She lived in Harrogate before Staithes. Add her to your list. And she says she had a car accident. 'Tourist in a Range Rover drove into the back of me.'"

"Did you get her reg number?"

"When she drove off. Here."

Brady wrote it on the piece of paper. Passed it to Frankie.

"Tim Carrick, boss. Did she say anything about him?"

"She'd known him for fifteen years. He paid for her conservatory and loft conversion."

"Bloody hell, how much did she charge?"

Brady laughed. "You're not thinking of a change of career are you, Detective Sergeant? 'Same as always' Carrick said in his text to her. 'Two hundred.'"

"Pounds?" Frankie leaned forward. Took the calculator

off Brady's desk. Did a rapid calculation. Shook her head. "I'm in the wrong job. By a factor of ten."

"She said she was living on her savings. And downsizing from Harrogate. She implied she'd made a few bob. Find out how much will you, Frankie?"

Frankie nodded. "You're certain she was telling the truth?"

"I am. You know that phrase I always use. 'The ring of truth.' She had it. She said she listened. Implied the conversation was just as important as..."

"The other stuff?"

"Right. She made the job sound a lot like police work."

"Just not at two hundred quid an hour? If I request a new pair of handcuffs tomorrow, you'll know why."

47

"What do you think, boss?"

"What do I think about Tim Carrick, Frankie?"

"No. About a change of career. We're here. The Old Carriage Works. Lochie went to see some web designers yesterday. The Old Toffee Factory. Let's forget law and order. Whitby's villains. Bloody paperwork. Re-brand the station as the Old Cop Shop. Dan Keillor can open a gym. You can do leadership and training."

"Where's that leave you then?"

"Me? My idea, boss. I'll just swan around with a Hazelnut Latte. Double shot of espresso and cinnamon on top, obviously."

"Right. I'll tell Dave to sprinkle chia seeds on your bacon sandwich. Come on, let's see what the boss of Carrick and Company has to say for himself."

BRADY SIPPED HIS COFFEE. Nodded. "I congratulate you, Mr Carrick. Twenty-five years of drinking coffee in other people's offices and this is the best. By the proverbial country mile."

Tim Carrick laughed. "I spent a year in Melbourne. Best coffee in the world. I had the machine shipped over. La Marzocco. Five grand." He raised his eyebrows. "Bloody ridiculous. But life's too short for Mellow Birds."

Brady smiled. Wracked his brain. Failed to come up with a law that allowed him to arrest a coffee machine.

"As I explained to you on the phone, Mr Carrick, we're investigating the death of Sarah Trueman. I understand you went to see her."

Jeans, a white shirt buttoned up to the neck. Hair pulled straight back into a pony-tail, receding at the temples.

'Widow's peak?' Is that what you call it?

Goatee beard. Two leather bracelets on his left wrist.

Tap 'new-age businessman' into Google and this is what you get...

He nodded. "I'm not going to deny it."

Good. Because there's no point...

"OK," Brady said. "The obvious thing is to say 'tell us about it.' But let's step back. Tell me about *yourself*, Mr Carrick. I have a bad case of office-envy. I'd cheerfully swap with you. How did the business start?"

"Twenty years ago. All but two months. Two of us working for McKinsey. We – "

"The management consultants?"

He nodded. "We decided we'd rather consult for ourselves. And they were threatening to send me back to Malaysia. So we started Reid Carrick."

"But now it's just Carrick?"

"Right. Ed got sick. I bought him out. Worked my bollocks off. Built the business. Now we've clients in Florida, clients in the Far East. Specialise in ESG. Started – "

"That's..."

"Environmental, social and governance. Telling businesses – and the public sector – how to tick the boxes that millennials and the media want ticking. We've just launched Carrick Wellness. We've got all the top floor. People working from home. But we'll have to move. And sorry..." He smiled at Brady. "I'll take the coffee machine with me."

"You personally?"

"You obviously know the answer to the question."

Yes, I do...

"I'm married. I have two teenage children. I play golf. Not very well, but every man has a cross to bear. I try not to, but I tick the 'conventional businessman' box."

"But once a month you saw... I suppose I have to say 'Anastasia.'"

Carrick laughed. "I think we'd both be happier with Julie wouldn't we? Fifteen years, she was bound to tell me her real name sooner or later. And yes, you have my secret. My dark, dirty secret. So am I fucked, Inspector?" Carrick shook his head. Looked rueful. "Professional bloody ethics, eh? Might as well have told my solicitor."

"Ethics or not a woman has been murdered. Brutally murdered."

"And I'm the last person to visit the house. Caught by the long arm of coincidence. The whole of Yorkshire to aim at and I pick two women practically round the corner from one another. Maybe I should do the lottery."

Brady shook his head. "You're not 'caught,' Mr Carrick. No-one's accusing you of anything. But you visited her house. No-one saw her alive after that. So I need to know what happened. You went for a tarot reading. Let's take it from there."

"One question, Mr Carrick," Frankie said. "You don't strike me as the sort of person – "

"Who'd believe in tarot readings? Blunt, bluff Yorkshireman? Cynical? Up to two years ago I'd have agreed with you. But I had a health scare. Heart attack. Completely out of the blue. There I am in my garden. Looking at the tomatoes. Don Corleone in *The Godfather*. Next minute I'm being rushed into LGI. Leads, electrodes. 'Just like on TV,' I think. Then it goes black. I hear someone shouting."

He shook his head. Looked out of the window again.

"And I'm on the ceiling. Looking down through a mist. Ten seconds? Five minutes? I have no idea. But then I'm back. So you're right, Ms Thomson. Or two years ago you'd have been right. Now? I don't eat red meat. Don't touch alcohol. I cycle. And I'm willing to accept there might be plenty of things I don't know."

"So you went to see Sarah Trueman?"

"I did."

"Why her? There must be plenty of tarot readers closer to home."

He nodded. "Unquestionably. But my wife went. She'd got the name from someone at one of her business groups. So off she went with her sister."

"You didn't tell your wife you were going?"

He shook his head. "No, I didn't." He shrugged. "Embarrassed, I suppose. And I don't talk to her about the business."

"So the tarot reading," Frankie said. "You had a specific question in mind?"

He nodded. "I told you. The health scare. I've been thinking about selling the business. But I'm fifty-one now. What the hell would I do? So maybe I sell part of it. The wellness division. Maybe it's a step too far. Maybe I look for a partner. I don't know."

"I'd have thought... well, a business coach – your accountant – rather than a pack of tarot cards."

"Maybe. But the wife's sister was impressed. She's an actuary. You know, someone who thought about being an accountant but decided it might be too exciting. The world's biggest sceptic. So if she's impressed... Besides, an afternoon out in the country. Fish and chips afterwards. And it's a chance to think. Business maxim number one. You want to think differently, you need to be somewhere different."

"Thank you," Brady said. "That's the background. You want to talk me through it? What happened?"

He nodded. "I'm late. Ten minutes maybe. I park by the village shop. What used to be the village shop. Walk up the path to her house."

"Take a step back. You made the appointment? How? Phone? Online?"

Carrick shook his head. Looked bewildered. "None of the above. I wrote her a letter. She didn't have a mobile. Wasn't online. Here's me worrying about artificial intelligence. Next minute the moon landings haven't happened."

So that's why we didn't find a computer. Or a phone...

"How did you get her address? From your wife? I thought you said you didn't talk to your wife about business?"

"I didn't. She told me that's how she made the appointment. So I was up early. Opened her handbag. Found her address book. Wrote to Sarah. Gave her a couple of alternative dates."

"What were they?"

"When I went and – hang on..." Carrick opened his

phone. Went to his diary. "And three days later. Friday and the following Monday."

"And she wrote back to you? Confirmed the date? Gave you instructions on how to find her?"

Carrick nodded.

Is that significant? The first date, not three days later. Three days food left out for the cats. Was she expecting to be away? Couldn't see Carrick because she knew she'd be away? Or did she just go for the first appointment because she was free? Leave space for someone else?

"So you're walking up the path to the house. Did you notice anything at this point?"

Carrick shook his head. "I'm not looking for anything, am I? I'm thinking about the reading. I've done some home-work. Know what cards I want. Not 'death' that's for sure. Not 'the fool' either. So no, I don't notice anything. The church. The graveyard. A big old oak tree in the corner of it. Nothing else. Like I say, I'm thinking about the cards."

"Nothing else?"

He shrugged. "It's quiet. Too quiet for me that's for sure. I could never live in a place that isolated."

"Then what?"

"The gate needed oiling. She'd taken care of the garden but not the gate. I went round the side. Knocked on the door."

"No post in the letterbox? Newspapers? Milk delivery?"

He shook his head. "Nothing. Red door, like she said. I knocked. Nothing."

"How long did you wait?"

"Five minutes maybe? Ten? I thought she might have gone out. I went back to the gate. Looked up and down. Nothing. I went round the back, knocked on the window. Same result. No-one in."

"Did you look in through a window? See anything?"

"Kitchen window. Looked like she enjoyed cooking. But all I saw was cat bowls. Nine of them – "

Three cats, three days. But I feed Archie twice a day...

" – But she needn't have bothered. I saw one of them. Mouse in its mouth. Grumpy looking bugger. The cat, I mean."

"Right. I can't believe the mouse was happy about it. Nothing else? Nothing looked out of place?"

"A pane of glass was cracked. I thought maybe... Maybe maintenance wasn't her strong point."

Brady nodded.

He's not telling me anything I haven't seen. Couldn't guess...

"What about the garden?"

Carrick laughed. "You're asking the wrong person. My wife's the gardener."

"Thank you," Brady said. "I'm tempted to spin it out to have another cup of your coffee, but we've taken up enough of your time."

Brady stood up. Carrick looked at him. "This is confidential, right? I've got a good marriage. But Anastasia. Julie." He shook his head. "I've got... needs. I can't help it."

Two points, Mr Brady. Number one, there is no limit to the distance a man will drive when he has an erection. Or needs to be a puppy. And punished when he's a naughty puppy.

Brady shuddered. Knew that was a mental image he'd never get rid of.

"I'm a policeman, Mr Carrick. I'm not here to judge your morals. But I have needs as well. I need to catch the person who murdered Sarah Trueman. So I will need the letter she sent you."

Carrick nodded. "It's still in the car. I'll walk down with you."

"And we'll need your fingerprints as well."

"Fingerprints? All I did was knock on the door. Touch the window maybe. The gate."

Brady smiled. "Good. Then your fingerprints won't be inside the house will they? And you won't have anything to worry about."

Tim

Thank you for your letter, and the two dates you sent me. The Friday is perfect for me, and I look forward to seeing you at 2pm.

I understand that this is your first time, and I ask only four things of you. Come with a specific question in mind: come with an *open* mind – and allow yourself to be guided.

Most importantly of all, trust. Trust the cards, and trust me to interpret them for you.

There are no good and bad cards. There are only answers – and trust me: I will help you find them.

I look forward to seeing on Friday.

Your guide

NB: My fee for the reading will be £150. Please note that the cards consistently warn me not to trust the banks, so please bring cash

48

———

"Thoughts?"

Brady pulled the Tiguan out of the Old Carriage Works. Turned left and pointed it back towards Whitby. Quickly sped up to sixty as a beat-up old Vauxhall Corsa raced toward him in the rear-view mirror.

"I would say we have our first suspect boss."

"You think he could have done it?"

"I think he would've needed help. He was well built, but not quite well built enough to haul a 70kg dead weight up a tree."

"So we're back to two people then. Do you think he had a motive?"

"Nothing that springs to mind immediately. That's if you buy his story though. It'll be interesting to see if we get a match on his fingerprints. If he was inside the house then we might be the ones making him coffee next time. Not that he'll approve of what we have in the station."

"A far cry from five grand *La Marzocco*."

Brady indicated left and made his way onto the A64 slip road. The Corsa immediately zoomed past him.

"You know, there are times when I wish I had lights in the car, Frankie. Stick a siren on and give a kid like that the fright of his life."

"Wishing yourself back into uniform boss? Most coppers work the other way around."

"I know. But there'll be a lorry trying to overtake another lorry in a few miles time. He'll get stuck behind that just the same as us. Makes you wonder what the point is…

"But back to Sarah Trueman. Let me talk to you, Frankie. Try and sound it out. I'm Carrick. I know Sarah from some-where in my past – a business deal gone wrong, an affair – we definitely can't rule that out based on what Julie Stott said about him. The mental images I had to put aside during that meeting. You're lucky she didn't want to talk to another woman."

Brady shuddered again. Indicated to get round a middle lane driver.

"The point is he knows her. Setting up a tarot reading is a guaranteed way for her to let me in. I park by the village shop. Walk up the path to her house. She doesn't know who to expect. Arranging the readings via letter – she can't have got much business that way? Relying solely on word of mouth. It seems strange. Risky. But either way, she doesn't know who she's meeting. So maybe when she opens the door, she's surprised, she's taken off guard."

"What about the cat bowls boss? The vicar said he didn't put them down. I'm not sure Carrick would have done that afterwards."

"No. You're right. So perhaps Carrick didn't go into the house after all. Perhaps he lured her out?"

"That still doesn't work boss. Why would she put the cat bowls down before she'd arranged a reading? Doesn't give off the best impression does it? *Hello, welcome to my cottage. Step over the bowls of cat food and I'll tell you your future."*

"So what are we saying?"

"She left the house intentionally boss. She knew she was leaving for a long time. So that was either before Carrick got there, or after he'd left."

"What time did she text the vicar?"

"Just after three."

Hope the wedding goes well. I'll miss you. Friday at 15:23

"And Carrick's reading was booked for 2pm. He arrives ten minutes late. That's just over an hour not accounted for, Frankie. We find out where Sarah was in that hour, my bet is we find the killer – or at least whoever took her."

"Two people then boss?"

"Two people? Carrick maybe one of them? I don't know. We'll get Dan to look into his background when we get back to the station, see what he can find. Right now Carrick is neither in nor out for me."

Brady sighed. He felt like he wasn't making any progress. So far all he'd done was rule the vicar out and speak to two widows with close to no information. Apart from informing him one of his officers was a thief. He sighed again.

"I've got a meeting with HR when we get back."

Frankie read his mind. "Jake?"

"Jake. Don't suppose you fancy one at the Black Horse afterwards? Give me the will to get through the meeting."

"Can't I'm afraid boss, I'm seeing Lochie."

"Invite him along?"

"No can do. We've got plans. Sorry boss."

Was she being deliberately evasive? Brady didn't feel like the most competent detective at that moment in time, but even he could tell there was something Frankie wasn't telling him. Something she didn't want to tell him...

"Another time then. Maybe when Jake is back."

"Have you managed to speak to him yet?"

"No. I thought I'd play this one by the book and go by proper protocol. But that means an awkward meeting with our station's HR rep. *Do I think he's been under unnecessary pressure? Could there be anything causing him anxiety?* Honestly you'd think they didn't know what we did for a living."

"When was that meeting you found? Gamblers Anonymous?"

"Every Monday morning. I'll drive him myself next week if I'm allowed. I have a feeling HR will tell me to try and take a backseat."

But that's not what Ian Henshaw said.

"First things first, come to the meetings. An' the sooner the better. Salvation Army, Admiral's Avenue. Monday. Seven-thirty. And what can you do to help? Be there. Just bloody well be there. 'Cos there's more bollocks talked about gambling than any subject under the sun."

And when have I been one to follow protocol...

49

S mooth, unctuous, unruffled. Brady shook hands with the headteacher.

I've met you a hundred times before. Someone who comes close to bullying anyone under him. Who magically manages to be somewhere else when the shit hits the fan.

Kershaw's twin brother. The one who didn't fancy the uniform. Who chose the education ladder not the police ladder...

Office overlooking the playing fields.

"You know what they say, Mr Brady. The Battle of Waterloo was won on the playing fields of Eton."

Not on the worn out astroturf of Whitby College...

"Were there any members of staff she was particularly close to?"

"We have a high turnover of staff. Lady Anne's looks idyllic. It *is* idyllic. But even I will concede it's isolated. The weekly trip to Sainsbury's can be a challenge, especially in the winter.

"The reason why she left is simple. Stress. An inability to cope. Frankly, her exam results were disappointing. And became more so. A steady decline over three or four years."

Headmaster Kirkup sat with his hands crossed in his lap. His chair tilted backwards at an angle. He looked relaxed. Comfortable. Like a man who wasn't worried about his position.

"You understand that parents are paying a great deal of money. And they're paying for a variety of reasons, chief among which is success. I know it's a dirty word in some wishy-washy liberal circles but not here. We don't believe that every child is a winner. That everyone deserves a prize. We believe in competition. That the race goes to the swiftest. We expect our pupils to go to Oxbridge. Represent regional and national sports teams."

He glanced out of the window. Stood up, beckoned to Brady. Pointed out of the window at a boy in cricket whites. A mop of blond hair, grinning at the boy next to him.

"Callum Macauley-Taylor. Remember the name. He'll play for Yorkshire by the time he's nineteen, England by the time he's twenty-two. Whatever records Cook and Root set he'll beat them. But *only* if we keep him focused. On the straight and narrow. That's what our parents pay for, Mr Brady. Promise delivered: potential realised. That's what we do. And that means pressure. Pressure on the pupils and pressure on the teachers. And some of them can't deliver."

"Sarah Trueman."

"Yes. Sadly, Sarah Trueman."

"So she left?"

"As you say, she left."

"Have you any idea what she did afterwards?"

He shrugged. "She said she was going to travel. Find herself. Some new age nonsense. Hardly in keeping with the traditions of the school."

"Were there any other teachers – any students – she was especially close to?"

"I refer you to the answer I gave previously, Mr Brady. We have a high turnover of staff. Pupils? No, not especially."

"This is a murder enquiry. If I have to I'll interview every teacher and every pupil you've had for the last five years."

Headmaster Kirkup hook his head.

"No you won't. Don't think I can't pick up that phone and speak to half a dozen QCs. If I think of anyone I'll let you know, Mr Brady. Your bluff and bluster may work in the whelk stalls of Whitby. Not here. Let me be blunt. Whatever answer you seek, it's not here."

"I'd like a list of all the members of staff who were here in her final year. And all the pupils she taught."

Brady did his best to keep his cool. Failed.

"And let me be equally blunt. Sarah Trueman was brutally murdered. I'll find the killer. A promise that will be delivered, Mr Kirkup. Whatever it costs. And, if we're being blunt with each other, I really don't give a rat arse for the school's reputation."

50

"I lost my temper with the head."

Frankie nodded. "That must have been satisfying."

"I was lied to for half an hour."

"How come?"

"Sarah Trueman. The teacher with no friends. Who never taught any pupils. And even if she had it was more than my job was worth to speak to them."

"How come?"

"I can pick up that phone and call half a dozen QCs, Mr Brady."

"I was really pissed off, Frankie. *Really* pissed off. But at the same time I was impressed. And envious. The facilities. And the confidence. The self-assurance. I spoke to a couple of the kids. It was just... Not Whitby College. And then I'm coming out. Walking across to my car – "

"Which looked out of place..."

"Which was the *only* one in the car park without a personalised number plate. And I'm walking across and there's a girl – Ash's age – with a horse. A *horse*, Frankie. She's got her bloody horse at school with her."

"Maybe Ash could go, boss. Take Archie with her."

Brady shook his head. "There's part of me that would love her to go, Frankie. The sports facilities. Four hockey pitches. Astroturf that professional footballers would happily train on. The extra-curricular stuff. Public speaking."

"You've been looking at the website."

"I have. Which parent doesn't want the best for their child? Except I don't have thirty grand a year."

"And you'd miss her sarcasm."

Brady laughed. "I would. But keep it to yourself."

"Besides, you did alright, boss. I did alright."

"If necessary I'll speak to every teacher who's ever worked there and every pupil she's ever taught. He told me she left because she couldn't handle the pressure. Because her exams results were getting worse."

Brady paused. Thought for a moment.

"I wouldn't be surprised if something hadn't happened at the school, Frankie."

"And they've kept it quiet? Omerta? The public school code of silence."

Brady nodded. "And they've kept it *very* quiet. Five hundred kids at thirty grand a year. Fifteen million quid a year? That's a hell of a cashflow to protect. And when someone threatens me with an army of QCs – "

"You get suspicious."

"He gave me a tip if you fancy going to the bookies. Callum Macauley-Taylor. Said he'll play for England by the time he's twenty-two. 'Whatever records Alastair Cook and Joe Root set he'll beat them. As long as we keep him on the straight and narrow.' Poor kid. Sounded like the head was going to personally supervise his cold shower every morning. And then sprinkle bromide on his cornflakes."

51

Brady opened his middle desk drawer. Shifted some papers around until he uncovered it. His little black book. One of the first pieces of advice he'd been given as a copper. Keep everyone's details. Suspects. Witnesses. And colleagues.

He flicked through the pages until he found Sam Waddington. They'd spent six years together on the force in Manchester. Sam was a Burnley lad originally. Meaning he and Brady had bonded over their struggling football teams. He'd continued to climb the ranks in the city while Brady traded gangs and gun crime for coastal walks and countryside murders.

But Sam also had a history with public school crime. He'd ran point on the case that uncovered a child labour camp at a boarding school just south of the Lake District. If anyone had crossed paths with Lady Anne's before, Sam Waddington should know the details.

"Sam, hi. How're things going over there?"

"We're good, Mike. Well, apart from the drugs. And the body we fished out of the Rochdale Canal. And Emily and I have finally decided to call it quits. So apart from drugs, dead bodies and divorce, I'm good. What about you?"

"Yeah, I'm fine. More than fine really. I've been here two years now. And my teenage daughter is still speaking to me, so all good."

"Someone told me you were dating a rock star?"

Brady laughed. "She's a musician, Sam. Working on a film at the moment. So 'dating' may not be the right word as there's currently about 500 miles between us."

"Just like the song then, you better get walking. Anyway – what can I do for you, Mike? I've got to go and interview a kid who crashed his BMW into a lamppost. Barely old enough to drive and he's got ten grand in the glove compartment."

"Lady Anne Clifford's school, Sam. We've got a murder case. Sarah Trueman, one of the ex-teachers. I was there earlier, hell of a place. You ever hear anything about her? Any problems with the school?"

"Apart from none of us can afford to send our kids there? No, Mike. You know where the school is. Ten miles up in the Dales. I can't think of the last time we had anything to do with them."

"No drugs? Rich kids with even richer parents?"

"If there's a problem they keep it all in-house. And rich parents is the key. The school brings a fair bit of money into the local economy. Cooks, cleaners, lab technicians. Teachers, obviously. Parents staying overnight. There's a fair few Russian kids there. One of the parents flew in by helicopter. Booked out two local B&Bs for three days. There's a couple of the parents on the watch-list, but nothing we'd look into unless some serious shit hit the fan. And the school likes to keep it that way I imagine. So no, nothing to report."

"Thanks, Sam. I'll leave you to your teenage drug dealer."

"You take care, Mike. Have a paddle in the sea for me. Put me some proper fish and chips in the post."

52

"Do you want me to pick up some dinner on the way home? Fish and chips?"

"I'm making pasta. Auntie Kate gave me a recipe when I went round for dinner the other night. Tomato and feta. You could get some garlic bread though?"

"Roger that. I'll be about twenty minutes. Can you see if we've any beer in the fridge?"

Brady waited. Heard his daughter sigh on the other end of the phone as she went to check. Heard the unmistakable noise of glass bottles rattling in the fridge door as it closed.

"Beer and cheese. About the only two things that are always in our fridge."

"Thanks Ash. Twenty minutes. I'll see you soon."

"Do you ever wish you had a horse?"

"A horse? I thought we were still paying off the house?"

"Your mum covered that, don't worry darling. And no – I'm not thinking about buying you a horse – Archie is enough to feed."

Brady bent down and ruffled his dog's fur. Knew he owed him a walk.

"But I was at a school today, Lady Anne Clifford's..."

"That boarding school in the Dales? We played them at hockey last term. The changing rooms were bigger than our sports hall. Didn't see any horses though."

"They've got them I can assure you. And plenty of other things too I bet. Some of the kids there – "

"Oh I know. They're mental aren't they? I think we lost maybe thirteen or fourteen one. And the one was a fluke. Check the garlic bread will you, Dad? And why are you interested anyway?"

Brady smiled. Cracked the oven door to check on the bread. Smelt the garlic. Felt his mouth starting to water. Should he be talking to Ash about this? Lately he'd felt like she was growing up faster. Drinking wine, cooking dinner. There was a part of him that liked it – liked having someone to talk to like an adult – but he didn't want to lose his little girl either.

"Just the case I'm working on. The victim used to be a teacher there."

"And you reckon one of the kids did it? She pushed them too hard in maths and so they've come back and got their revenge?"

"Not quite."

Although could it be an ex-pupil? That's not an angle I've considered yet. And chemistry is never a favourite subject...

"You never know, Dad. There was a group of boys there who were watching the hockey. I swear they could've been straight out of the mafia."

"You didn't get jealous then? Wish I'd shipped you off to Lady Anne's?"

"No chance. You'd miss me too much. And who would feed Archie when you're late home every night? Now set the table. The pasta's nearly ready."

Brady laughed.

"You know you get more and more like your mother every day."

And she would've been so proud of you.

You really would, Gracie. I wish you could see her now.

53

Brady pushed open the balcony door as quietly as he could and stepped outside. Whitby sparkled in the moonlight. One of the boats in the harbour had fairy lights adorning the mast. The bright colours reflected off the water. Drifted with the gentle tide. He reached for his chair and sat down.

"I miss you, Grace."

He spoke out loud to himself. Looked in the direction of the cliff top. Couldn't see it, but knew it was there. How long had it been since he'd walked up to Grace's hill? Too long. Brady felt guilty. His life was moving forward but he wasn't yet ready to leave his past behind.

"Someone told me you were dating a rock star?"

"She's a musician, Sam. Working on a film at the moment. So 'dating' may not be the right word..."

But Brady wasn't thinking about Siobhan. He looked across Whitby and realised it wasn't Siobhan he wanted in his bed tonight. It was Grace.

Ash was so much like her mother now. Sitting opposite her at the table, eating pasta, Brady couldn't help but see the similarities. The way she tucked her hair behind her ears to stop it falling in the sauce. The way she wiped her mouth with a piece of kitchen roll after every couple of bites. Even just the way she smiled.

"I wish you were here, Gracie. I wish I could see you just one more time."

Despite his best efforts, as always, Brady's thoughts drifted back to his case.

Did Sarah Trueman think of someone as she hanged from the tree? Was it the person watching her? Or someone else? And why was she positioned like that?

Brady dug his phone from his pocket. Opened his email. Read the message he'd received earlier that evening.

DEAR MR BRADY,

I am sorry to let you down, but I have decided I will be unable to help with your investigation.

The cards do not predict it to be a wise decision on my part and they have never steered me wrong.

I can recommend a friend of mine – George – who you can find online at www.wintersongreadings.co.uk who might be able to help you instead.

Best of luck with your work.

Yours,

Elvina.

AT LEAST ELVINA had the courtesy of recommending someone else. And at least that someone else had a website. If only Sarah Trueman had been online.

A murder? Don't worry, we'll print out a list of everyone she's been in contact with in the last month. You'll find the killer in no time...

So that was his morning. Call George at *Winter Song Readings* and finally, finally speak to Jake. With the surprising blessing from HR.

54

"Boss, there's someone to see you."

"Bloody hell, Sue, it's only three days since the last one. The power of TV, eh?"

"I don't think it's TV, boss..."

A woman in her late fifties. Grey hair cut confidently short. No-nonsense glasses. Lean, already tanned despite the weather.

Brady held out his hand. "Michael Brady. And... We've met, haven't we?"

She nodded. "Not officially, Mr Brady."

"But you were at Lady Anne's..."

And you spend your weekends walking in the Dales...

"I *am* at Lady Anne's. But only four days a week."

Brady nodded. "And on Friday you go walking on the hills. Except for this Friday. Can I offer you a cup of tea, Ms..."

She held her hand out. A cool, firm handshake. "Carolyn Armer."

"So can I offer you a cup of tea, Ms Armer?"

She shook her head. "You can offer me a walk, Mr Brady.

The last time I was in Whitby was thirty years ago. Let me see if the town is as beautiful as it was."

Brady smiled. "It is. And a walk sounds perfect, Ms Armer. I have a bandstand with a view..."

"Your best mug, Dave," Brady said ten minutes later. "No chips if you've got one."

Dave sighed theatrically. Shook his head. "Bloody demanding customers. Here."

He reached for a black and white striped mug, a blue star on the side of it. "Newcastle United retro. My favourite. I hope she's worth it."

Brady passed Carolyn Armer the mug of tea. "You're sure I can't tempt you with a bacon sandwich?"

She smiled back at him. "You can certainly tempt me, Mr Brady. But the answer will be 'no.' You know the old saying. We dig our graves with our knife and fork."

"I've heard it..."

And thanks to Dave I've ignored it...

"Anyway – "

"You didn't drive ninety miles to discuss diets?"

She shook her head. "Or to admire your view. Beautiful as it is."

Carolyn Armer sipped her tea. Hesitated for a moment. Then told Brady her story.

"I'm not a religious woman, Mr Brady. I don't believe in God. I do, however, believe in doing the right thing. And if that sounds pretentious – or outdated – " She shrugged. "I am who I am. So that's why I'm here. To give you some background. Tell you that your trip to the Yorkshire Dales this week wasn't the dead end the headmaster might have suggested it was."

Brady nodded. Knew when to keep quiet.

"I've been the Head's secretary at Lady Anne's for ten years, give or take a few months. One Head who retired. And the current incumbent."

Her tone of voice left little doubt which she preferred.

"The Head has one priority, Mr Brady. Make sure the fees keep coming. You may think the way to do that is good academic performance. Success on the sports field. All the traditional boxes that a school needs to tick. But we have a new breed of parent. With *one* box to tick. And for whom thirty thousand a year isn't even petty cash."

"You're talking foreign parents? Ticking the 'English public school' box?"

"I am. Russian and Chinese. Lady Anne's is far from alone but we have, effectively, a school within a school."

"And they're treated differently?"

"Very differently. If the hockey match is played on the brand new, state-of-the-art, Alexei-Kamenev-sponsored astroturf..."

"Then the normal rules don't apply to Dimitri Kamenev?"

"Sasha in this case. But yes, precisely."

Brady watched Ms Armer carefully. Saw the same level-headed principles that he'd seen in Julie Stott. Though perhaps behind a softer face.

"What does this have to do with Sarah Trueman?"

"I'm now entering the realms of informed guesswork, Mr Brady. But I wouldn't have driven over here if I wasn't sure of my guesswork."

Brady nodded. Finished his coffee. Wondered if he'd hear 'we dig our graves with our knife and fork' every time he stood at Dave's counter.

"The school has a tradition. At the end of the summer

term those pupils who are going into the sixth form are entertained by their teachers. It takes – "

"So the pupils are sixteen?"

She nodded. "Sixteen. The entertainment is what's commonly known as a safari supper. Many of the teachers live in the boarding houses. They cook for the students."

"So starter with one teacher. Main course with another?"

"Exactly. And five years ago Sarah Trueman, Chemistry teacher at Lady Anne Clifford's, was cooking for her students."

"That was her last year wasn't it? The head said she left due to consistently poor exam results."

"Yes, I'd imagine that's what he said. But any teacher can have poor exam results for a couple of years. It's the same in any school. You have years that produce an outstanding rugby team. You have years that produce outstanding exam results. Gloss over it all you like, but some school years are just not very bright. Sarah Trueman wasn't a bad teacher. She was just unlucky. Her last exam cohort only cared about one thing when it came to chemistry and it wasn't going to be found in a text book."

Carolyn Armer sipped her tea. Looked out to sea.

"In the summer holidays one of the girls – Natalya Petrov – died. Her family owned a villa in Tuscany. She collapsed in her father's arms. Not sure they ever publicly announced the cause of death."

"And she's sixteen?"

The age Ash will be next year...

"Sixteen. She'd been having problems with drugs. Psychosis. I'm not an expert, I won't speculate."

"You're going to tell me she was one of the students who went to Sarah's?"

"I am. They went in fours. I only know the name of one of the other students – these were very informal affairs."

"Should I take an informed guess?"

Carolyn Armer nodded. "And you'd be right. Sasha Kamenev was widely suspected of having some involvement. He was one of the students at Sarah Trueman's that night. But I've already told you – "

"A school within a school?"

"A very lucrative school within a school. If Sasha was expelled there'd be no new hockey pitch. He had two younger siblings at the school. They were far from the school's only Russian students. And they wouldn't risk other wealthy parents deciding they'd prefer a more..." She paused.

Looking for the right word...

"...a more liberal regime for their children."

"But someone had to take the blame." Brady made it a statement, not a question.

"As you say. There was a suggestion that the children were already drunk – or high, or both – when they arrived at Sarah's. She took no action. Fed them and let them wander across the quad to a rack of lamb."

"But surely the other teachers – "

"Were equally culpable? They'd been at the school for longer. Were more senior. And happy to play the game."

"And more expensive to pay off?"

"Very possibly. Either way Sarah Trueman was the scapegoat. The school's sacrificial lamb. Her exam results were a convenient smokescreen."

"So I need to find Sasha Kamenev? And the other two students who were there that night?"

She shook her head. "Sasha will, I'm afraid, be a little elusive."

"He's back in Russia?"

"He's dead, Mr Brady. His father gave him a Ferrari for his eighteenth birthday. Two weeks later Sasha wrapped it round a tree in the South of France."

"So how do I find the other two students?"

She shook her head. "There I can't help you. These were informal, ad-hoc arrangements. But you could find a PE teacher. Ben Moxon. At the time head of boys' games at Lady Anne's. And when he wasn't organising boys' games, indulging in some other games with Ms Trueman. So the gossip had it..."

"And the gossip is reliable?"

"As I said to you, Mr Brady. I don't believe in God, I do believe in right and wrong. I liked Sarah. She was a bit – " She made the inverted commas gesture with her fingers that always annoyed Brady – "... 'new age' for me, but at heart she was a good woman and a hard-working teacher. She was seeing one of the other teachers. So what? Why else do teachers arrange field trips? Yes, the gossip is reliable. Like I said, I wouldn't have driven ninety miles if it wasn't."

"And where do I find Ben Moxon? Don't tell me he's dead as well?"

She laughed. "Far from it, Mr Brady. He's in York."

And if what you've told me stirs up some shit and some of that sticks to the Head you'll consider it a morning well spent, Ms Armer. So will I. Thank you...

55

"I've just had an interesting conversation."

Frankie raised her eyebrows. "That sounds suitably cryptic."

"The school secretary from Lady Anne's came to see me. She wanted an unofficial, off-the-record, cup-of-tea-by-the-bandstand conversation."

"Why?"

"Because she believes in doing the right thing. Because she was a friend of Sarah's and thought she'd been unfairly treated. Most of all, I suspect, because she's close to retirement and thinks the Head's a shit."

"An opinion you share."

Brady nodded. "I do. She told me about something five years ago. A dinner party. The kids finish their exams. GCSEs. The ones that are going into the sixth form are entertained by the teachers. Safari suppers – you know – "

"Starter in one house, main course in another and the thought of walking half a mile for Brenda's Black Forest gateaux makes you strategically twist your ankle? I do know."

"Remind me not to invite you. Anyway, the end of term comes and Sarah Trueman is cooking. Four kids are coming to her – sixteen year olds. One is Natalya Petrov, another is a boy called Sasha Kamenev. She doesn't know who the other two are. 'Very unofficial,' she said."

"Like your conversation?"

Brady laughed. "Exactly. Anyway, Natalya dies during the summer holidays. Drug-induced psychosis is the best I've found online. Sasha is widely suspected of being the supplier, but nothing can be proved. But the school needs a scapegoat."

"Why? Natalya didn't die while she was at the school."

"No. But her problems can be traced back to it. And her parents want to know the full story. And they're only human. They want someone to blame."

"And that's Sarah Trueman?"

Brady nodded. "Bingo. For not seeing that the kids had been drinking – "

"And smoking something probably."

" – When they arrived. For letting them go on their merry way. What did she say? 'Across the quad for rack of lamb.'"

"So you need to find Sasha?"

"I can't find Sasha. His dad gave him a Ferrari for his eighteenth birthday. He wrapped it round a tree in the South of France. About three years ago."

"You want me to check that? Easy enough."

Brady nodded. "I can't see any reason why she'd lie. But yes."

"What about the other kids? Not to make an assumption based on the names you've given me so far – but can we assume they were Russian too?"

"Quite possibly. Ms Armer said the school was half filled

with Russian's and Chinese. It's their money that kept the place afloat."

"If Sasha was expelled there'd be no new hockey pitch. He had two younger siblings at the school. They were far from the school's only Russian students. And they wouldn't risk other wealthy parents deciding they'd prefer a more liberal regime for their children..."

"She must have told you something else, boss."

"She did. Ben Moxon. At the time, head of games. Sports Director, or whatever fancy title he'd have had. And when he wasn't signalling four leg byes, conducting an affair with Ms Trueman. And now to be found in York. St. Peter's, at a rough guess."

"So you're going to see him?"

"*We're* going to see him."

"Boss? One more question?"

"What's that?"

"How do you do that?"

"How do you do what?"

"Signal four leg byes?"

"Seriously?"

"Seriously, boss."

Brady shook his head. "Didn't you pay attention at school, DS Thomson?"

He stood up. Lifted his right knee and tapped it with his right hand. Then he extended his right arm and swept it across his body three or four times, finishing with an exaggerated flourish.

Frankie looked at Brady. Held his eyes. "My God," she said. "No wonder she found him irresistible..."

56

"Dan –" Brady looked around the empty police station. Searched for the other members of his team. "Where is everyone?"

"This is it boss. Anya is back tomorrow. Claire says Jake is still unwell."

"Christ we might have to draft in some uniforms. Or drag Geoff out of the underworld."

"We could ask Kershaw to come back if you're that worried boss?"

"Let's not be hasty now. Lesson one of detective work – never make impulsive decisions."

Though if the team gets any smaller, we might not have a choice. I can almost hear my voice echoing off the walls.

"How have you been getting on, Dan? We've a few more names we need you to look into."

"Nothing to report boss. I went over to York to track down our two partial prints from the house. Spoke to the drink-driver. Definitely not the type. Nearly had a panic attack when he opened the door. He hasn't touched a drop of alcohol since. The incident scared him shitless. And he was at work all day Friday, then at a charity event in the evening with his wife. Showed me the photographs to prove it."

"And the car thief?"

"Solid alibi. He saw a shiny new Merc last month and couldn't resist. Currently serving nine months."

Brady sighed. "What about Carrick?"

"Everything I've found so far matches with what you said boss. No dark links from his sordid other life yet."

"So we're no further forward? Brilliant. Sorry Dan – that's not aimed at you. I'm just frustrated. Here –" Brady handed Dan Keillor a scrap of paper with a breakdown from Carolyn Armer's informal interview on it. "See what you can get from that will you? A past lover. There's got to be something juicy there. Please God let there be something..."

57

Brady closed his car door. Put his hands on the steering wheel. Dropped his head into the cradle his arms made. Exhaled deeply.

It was over a week since they'd found Sarah's body. Nearly two since she'd left her house. And Brady was no closer to catching her killer than he was to winning the lottery.

Not only that, but he still didn't understand why she'd been killed. What relevance did the tarot cards have? The Hanged Man? He shook his head and pressed the ignition. Perhaps his next meeting would help him figure that out.

THE DRIVE to Scarborough was teeming with life. Brady loved this time of year. Lambs in the field. Blossom on the trees. He dropped down a gear as he took the hill into High Hawsker. Smiled at a field full of lambs. Saw the bright red numbers printed on their backsides.

There was a certain unpredictability to Spring on the Moors. One minute he was driving past a field of lambs, the next there was a churned-up mud bath resulting from the rain.

Brady passed the turning for May Beck. Thought about what Carolyn Armer had said.

"You could find a PE teacher. Ben Moxon. At the time head of boys' games at Lady Anne's. And when he wasn't organising boys' games, indulging in some other games with Ms Trueman. So the gossip had it..."

"And the gossip is reliable?"

"As I said to you, Mr Brady. I don't believe in God, I do believe in right and wrong. I liked Sarah. She was a bit 'new age' for me, but at heart she was a good woman and a hard-working teacher. She was seeing one of the other teachers. So what? Why else do teachers arrange field trips? Yes, the gossip is reliable. I wouldn't have driven ninety miles if it wasn't."

Brady pictured his PE teacher. Mr Adams. He had been tall. Well over six foot. And he had muscle too. It meant his bowling had been a bit lopsided. But he could bat. And when rugby season started his full skillset was unleashed. Could he hoist a woman into a tree? Undoubtedly. Mr Adams would be in his sixties now, but Ben Moxon...

And when he wasn't organising boys' games, indulging in some other games with Ms Trueman.

The tarot cards. The Lovers. Could this be the most obvious clue that Brady had been overlooking?

Brady drove down the White Way into Cloughton. His mind returned to Carrick. Another man in Sarah's life. Working alone Carrick didn't look like the sort of man who could have killed Sarah Trueman. But with someone else? Maybe with Moxon? Brady willed Dan Keillor to find a connection between the two men.

The green fields of the Moors gave way to brick buildings again as Brady approached Scarborough. He dropped down a hill next to a caravan park. One of the many access points to the Cleveland Way signposted beside it.

He'd walked part of it many years ago. One summer when he'd brought Grace over to Whitby. Ten miles to Ravenscar. Just over four hours. They'd spent the night in a hotel overlooking the North Sea. Watched the waves crashing against the cliff through the night. Missed breakfast the next morning. Walked back considerably slower than the day before.

Brady looked out to the sea as his sat nav told him to continue straight on into the town. Murmured *I miss you* under his breath. Tried to focus on the tarot reading instead.

George had instructed him to come with a question in mind. Just like Carrick had told them. Just like Sarah Trueman had written to Carrick. Brady was unsure how specific this needed to be.

Who killed her? Will I catch the killer? Where will I find them?

The options circled in Brady's head as he parked outside an Italian restaurant. One that looked like it needed some serious work doing. That likely only catered to regulars and visiting families with small children.

The Market Halls were just ahead of him and so, he hoped, were some answers.

A yellow door that even Brady thought had been badly painted. A brass stag's head mounted on the top panel, plastic purple roses entwined through the antlers.

He knocked. Gently pushed it open. Found himself face to face with a skeleton, perched jauntily in a corner. A pirate's bandanna round his head, a tarot card clasped between his fingers, grinning cheerfully at Brady.

The room was empty.

But unlocked.

Which means I don't have long to wait...

Brady turned round. Saw a door in the wall opposite him. Watched it open. A tall, thin man come out.

Brady smiled. A man who'd been to a music festival in the 80s and decided that his clothes were just fine. Who'd aged gracefully inside them. Whose hair had turned grey as the tie-dye headband had gradually faded.

"George?"

He smiled. Raised his eyebrows. "George? It depends.

Are you taking the shop next door? Are we going to be neighbours? Or is it the cards?"

Brady laughed. Gestured behind him. "The cards. I emailed..."

"Leo then." He pointed at a sign on the door.

If the Soul Moon is closed please call Leo Wintersong to book a reading.

A mobile number.

"But you don't need to call Leo Wintersong. You're here. How can I help you?"

A soft, reassuring voice. A hint of a familiar accent.

Not many miles north of Whitby...

Brady held his hand out. "My name's Michael Brady. I'm a police officer. I'm – "

Leo smiled. "Brady? That's an Irish name. Mac Brádaigh, son of Brádaigh. From *bradach*. Spirited, fiery, argumentative. I've been waiting for a man like you, Mac Brádaigh."

"A man like me?"

"The King of Swords. He spoke to me yesterday. Structure, routine, self-discipline. Mind over matter. Head over heart. Logic and reason. Law enforcement. The police, the military. A man who's self-disciplined, intelligent, honest. Who uses intellect over emotion. An Aquarius, Gemini or Libra."

Bloody hell, I'm a Libra. But come on, that's part of the sales pitch. 'I've been waiting for someone like you.' He'll say that to everyone. Do I look like a copper? Clearly. And who doesn't want to think they're intelligent and honest...

"I'm investigating a murder," Brady said. "A colleague of yours changed her mind. Didn't want to help me. So that's the first question. Tarot cards were involved in her death. I need some help. I can't make you say 'yes...'"

Leo laughed. "Helping the police with their enquiries? I

always assumed it was a prelude to eating porridge. Anything I can do to help. Come in. Ask away."

He pushed the door open. Led the way into a small, square room. A purple curtain on the back of the door. What might once have been a fireplace on the far wall. Black drapes dotted with golden stars. A rocking horse standing incongruously on a table. A picture above it that might equally have been Oscar Wilde or Aleister Crowley. The skeleton's grin even broader.

Leo gestured at a seat. A small, square table covered with a black cloth. A white pentangle in one corner. The skull of a small animal resting opposite it.

A snake?

Brady realised he had no idea what a snake's skull looked like.

Glanced down at the skull again.

It can't be a snake. No fangs.

Put his phone down on the table. Almost unbalanced it. Didn't know whether to worry about knocking the table over or not being able to recognise the skull. Wasn't sure how to start. Took refuge in small talk.

"How long have you been doing this?"

Leo shrugged. Spread his hands. "Thirty years? Ten seriously. I grew up in Redcar. My nan had a B&B. Winter in Redcar... There's not much call for B&Bs. So she started doing readings."

"She taught herself?"

He shook his head. "The cards? To some extent. The insight? No, you can't learn that. It's a gift. Like many things in life, you've either got it or you haven't. Her family came from Ireland. Irish Romany." He laughed. "Maybe we're related, Mac Brádaigh? Or maybe that's *too* romantic."

"So you picked it up from her?"

"I was at Nan's a lot. Mum and Dad... They liked to go out on a weekend. So I was shipped off to Victory Terrace. And I'd watch her. I don't know how old I was. Eight or nine. I'd sit at the top of the stairs. She winked at me one day. Left the parlour door open a touch wider. And the women would come round. Wanting to know. Pregnancies, abortions, affairs. And some of the men. Furtive. Embarrassed. Fresh off their shift at the steelworks. Sweat still drying on them. So Nan earned a few coins. Then she was making more from the cards than the B&B. But life take its course, doesn't it? I was a teenager. And you can't tell the careers master you want to be a tarot reader."

"So what changed?"

"I lost someone. Ten years ago. Needed answers. And the cards spoke to me. Helped me. So I started to take it seriously again. 'You've got Nan's gift,' I told myself. 'Don't waste it.'"

"And here you are?"

He nodded. "Here I am. Finally in the right place."

"I've read a book," Brady said. "'Teach yourself tarot' I suppose. Been online. But I need to speak to someone. There seem to be different interpretations for the cards..."

"There are. But I'm a traditional reader. I believe every card has a specific meaning. So ask your questions, Mac Brádaigh. Let's see if we can find some answers."

59

Brady nodded. Reached for his phone. Did his best not to tip the table over. Stole another glance at the skull.

Still couldn't work out what it was.

A rabbit?

"You're definitely alright with this?"

"I'm very alright with this. Let's find some answers."

Brady opened the picture. Passed it across the table.

"This was in her house. Laid out on a table. We don't know if it was a reading for someone. Or – "

Leo looked at it. Nodded. "It's not a reading," he said. "It's a question. The curious fan. She wanted an answer."

"The curious fan?"

"I know I sound like Lady Windermere. But if she wanted the answer to a question... You can cut the cards. Turn one up. But I use this. Fan the cards across the table. And like your picture, take three cards."

"Is it yes/no? Or deeper than that?"

Leo shook his head. "Tarot cards are not really yes/no. Someone with the gift, the spirit, they'd use a pendulum for a straight yes/no. Clockwise for yes, anti-clockwise for no. Here... You mind if I expand the picture?"

"Not at all. Go ahead."

"These cards. They tell a story."

"The cards together?"

He nodded. "I say that all the time. On their own the cards are just words on a table. My job is to make a sentence out of them. So this one, the first one she's turned over. The Two of Cups. Two people exchanging cups, pledging their love. With the lion's head above them. Passion. Sexual energy. So the Two of Cups, that's your soulmate. Antony and Cleopatra. Romeo and Juliet."

"Except Romeo and Juliet didn't live happily ever after."

"What everyone says to me. Can't live with him, Leo. Can't live without him."

"The card's upside down."

Leo nodded. "Reversed. Which means it's obsessive love. Possessive. Sometimes it means a break-up. Especially..."

He tapped Brady's phone. "Especially with this second card. The Lovers. That one's reversed as well. So lack of trust. Conflict. Not being sure of the direction your life is taking."

Brady nodded. Realised he was starting to be impressed. Pushed the feeling to one side. "What about the third card?"

"The Tower? People are frightened of the Tower. One of the cards you don't want, supposedly. The Tower. The Devil. The Ten of Swords. No-one wants the Ten of Swords."

"The guy with the swords in his back?"

"Right. Ruin. Failure. Dead end. Betrayal. No-one wants that one. Sorry. Where was I? The Tower. You can see it here. Lightning strikes. It's on fire. Two people are falling, head first."

"Nine-eleven?"

"That's the obvious parallel. But it's about change. *Real* change. *Escaping* the chaos."

"So the three cards together?"

"It's hard, not knowing her. Not knowing the question she asked. But if it was me – "

He sighed. Gave Brady the impression he was remembering someone.

"If it was me... She's gone to meet someone from her past."

"A lover?"

"Definitely. *Very* definitely. And it was intense. She's asking herself a question. Meeting him will give her the answer."

"Do I go back to my ex?"

"Maybe. Maybe it's about taking back control. Maybe she thinks she's drifted into something. Wants to break free."

What am I supposed to say? It fits. She'd drifted into a relationship with Croft. Was angry with herself. Met someone from her past. Moxon? Carrick? Someone else?

Leo looked at him. Raised his eyebrows. "You were sceptical weren't you? Not quite cynical, but well on the way..."

Brady nodded. "I was. Cold, hard evidence. Three words I've lived by. But recently..."

"The older you get the more you realise there's only one thing you know for certain? How much you *don't* know?"

Brady laughed. "More or less."

'How much you don't know.' Exactly what the vicar said about Sarah...

"So what do you need to know?"

.   .   .

BRADY'S PHONE RANG. He glanced down at the display.

Frankie.

"I'm sorry, I need to take this. Two minutes. I have one more question... Frankie, one minute. Just let me go outside."

Brady opened the yellow door. Walked the twenty yards to the entrance. Stood on the pavement outside the Market. St Mary's Church up to his left, the Castle walls in front of him guarding the Old Town, a glimpse of the sea to his right.

"Frankie, sorry. What can I do for you?"

"Jake, I thought you'd like an update. He came in shortly after you left. So far so good. He's chatting with Dan. Helping with the investigation."

"Brilliant. Thank you. I need to talk to him. But it sounds like he's doing his best. That's all we can ask."

"How's it going? What've you seen through the mist?"

Brady laughed. "He's confirmed what we thought. She went to meet an ex. Probably feeling stifled by the relationship with Croft. But a jealous, possessive ex... Who knows why she met him? But she did. Or this guy says she did. And I suspect he killed her. So we need to find out as much as we can about Ben Moxon from the school. And we need to go and see him. Soon. Tomorrow. I'll be back about four. Strategize in the Black Horse?"

"I'm leaving early if that's alright, boss. I need to be at the doctor's."

"Sure. No problem, Frankie. I'll see you in the morning."

Brady walked back into the vaults. Out of the sun, back into the half-light.

'So what do you need to know?'

Need to know? What's wrong with Frankie. That's twice now

she's evaded me in the Black Horse. Who killed Sarah Trueman. What the Hanged Man means. But that wasn't your question was it, Leo? What do I really want to know? Who killed my wife? Will my daughter be happy? What happens with Siobhan? What do I want to know? A hundred things...

60

"I'm sorry," Brady said. "My DS. Detective Sergeant. Just one more question, Leo."

Leo smiled. Gestured for Brady to sit down again.

Brady remained standing. "One more card I'd like to know about," he said. "The Hanged Man."

Leo nodded. "Another card people are always afraid of. They think it means death. The suicide card. You know, the old Hammer horror films. Peter Cushing hurls it down dramatically. But they shouldn't be afraid. The Hanged Man is there of his own free will." He went through the deck. Found the card. "There, look at his serene expression. The red trousers represent the physical body. The passion. The blue shirt signifies calm emotions. You see the same combination in saints. Maybe he's making a sacrifice."

"What if the card is upside down? Reversed?"

Because Sarah Trueman sure as hell was upside down...

"In a word, frustration. You're making a lot of effort, but you're getting nowhere. Nothing is turning out as it should."

Brady laughed. "That sounds like a summary of my life."

He held his hand out. "Thank you again, Leo. You've been really helpful. And I've learned – "

Leo shook his head. Gestured again for Brady to sit down. "I haven't been helpful at all. Not yet."

"You have. The Two of Cups. The – "

"I haven't answered your question. What do you need to know, Mac Brádaigh?" He held the cards out. Offered them to Brady. "Go ahead. Shuffle them."

Brady hesitated. Slowly sat down. Retreated behind small talk again. "How long have you had them?"

"Those cards? Since my nan died. And they've never been cleaned. Everyone that's ever held the cards. I keep them with me."

Brady reached for the cards.

Leo held his hand up. "One last thing."

He fanned the cards out on the black cloth. Picked up a brass bell. Lightly tapped it with his finger. Traced the bell across the cards as the echoes died away. "Clear the energies," he said. Closed his eyes, brought his hands together in prayer. "And see if there's anyone with us."

Brady suppressed a smile. Accepted that cold, hard evidence had given way to a tarot reading. Wondered what Grace would make of this. Forced himself to focus on his question.

What happened to Sarah Trueman?

Brady started to shuffle. The cards felt thick. Well used. But not greasy, as he'd expected.

He's right. I can feel them. All the hands that have shuffled these cards before me...

"Supposing it's bad news? What was it? The Ten of Swords?"

Leo shook his head. "Don't worry. And don't try to second-guess. You don't find the right cards. The cards will find you. Now, cut the pack into four. Roughly equal. Push one towards me. And think about your question."

"I'm not supposed to tell you am I?"

Leo shook his head. "No. But focus on it."

Brady looked down at the four piles.

Second from the right...

Pushed them across the black cloth. Watched Leo turn over the first card.

"This first card. This is you."

"The Fool, I expect."

Leo smiled. Turned the card over. "The Wheel of Fortune. And upright. Turning in your favour Mac Brádaigh. Good luck. Destiny. A decisive moment. A turning point. If you're going to gamble..."

Brady looked down at the card. A giant wheel, covered in symbols. Different creatures surrounding the wheel. An angel, an eagle, a bull, a lion.

The Wheel of Fortune. As far from a cold, rational copper as you can get...

"If I'm going to gamble now's the time to do it? What are the four creatures?"

"The four evangelists." Leo looked at Brady. "Remember though, the wheel turns. When you have good times, make sure you enjoy them. When there are bad times – "

Switching off my wife's life support...

"– Know that they won't last forever."

Brady nodded. Looked around the room. The skeleton in the corner continued to smile back at him.

"I – "

The door suddenly opened. A woman's head appeared. A tourist. "I wondered if we could look round?"

Leo shook his head. "No, I'm sorry. I'm in the middle of a reading. Tomorrow maybe."

"I'm sorry, we'll come back." The head disappeared.

"My apologies," Leo said. "I forgot to put the sign up."

"No problem," Brady said. "I..."

"The second card. More about you. The Three of Pentacles."

A young man standing on what looks like a workbench. An older couple looking up at him. Is he in a cathedral? Or a university...

Leo raised his eyebrows. "Someone at the top of his game. A master builder. High learning. A Master's degree. A PhD. There's nothing this person can't achieve. But – " he added. "It comes from hard work. There's no luck involved. The hard yards, that's what we're supposed to call them now aren't we?"

Ash. Going to university. Qualifying...

"Now. Three decks left." Leo reached forward. Centred them with a precision Steven Croft would have envied. Placed a gold coin on each of them.

"Put your finger on the coins. Each one in turn. Feel which deck speaks to you."

Brady put his forefinger on the first coin. Felt nothing. The second one. Wasn't sure that he felt anything. Tried to convince himself his finger was tingling. Failed. The third coin.

Something? Maybe...

He pushed the deck towards Leo.

61

"I'm going to make a Celtic Cross. Ten cards. Six cards making the cross. Then four more. The staff that supports it."

He laid the cards out one-by-one. "The present," he said. "Your signature card. Maybe the most important thing in your life."

Finding Sarah Trueman's killer.

But Ash... Ash is the most important thing in my life...

He placed a second card across the first one at a ninety degree angle. "The problem. What's stopping you."

A card to the left – "The past" – and to the right. "The future."

A card above the signature card. "Your conscious. What you know now." And a card below.

"My unconscious?" Brady said.

"As you say. What you *don't* know. And there you are. The Celtic Cross. These cards have touched one. On Iona. A windswept Scottish hillside. I stumbled up the hill. Kissed the cards. Touched them to the cross. Seventh century?

Eighth? Now... Four cards that form the staff. To support the cross."

He laid them out to Brady's left. "Your influence: the here and now. The environment: the external influences." Leo paused. Looked up at Brady. "This one. Your hopes and fears. And the last card. The outcome."

Finding Sarah Trueman's killer...

Leo took the final card off the deck. Reached forward to place it on the black cloth. Suddenly shook his head. "No. That card's not appropriate. I'm taking it out."

"Why? It's – "

"No." He shook his head vehemently. "No, it's simply not right for the reading." He put it on one side, just above the skull. Took the next card off the deck. "This one," he said. Placed the card at the bottom of the staff.

Brady gestured at the card he'd removed. "You're sure? I can take bad news. I'm a big boy."

"No. Trust me."

And now I need to know what that card is. More than anything...

Leo turned over the first card. "Your signature card. The Page of Pentacles. A young person." Looked up at Brady. "You have children?"

"I have a daughter."

"She's grounded. Loyal. Responsible. But she's ambitious. Career. Education. She knows what she wants."

'I've decided what I want to do, Dad. I'm going to be a human rights lawyer. Like George Clooney's wife.'

Brady tapped the Three of Pentacles. "There's nothing this person can't achieve? Is that her?"

But this is about Sarah Trueman, not Ash. And education. Sarah was a teacher. It couldn't be more obvious...

"Maybe. Let's see what the other cards say."

Leo reached forward. Turned over the second card. "The problem," he said. "The obstacle." Raised his eyebrows. "The World."

"The world at her feet?"

"Travel, for sure. Distance. But new beginnings as well. One project ends, a new one starts."

Travel. Sarah Trueman. All that time in South America. Then it ends. She comes home to look after her mother.

Or Ash. Again. 'I'm going to study in America, Dad.'

"The past," Leo said as he turned over the third card. "The Lovers again. Reversed again. Like I said, conflict. Not knowing which direction your life is taking. Maybe a relationship that needed working on? And the fourth card. The future. Ouch! The Three of Swords. Betrayal – "

"In a relationship?"

"This time... Yes. Remember what I said? The cards don't have a meaning on their own? But The Lovers. Then the Three of Swords."

Brady looked down at the card. A bright red heart. Pierced through by three long swords. Clouds behind it. Heavy rain.

'The cards tell a story.' Possessive love. She betrayed him. And he took revenge...

"There is another meaning to the Three of Swords."

"What's that?"

"Grieving. Taking a long time to get over something. Not being able to move on."

Sarah Trueman remember. She's the reason you're here. Not Grace.

But it fits. 'I need to know what happened to her, Dad.' Me too, Ash. Me too...

"What's next? My conscious? What I know?"

"The Six of Pentacles. Giving and receiving. Usually money. Your daughter's not planning a wedding?"

"I bloody well hope not. She's barely fifteen."

Leo laughed. "Sorry. But not just money. Wisdom, learning, knowledge."

Speaking at the school. But Sarah Trueman spent her working life giving knowledge. Five out of five so far. And the other card. Education. The one I thought was Ash at university.

At what point does this start to unnerve me...

"The last one in the Cross," Leo said. "Your unconscious. What you don't know."

"You'll need a bigger sheet of paper..."

"We'll see..." He reached forward. Turned the card over. A woman sitting on a stone bench. Blindfolded. The sea behind her. A crescent moon in the sky. Her arms crossed, a long sword in each hand.

"The Two of Swords. Confusion. A difficult choice, the swords pointing in opposite directions."

Sarah Trueman. Unable to decide. The curious fan. Asking her own tarot cards for an answer.

Or is it Ash? Studying in America. Not sure whether to come home.

Bloody hell, this is giving me more questions than answers...

"Onto the staff. Mac Brádaigh. Your seventh card. The here and now." He reached for the cards on Brady's left. Turned the first one over. "The Empress," he said. "Reversed. Some readers would say that means you have a fear of someone else controlling you."

Brady laughed. "This bloody case is controlling me. Until it's done – "

Leo shook his head. "I told you I was a traditionalist. The old meanings. And I don't like to sugar-coat either. The

Empress is a mother figure. Reversed... A child. A pregnancy. Unplanned, probably."

"Back to your nan's? I don't – "

Brady stopped in mid-sentence.

Frankie. Those visits to the doctor. The ones she won't discuss with me.

'I'll see you about four.'

'I'm at the doctor's at four.'

I knew it. I bloody well knew it.

"You look worried," Leo said. "Maybe I'm wrong. Maybe the other readers are right. Take back control. But I stand by it. A child."

Brady shook his head. "I don't know. A child? I don't think so. I hope not."

I can't lose Frankie. Not for a year's maternity leave. I simply can't.

"What's the environment got to say? What was it? External influence?"

Leo turned the card over. Drew in his breath. "Remember I said I was expecting you? The King of Swords? Law enforcement. Intelligence? Honesty?"

Brady nodded. "I remember."

"Meet your enemy. The King of Pentacles. Reversed. A gangland boss. Status, money, power, control. And he doesn't care who he hurts on the way. Especially women. The bad boy women are attracted to. Know they shouldn't. But can't resist."

"There's nothing good about him?"

Leo shook his head. "Ronnie and Reggie Kray. Al Pacino in whatever that film was. Tony Soprano."

"Tony Soprano saw a shrink. He loved his family."

"Ah well, we all have a weakness." Leo leaned forward. Tapped the card. "This is your enemy, Mac Brádaigh. The

King of Pentacles. You'll need all your logic and reason. And you'll need the Wheel of Fortune to be in your favour."

Sarah Trueman's killer. Don't worry, pal. I'm coming...

"What about my hopes and fears? As if this isn't enough?"

Leo turned the card over. Laughed out loud. "The Ace of Wands," he said. "Reversed." Reached across the table, clasped Brady's arm. Looked into his eyes. "I'm so sorry. And at such an early age. Erectile dysfunction."

62

"**E**rect – "

"I'm joking. Or maybe I'm not. Look at the card. The hand coming out of the cloud. Holding the branch. The club, if you want to call it that. The hills, the river in the background. The new leaves coming from the branch. It's clearly a phallus. A fertility symbol. But yours is reversed. Trials and tribulations. I should tell you to have some time off. Take a sabbatical. Find what you really want from life."

Brady shook his head. "That's impossible."

And the reading's not about me...

"So you need to be patient. Wait for the right time. And the right outcome."

The outcome you don't want to show me...

"What about the last card? The outcome?"

A conviction. Life. With no chance of parole...

Leo turned the card over. "The Page of Wands."

A young man. Well-dressed. Holding a staff with green shoots.

"Passion," Leo said. "You can sense his excitement.

Curiosity. New worlds to explore. And he's got the vision. He can see the big picture."

"That's my daughter," Brady said. "How can it be anyone else?"

Or Sarah Trueman. Off to South America...

"You worry that she won't come back?"

"What father wouldn't worry? She's my only child."

"She will. It won't be an easy decision. She'll spend a long time thinking about it. The Two of Swords, remember. But the Page of Pentacles. Your signature card."

Brady nodded. Looked down at the cards. Couldn't help feeling he'd been told more about himself than about Sarah Trueman.

"What about the Three of Swords? The betrayal?"

Does that mean Ash will stay in America?

"Grieving, Mac Brádaigh. Ten years ago. It took me a long, long time. Don't rush it."

Brady stood up. Realised how long he'd been sitting down. How stiff he was.

"I owe you some money,"

"Dare I ask for cash?"

Brady laughed. "I'm a copper, not the taxman." He counted the notes out.

Brady hesitated. Looked at Leo. "The card you took out. What was it?"

Leo shook his head. "Not relevant to the reading."

"No, I need to know. I saw the expression on your face."

Leo sighed. Shook his head a second time.

No good will come of this...

Reached down. Turned the card over.

Brady stared at the card. Saw a man lying on a beach. A shoreline. Mountains in the distance. Black clouds. Lying on his front, his right arm flung out. Ten swords piercing his back. Blood on the ground. A red cloak across half his back.

Then you realise it's not a cloak. It's blood...

The Ten of Swords.

The card no-one wants...

"You saw it. You took it out."

"Yes, because it wasn't relevant."

"Supposing you'd left it in? What would the outcome have been? *My* outcome?"

"You want me to put it in one sentence?"

Brady nodded. "Like I said, I'm a big boy."

"You'll get the answers you want, Mac Brádaigh. *All* the answers. But you'll pay a heavy price. Three sentences. I'm sorry."

"And you're telling me not to look?"

Leo shook his head. "What would be the point? You came to me for answers. And you'll go on looking for answers. Just remember the Wheel of Fortune. Enjoy the good times. Remember that the bad times won't last. And don't gamble, Mac Brádaigh. Not until the Wheel has turned in your favour."

"One final question," Brady said.

Leo laughed. "I saw you looking. My partner's idea of a joke. A sheep. I'm an Aries."

BRADY BLINKED as he stepped out onto the street and his eyes re-adjusted to the sunlight. Wanted to sit down with a coffee and a notebook. Make sense of everything he'd been told. Knew he didn't have time. That he had to get back to Whitby for Ash.

I hope you're right, Leo. I hope she does decide to come back. I want her to be happy. I want her to be successful. Fulfilled.

But not four thousand miles away...

Walked back up New Queen Street.

'You'll get the answers you want. But you'll pay a heavy price.'

Fair enough. That's what I signed up for. And however much I pay, it's not what Sarah Trueman paid. The Hanged Man. 'You see the same in saints. Maybe she's making a sacrifice.' That doesn't make –

Brady glanced up. Noticed that T L Chapman and Son's blue shutters were up. A hearse was halfway out of the garage. Parked straight across the pavement.

Laughed to himself.

'Frustration. You're making a lot of effort, but you're getting nowhere.'

Even the path back to my car is blocked...

Then Michael Brady suddenly shivered.

Looked at the hearse blocking his path.

Told himself it wasn't an omen.

That it had nothing to do with the Ten of Swords...

———

63

Brady tried to push his questions from the tarot reading to the back of his mind as he walked from his car to his front door. He clutched a bottle of *Pinot Noir* in his left hand. Flowers in his right. He tried not to crush the stems as he twisted the key in the lock. Heard one of them snap.

Siobhan was on her way over. She'd sounded semi-serious on the phone. Said she had something to tell him.

He knew he should be more worried. Bothered at least. But he couldn't concentrate on Siobhan at all. He needed to get his notes from the reading down on paper. Look up the cards in his book. Try and work out what it all meant.

"Alright mate," Archie whined as Brady put the wine and flowers down on the table. "I know I owe you a walk. Early tomorrow morning, OK? Before I'm back in the office. See if you can help me make sense of everything."

There was a note on the kitchen table. His daughter's elongated handwriting scrawled across it.

I'm spending the night at Jess'. Around this weekend though. Let's hang out?

Brady smiled. Tried to push the Two of Swords from his head. "At least she's not gone yet Arch. We'll all do a big walk together. Somewhere out on the Moors. Walk for miles. See if her heart is still set on America..."

"Knock, knock!"

Brady turned as Siobhan walked into the kitchen. Archie bounded over to her. Jumped up her legs until she gave in and tickled under his chin.

"He always makes me wait my turn doesn't he." Brady laughed. "How are you? How was Ireland?"

"Cold. And wet."

Archie finally felt satisfied. Padded over to his bowl in search for biscuits instead. Allowed Brady and Siobhan to embrace. Brady breathed in Siobhan's perfume. Kissed her. Smiled.

"As you'd expect then. Did everything go OK? You sounded a bit worried on the phone."

"Oh it's nothing – I'm fine. The recording was good. Great even. The final product looks incredible. I can't wait for everyone to see it."

"Are you sure? You said you had something to tell me?"

You'll get the answers you want, Mac Brádaigh. But you'll pay a heavy price.

"It can wait. Do you want to order pizza? I'm starving."

"Sure."

Leo's words echoed in his head as Brady opened the wine. What wasn't Siobhan telling him? Why had she changed her mind?

And the fourth card. The future. Ouch! The Three of Swords. Betrayal –

In a relationship?

This time... Yes. Remember what I said? The cards don't have a meaning on their own? But The Lovers. Then the Three of Swords.

He'd thought the cards were about Sarah Trueman. What if the reading was about him? Him and Siobhan. Had she betrayed him in Ireland? Had she met someone else?

"Hello? Earth to Michael. Are you in there?"

Siobhan waved her hands in front of Brady's face. A look of amusement sat on her own.

"Sorry. I had a tarot reading today. I was just thinking about what he said."

"You had a tarot reading? Now I've heard it all." Siobhan teased him. "Go on then. What future did he reveal to you?"

"I'm not sure. I didn't go for me – the case – there are links to tarot cards in it. But none of his answers were straightforward. I can't help feeling he was saying one thing and telling me something else."

"That's how they work isn't it. Leave you with more questions than you started with? It's a sure-fire way to guarantee you go back and hand over more money. Let me ask you one thing though..."

"What?"

"Did your tarot reader predict pizza? Because like I said, I'm starving. And make sure you order without mushrooms this time."

Brady picked up the last slice. Looked at Siobhan with an '*are you sure you don't want this glance*'. Dipped the end of it in the last glob of sauce. Leant back on the sofa. Tried not to get it on his shirt.

"So," Siobhan started, "there was something I wanted to talk to you about."

Brady forced himself to swallow. "I knew it! Why didn't you say so earlier?"

"I didn't want to talk before we'd eaten. I didn't want to

have another fight. You're always touchy if you haven't eaten."

"Am I?"

"I don't know. Maybe. I definitely am. Anyway – "

Brady looked at Siobhan. Had the feeling he wasn't going to like what she was about to say. Saw the Three of Swords again. Betrayal...

"I've been offered another job. We have. Helen and I. The same director. Another film. An art-deco piece."

"What? That's amazing Siobhan. Well done."

"Just wait."

Siobhan shuffled an inch away from him on the sofa. *Was there something more?* Brady did as he was told.

"It's in America."

"Oh."

Brady didn't know what else to say. He'd been expecting her to tell him she'd met someone else. That she'd had an affair in Ireland. Reunited with an old lover.

"Where?"

"LA. Where else. It's got a great cast. And apparently some critics are already talking about it. It's just – well – it's in America. That's not exactly a hop-on-a-plane-and-visit-for-the-weekend kind of place."

"How long would it be for?"

"I don't know. That's the thing. Eugene – that's the director – he seems to think that if it goes well, it could lead to lots more. It's sort of an open-ended thing..."

"So, indefinitely?"

"Maybe. I don't know. I'm sorry Mike. I don't know if I'm going to say yes yet. I need to speak to Helen about it. The whole thing was just sort of dropped on us as we were leaving. She caught a separate flight. I don't know if..."

"Do you want to do it?"

"I think so. Yes. No. I don't know. I sort of feel like I'm getting another opportunity with my music. There's a part of me that feels like I shouldn't turn it down. But it means... for us..."

Brady reached out. Took Siobhan's hands. Looked at her. Smiled.

"You should go."

"But – "

"You're right. It's an amazing opportunity for you. You shouldn't turn it down. Especially not because of some tired old copper from Whitby."

"But what are we supposed to do now?"

"What we always do. Eat pizza. Drink wine. And just enjoy the time we have together."

Brady leaned forward. Put a hand on the back of Siobhan's head. Kissed her. Wondered why he didn't feel more upset...

64

"You wanted to see me boss?"

Brady looked up. Smiled. "Jake. Come in. Close the door. Don't look so nervous. I'm sorry it's taken me this long to speak to you."

"It's fine boss. Claire told me about – I mean – I should have... I'm sorry boss."

"Jake. First thing's first, you don't need to apologise. Not to me. The second thing – and arguably the most important thing – are you okay? Physically. Mentally. Just are you okay?"

Jake looked down at the floor. Then out of the window. Then to the picture behind Brady's desk. He shifted in his seat. Looked nervous. His eyes were bloodshot. His hair messy and unkept. He didn't look like he'd slept properly for weeks. Brady sympathised with him. Knew what he was dealing with was a disease. Wanted more than anything to be able to help him.

"I don't really know how to answer that boss. I'm ashamed. I'm embarrassed. I feel like I've let everyone down."

"Let me stop you there Jake. And let me talk – is that okay?" He paused and looked at Jake. Saw him nod. "I can understand that you don't want to speak about it. And I'm not going to try and force you. But you're my responsibility, Jake. Absolutely within these four walls and – to be honest with you – out of them as well. You know I'm not the sort of copper that switches off and forgets about the case the second he goes home. Well that goes for my team too. Just because I'm sat at home in my pyjamas doesn't mean I'm not thinking about you. That I'm not worried about you."

"I'm sorry boss," Jake repeated. "I didn't mean to – "

"I know you didn't, Jake. And I've told you – you don't need to apologise to me. What I do need you to do however, is get some help."

Brady looked at Jake. Imagined how he might have looked at his son if he and Grace had ever had a second child. He just wanted what was best for him. Jake Cartwright was nothing more than a young man who had lost his way. He deserved a second chance and, in that moment, Brady felt determined to give it to him.

"I've spoken to a guy in Middlesborough. Ian Henshaw: Gamblers Anonymous. They meet on Monday mornings. Seven-thirty. I know it's early. If you need a lift, I'll take you. I'll *happily* take you. And Jake, I know it's hard too. You're embarrassed, I get that. But just being here – you've taken the first step. What's happened at work over the last few weeks, I'm willing to sweep that under the rug. But you've got to do something for me in return. You've got to try. You've got to go to the meetings. You've got to close down your accounts. Sign your pay check over to Claire if that's what it takes. *Whatever* it takes. Because you can't keep going on like this Jake, you just can't."

Brady breathed. Looked at Jake. Noticed he still wouldn't make eye contact.

Have I been too harsh on him? Have I said the wrong thing?

No – he needed to hear all of that. I needed to speak to him. He must understand I just want what's best for him. That I just want him to be okay. Screw protocol and the thirty quid, the health and happiness of my team is worth a lot more than that...

"Thanks boss." Jake finally spoke. Finally made eye contact. Looked up at Brady and forced out a hopeful smile. "That meeting... have you got the details?"

Brady handed him a piece of paper. "Of course. And I mean what I say – if you need someone to take you, someone to be there for support. I understand that you've got Claire, but if you ever need anyone else..."

"Thank you." Jake shuffled in his chair again. "The rest of the team boss. Do they know?"

"Frankie does. No one else. And it'll stay that way unless you want it any different, Jake. Now – the complicated bit – I hope you understand that I can't have you working on this case anymore. Not because of what happened with Mrs Hornby –"

Though we will have to come back to that later, once everything else is sorted...

"– But just because I can't. I need everyone to be at their best for this one."

And frankly Jake, that's far from where you are right now.

"I understand. What do you want me to do boss?"

"Desk duty I'm afraid Jake. Paperwork. I'd like you to be in the building. Try and reintegrate yourself back into a normal routine. Once all this mess is over and done with, we'll sit down again and talk about what's next. Does that sound okay?"

"Yes boss. I understand. Thank you and – I know you

don't want me to say it boss – but I am sorry. I know I've got a lot of making up to do."

"Let's just start with the paperwork and take things from there. We've got through worse Jake. There's always a way out."

Jake Cartwright nodded. Stood up from his chair. Held Brady's gaze confidently. Looked a different man from the one at the start of the conversation.

"And Monday. I'll be there boss. I promise."

I hope so Jake, I can't lose anyone else...

65

B rady held the door open for Frankie. Let her walk in first. Glanced around Ben Moxon's office. The walls were lined with pictures of school teams. Cricket. Rugby. Football. Lacrosse. St Peter's covered them all it seemed – and covered them well.

Two pairs of trainers were lined up against the wall to the right of Moxon's desk. A cricket bat sat on top. A spool of grip tape waiting beside it. There were a few books on a shelf behind the desk. Brady could only make out the title of one: *Legacy by James Kerr. What the All Blacks can teach us about the business of life.*

Brady smiled. Could tell he was in for an interesting conversation.

"This'll set the tongues wagging then. Two of you as well. How can I help?"

Brady guessed that he was about forty. Tall, a neatly trimmed beard. Hair fashionably long. Brown eyes, a ready smile. Tracksuit bottoms and a well-worn, short-sleeved rugby shirt. Bare feet in flip-flops.

"And sorry, you don't mind if I keep taping my bat up

while we talk? Had this one a while. Getting sentimental in my old age."

Brady laughed. On first impressions Ben Moxon didn't seem like the type to drug someone and hang them upside down from a tree. But first impressions had steered him wrong before...

"I don't mind at all. I'm old enough to remember the days when a new bat needed knocking in."

Ben Moxon nodded. "Happy times. Sit in the front room with a ball in an old sock. Drive your mother mad."

"And linseed oil..."

"When you two have finished talking in riddles..."

Ben Moxon smiled at Frankie. "It's the best thing about cricket. A sport with a secret language."

She nodded. "So I realise. I'm an expert in leg-byes, apparently."

"You were at Lady Anne's five years ago," Brady said. "And you were having a relationship with Sarah Trueman."

Moxon nodded. Didn't try to hide his feelings. "I was. And I've seen the news. So it was obvious why you were coming. And who told you. Give my best to Carolyn Armer, won't you? A woman born to look through keyholes."

"Sarah..." Brady prompted.

"Sure, we had a thing for three, maybe four months. I'd split up with my first wife. She was on her own. She was a few years older than me but... It was good."

"It lasted three or four months? Why did it end?"

"She'd left the school. She was going travelling. South America. And I'd met Beth. Now Mrs Moxon. And currently very pregnant and very pissed off. But Sarah and me – we parted on good terms."

Brady nodded.

So far, so believable. But that's exactly what I expected him to say...

"Why did Sarah leave the school?"

Moxon put the bat down. Weighed his answer carefully. "The Head decided to part-exchange her for a new hockey pitch."

Don't say anything. Let him elaborate...

"You obviously know about Natalya. Patrov? Petrov? One of the two." He shook his head. "You see it all the time. This place. Annie's. Affluent neglect it's called. Parents who think money replaces time. Not me. I'll never make that mistake. Beth teaches at a local school. We've got a house around the corner. And I'm not going to miss a bloody minute. Every game he plays I'll be there on the touchline."

"Natalya Petrov..."

"Sorry. Yeah. I had a girlfriend at uni who was the same. Needy. 'Do you love me, Ben?' All the time. So what she didn't get from her parents she got from drugs."

"And the school turned a blind eye?"

"If the UK's public schools expelled everyone who smoked a bit of pot they'd be empty. And bankrupt."

"But Natalya went a lot further than that?"

"She did, sadly. Silly girl. Whatever she wanted Comrade Kamenev was on hand to supply it. But he was never going to take the blame. Daddy's hockey pitch saw to that. And two more thirty-grands-a-year lower down the school."

"So Sarah was fired?"

Moxon pursed his lips. "No, not really. They reached an agreement. Sarah accepted a pay-off, the school's reputation stayed intact. Natalya Petrov's parents salvaged what they could from it."

"Was Sarah angry?"

"What do you think?"

"My guess is yes. Or it would have been my guess..."

Until you asked that question...

Moxon shook his head. "She was a willing victim. She'd had enough. She was going to quit anyway. Probably at the end of the Christmas term. It got bloody cold up there in January and February. She liked her sun did Sarah. She played her hand really well. Took her money, kissed me goodbye and caught the first plane to Bolivia."

"But she must have known she wouldn't get another teaching job."

Moxon shook his head. "She'd had enough. She didn't want one."

"South America... What did she do there?"

A second shake of the head. "That I don't know. Like I said, I'd met Beth. I left Annie's a year after Sarah. Moved over here. You know what it's like. New relationship. Determined to get it right. Especially if you fucked up the first one."

"One last question," Brady said. "What else was Sarah into? Apart from teaching. Hobbies, interests. That sort of thing."

'A bit 'new age' for me. But she was a good woman. And a hard-working teacher.'

"She cooked. What she couldn't do with a wok was no-one's business. She kept herself fit. She'd run a marathon when she was younger. She read a lot. She was too intelligent for me, that's for sure. But we had a good time."

"She wasn't..."

How the hell do I phrase this?

"She didn't have an interest in knowing what was going to happen? The future? The occult?"

Moxon laughed. "Fortune telling? What's happened? You short of a gypsy on Whitby seafront? Only that she wanted to travel. And that it wouldn't last. She said that to me all the time. 'It won't last, Ben.' I knew it as well. So we made the most of it while we could. And like I say, then I met Beth."

hat did you make of that, boss?"

"On the face of it, fine. He ticked every box..."

"But digging a little deeper?"

Brady nodded. "That's what I thought. 'She liked her sun did Sarah.' If she liked the sun so much, Frankie, what was she doing in North Yorkshire?

"That's not fair, boss. There was a sunny day last week. Or the week before."

"And she might have been planning to move. Once her mother had died. We don't know that. We'll never know that."

"Except she'd modernised the place."

"We might, boss. If we phone the local estate agents. Just because there wasn't a board up..."

"Good point. I'll get Dan to phone them."

"Something else she said, boss. 'It won't last.' What did you make of that?"

"Ben Moxon thought she was talking about the relationship, didn't he?"

"He's a man. Men always think you're talking about them. Like a woman couldn't possibly have anything else to think about."

"Nothing about tarot cards. Or any reason why he might want revenge."

"Maybe they didn't have that sort of relationship. Maybe it was just sex. Good-looking younger guy. Middle of the Dales. You can understand it. And if he did string her up in that tree, he's not going to come out and tell us why the first time we meet him is he?"

"Valid point. I still think there's something there. Suppose she was talking about something else?"

"Something from her past."

"But what…"

67

"Now then Dan – what have you got for me? Something good I hope?"

"She was pregnant."

"What? When she died?"

"No, boss. Years ago. Just before she left to go to South America. There's a doctor's report – miscarriage."

Brady took the report from Dan Keillor. Looked at Frankie. "No prizes for guessing who the father was."

The Empress is a mother figure. Reversed... A child. A pregnancy. Unplanned, probably.

Could Leo Wintersong have been right after all...

"That's one thing that Ben Moxon didn't tell us. Do you think he knew?"

"A miscarriage and then she flees to South America? Of course he knew Frankie. Why he didn't tell us is the more pressing question."

"Because it makes him look guilty."

"It makes him look very guilty. But why now? If Sarah Trueman had a miscarriage five years ago, why would Ben Moxon suddenly decide to kill her now?"

"Didn't he say his wife was pregnant boss?"

I'd met Beth. Now Mrs Moxon. And currently very pregnant and very pissed off.

"Bingo Frankie. Bloody brilliant bingo. Shall we go back and slap the cuffs on him? Get this one wrapped up in time for fish and chips at dinnertime? Got anything else in this report for me, Dan? Found out where she was held… established a chain of events…"

Dan Keillor grinned. "Close. I think Moxon and Carrick knew each other."

For once, Brady didn't know what to say. Dan handed him another piece of paper. Brady looked down at the printed report. Wanted to hear the words for himself.

"How?"

"The York and District cricket league." Dan looked proud of himself. "They both played in it – for two separate teams – for six overlapping years."

"Six years. Two matches a summer, maybe more if you include friendlies. The occasional evening. That's somewhere north of twelve to fifteen meetings. Do you think they could have become friends?"

"It's likely isn't it, boss? I play rugby at the weekend. There are lads I've been playing against since I was fourteen, fifteen. Same lot. You're in the club bar after a game. You get talking. A few of them I've met for a beer outside of the season. I'm willing to bet that happens in cricket too."

"What's the age difference?"

"Four years. Nothing really."

"So they *definitely* could have been friends. Good work, Dan. Great work in fact. Drinks on me in the Black Horse this Friday. Let's see if we can get this wrapped up by then."

68

Brady sat in his office. Couldn't help feeling that things were finally starting to fall into place. He deserved a break on this one. They'd been round the houses with all the evidence. The vicar. The Roxby widows. The tarot cards. Now – as much as Brady hated to admit it – he felt like his tarot reading had given him more insight into what had happened to Sarah Trueman than the entire first week of police work.

Picking up his phone he started to dial Carolyn Armer's number. If Sarah had been pregnant then surely someone else at the school had to have known. The school secretary seemed more than happy to talk about Ben Moxon, but would she have kept secrets about Sarah Trueman if the two of them were friends? Brady needed to find out.

"Hello?"

"Hi. Ms Armer? It's DCI Michael Brady. Do you have five minutes?"

"Mr Brady. I wondered if I'd hear from you again. Now that I have – I assume you've been to see Ben Moxon."

"You assume correctly, Ms Armer. Though it's not

directly off the back of that conversation that I am ringing you. It's down to good old fashioned policework for once. Sarah Trueman – " Brady paused. Wondered whether he needed to be careful with the words he chose. Decided not to bother.

"Did she ever tell you about her pregnancy?"

Silence. Brady heard a short intake of breath from Carolyn Armer, followed by what he imagined was her pursing her lips and making a decision.

"She did, Mr Brady. However I fail to see the relevance..."

"So you knew Ben Moxon was the father?"

"I did. And I gave you his name. You surely don't want me to carry out the investigation for you?"

"No – thank you, Ms Armer – I'm just trying to fill in a few blanks..."

"I gave you his name. I told you about the dinner parties. Forgive me, Mr Brady, but I'm not sure what else you want from me?"

"Just to see if there is anything else you know about Ben Moxon's relationship with Sarah Trueman that you haven't already told me. Was it a good relationship? A happy relationship?"

Carolyn Armer laughed on the other end of the phone. "I wouldn't call it much of a relationship at all Mr Brady. It was more of... an arrangement. They were both teachers at the school. Both young. Attractive. There wasn't exactly much of a social scene. Men and women have needs. I believe they filled that need for one another."

"They were never outwardly seen together? They didn't appear to go on dates or show off their relationship to others at the school?"

"Inter-faculty relationships are never something to show

off, especially at a school like Lady Anne's. So no, they didn't flaunt it. There were rumours – as I imagine there are in most schools if two teachers are ever seen together. The students loved to gossip. But officially, I doubt anyone else knew much about it."

"And when Sarah left for South America – did you notice any change in Ben Moxon? Did he do anything or say anything that surprised you?"

"Not that I can recall. It was many years ago. Teachers come and go. There is no mourning period before the empty role is filled."

"Thank you, Ms Armer. I trust I can call again if anything else changes?"

"You can, Mr Brady. Though I doubt it will. Goodbye."

Brady put the phone down. Wondered what Carolyn Armer was hiding. It was almost like he had spoken to a different woman to the one who had walked into the station. She was stand-offish. Blunt. Definitely secretive.

There was undoubtedly something else that had happened at Lady Anne's. But what?

Brady sighed. Wondered if Ash would want fish and chips for dinner. Knew he at least knew the answer to that question...

69

"Steady on Arch." Brady pushed his front door shut with his foot. Balanced the fish and chip boxes in one hand. Tried to stop an over-excited dog from knocking them over. "Yes I've got you a sausage. When do I not get you a sausage? Just let me put them down first."

"Hey Dad, did you remember to get scraps?"

"Do you really think I'd forget, Ash? Sausage for Archie. Scraps for you. It'll be remarkable if I get my own dinner at this rate."

"Doesn't look like you've missed many meals recently." Ash grinned. Nodded sarcastically at Brady's stomach.

"I'll throw these out then, shall I? Make us a salad instead."

"No! Come on," Ash took one of the wrapped parcels from Brady. Peeled back the greasy newspaper. "This one's yours."

"I've not seen Siobhan much lately."

Ash posed the statement as a question. Archie sat at Brady's feet looking up hopefully. The sausage long gone. Ash was to his left. She perched on the edge of the sofa, hunched over her fish and chips. She didn't look up. But the question hung in the air unanswered.

"I think she's going to America."

"Oh." Ash paused. Glanced at her father. "That's a shame. Are you okay?"

"I'm fine," Brady replied. Realised he was telling the truth. "I'm not sure I was ready for a proper relationship in all honesty. I liked Siobhan. I do like her. But..."

"She's not mum."

"No one will ever be your mother sweetheart. And I don't want you to think I'm looking for a replacement. It's not that anyway – it's just – too soon I suppose."

"I get that. Jess has started dating this new guy. Lucas. But I don't think she's properly over Aaron. I think Lucas is just a rebound. She wants me to go on a double date with them this weekend but I'm not sure I want to fake it."

"Have you said that to Jess?"

"What, that I think Lucas is just a rebound? Yeah right, Dad. I'm sure that would go down well."

"If she's your friend isn't it better to be honest with her?"

"Not if it'll just upset her. Lucas won't last – it might just be easier to go along with it for the time being."

"Hold on. If she wants you to go on a double date... does that mean you've got a new boyfriend? What's happened to Spencer? I thought he was away this weekend."

Ash rolled her eyes. "And you're the best detective Whitby has to offer? No, Dad. I don't. Me and Spence are still together. Jess just wants me to tag along with one of Lucas' friends. Sort of a group hang. But I don't really want to. They're all a bit weird and posh. His cousin goes to that school we were talking about actually – Lady Anne's."

Brady thought back to the kids he'd seen on his visit to the school. The boy playing cricket.

He'll play for Yorkshire by the time he's nineteen, England by the time he's twenty-two. Whatever records Cook and Root set he'll beat them. But only if we keep him focused.

"Maybe you should go for the cousin instead. He might have better prospects if he's at Lady Anne's."

Ash laughed. Dug her phone out of her pocket. Tapped away on it for a couple of seconds. Held it out to Brady so he could see the screen.

"If you insist..."

Brady looked at the photo. A group of young boys. Sixteen or seventeen. Lady Anne's in the background. It was taken in black and white. Each of them wore a leather jacket. Rolled cigarettes in their hands. Two of them were flipping off the camera with the other.

"Christ. *They're* the boys from Lady Anne's? They're nothing like the one I saw playing cricket."

"Course they're not. That place is all about image isn't it? They're not going to parade the bad kids around when someone comes to visit. I'll bet they were all locked away in detention."

Brady paused. Thought for a moment. "Ash..." He spoke hesitantly. Unsure whether he wanted to broach this topic with his teenage daughter. Knew he shouldn't. Couldn't resist.

"Do you think you'd be able to find pages belonging to past pupils of the school? You're not friends with that boy are you? Yet you found his photo pretty easily."

"Well yeah, it's the Internet Dad. Nothing is private."

"So could you find students who've left the school? Were there a few years back. Didn't necessarily live in the area."

Ash shrugged. "Probably. There'll be groups for each leavers year I bet. Who are they?"

Brady paused again. Should he really be doing this? But

what if Ash could find him something Dan Keillor hadn't? Maybe a teenage perspective was what they'd been missing. He sighed. Gave in. Went to retrieve his notebook and duly handed over the details to his teenage daughter.

"Natalya Petrov and Sasha Kamenev. Yep." Ash tilted the laptop screen so Brady could see. "They're both in this group. Looks like... oh. Natalya died? There's a memorial page linked for her. Do you want me to look at that?"

Brady nodded. Ash clicked. He leaned over his daughter's shoulder as she scrolled slowly down the page. Read the outpourings of sadness and remorse from fellow students as they reacted to her death.

"Maybe I should go through this myself. You don't need to read all of this stuff."

"Are you sure? There's probably more I can find."

"No it's fine, thank you sweetheart. You've done enough. Maybe don't mention this late-night detective work to Frankie the next time you see her? You don't want to get your old man in trouble do you..."

"OK, Dad. Don't stay up too late."

"I won't. I'm in Scarborough tomorrow morning. Leaving early so I probably won't see you before school."

"What for?"

"Seeing a psychologist. And no, before you make the joke, not because I'm losing my marbles. For the case, of course..."

"If you say so. Night Dad. Love you."

"Love you too Ash. Sleep well."

Brady watched his daughter go upstairs. Waited until he heard her door close. Returned to the laptop screen.

There was a post on the page that had caught his eye. Written by a girl called Martha. It contained an outpouring of emotion. *I wish I could have done something. I'll miss you so much. How could we not have realised?*

But it wasn't the words that caught Brady's eye. It was the different coloured text that Natalya's name was written in. Light blue. Hyperlinked. He moved the cursor over the name and clicked. Found himself on Natalya Petrov's personal page. Her smiling face looking back at him.

Brady scrolled slowly down the page. Most of it was archaic now. There were a few people that posted on her birthday each year – sharing messages of sadness and how much they missed her. The messages grew more frequent the further back in time Brady scrolled.

Time really does heal all wounds.

His index finger continued to scroll. Past the moment of Natalya's death. Further back into her final few weeks alive. Then he saw it. Stopped. Double clicked. A photo. Four students sat around a dinner table. Natalya Petrov. Sasha Kamenev. And two others. The missing students. He'd found them.

70

"And what can I do for you this morning, Inspector Brady?"

Susanna Harrall smiled. Tucked a strand of her half brown, half blonde hair behind her ear. Leant back in her chair.

"Michael. Mike. I thought we agreed we were on first name terms now?"

She laughed. "I'm sorry. We are. Given the subjects we've already discussed. And I saw you on TV. So it's not hard to work out why you're here.

"First things first, though. Would you like a cup of NHS tea?"

"Is it any better than police canteen tea?"

"What do you think?"

Brady laughed. "Then I'm fine. But thank you."

Susanna made herself one anyway. She looked tired. Like she was working too many hours – a fate more than likely considering the state of things in the NHS.

Brady watched as she heaped two sugars into her mug. Sat back down. Took a comforting first sip.

. . .

"LET me tell you the story. Some of this isn't publicly available – "

"But you're going to trust my discretion?"

Brady nodded. "As you say. Given what we've already discussed."

Brady took a deep breath. "To the best of our knowledge Sarah Trueman left her house on Friday. The local vicar reported her missing on Monday and her body was found on Wednesday. She was found hanging from a tree at May Beck – "

"I used to take my children there. Harry was always cross I wouldn't let him climb down to the waterfall."

"She was hanging from the tree, her left leg crossed behind her right leg in this position."

Brady passed her his phone. Showed her the picture of the tarot card.

"That exact position?"

"Exactly. The cause of death was a brain haemorrhage."

Or as Geoff put it: a madman. A fucking madman hung her upside down from a birch tree.

Susanna shook her head. "I've been to May Beck count-less times. With my children. It's... well, it's a nice place to walk. The kids would run around. Climb trees... How did he do it?"

"You're asking about the logistics of getting her up there? He tied by her right ankle. Swung a rope over the branch. Hauled her up."

"So he took the body, the rope – and whatever else he needed?"

Susanna paused. Took another long sip of her tea.

"Did she cooperate? She must have been – "

"We found traces of a sedative in her bloodstream."

"That makes sense."

"This is what we think so far. One, he's strong. Bodies are bloody heavy things. Bodies on the end of ropes – even when you're using leverage – are even heavier."

"Until gravity lends a hand."

"Right. But he's still got to get her up there. And she wasn't just a couple inches from the ground, Susanna. He definitely had to be strong."

"And he obviously kept her somewhere. Based on your timeline he held her for what – two, three days? Which means he planned this carefully. Meticulously."

Susanna stopped to think. Considered the information.

"You're asking me who I think could have done this?"

Brady nodded. "What type of man? What personality traits? We've some theories. But right now they're only theories."

"And you'd like some more?"

"I'd like some professional insight."

"Surely you have access to police profilers?"

Brady nodded. "I do. But once you've worked with them two or three times you know how they think. I want…"

"You want someone who thinks outside the box?"

"Bluntly, Susanna, I want someone who will ignore the bloody box completely. So I'd like your opinion. One, because I value it. Two, because you won't think along traditional police lines."

She laughed. "You realise you've just used the four most persuasive words in the English language? 'I value your opinion.' Who can resist that?"

Susanna Harrall looked across the desk at Brady. Narrowed her eyes slightly. "Do you have a twin brother, Mike?"

"No, I've – "

"An evil twin, separated at birth?"

"You're saying he's like me?"

"I'm saying he's very much like you. What you've described to me is someone who does his homework. He clearly didn't arrive at May Beck and think, 'this'll do.' He'd been before. He came prepared. Knew what he needed to do to her. How long he'd need the drugs to last. Just the right amount so she could walk down there, not too much so she could run away. So, yes, homework. And preparation."

Another sip of tea. A moment of thought.

"But not only that, he's prepared to take a risk. What time does it get dark? He can't have done his work in the dark, so he has to risk someone coming. So calculated risk."

And that means he was prepared to deal with the consequences of getting caught too...

"Remember: risk is part of the thrill. What you're describing, Mike, is someone like a professional gambler. Someone who gets a kick out of taking risk. But someone who thinks it through at the same time. Someone calculated. Someone without any fear. Or without the brains to be afraid when he should be."

"And you think that's like me?"

"Can I be honest with you?"

This doesn't sound promising...

"Yes, of course."

"You do your homework. You're here speaking to me. But you've access to police profilers. That's what procedure says you do. But you're ignoring procedure. You're prepared to put yourself in danger. And there's a small part of you that needs it, Mike. That man you followed down the pier – "

"He had someone with him. I had no choice."

"Back up?"

"I was a civilian. At the time..."

"This is what, Mike? Our third conversation? Every time you've been prepared to ignore procedure. Step outside the boundaries. That's what your killer does. Every day of his life."

"I don't do it every day..."

"Even so. But those are my insights for you, Mike. This is someone who does his homework. But he's prepared to take risks. Big risks. This isn't someone I'd advise you to play poker with."

"There's another thing. She's tied like the tarot card. That's clearly a message. Either to her. Or to himself."

"Or to whoever finds her. I'd say he has a sense of humour. And a sick one at that."

71

Brady climbed back into the Tiguan. Checked his phone. One missed call. One voicemail. A number he didn't recognise. He clicked on the recording. Pressed play. Heard a woman's voice.

Mr Brady. I'm Beth Moxon. Ben's wife. I know you spoke to my husband recently and I know what sort of questions you asked him. But even though you have spoken to Ben, I'm not sure you will have understood him. Call me back when you can. I think we should talk.

Brady looked at the time of call. 09:27. He'd only missed her by fifteen minutes. He pressed her number again. She answered after the first ring.

"Hello?"

"Beth Moxon? This is Detective Chief Inspector Michael Brady. I'm sorry I missed your call. Is now still a good time?"

"Ah, Mr Brady. Yes. Now is fine. Let me tell you about Ben, shall I?"

Brady nodded. Sensed he didn't need to reply. Wondered what was coming.

"Ben was a really good cricketer when he was young. Thirteen, fourteen, he was at the county nets. But not just cricket. He played rugby. Football. He had trials with Leeds. He could swim. Bloody hell the first time I went on holiday with him. Half-man, half-fish…"

Where's she going with this?

"And I know what you're thinking, 'cricket, football, I wish I'd been that good.' They all do."

Yes, I was…

"But you know what? It nearly destroyed him. Teachers? Men amongst boys, boys amongst men? That's Ben Moxon. Sporting ability? Right up there. Confidence, self-belief? He hasn't got any."

Brady didn't speak. Began to realise where it was leading. Remembered the day he'd felt the same way.

"Ben's the best in his school. Football, cricket, swimming. He's the best at everything. Everyone tells him he's going to be a professional footballer. 'Football for England in the winter, Ben. Cricket for England in the summer.'"

Yep, exactly what I thought when I was nine or ten…

"And so he goes for the trials. Leeds United. Yorkshire nets. Under-sixteen, under-seventeen, he plays for the county. You go to his parents' house. There's more medals and trophies than a bloody trophy shop. Pictures on every wall."

Brady finally spoke. "But he wasn't good enough?"

"No he wasn't. He said something to me once. 'You've got to be bloody good to realise how good the top people are.'"

Brady nodded. "You do." Understood what she meant.

"He said in the end he didn't want to play. Everyone's telling him how good he is, except the people that really matter. The pros. Said he couldn't stand the look on his mum and dad's faces. His mates asking him how it went. When he was signing professional."

"So he became a teacher."

Beth Moxon paused on the other end of the line. Let out a faint sigh.

"He became a teacher. And a bloody good one at that. But after he started, he told me he didn't play a game of cricket for five years. 'Cos if he did all the pressure, all the expectation, it just came flooding back. We had a relationship. A year give or take a week, at the beginning of his teaching career. But he wasn't a man you could have a relationship with. He was in this dark, dark place. Still thinking he'd let everyone down. So we separated, went our different ways. I didn't see him for a couple of years. Then one summer, I bumped into him. In the supermarket of all places – can you believe that?"

I can. In fact meeting someone in a supermarket sounds all too familiar...

"I see him in the supermarket and... he's changed. He's different. He seemed lighter somehow. Happy. Not tormented by his past."

"And that's the summer he was seeing Sarah Trueman?"

"Yes." Beth Moxon replied, her voice distant and delicate. "I don't know what buttons she pressed but she pressed the right ones. He's smiling, he's confident. He's... Finally he's at peace with himself."

"And..."

Bloody hell. She's married. She's pregnant. And she knows she's second-best...

"Right. She left. Went to South America. See you, Ben, I'm having a mid-life crisis. Or I'm having something. And whatever it is it doesn't involve you. You're on your own again, pal. So I see him again one day – by chance, completely by chance – and he's a shell. Broken. Back on the anti-depressants. After all that time – I couldn't bear to see him like that. So we started talking again. One thing led to another. But as much as I want to believe otherwise, he's never been like that day in the supermarket. He's never had that same twinkle in his eye. That lightness. The scars from his past are still there, Mr Brady. And Ben isn't the type of man who has the courage nor the capability to do anything about them."

BRADY HUNG UP THE PHONE. Started his engine. Made it five minutes down the road before he decided he needed to speak to Frankie.

"I just had the strangest conversation with Beth Moxon."

"The pregnant wife boss? What did she want?"

"She rung me effectively to tell me that Ben Moxon couldn't have been responsible. She says he's a guy with no self-confidence. Prone to depression. 'He was a shell when I found him,' she said. 'Back on the anti-depressants.'"

"Anti-depressants?"

"Apparently he's a track record with them. I'm sure medical records could prove it. She said that when Sarah Trueman left, Moxon was a wreck. Barely holding himself together. That he was haunted by his past sporting failures. His almost-good-enough-but-not-quite youth."

"Do you believe her boss? When we met him, he didn't seem particularly damaged..."

Brady paused. Thought for a moment.

"I came up against Steve McManaman in a tournament once."

"Who?"

"He played for Liverpool. Then Real Madrid. And he was light years ahead of me. Of everyone on the field. Light years. And I realised there and then I wasn't going to be a footballer. That maybe I ought to pay attention in class. But I can see that. Maybe that's what happened to Moxon. Your coaches, your teachers are telling you, 'Yeah, you can do that. Train more, practice more. Focus...'"

"So he's a frustrated footballer, cricketer, whatever. Surely that plays in our favour? Spent his life being just not good enough. It happens again – except this time in a relationship – he decides to finally do something about it."

"Maybe. But I don't get the feeling this one is the result of someone just snapping like that. The detail. The precision. That hanging had been planned. Plus it goes against the other conversation I've had this morning Frankie. My psychologist – I'm just driving back from Scarborough now, I'll be in the office in about thirty minutes – she said our guy was someone who's in control. Not someone prone to depression. Our murderer – whoever he is – he doesn't see himself as one of life's victims."

"So where are we? Who are our main suspects?"

"It's between Carrick and Moxon for me boss. I'm happy to rule out the vicar."

"Me too, Frankie. And I'm leaning towards Carrick after today's calls. Susanna Harrall said we were looking for someone who does his homework. Someone who had been there before. Who came prepared."

She also said we were looking for someone very much like me. My evil twin. I'm not sure that's information I want being made public...

"That could be Carrick boss. He's intelligent. Set up his own business. You've got to do your homework for that."

"Right. He fits the profile better than Moxon. But he lacks the motive. Moxon on the other hand…"

"There's the miscarriage. The scorned lover. Moxon is still my bet boss. Anyone can plan a murder, but you're only going to go through with it if you really want to hurt your victim."

"And hanging them upside down from a tree definitely counts as hurt."

Brady picked up a cricket ball from the bookshelf in his office. Chucked it up in the air a couple of times. Thought back to his playing days.

"What if they worked together like Dan suggested? Moxon has the motive, Carrick has the plan."

"It's possible boss. In truth, I think it's more possible than either one of them doing it alone. But I'm still not convinced."

"We need more information. Why do background checks take so bloody long to get done? If we were in Russia or China Frankie… there'd be no end to the information we could find in a heartbeat."

72

B rady parked where he always parked in front of the Zetland Hotel. He glanced out across the sea. Remembered his first time standing there. Waiting. Unknowing. This time he didn't have to wait. He walked straight into the building. Directly to Mozart's front door. He was buzzed in like an old friend.

Is that what am I now? The old friend of a hacker? Maybe...

Mozart looked the same as he always did. His hair was neatly trimmed. His jumper carefully pressed. The leather elbow patches the only part of his appearance showing the passing of time. Brady stepped inside. Shook his hand.

"It's good to see you," Mozart smiled. "Though I trust this isn't a social visit?"

"Not unless Whitby's murderers decide to give me a day off."

"I thought not. Earl Grey?"

Brady thanked him. Walked into the living room and sat down in an armchair while Mozart disappeared into the kitchen. The computer desk with its multitude of screens still dominated the room. Brady thought back to Carrick's office. He'd had two. Moxon's? He couldn't even remember seeing a laptop.

"Quite a unique case you're working on, isn't it?" Mozart reappeared. Handed Brady the same art-deco mug he always did. "I did wonder whether you'd decided to seek guidance from a more fitting source on this one. The stars perhaps..."

Brady laughed. "I did. A tarot reader. Though I think he just added to my questions."

Mozart couldn't help but smile. "I have to say Michael, that's not an angle I ever saw you pursuing. But you've come back to your senses now at least. How can I help you? Or rather, who can I help you with?"

"Ben Moxon and Tim Carrick. A PE teacher and a management consultant."

"And you want to know if they're connected?"

"I know they're connected. Or they were. The York and District cricket league. Police work has got us that far at least. I want to know if they're *still* connected. And if they might have had any recent contact involving Sarah Trueman."

"Leave it with me Michael, I'll see what I can do. Is that all?"

Brady dug his phone out of his pocket. Opened the *Photos* app. Selected the grainy image he'd taken the other night. Zoomed in slightly to remove the wavy lines that appeared when you took a picture of something on another screen. Handed it to Mozart.

"Not quite."

"Some old school friends of yours? Or more your daughter's age?"

"Pupils of Sarah Trueman. I know two of them: Sasha Kamenev and Natalya Petrov. Both now dead. It's the other two I'm interested in."

"Do you have names?"

"Martha."

"Just Martha?"

"Yes." Brady reached over and took his phone back from Mozart. Flicked through until he found what he was looking for. Handed it back.

"I found this old profile for her. But there's no last name. No more information. It's no longer active..."

"Maybe not for you." Mozart smiled. "Give me a couple of days. I'll be in touch."

"Thank you." Brady stood up to leave. Shook hands with his friend – realised that was truly how he thought of Mozart now.

I wonder if Scholesy would be proud...

73

B rady stared at his computer screen. Wished Mozart would hurry up.

Why can I not solve a case without him? Should I be disappointed in myself? Is my detective work getting tired?

"Boss?" Brady looked up as Frankie knocked on the door.

She closed the door behind her. Stared at Brady. Drew her breath in. Half way between a sigh and a sob.

"Frankie? What's wrong?"

Ashen. In shock. Something to do with her recent appointments? Bad news. Really bad news...

Brady stood up. Stepped out from behind his desk. Two strides. Took her arm.

"Frankie. What's the matter?"

She looked up at him. Eyes barely focused.

"Jake."

"Jake? What about Jake? He should be on desk duty downstairs – "

"Jake's dead, boss. He shot himself."

. . .

BRADY WAS BACK AT HOME. Waiting for *Grandstand* to start. *Football Focus*. Interrupted by the phone.

'Can I speak to Mrs Brady?"

'She's out. I'm her son, can I take a message?'

'It's the nursing home. I'm really sorry to tell you. Your father has passed.'

'Passed?'

Passed what? What the hell does 'passed' mean?

'It was very quick. He wouldn't have felt anything. If she'd let us know about the arrangements.'

What arrangements? Passed what for God's sake?

"WHERE?"

"His uncle's farm. Smallholding. Eskdaleside. In the barn. His uncle keeps a gun…"

Frankie lost her nerve. Broke down into sobs. Brady didn't know what else to do. He put his arms around her. Held her until she stopped. Said the only thing he could think of saying.

"I'm going out there."

Frankie sniffed. Wiped her nose with her sleeve. Looked at him. "You think that's wise? The paramedics – "

"We owe it to him, Frankie. *I* owe it to him. You don't have to come. And I'm not blaming you. Especially with…"

Don't say it. Her sister committed suicide.

"That was a long time ago. You weren't the only one he could have talked to. If you're guilty, then I'm guilty too. And like you say, we owe it to him."

BRADY WALKED INTO THE BARN. It looked exactly as it was supposed to. Straw bales. Gaps in the back wooden wall. In need of a repair. Sunlight filtering through. Farm equipment lining the walls. Harnesses. Horse collars. And Jake. In his uniform. Minus the back of his head.

Brady felt a sob catch in his throat. Felt his eyes fill with tears. Didn't try to blink them away.

He took in the barn again. Saw it in a different light. Jake's blood decorated almost every surface. The straw. The harnesses. Everything.

"Mike?"

Geoff Oldroyd was already on the scene. He held two envelopes in his hand.

"You know you don't need to be in here?"

Brady swallowed. Didn't know what to say.

"Claire's outside with Frankie. Maybe you should go and talk to her?"

"Sure, Geoff." Brady's voice felt scratchy in his throat. "Thanks."

"His uncle found these in the house. One for Claire. Looks like one for you."

Brady took the two envelopes from Geoff. Saw the word 'Boss' on the front of one. Swallowed again.

It didn't seem real.

Brady stepped out of the barn. Saw Frankie. Saw Claire.

The farmyard was alive with activity. Paramedics. Jake's Uncle. His wife. Their kids. Dogs scampering around. And Jake lying just yards away with a gaping hole in his head. Brady felt sick. Wanted to run. Couldn't. He tried to force the image of Jake's splattered brains out of his head. Walked over to Claire.

"I'm so sorry."

Claire looked up at him. Mascara lined her cheeks. She held his gaze for a moment. Burst into tears again.

"He left this for you."

Brady held out the envelope with 'Claire' on the front. Waited for her to take it.

"I can't." It was barely a whisper. "Will you read it to me?"

Brady gritted his teeth. He'd been afraid she'd say that. But what choice did he have? He'd had a duty of care towards Jake and look where that had got him. Now he had one to Claire. He had to do as she asked.

Claire. I love you. I'll always love you. But I'm no good for you. Find someone who'll make you happy. Find someone who won't gamble away your holiday. Find someone better than me. It won't be difficult. You deserve better. And I'll never beat gambling. It'll always be there. It's like a demon sitting on my shoulder. All the time, wherever I turn. Every time I open my phone. I stole money from an old lady. That's how bad it is. I'm sorry, Claire. Really sorry. I'm crying as I write this. But I'm an addict, who's going to lose his job.

You deserve better than me.

I'm sorry.

I love you. Jake xxx

Brady didn't try to hide his tears. He handed the letter to Claire. She grasped it like she was holding onto Jake himself.

Brady turned away. Forced himself to strike while the iron was hot.

Boss. I'm sorry. By the time you read this, I'll be dead. I understand why you did what you did. Can't have a thief being a copper. I know you'd have to sack me in the end.

I should have told you earlier. But I didn't have the courage. I was frightened of what people would say. I've let you down. I've let everybody down. You said once that everybody got one chance. I reckon you gave me about ten. But I still fucked up. And I couldn't beat gambling. This was the only way.

I'm sorry, boss.

Jake.

PS – catch him, won't you? I can swear at you now. I won't be around to get a bollocking. You're a fucking brilliant copper boss. I know you'll nail him. Do it for me.

Brady took a deep breath. Read the letter again. Finally looked up. Made no attempt to hide the tears running down his face.

I'll do it, Jake. I promise.

74

Brady sat on his sister's sofa. Shoulders slumped. Mug of untouched coffee on the table in front of him. Box of frequently touched tissues beside it.

He still didn't believe it was real.

"I get there, Kate. Busiest scene I've ever been on. Dan's already there. The paramedics. His uncle. The wife. Kids running round. Dogs barking. It's chaos. Absolute bloody chaos. And then I go into the barn and it's like all that noise just fades into silence. Jake's there and..."

Brady sobbed. Reached for another tissue.

"He's wearing his bloody uniform. Told his uncle he was just calling in for a cuppa on his way back to the station. Wanted to have a look in the barn to help him figure out something on a case. Then his uncle hears the shot... It was everywhere. *Jake* was everywhere. Oh God."

Brady felt bile rise in his throat. Saw Jake in front of him. Forced himself to swallow.

"I'm sorry, Mike."

Kate put a hand on her younger brother's knee. Let him know she was there for him.

There wasn't anything she or anyone could say to bring Jake back. Brady knew that. But he was glad she was there nonetheless.

"I can make up the sofa if you want. You can stay here tonight."

Brady sniffed. Shook his head. "I can't, Kate. Thank you – but I need to be home for Ash."

"She could come over too. I'm sure the girls wouldn't mind."

"No, it's okay. But dinner soon? Do you want to come round? Pick an evening when the wind isn't blowing a gale and we can sit out on the balcony."

"Sure, Mike. I'd like that. You do need to let someone take care of you every once in a while, you know. You can't do everything by yourself."

Brady looked up at his big sister and smiled.

"Ash does that plenty, don't you worry. You know what she's like."

———

75

The next morning was cold. Brutally cold. Brady didn't feel any better, but he dragged himself out of bed all the same. Kate was right. He needed to take care of himself. He needed to stick to his routine. He needed a proper breakfast...

"I HEARD, Mike. I'm sorry. He was a good lad."

Brady clutched his coffee like it was a lifeline. Looked out across the harbour. Watched the boats bobbing on the water. Shook his head.

"The first man I've lost, Dave. And it's my fault. Absolutely, one-hundred-per-cent my fucking fault."

Dave opened his mouth. Started to speak. Brady cut him off.

"My door's always open. Any problems come and talk to me. That's what I always say, Dave. Cliché after fucking cliché. And he didn't. He couldn't. 'Frightened of what people might say.' What sort of boss does that make me, Dave? Obsessed with catching the killer. Make sure I'm a good dad. Lying in bed with my rock star girlfriend. And someone pays the price. And it's Jake. His whole fucking life in front of him. Not anymore..."

"Mike. Can I say something to you? We're friends. You won't fall out with me? Jump over the counter and punch me?"

Brady shrugged. Shook his head. "Say what you like Dave. It won't bring him back."

"It's *not* your fault, Mike. And when you're thinking clearly you'll see that. You're *not* the only person he had to talk to. What about his mates? Relatives? He must have had someone."

"His mum and dad? What the hell am I going to say to them, Dave? I sent your son home? Put him on desk duty? Wasn't there when he needed someone to talk to. Twisted the bloody knife."

Brady felt his phone start buzzing in his pocket. Pulled it out. *Kershaw.*

"Oh bloody hell. This is exactly what I need right now."

He nodded goodbye to Dave. Started walking in the direction of home. Pressed the green button.

"Sir."

"Brady. How are you? Nasty business with Cartwright. Some people just aren't cut out for the force."

Shows how little you know. Jake was a great copper. I just let him down...

"I've seen two or three like that down here in London. One jumped in the Thames over Christmas. Not the way I'd want to go. And there's a mountain of paperwork."

"We'll manage sir."

"Good, yes. I'm sure you will. But that's not what I wanted to speak to you about Brady. It's rather strange timing. But I've been offered an opportunity."

"Sir?"

"A permanent role down here. Advisory. Helping to bring more of the force into the 21st century."

And you're the man to do that? The public sector really does need help.

"Anyway it's not just an opportunity for me. There's one for you too, if you want it. Take over my office. Upgrade that view of the car park..."

"You're offering me your job?"

"It's yours if you want it, Brady. A healthy pay bump too. More control. Maybe you could persuade Thomson to stick around and fill your role."

"What do you mean?"

"You must have heard, Brady? You didn't think she was going to stick around in Whitby forever, did you? She's bright. She's getting out. But you never know – if you offer her the DCI role you might convince her. Think it over, will you? No need to give me your answer today. And best of luck with the paperwork. Plenty more of that if you do take the step up the ladder..."

Brady felt the line go dead in his ear. Realised he was outside his front door. Tried to process what Kershaw had just said.

Maybe you could persuade Thomson to stick around.

Frankie is leaving?

Brady pushed open the door. Walked inside. He couldn't lose Frankie as well. He just couldn't.

76

After sitting in the house for fifteen minutes, Brady knew he needed to be outside. There was too much on his mind to sit and think about it. He needed to walk. He needed to figure some things out.

"I'm going out for a walk, Ash."

"Where, Dad?"

"May Beck."

"May Beck? That's miles away. And it's raining."

"I know. I just want – "

What do I want? I want to be alone with my thoughts. With the killer. Feel him. Understand him.

"So you're going for a walk in the woods? In the rain?"

Brady nodded. "Yes. It doesn't get dark until after seven. I'll be back before then. Get something to eat on my way back."

"Supposing you meet a mad person, Dad?"

Brady laughed. "Supposing I'm the mad person, Ash?"

She didn't reply.

. . .

BRADY TURNED SHARP LEFT, crossed the cattle grid. Realised that he hadn't really seen the road the last time he'd driven down it. The gorse coming into bloom, a lonely tree off to the left, a field on his right patrolled by a solitary seagull.

There was fog in the valley between the small hills. Low cloud blocking out the sea. Arching across the moors as if God had turned a sprinkler on. He drove in and out of the showers, flicking the wipers from full to intermittent. And back again. One of those irritating days when the rain was halfway between the two.

He carried on driving. Slowly, as a sheep sauntered across in front of him. Noticed how dense the woods were on his right. A break for the entrance to the caravan site. Another fifty yards and there was a rusty, corrugated iron shelter in the woods.

For the sheep? Or does someone live there?

The road started to drop down towards the beck. Bent round to the right. An isolated farmhouse came into view. Two tractors, one red, one blue, standing in the yard. Brady braked again. Two defiant sheep strolling sedately down the middle of the road. The one with horns turned and looked back at him. A splodge of red paint on its back, a black face.

He was at the bottom now. Saw a bedraggled tourist walk off the path, navigate the puddles on the bridge. Walk into the car park. He drove across the bridge. Turned right. Parked. Glanced up into his rear-view mirror. Watched the tourist climb into a white 4x4. Saw it drive off, leaving him alone in the car park.

He climbed out of the car. The rain was getting heavier.

Listened. The only sound was the rain falling on the trees. One solitary coo from a pigeon. And then the rain again.

'Suppose you meet a madman, Dad?'

If I do they won't find me until morning...

There was a seat at the back of the car park.

There isn't a plaque on it. The only seat in Whitby without a plaque.

He walked over to it. Finally saw a small, oval plaque. Almost the same colour as the seat.

In loving memory of Olga Mary Tindall. 1926 – 2014

Eighty-eight. A good innings, Olga. Some people don't even get half that...

Brady walked back across the bridge. Now the puddles on either side were nearly meeting in the middle. Saw two Coast to Coast signs, one pointing straight up the hill.

Fourteen days of walking. Five miles from the end. And there's one last hill to climb...

He started walking towards Falling Foss, trees between him and the beck, ferns on his right.

The sound of the beck mixed with the rain.

Walk along here on a sunny day and it's beautiful. The beck running over the rocks. A coffee and a slice of cake at Falling Foss.

But when you're on your own. The light fading. The rain. Low cloud...

Brady heard the sound of the beck being played over the opening credits of a horror film. Forced himself to concentrate as he walked over stone and tree roots.

That'd be sensible. Twist your ankle. Crawl back to the car...

Had the rain stopped? All he could hear was the noise of the beck. Water dripping off the trees. He couldn't escape the feeling that he was being watched. Expected someone to tap him on the shoulder any minute.

We need a word for that as well, Frankie...

Went round the slight bend. Up the hill. Found the tree. Stared up at Sarah Trueman...

.   .   .

THE PUDDLES on either side of the bridge had joined in the middle. Brady picked his way through the shallows. Caught a glimpse of movement ahead of him. Thought for a minute – but it was only his defiant friend from the middle of the road. It turned round, saw Brady. Broke into a gentle jog.

Brady sneezed. Again. And a third time.

Three. Lucky? Or unlucky? Or just a sign that walking through the woods in the rain isn't a good idea?

He turned into the car park. Looked up. Saw a cream Nissan Micra parked next to his car. Glanced across. Couldn't see the driver.

Brady walked back to his car. Hesitated. Walked back towards the bridge. Looked up at the tree growing next to it. Looked at the branches. Nodded. Knew he'd found what he wanted.

A clearing. He could see the beck clearly. A branch reaching out over it. A rope. Six, maybe seven feet long, ending two feet above the water. A thick knot at the end of the rope. Cling on to the rope, put your feet on the knot, swing out over the beck.

He'd done it as a child. In the days when he only went to the woods when the sun was shining. Before people were hung from trees. Brady looked at the rope again. Shivered.

Drove back up the hill. Saw a sign halfway. Some respite for the coast-to-coast walkers.

Littlebeck 2½ miles.

That looks lovely. I should do it with Archie one day.

Sighed.

Knew he had far more pressing concerns than finding a new walk for Archie...

77

Brady let himself back into the house. Took his shoes off. Didn't want to traipse mud on the carpets.

"Next time Arch. I'm sorry. I know I owe you one. Here."

He dug into his pocket and pulled out a dog biscuit. Felt guilty for leaving his dog behind. Knew he owed him a really long walk.

Brady walked upstairs toward the bathroom. Heard the shower already running. Went into his office instead. Had to wait his turn. He knew there would be a mountain of paperwork waiting for him when he went back into the office. People to talk to. Explain about Jake. And now there was Frankie to worry about too. Should he talk to her? Confess what Kershaw had said? Brady didn't know whether he could do his job without Frankie. Even before he'd re-joined the force – when everything happened with Patrick – knowing she was part of the team had been integral in making his decision. If she left there was only him and Dan Keillor. How long would that last?

Brady lifted the lid on his laptop. Checked his email. Saw a familiar sender. Mozart.

Please let this be good news...

50% of this I could have done with my eyes closed, Michael. Maybe the police department does need to work harder... Still looking into Ben Moxon and Martha however. Should have more information for you on Monday. Attached as per.

Brady clicked the attachment. Saw Tim Carrick's name at the top, accompanied by another word that made his heart sink.

Tim Carrick: alibi.

On the date of Sarah Trueman's disappearance Mr Timothy Carrick was engaged in extra-marital relations with one Madame Bellatrix. She keeps a digital appointment book with the date, time and duration of visit. Enclosed in appendix.

Brady scrolled down. Found the copy of the appointment book. Saw Carrick's name. Realised there was no way he could have been the one to hang Sarah Trueman. Doubted based on this recent evidence whether he could have been involved at all. Knew he had to rule the man out. Sighed. Scrolled back up to the other information.

Unidentified male from photograph: Giles Quinn. Senior Analyst at Quinn Capital (his father's firm).

There was an address in London. A link to a website.

And a long drive in the calendar...

78

Brady took a deep breath. Knew he couldn't put it off any longer. The team was waiting for him. What was left of the team...

He walked into the briefing room and made his way to the desk at the front. Chose not to sit behind it. Perched on the edge instead. Frankie and Anya were talking in hushed tones. Dan Keillor was staring out of the window. That was it. The four of them. The best that Whitby had to offer.

Brady waited for Frankie and Anya to finish speaking. Clasped his hands together. Addressed his small team.

"I'm not going to brush over what happened on Friday. Jake was one of us and he doesn't deserve to be forgotten about or swept under the rug. We'll each be grieving in our own ways. Dealing with it in whatever manner works. But I will say this – talk to each other. For the love of God please talk about how you're feeling. We've all seen first-hand what bottling it up can do. So don't let that be an option for you. If you need to take some time off – we'll manage. If you need to finish early to go and see your family – do it. I don't ever want anyone cutting any corners when it comes to how they're feeling. Each of you is the priority here and I take that very seriously."

Brady paused. Looked from Frankie to Anya and to Dan. Held each of their gaze. Made sure they understood him.

"Now to the case – Jake says we need to nail this guy. So we will. Simple as that."

Frankie nodded. Dan looked resolute. Anya stood up a little straighter. Folded her arms in front of her. They all looked straight at Brady. Focused. Ready. Prepared to do anything for their team.

"I've come across some new information about our man Tim Carrick." Brady paused and handed the page he'd printed at home over to Frankie. She read it before passing it to Dan.

"I think based on this we can rule him out. I've also got another lead: Giles Quinn. He works at a hedge fund in London. I'm going down there this afternoon. Dan – I need you to pull everything you can on this guy before my meeting at 4pm. Email it over to me. Anything you can find. Nothing is too small."

"Am I looking for anything in particular boss?"

"He was one of the kids at the dinner party Sarah Trueman held five years ago. So anything from his past. Links to the school. To our victim."

"On it, boss."

"Frankie – I want you to look back through everyone we've spoken to. The widows in Roxby. The vicar. Julie Stott. Carolyn Armer. Ben Moxon. I can't help feeling we've missed something. We spoke to each of them for a reason. Find it. And find out what we're missing."

"Sure thing."

"Anything you need from me boss?"

"Anya." Brady paused. She would have been one of the

last on the scene at Jake's suicide. Being a scene of crime officer was one thing. Being a scene of crime officer when the scene is someone close to you is something else.

"Are you okay? Do you still have anything to follow up on from the farm?"

"A couple bits. And yeah. Or at least – as okay as I can be. I signed up for this boss."

"Not exactly…"

No one signs up to seeing their friend blow their brains out.

"But finish whatever you need to do with that. Then look into the window catch, will you? And the tassel. See if we've missed anything. There has to be another clue somewhere."

"Yes boss."

Brady looked at his small team. Saw the determination on their faces again. Knew each of them would do whatever it took to see this case through. To find justice for Sarah Trueman. And to honour Jake's wishes.

79

B rady walked out of Kings Cross station. Was glad he'd decided to get the train. The rain was coming down sideways. So much for Spring...

He turned right and headed toward the taxi rank. Joined the short queue. Didn't have to wait long.

"Cheers, guv. Where you headed? Tourist are you? You don't look like one."

"Quinn Capital," Brady said. Gave the address.

"That the hedge fund isn't it? Whatever the hell one of those is. Sharp lads. Would've sold your wife a pair of nylons in the War. Need to watch out around them."

The black cab pulled out into London traffic. Swerved across a few lanes.

Should I? Why not? Give him something to tell his wife over dinner.

"I'm a Detective Chief Inspector. I'm here to interview one of the 'sharp lads' about the sins of his youth."

The cabbie shook his head. Laughed. "Good for you. And sins of my youth? Can't remember that far back. Married thirty-eight years. She never lets me forget it."

Brady smiled. Sat back in his seat. Let the city rush by through the window until they pulled up outside Quinn Capital.

He handed over a £20 note. Told him to keep the change.

"Cheers, guv. Good luck in there."

I wonder if I'll need it...

BRADY REACHED HIS HAND OUT. The plate glass doors slid open before he could touch them. Found himself in a reception the size of the main office in Whitby. A security guard looking exactly like an ex-copper should look.

"Quinn Capital?"

"Thirty-second floor. And the two above it. But reception's on thirty-two."

Another reception you could play cricket in. A receptionist taking a rest between perfume commercials.

The London Eye visible from one window, the Shard from the other.

"You can spend the rest of the day as a tourist if you like. There's a restaurant at the top."

Brady turned round. Early 20s, straight out of an aftershave commercial. The sort of man who once strolled out to bat for England. A gentleman, not a player.

'Confidence, not arrogance, Mr Brady.'

Maybe not, Headmaster...

"It's spectacular."

Giles Quinn shrugged. "It's London. It *looks* spectacular from up here..."

But down there. Where the little people live...

"How can I help you, Mr Brady? I've a conference call with a client in twenty minutes."

Don't waste my time. You know what, Giles? I couldn't care less.

"I'm looking into the death of a woman called Sarah Trueman. She was – "

Quinn raised his eyebrows. Smiled. "Freddie Trueman?"

"I'm sorry. I – "

"She was from Yorkshire. She was called Trueman."

'Sharp as a whip.' Which clearly I'm not...

"Her nickname at school, Inspector."

"Right. I apologise. She was found hanged from a tree, Mr Quinn. It didn't seem appropriate to give her a nickname."

Quinn nodded. "I can see that. Wouldn't look so good on the file. Operation Fiery Fred. Sorry, Inspector. I'm in a good mood. Closed a deal. Flippant. I'm sorry."

Don't let him piss you off. The information. That's all you want.

"I'd like to ask you about a dinner party, Mr Quinn – "

"Last week? The week before. One goes to so many..."

Brady sighed. "Please don't piss me off, Mr Quinn. I know I'm a long way from home but I'm still a police officer. I can still arrest you. So answer my questions. Then I'll fuck off back to the frozen wastes that are the Northlands and you can do your conference call."

"Sorry, Inspector. Wrist slapped. Five hundred lines." He smiled his charming smile. "And trust me, if we're comparing icy wastes I'll see your Whitby and raise you the frozen fucking fells around Annie's." He led Brady into a meeting room. "Ask away."

Is he strong enough? No. Is he bright enough to plan it out? Yes. Is he the sort of person who'd dress her like a tarot card? Yes. But would he commit to holding her all that time?

Maybe not alone...

"You were at a dinner party. The end of term."

Quinn nodded. "I was. Rack of lamb. Very good. Very, *very* good. Some bloody vegetarian thing for the starter. But I'm deeply sorry, I was too stoned to remember the pudding. I did detect the faint whiff of a Sainsbury's shelf in the wine if that's any help."

All you want is the information...

"There were four of you there."

"There were. 'Were' being the operative word as I'm sure you know."

"I do. Sasha and Natalya..."

Quinn shook his head. Looked half-wistful, half-amused. "I miss her. Nat. She was... Interesting doesn't come close. Funny. Manic. On the edge all the time." He winked. "And what she couldn't do with her tongue..."

Brady made one final effort not to lose his temper.

"Do you know how she died?"

"I know the line they gave everyone. Something related to her drug-use. Psychosis, was it? Outside of that I have no idea."

You're lying. Lying through your very expensive, perfectly-straight teeth. And you don't care that I know.

"And Sasha, of course," Quinn said. "How you start as an underwriter, I suppose. 'Here's a Russian teenager. Likes to take drugs. Thinks he's James Bond when he climbs into a car. *Papochka* gives him a Ferrari for his birthday... Perhaps we won't offer him life cover.'"

"What was he like?"

"What was he like? I've just told you. A death waiting to happen. Either himself or someone else. Got changed for PE and flashed his first Mafia tattoo. Little Miss Martha seemed to like it though..."

"They were having a relationship?"

Quinn pursed his lips. Considered his answer. "Having a relationship. A phrase straight from the Northlands. Martha *thought* they were having a relationship. Sasha knew he was fucking her. The lure of the bad boy, Inspector. If only I could be so attractive to women. I suppose I shall have to join the Young Conservatives."

"Where is she now?"

"Martha? Well she's alive, I think. Only fifty-fifty when we tucked into Freddie's rack of lamb. But where I have no idea."

"You don't keep in touch? Facebook?"

"Facebook? Good God, my parents use Facebook. Don't be ridiculous."

"So you've no idea?"

"Where she is? None at all." He shrugged. "Why should I? Martha was a card of a very low order, Inspector."

Sarcasm. Jokes. Lies. The sum total of which is fuck all.

"So the four of you went for dinner. Stoned?"

Giles tipped his head to one side. "I'm disappointed, Inspector. Half-stoned. As I said earlier. Otherwise I wouldn't remember the stellar rack of lamb, would I?"

"What did you do after the meal?"

Quinn blew his cheeks out. "Six years ago? Without my diary I can barely remember last week. I'd assume Sash took the delightful Martha behind a convenient hedge. Or possibly he didn't bother with the hedge. Nat and I smoked something. God knows what. She had an inexhaustible supply."

"From Sasha?"

He shook his head. "From anyone and everyone. She was like a truffle hound where dope was concerned. She had a supplier at the school. Someone down in the village, I think. One of the local boys in blue maybe? It's certainly a lucrative second income for a couple of Met officers I know..."

"Who's your client?" Brady said.

Quinn laughed. "You know I can't tell you that."

And even if you could I wouldn't have heard of him. Or them...

80

"Honestly Frankie. There's a certain type of person who works at a hedge fund. And I do not like that person."

Brady glanced around his train carriage. Wondered if there was anyone who might fit the description listening in.

"Really boss – can you say you're surprised? Those big city boys don't really strike me as your type."

"Did you forget I moved to Whitby from Manchester?"

"It's still not exactly on the same scale as London is it boss? Swapping Rochdale canal for the Thames. Anyway – I think I've found something."

"Go on."

"Julie Stott. We need to go and see her. I've made the arrangements."

"Why?"

"She has a daughter..."

"WHAT IS it with this bloody case?" Frankie said. "First Sarah Trueman, now this. I've got cottage-envy."

Whitewashed walls, a red pantile roof, a bright red door, flowers Brady didn't recognise growing up the side of it. The obligatory lobster pot decorating the patch of front garden. A view of the bridge over the beck.

"Airbnb must be salivating," Brady said. "Let's see what she has to say."

"JULIE. You came to me. Told me about Carrick. Now, he's not quite the knight in shining armour he likes to think he is, but he's not a murderer. I understand though. You wanted to help us find Sarah Trueman's killer. But you were wrestling with a difficult decision."

"Ethics. I told you. Even in my profession. My former profession."

Brady shook his head. "No. That's where we part ways, Julie. Sarah's a friend of yours. You've met her through the church. You're a similar age. But she disappears on Friday. You don't come into the station until ten days later. We all struggle with decisions, Julie. But not for ten days."

Brady reached forward, sipped his tea.

"Someone came to see me. The weekend before you did. They gave me some information. Confidential information. About one of my team. If I acted on it I was betraying a confidence. But if I didn't do anything... It could affect other people. So a tough decision. And I thought hard about it. But here's the thing, Julie. I thought hard about it for ten minutes. Not ten days."

"I – "

Brady held his hand up. "Here me out. Like I say, that decision was about one of my team. Jake Cartwright. His whole life in front of him. He shot himself three days ago. Went to his uncle's farm. Into the barn. Knew where he kept his shotgun. I don't think I got my decision about Jake wrong. But I wasn't there when he needed to talk. I'll carry that with me forever.

"So that was Jake, God bless him. Ten minutes thinking. I knew what I had to do. But supposing the decision *isn't* about Jake? Supposing it's about my daughter? She's fifteen, Julie. Sixteen in a week. A tough decision to make about my daughter. Something personal. I'm going to lie awake at night. I'm going to make a list of pros and cons. I'm going to make a decision. Then I'll change my mind. Change it back. Do that half a dozen times. Spend another night wide awake. That's what I thought when you walked into the station, Julie. 'Here's a woman who didn't sleep through the night.' At first I put it down to Carrick. Back pain maybe. But then I thought, what keeps me awake at night? Two things. Cases I'm working on. And my daughter."

"I – "

"No, Julie. I know you're used to men doing as they're told. Not this one.

"Sarah Trueman, Julie. She's murdered, and you agonise about coming forward. Why? Why does it take ten days? The same reason it would take me ten days. Because I'm making a decision about the one person I love more than life itself. My daughter. So I need to speak to your daughter, Julie. I need to speak to Martha."

Julie didn't speak. Stared at Brady.

"And that's how you know Sarah. Because Martha was at the school. Sarah taught her. Befriended her. Maybe felt sorry for her. She didn't have the wealth, the privilege of the others. Martha got into trouble at school and Sarah protected her. You move here and you find her in the next village. She's not the reason you moved here, but it's one of life's happy coincidences. And you're in her debt. Whatever she did, you're in her debt. But still you wait ten days before you come to me. Because you're worried you'll put Martha in danger. Because she's got her life back on track. And you don't want to take any risks. I sympathise, Julie. I really do. But in the final analysis I have to find Sarah's killer. And I need to speak to Martha."

Brady heard the door open behind him.

"What about?"

81

A bright, inquisitive face. Wide brown eyes. Slightly tanned. Ripped jeans, a sweatshirt, hair pinned up.

"I tried to tell you," Julie said. "You wouldn't let me speak."

"Martha?"

She nodded. "Home for the weekend. It's not unknown."

"Where – "

"Where am I now? I'm in Glasgow. Strathclyde University. A Psychology Master's. Specialising in Addiction."

"And you're home for the weekend?"

Frankie reached across, put her hand on Brady's arm. "Boss, you're doing a Master's in stating the obvious."

Brady shook his head. Reached forward. Realised he'd finished his tea.

"I NEED to ask you some specifics. The dinner party..."

She nodded. Reached up. Re-fastened her hair.

Getting serious...

"Tell me about it..."

"There were four of us. You knew that. Giles and Nat – "

"Natalya?"

"No-one called her that. Nat. Nattie. Sorry, it sounds ridiculous now. We were sixteen. But Giles and Nat were there on merit. I'd drawn the short straw."

"Bolognese Bill?"

She laughed. "Right. I can't remember where Sasha was supposed to go. Two hours and he'd re-arranged it. Bribes or blackmail. He'd learned from his father.

"I was infatuated with him. Good-looking, rich, funny. God knows what he saw in me."

"Talk me through it. What happened when you got there? Did Sarah let you in?"

"She's not really ready when we get there. Nat and I said maybe Ben Moxon had been round."

Brady forced himself not to speak. Keep the excitement out of his voice.

"Ben Moxon?"

"The games teacher. Cricket coach. Director of Linseed Oil Giles called him. Not the sharpest knife in the drawer. Sorry, I'm not supposed to be judgemental."

"Why would the cricket coach go to see Sarah?"

Julie raised her eyebrows. "Why does any man go to see any woman? The oldest reason in the world."

"They were having an affair?"

I need to hear it from the source...

Martha nodded.

"Did you see them together? What sort of relationship was it?"

Martha shook her head. "It was common knowledge. School gossip. But see them together? No."

"I did," Julie said. "Speech day. The one where you won

the Psychology prize, love." She shook her head. "It wasn't pretty. Or healthy. Have you seen *Forrest Gump*, Mr Brady? Forrest Gump and Jenny. But with an edge. An unhealthy edge."

"You think he'd harm her?"

"I think men will do a lot of things when they don't get what they want. Hell hath no fury like a man scorned. Especially an insecure one."

Brady scribbled down some notes. Tried not to let his excitement get the better of him. Knew he needed the rest of the story.

"So you get there. Sarah Trueman isn't ready. What do you do?"

"We went upstairs. Sarah's bathroom. I've got some coke. She'd got this wooden top in the bathroom. The sink on top of it. One of those taps where the water runs along a little channel. So Nat gets her bank card out. I remember it. UniCredit. A gold debit card. We both snort a line of coke. Then Nat goes back for seconds. And we're joking about leaving a tiny bit on the worktop. Do we wipe it up? 'Leave it,' Nat says. 'It'll be the most fun she's ever had brushing her teeth.'"

Martha drew her breath in. Shook her head. "I'm not very proud of that. Given what happened. At the time I didn't see the whole picture."

"You do now?"

She nodded. "School's like Annie's... They'll do anything, say anything to protect their reputation. Their fee income. So they needed a scapegoat."

Brady nodded. "Trust me, I know. I've been there with my own daughter. 'The school doesn't have a problem with bullying, Mr Brady.'"

"You dealt with it?"

Brady shook his head. "My daughter dealt with it. I did a

bit but no. She sorted it out for herself. So I sympathise. Tell me more about Natalya. Were the two of you close?"

"Her mother committed suicide. Nat told me one night. Her dad covered it up. And Nat found her. That's why he was so protective of her. She was eight."

"How? Did she tell you that?"

"She hanged herself. Probably gave Nat the idea."

"Excuse me?"

Martha paused. Reached for her mother's hand. Looked to be battling some internal demons.

"I don't think Nattie died after a run, Mr Brady. I think she killed herself."

Brady tried not to let the surprise show on his face. Failed. Did his best to continue the conversation.

"Why?"

"She did the Founder's Race."

"What's that?"

"Another of Annie's traditions. Three miles up the fells, three miles down them. Preferably in the rain. Or the fog. Your parents have to sign a disclaimer. Just in case you go over the edge."

"How high?"

She shook her head. "I don't know. About a thousand feet of ascent someone said. And if you're not going up, you're falling in a bog. But Nat did it. And if she had the slightest inkling of a heart problem that race would have found it."

"So you think she committed suicide?"

"No, Mr Brady. I don't think she committed suicide. I *know* she committed suicide. Her mother was depressed. Clinically depressed. If a close family member has depression you're forty or fifty percent more likely to suffer it yourself. There's plenty of research that suggests addiction is the same. You add drugs into that mix. And there was the text..."

"What text?"

Martha took in a deep breath. Her eyes glistened with tears.

"It was the last thing she ever said to me. I didn't even reply at the time. It was early. Like five in the morning. When I saw it I thought maybe she was still high from the night before. I don't know. I didn't reply. Now... I wish I'd been awake. I wish I'd seen it."

"What did the message say?"

"Just one line: *time to be with mummy.*"

"The school didn't know?"

She shook her head. "Maybe. Nat didn't want to talk about her problems; the school didn't really want to know. Mental health issues? Fresh air and exercise were the answer. For Nat, the answer was drugs. And they were far too easy to get access to."

"But you did them with her?"

She shrugged. "Everyone did them. But yes, I stood next to her in Sarah's bathroom and watched her do a line. Then rub what was left into her gums." She wiped a tear away, reached for a tissue. "I'm not proud of that. And it's a debt I'm trying to repay. Whether I ever will... Well, I'll do my best."

Julie put her arm around her daughter. Pulled her into her chest. Martha looked exhausted. Like telling the story had wiped her out. Julie noticed. Picked up the tale.

82

"About a month after we hear about Natalya's death we get a letter. We're summoned to the school. 'Enquiries into the death of Natalya Petrov. Reason to believe your daughter may have been involved in activities not in keeping with the school policies on drug misuse.' Some such bollocks. It's obvious what they want. A scapegoat. And this girl whose mum doesn't pay the fees in the most conventional way is a good place to start.

"So there we are in the Head's study – "

"Kirkup?"

"The one before him. An oily bastard if ever there was one. And the matter's resolved. 'A complete misunderstanding, Ms Stott. The matter is resolved to everyone's satisfaction.' She phoned me as we were driving home."

"Sarah?"

Julie nodded. "She'd agreed to take the blame. Vasili Petrov blamed the school. Drugs in his daughter's system. Psychosis. Heart failure. Whatever spin they put on it. The staff should have done better. Should have seen something. Sarah was Natalya's boarding house mistress. She happened to host the dinner party that Nat went to. She was the perfect scapegoat. She leaves. The school keeps its reputation. Sarah flies off to South America. No more harm done. Except she didn't know what sort of man Natalya's father was."

"What do you mean by that?"

"Come on detective," Julie Stott looked at Brady. Challenged him with her gaze.

"You said it yourself. There's a reason I waited ten days to come forward and tell you about Tim Carrick. There's a reason I wanted to keep Martha out of this. Vasili Petrov is not a man you cross. Sarah losing her job might have been enough for him at the time. But now she's dead. And I'm frightened even mentioning his name is going to get me on his hit list..."

"His hit list?"

"I can't do all your work for you, Mr Brady. But Sasha Kamenev is dead."

"He died in a car accident."

His father gave him a Ferrari for his eighteenth birthday. Two weeks later Sasha wrapped it round a tree in the South of France.

"I'm sure that was the story. Just like how Natalya keeled over after a run. He clearly didn't bother to cover up Sarah's death. Why? Maybe he blamed her most of all. But does that mean I think he's finished? I think my daughter changing her last name can answer that question for you."

Brady looked at Julie Stott. At her daughter. Couldn't miss the fear in their eyes.

"If you knew all of this Ms Stott – if you truly believe it all – why didn't you say anything sooner? Why have you kept us from the man you believe is responsible?"

"You have a daughter don't you Mr Brady?"

"I do."

"And you would do anything to protect her. Even if it meant putting yourself in danger. Even if it meant breaking the law."

Brady didn't answer. Julie Stott hadn't asked a question. It was a statement. It was fact. He would do anything for Ash.

Even if that meant crossing a line that shouldn't be crossed.

83

"What did you make of that?"

"What I made of it, boss, was that they were telling the truth. What was it your old boss said?"

"Jim Fitzpatrick? 'The ring of truth, Mike. You'll know it when you hear it.'"

"And we did. Except it leaves us with some questions."

Brady nodded. "More than some questions. A mountain of them. And a brand-new suspect. Julie Stott certainly seems to think Vasili Petrov is behind this. But why? He had his revenge on Sarah Trueman years ago. Why decide to come back and kill her now?"

"She's clearly frightened boss. If she's right – we could have her done for perverting the course of justice."

"Do you think she's right? That Vasili Petrov is picking off the people at that dinner party one by one?"

"Maybe. But you spoke to one yesterday. I assume he was alive for that conversation?"

"Alive and very much kicking, Frankie. Let's get back to the station – Dan's already done a background check on

Petrov – nothing came up. After that conversation, I want to know why."

"Fuck. Just fuck."

Brady held a badly translated French newspaper report in his hand. Still managed to understand it. Suspected foul play. The death was officially ruled an accident, but there were question marks around the state of the car. The brake fluid. Or lack of it.

"This was over four years ago, Frankie. If Vasili Petrov was responsible – and that's a big if – why would he come back now and start again? Why have Sarah Trueman kicked out of Lady Anne's, drain this poor kids' brake fluid and then five years later decide 'oh that was fun, maybe I'll have another bash at it'?"

"I might have the answer to that boss?"

Dan Keillor appeared in the doorway. More reports tucked under his arm. His face told Brady everything he needed to know. They should have been looking closer at the kids from the dinner party.

Julie Stott had led them on a wild goose chase with Tim Carrick. There was a large part of Brady that wanted her to see justice for that. But the murderer had to come first. They needed to find Vasili Petrov.

"First have a look at this," Dan handed Brady a sheet of paper. Still warm from the printer tray. "Natalya Petrov's mother: Marina. She hanged herself from an olive tree at their family villa in Tuscany."

"Just like Martha said."

"I had to dig pretty deep to find that, boss. All the public reports – even the official cause of death – say drowning. Had one too many martinis and fell asleep in the pool."

"Petrov tried to cover it up?"

"Tried and succeeded boss. I stumbled across that information in the comments section of some tabloid site. Tracked down the person who wrote it – they died shortly after. Another drowning…"

"Okay. I'm starting to believe this guy is behind it. But why now? Why come back for Sarah Trueman?"

"His son, boss."

"His son?"

"He died two months ago. A skiing accident. *Actually* an accident this time. He was at their family lodge in Val d'Isere – "

"Bloody hell how many homes do these people have?"

"More than we can ever hope for boss. But they're all empty now. Except for Vasili Petrov. That was his only other child. His eldest. His heir. Tried to backflip off a ramp and landed on his back. Broke his spine. Snapped his neck. Died instantly."

"Two months ago?"

"Yes boss."

"Fuck."

"Where is Vasili Petrov now, Dan? Did you manage to find that too?"

Dan Keillor shook his head. "There's no record. Nothing. He attended his son's funeral the week after his death. No one has seen him since."

No one except Sarah Trueman I'll bet…

84

Brady glanced out of the window. The rain bouncing down in the car park. The sun lost behind the clouds.

Pathetic fallacy.

Ash had taught him the literary term last year. When the weather reflects your mood or the situation you are in.

Well, there's a murderer on the loose and I've no idea where to find him. My girlfriend – if I can still call her that – is leaving for America and I haven't spoken to her in days. One of my team has killed himself. Another one is apparently leaving for a new job. And it's my daughter's birthday this week and I still haven't bought her a present. That's got to be the most pathetic pathetic fallacy there is.

"Boss?"

"Hm?" Brady looked up. "Sorry Frankie I was miles away. Watching the rain. Thinking about how I still need to get Ash a birthday present."

And how you might be leaving me...

"Still? It's her birthday in two days, isn't it?"

"It is. And yet another one that I'm likely to be very

absent for. Unless you've found Vasili Petrov hiding out in your spare room?"

"Sadly not, boss. Though I have been thinking. Have you got five minutes?"

"Of course. Is this a serious let's-sit-down conversation or do you want to walk with me to the coffee machine? Try my luck as I'm clearly not making it to Dave's…"

Unless you're going to tell me that you're quitting…

"It's broken boss. I think someone's put some *Nescafe* next to the kettle though."

"The police budget stretches to *Nescafe* now? Maybe there is hope for us after all."

Frankie laughed. Held the door open for him.

So it's not time to hand your notice in yet, DS Thomson. Though according to Kershaw I won't have to wait long…

"I've been thinking about the cats, boss. Nine bowls. That's definitely an overnight stay. So she must have agreed to meet someone. Someone she knew."

"We already know she didn't drive anywhere. And none of the local taxi firms were called to that area on Friday afternoon."

"So someone picked her up. Someone she trusted and wasn't nervous about potentially being seen with."

"A lover?"

"That's what we all thought initially. Ben Moxon is still an option. But I think it was someone else boss."

"Who?"

"A friend."

85

"I didn't expect to be called back here, Mr Brady. Especially not like this. Tell me – what can I do for you today?"

Julie Stott looked calm. Confident. Her face gave away nothing. Her mouth remained set in a firm line. A scarf tied loosely around her neck. Hair neatly sitting on top of it. Not a wrinkle or a whisper out of place.

"I had a few more questions for you if you don't mind Ms Stott. About Sarah Trueman."

"I wouldn't imagine it would be about anything else."

Julie Stott adjusted herself slightly in the chair. Rested her hands in her lap. Kept her cards close to her chest.

What had she said before? 'I've never been in a police interview room.' Well this makes twice, Ms Stott. And this time I'm not letting you leave until I get the answers I've been searching for...

"We've established by now that you and Sarah were closer than you originally let on. How often did you see her, Ms Stott?"

"Most weeks at church. More than once if there was a fundraiser or a committee meeting."

"Did you ever go round to her house to visit her? For a reading perhaps?"

"No. I knew about her tarot cards but it never interested me much. After living a life like mine Mr Brady, there is very little you leave up to chance."

"Just for a visit then. Did you ever go round for tea? Have a bottle of wine in the evening?"

"Once or twice maybe. We weren't especially close."

"Do you have many female friends?"

"Excuse me?"

"Female friends, Ms Stott. Or friends in general – have you got many?"

"I suppose I have the normal amount for a woman of my age. One or two less perhaps. My line of work doesn't exactly lead itself to long-standing relationships. You can't swap office gossip or complain about your co-workers like everyone else. But I don't see what that has to do with Sarah?"

"I think it has everything to do with Sarah, Ms Stott. I think it has everything to do with Sarah because you *were* close. You were friends. You're women of a similar age. You've both had challenging careers – worked with men in a disciplinary sense one way or another. I think that bonded you. And I think that made you very close friends indeed."

Brady paused. Looked at Julie Stott. Saw her hands now clasped tightly in her lap. Her knuckles blanched.

"Where were you the Friday Sarah Trueman went missing, Ms Stott? Where were you over that weekend?"

"I was at home. I – "

"By yourself?"

Julie Stott didn't answer. She dropped her head. Closed her eyes. Let out a long breath. When she opened her eyes all the confidence and bravado she'd entered the interview room with was gone. Replaced by a frightened, small, aging woman. She spoke quickly. Desperation in her voice. Pleading. Doing her best to explain.

"You have to understand I did it for Martha. I had no idea what he was going to do to her. He just said I had to get her. I had to bring her to him. It was Sarah or Martha. I didn't have a choice."

"You always have a choice Ms. Stott. Always."

Detective Chief Inspector Brady stood. Looked down at Julie Stott. Silent tears rolled down her cheeks.

"I'm going to get a cup of coffee. Tea? Two sugars was it?"

86

"Well?"

"You were right, Frankie. She did it. She lured Sarah Trueman out of her cottage and walked her towards her grave."

"Did she know he was going to kill her?"

"I haven't got all the details yet. Let her stew for five minutes while I make a cup of tea. Have you brought her daughter in?"

Frankie nodded. "She's down the hall. Safe. Dan Keillor is keeping an eye on her."

"Good. We can't let that girl out of our sight until we know the whereabouts of Vasili Petrov. Consider this Whitby's very own witness protection programme."

"Are you going to tell her about Giles Quinn?"

Brady sighed. He hadn't liked the man at all, but he didn't deserve the ending he got. Slipped and fell in front of an oncoming tube. At least that was the line. Officers on the scene reported it as an accident. Brady had already sent a note to the Met explaining what he thought might have happened.

"That depends how forthright she is with information. I don't doubt knowing that her daughter is the only one left alive from that dinner party will help her open up and sing if she's struggling."

"Go easy on her boss. She did it for her daughter after all."

"I have a daughter too, Frankie. That doesn't mean I'm willing to let an innocent woman die for her."

But if you didn't have a choice? What had Julie said?

'You would do anything to protect her. Even if it meant putting yourself in danger. Even if it meant breaking the law.'

And she was right...

BRADY HANDED Julie Stott the mug. Saw her hands shaking slightly as she took it from him. Her entire persona had changed. She was afraid. And she was guilty.

"I need you to talk me through what happened, Ms Stott. From the very beginning. From the first moment Vasili Petrov contacted you."

Julie nodded. Took a sip of her tea. Braced herself.

"Just over a month ago I received a letter. No idea who it was from. No return address. But addressed to me. At my home. Delivered with the morning paper and the gas bill. It was handwritten and it contained only one line: you can't hide the truth forever.

"At first, I thought it was from an old client. Or maybe even one of their wives. You've heard about that sort of thing happening before. A husband lets the truth slip. The wife blames the dominatrix. Can't believe their husband could have been responsible. Plans to destroy 'the whore who corrupted him' instead. It's a bit soap-opera-drama for me, but it happens."

"I can believe you. Only in this case, it wasn't a scorned wife. It was Vasili Petrov?"

Julie nodded. "Or someone who worked for him. Two days later I'm confronted. Cornered in the Bank Top public toilets of all places. It was dusk. I walk down to the lifeboat station and back every evening after my dinner. Ever since my accident – it hurts like hell – but if I don't keep moving it hurts a hell of a lot more. So I make myself do it. Every night. Twenty minutes there, twenty minutes back. Twenty-five if my back is playing up. Or if I need to stop and relieve myself. Like I did that night."

Staithes public toilets. Not somewhere I'd ever choose to stop. What is that – halfway? Ten more minutes and you're back at home. But then supposing Petrov knocks on the front door instead...

"Can you describe the man you spoke to? What did he say?"

"I couldn't see his face. He wore a dark beanie hat. A scarf pulled up over his mouth. It looked expensive though. I remember thinking that. 'Am I about to be mugged by a man in a £100 cashmere scarf?'"

"What else?"

"He was big. Tall. Broad shoulders. Filled out the doorway. Wouldn't let me past. He stood there for maybe thirty seconds before he spoke. Arms crossed. Just looking at me. Sizing me up. It was like he was assessing me. Seeing if I was going to challenge him."

"But you didn't? What did you do?"

"What could I do? I waited. I looked at him and I waited to see what was going to happen next. A more astute woman might have screamed. Maybe I should have. But after spending my life dominating men, I've learnt to understand them. This man made me nervous. But he didn't make me feel afraid. I wasn't worried about what was going to happen. I – it's hard to explain. But I just felt like everything was under control. Like our meeting had been planned."

Brady raised his eyebrows. Analysed Julie Stott. Waited for her to continue.

"When he finally spoke, he mentioned Martha by name. Her new name. We made the decision when she moved up to Scotland that she was going to change her last name. The fear of what had happened at Lady Anne's never went away. She knew Natalya had killed herself and she was terrified something was going to happen to her.

"When that other boy died – Sasha – Martha was convinced it was because she'd told him her true feelings about Natalya. Martha was obsessed with him. Teenage girls and their first love – I'm sure you know what it's like. But she told him and then two, three weeks later, he winds up dead. Call it a coincidence. Call it whatever you like. Martha was terrified. She was convinced Natalya's father was going to come for her. So we changed her name. Took the steps that were needed to protect her and hid her away as best we could."

"That's not much of a life for a child – did you not consider coming forward? Talking to the police?"

"Only for about thirty seconds. Martha said that was exactly what Sasha said when she told him she thought Natalya killed herself. He said he could get his father to look into it. They were both from Russian families. And then Sasha winds up dead. You can understand why we were afraid."

Brady nodded. Realised again that he would do anything to protect Ash if she was ever threatened like that.

"Okay – back to your meeting. The man, Vasili Petrov or not, he mentioned Martha by name. What else did he say?"

"In short, he said that if I wanted my daughter to remain protected – unharmed – then I needed to deliver Sarah Trueman to him. He said he knew we were friends. He gave me a date: Saturday morning. And a location: an old farmhouse between Staithes and Boulby. He told me to get Sarah there early Saturday morning and Martha could remain hidden."

"And if you failed?"

"He didn't need to go into detail there. I knew that if I didn't do what he instructed then Martha would be next. I knew I didn't have a choice."

87

"I invited her over on Friday afternoon. I told her I'd started going swimming in the sea early Saturday morning. Told her it was good for my back. Why wouldn't she believe me? Sarah seemed to like the idea of watching the sunrise too. So that was it – she came over on Friday afternoon, we had dinner, shared a bottle of wine and then the next morning we left before it was light out and made our way down to the sea."

"Didn't anyone see you? I know it's Staithes on an early Saturday morning, but there had to be someone around. Fisherman? The local milkman?"

Julie lowered her head. "I wished that there was. Every window that we walked past I hoped a light would come on. I hoped we'd see a mutual acquaintance drive past. Anyone who would stop and say hello. Give me a reason not to go through with it. But it was quiet. Too quiet. At one point I even thought Petrov had planned it somehow. Made sure nothing would get in our way."

Brady scribbled down some notes. Wondered whether anyone could have the power to do such a thing. He had no idea who Vasili Petrov was or what he was dealing with, but he had dealt with similar in the past.

Marko Vrukić's face appeared in front of him. The Serbian warlord. One of the most prominent figures in the civil war. A mass murderer. A man who's committed war crimes. If Vasili Petrov was anything like Marko Vrukić then Brady knew he was capable of anything.

"We made it down to the river bridge and turned right along the Cleveland way. I told Sarah there was an old farmhouse a little way out. Steps down to a quiet and secluded patch of beach where no one would see us. She had no reason not to trust me. No idea what was waiting for her."

Julie Stott stifled a sob. Brady didn't feel sorry for her. He couldn't. Julie Stott hadn't seen Sarah hanging from a tree. She hadn't seen the lengths she'd gone to to try and leave a clue behind. The window catch. The tassel from an old beach towel.

At least the morning swim explained where the towel had come from.

"This farmhouse," Brady asked. "Can you identify it for us? I assume that's where Sarah was held."

"Held?"

"For several days, Ms Stott. You didn't just walk Sarah Trueman to her death. You left her to be tortured for days. You dropped her off with a murderer, walked home and never looked back."

Julie Stott couldn't hold it together anymore. She broke down. Tears streamed down her face. Her body trembled. The once strict, unwavering persona of Mistress Anastasia was broken.

"I had to keep Martha safe. I didn't want Sarah to get hurt. But I didn't have a choice. If I hadn't – he would have come for Martha. He would have come for all of them."

"I'm afraid he already has, Ms Stott."

Brady paused. Rearranged the papers in front of him. Saw Julie look up at him with wide eyes. Her expression etched with terror.

"What's happened? Where is Martha? Is she okay?"

"Your daughter is fine, Ms Stott. She's in this very building in fact. Under our protective custody. The same – unfortunately – cannot be said for Giles Quinn. He was found last night on the Victoria Line. Literally. The story will say that he jumped. Or slipped. But based on what we have learned I think you and I know the truth."

Julie Stott didn't speak. Her bottom lip quivered. The knowledge that what she had done hadn't changed Vasili Petrov's plans at all seeped into her. She seemed to shrink. The shame swallowing her whole. Eating her alive.

"Please," she begged. "Please keep Martha safe."

Brady stood. Looked down at Julie Stott. Wondered if he would ever go this far to protect Ash. Didn't want to know the answer.

"We will. But we have to catch Petrov first."

88

"Do you think he'll still be there?"

Brady, Frankie and Dan Keillor crowded round a computer screen. The farmhouse Julie Stott had described on the screen. The path that walkers took in the summer curved past the old building. Still about two-hundred yards between it and the front door. A distance long enough that when coupled with the wind off the sea and the noise from the gulls, no one would hear a whisper of what happened behind the old stone walls.

No one would be able to hear her scream.

The farmhouse itself had taken its fair share of battering from the North Sea. The once white-washed walls were a dirty grey. The roof caved in at one corner. Two of the front windows smashed. There was a small outhouse to the rear of it, next to a path that led down to the beach.

'I told Sarah I normally changed in the little outhouse round the back. I let her walk in first. I didn't follow. I didn't step inside.'

So you just left Sarah to fend for herself. What happened when she crossed that doorway? Was Petrov lying in wait for her? Did he snatch at her straight away, or did Sarah Trueman

enter the dark room, turn around to search for her friend and find
Vasili Petrov standing in her place?

"If he's in there he'll be expecting us now. I've no doubt
he's been keeping tabs on Julie Stott since we visited her
cottage the other day."

"Should we call for backup boss?"

"Not until we know for certain. It'll need to be just me
and you at first, Frankie. Dan – I need you to stay here and
watch over Martha. She's in danger too now. Remember
what I said: Whitby's very own witness protection
programme. And you're in charge."

"Got it boss."

"So what's our plan then? You go in the front, I go in the
back. Hope that Vasili Petrov hasn't filled the place with
armed Russian guards?"

"There's no need to sound overly confident, Frankie. You
forget about our twice-yearly hand-to-hand combat
training."

"Seriously though boss, what's the plan once we get in
there?"

"Honestly? I'm not sure. But..." Brady thought for a
moment. Was it worth the risk? Even in theory. "We do have
a bargaining chip. Martha. Perhaps we can use her to our
advantage?"

"You mean like bait?"

"Not in the literal sense, but maybe. Figuratively. There
could be something we can imply..."

Brady had used Anya as bait once before. And he
remembered all too well how that had gone. Doused in
petrol three days before Christmas. A killer who was determined to set her hair on fire. A year where not just the
turkey was burnt.

And I promised myself I'd never do it again.

"We'll think of something in the car, Frankie. We always do. Besides – I get the impression that Vasili Petrov likes to talk. To show off. If he's there, I'm sure he'll give us time to come up with a plan."

BRADY AND FRANKIE climbed into the Tiguan. He glanced over at her. Black leather jacket zipped up like a layer of armour. Face set in a determined line. But a face that was hiding the truth.

I wonder if this will be one of the last cases we work together. If she's waiting for it all to be over before she hands in her resignation.

Brady started the engine. Looked at Frankie again – her eyes forward, ready to go into battle. He remembered the first time he'd really spoken to her, in Patrick and Kara's kitchen. His best friend had just been murdered. His brother-in-law was determined to close the case before it had even been looked into.

Frankie had given him a chance. A lifeline. In the form of a backpack and a laptop. She had been one of the main reasons Brady decided to go back to work. The knowledge that he would work alongside someone like her made dealing with the Kershaw's of the world all that easier.

There were days where he'd wanted her to be a lot more than just a colleague. But they'd both agreed work was the most important thing to each of them.

'As good as it gets.'

Maybe next year they wouldn't even have that...

"Are you alright boss? Should we get going?"

Brady snapped back to reality. Sniffed. Looked at Frankie for a third time. Smiled. Apologised. Started the engine. Knew he had to make the most of what he had whilst it was there.

89

They stood on the Cleveland Way. The path took you right past the farmhouse. Climb over the stile, walk a couple hundred yards and knock on the door. Easy. Unless there was a Russian murderer lying in wait.

But if Vasili Petrov is inside, he already knows we're here.

"Ready?"

Frankie put one foot on the bottom slat of the stile. Swung her other leg over the stop. Stopped to reply. "Let's do this."

She jumped down gracefully on the other side. Brady tried to follow suit. Landed far less impressively. Straightening up, he took the lead as they walked toward the farmhouse. They'd discussed one of them going round the back, but preferred their chances together. Besides, after what Petrov had done to Sarah Trueman, neither one of them wanted to be cornered alone.

Brady reached the door first. Balled his right hand into a fist. Knocked. Waited, Knocked again.

"Hello? Anybody home?"

"Bit of a long shot don't you think, boss? If he's in there he's not giving himself up that easy."

"I know." Brady shook his head. Knocked one more time. "It's times like these I wish we carried more than just a taser."

Brady put his hand on the doorknob. Twisted it. Felt the door give way to him with very little resistance. It swung open. Welcomed them both inside.

"For an old farmhouse, I'd say that door works rather well."

"A little too well, Frankie. Feels like someone has done a once around with a can of WD40."

They stepped inside. Found themselves in an old kitchen. A few plates and mugs were piled in the sink, evidence of several years of dirt and grime resting on top of them. Brady and Frankie moved through the room as quietly as possible.

To the right of the kitchen was an old utility room. Rusted taps sticking out from the wall. The linoleum ripped up from the floor. Cold stone slabs underneath. None of it looked like it had been touched for years. Dust balls gathered in the corners. The wind the only noise as it rattled through the old building.

"Let's try upstairs."

Brady walked as carefully as he could manage up the old staircase. Each step groaned beneath him. He imagined the wood giving way. Falling to his death in a cloud of dust and debris. When he reached the top he let out a breath he didn't realise he'd been holding. Frankie stood next to him. Listened for a moment.

"It's too quiet. There can't be anyone here."

"I agree. Let's split up. You take that back bedroom. I'll go in here."

Brady nodded to the master on his left. Edged the door open with his foot. The room was bare. A bed positioned in the centre of the back wall. A battered, stained mattress on top. There was no bedding. No carpet. No curtains.

He walked over to the window. Looked out onto the Cleveland Way. If someone was walking past and they looked up – would they see him? If he shouted – would his voice be heard?

"Boss? In here."

Brady heard Frankie's cry from the other room. Stepped out into the hall. Crossed into the back bedroom. Found her standing by a window too. Looking out over the North Sea. The waves crashing against the cliff. The gulls swooping down and picking small fish out of the water.

"Look."

Frankie turned round. Held out her hand.

Brady stared at the object. A small pewter-coloured locking nut, maybe half an inch across.

Something he'd seen before.

"This window has one," Frankie said. "That one," she nodded to the other window in the room, "does not."

Brady took a step back and looked around the room. It was just as desolate and bare as the other bedroom. No bedding. No carpet. No curtains. Not even a light bulb swinging from the ceiling. Nothing you could use to leave behind a clue for someone. Nothing – he swallowed – except the window catch.

Brady reached into his pocket and pulled on a pair of gloves.

"We need to get Anya here now. See what – "

Brady's phone started to ring. He looked at the display. Saw Dan Keillor's number.

"Dan. What is it? We're at the house. She was definitely held here. Tell Anya – "

Dan Keillor cut him off.

"She's gone boss."

"What? Who's gone? Anya?"

"Martha. She asked me to get her a coffee. I had to go into the kitchen and wait for the kettle to boil because the machine's still broken. When I got back, she was gone."

"Gone? Gone where?"

"She left a note boss."

"Well for Christ's sake what does it say, Dan? Where's she gone?"

"*It's time this ends. I'm your bargaining chip. I'm the one he wants.*"

"Fuck."

Brady balled his hand into a fist again. Smashed it into the window frame.

"She heard me. She bloody heard me saying that. Fuck. Is that all it says, Dan? Nothing else? No idea where she went?"

"That's it boss. She can't have gone far though. I'm walking out now. I'll search the area."

"Find her, Dan. We'll head back. But we need to find her. Petrov can't win this one."

90

"She must have heard me, Frankie. She must have heard me when we were talking about using her as bait. And now she's decided to be the hero. Fuck. This is all my fault."

"It's okay, boss. We'll find her. Like Dan says, she can't have gone far."

The two of them hoisted themselves over the stile onto the Cleveland Way. Started to jog back toward the car.

"We need a bigger team. Three bloody coppers." Brady panted as he pumped his legs. Tried to keep up with Frankie. "We need more than that."

DAN KEILLOR WAS WAITING for them at the station as Brady pulled up. Alone. He shook his head. Martha was gone. Brady swore under his breath again.

"What about Julie? Have you spoken to her?"

"No boss. She's still inside. She doesn't know."

"Good. Keep it that way Dan. We can't have her mother trying to break out as well."

"Wait – what about her phone boss?"

"What about it, Frankie?"

"Julie's phone – she might have a tracker on it for Martha. *Find my friends.* I've seen people use it before."

"Brilliant. Bloody brilliant. Go and check will you, Frankie. We'll have her phone in evidence. Get it unlocked. Get the app. Try not to tell Julie what's happened. Dan – where have you looked so far?"

"I've gone down to the harbour, no one has seen her boss. I didn't leave her for more than five minutes I swear. I had no idea she was going to do a runner."

"It's okay Dan, I don't blame you. It's me she overheard. *I'm your bargaining chip.* That's exactly what I said she was. But I was never planning on going through with it."

"Do you think she knows where Petrov is? Or knows how to find him?"

"Right now I have no idea what she knows, Dan. I just know we have to find her. Have to get to her before Petrov does. I've had enough of people trying to be the hero."

"I'VE GOT HER BOSS."

"Where?"

"We probably drove past her. She's on the move. Heading back toward Staithes."

"Back home?"

"Or to the farmhouse. Did you already send Anya out?"

Brady nodded.

"We've got to get there first. Dan – take a squad car. Go and check Julie's cottage and make sure Martha's not gone there. Frankie, you're with me. I've a hunch we won't find the farmhouse empty this time."

· · ·

BRADY SPOTTED Anya just before a bend of the Cleveland Way. Another hundred feet and the farmhouse would come into view. They'd caught up with her just in time. He closed the last few meters between them. Leant over. Put his hands on his knees. Caught his breath. Let Frankie explain why they were there.

Anya paled slightly at the thought of what she nearly walked into. But then she straightened up. Set her face into a determined expression. Balled her hands into fists.

"What do you need me to do, boss?"

Brady finally caught his breath. "Be our backup. Wait here. Stay out of sight. If you don't hear from us in say, twenty minutes. Call for backup and follow suit."

"Twenty minutes?"

Brady nodded.

"Frankie – let's get going. We don't know what Martha's just walked into."

The two of them approached the farmhouse as quietly as possible. Part of Brady thought it was pointless. Petrov must know they were on their way.

Had he been there earlier? Had he been watching us?

Still years of policework reminded him to keep a low profile. To at least try and maintain the element of surprise.

Frankie peeled off before Brady reached the door. Just as they'd discussed. He watched her walk away into the fading light. Wondered if one day soon he'd be watching her walk away for good.

Not now. Save Martha. Arrest Petrov. Then you can worry about Frankie...

Brady steeled himself. Knew how he had to play it with Petrov. Didn't knock. Walked inside. Prepared himself for the worst.

The kitchen was just as they'd left it. A breeze shuddered

through the door behind Brady. Picked up wisps of dust with it.

Brady watched them swirl in front of him. Couldn't stop himself thinking of Grace. Scattering her ashes on the cliff top. Watching them swirl on the wind. Almost hang in front of him for a few seconds. Like she was saying goodbye.

Brady blinked Grace out of his mind. He needed to focus. If he had his way, then no one else had to die.

"Petrov!"

Brady shouted confidently. Showed no fear.

"I know you're in here. Let's talk. Like men. Martha isn't the only one who knows the truth about your daughter..."

91

"Mr Brady. I was wondering when we might meet."

Vasili Petrov stood confidently in the centre of the sitting room. A fire burned brightly in the old stone fire place to his right. The flames casting shadows on the walls.

Martha trembled in his grasp.

Petrov was tall. A shade over six foot. Greying hair cropped close to his skull. An already-grey goatee beard. Tanned. His frame packed with muscle. Pale blue eyes.

Brady looked again.

The palest eyes I've ever seen...

"I know why you're doing this." Brady spoke softly. Calmly. "You know none of this will bring your daughter back."

Petrov laughed. Shook his head in a condescending fashion.

"My Natalya has been lost for a long time. You think I do not know this?"

"I think you're trying to keep how she really died a

secret. I think you're willing to do anything to try and maintain your family honour. Especially now your son is dead."

"Do not speak of my son."

Martha let out a whimper as Petrov tightened his grip on her arm. His pale eyes narrowed into slits. Brady knew he had hit a nerve.

"How did your son die, Vasili? A skiing accident? Was it really an accident? Or did he take his life like your wife and daughter. Tell me... Were they all trying to escape you?"

"You know nothing about my family. How dare you – "

"I know a lot more than you think."

Brady watched as Petrov's face grew redder with anger. Martha squirmed beside him. Desperate to be released.

Just a little longer, Martha. Hold on just a little longer...

"I know that your wife hanged herself. Tired of your dominating rule and cold-heartedness. I know your daughter found the body. That you tried to cover it up. Did everything you could to maintain your family's reputation. To stop people from believing you weren't the family man you'd built your brand around.

"It's probably what gave your daughter the idea – don't you think? Tell me, what do you think was going through her mind that morning when she walked down to the olive grove? Do you think she was sad? Or do you think she was happy to finally be saying goodbye to you? If you ask me, I think Natalya made the right decision."

"You take my daughter's name out of your goddamn mouth."

Brady had done it. He'd hit the nerve. In one movement Petrov let go of Martha and lunged toward Brady. His eyes bulging with hatred. His hands reaching out for his throat.

Brady ducked. Avoided Petrov's reach just in time.

Watched the man stumble and struggle to regain his balance.

"Go, Martha! Out the back door. Find Frankie!"

Brady pushed the young girl out of the room. Turned. Faced Vasili Petrov. Heard the door open and close behind him. Knew at least she was safe.

Petrov let out a deep sigh. Cracked his neck from side to side.

"No matter." He shrugged. "My men will get to her before yours do."

Brady had no idea if Petrov was bluffing. There wasn't time to consider it. He trusted Frankie to take care of things outside. He had to focus on the man in front of him.

"Besides," Petrov continued. "It's time you and I had our little chat. Man to man. Father to father."

Brady watched Petrov carefully. Waited for the Russian to make his next move.

"Ashley, yes? She is nearly the same age as Natalya was when she died. The relationship between a father and his daughter is something else. Something special. You only hold her hand for a few years. You hold her heart forever."

Petrov paused. Put his hands in his pockets. Rocked on his heels.

"You are right, Mr Brady. Natalya hung herself. At the end of my olive grove, just like her mother. You have done your research. I am impressed."

"It comes with the job."

"It was nothing special. Two dozen olive trees maybe. Some of them three hundred years old. I walk down there every morning. Or at least I used to. I watched the sun rising. One thing you can count on in Tuscany. You can always watch the sunrise. Not like back home. It was one of the things that drew me to the place. That and Natalya's mother…

"So there I am, walking down my olive grove. Wondering if I can arrange to be back again for the harvest. Late October. Early November. There's something special about your own olive oil. Not that you'd know, Mr Brady. You strike me more as a… supermarket sauce kind of man. Not quite the same, is it?"

Brady continued to watch Petrov. Remained quiet. Refused to rise to the bait.

"It's a Saturday morning. The sun rising on another beautiful day. Natalya had told me she was going for a morning run. That girl could run, Mr Brady. Like the wind. There was a smile she'd flash at me when she ran past. A smile that said 'I can do anything'. I think to myself – if you could do anything my girl, why did you do that?

"I'm trailing my hand through some long grass. Thinking about the harvest. And there's my child. My daughter. My only fucking daughter. She was hanging from a tree at the end of the olive grove. A redbud tree. Purple flowers. Cercis siliquastrum. You know what's significant about the redbud tree, Mr Brady?"

Brady shook his head.

"Judas, Mr Brady. Legend has it that Judas hung himself from a redbud tree. After he'd betrayed Our Lord. Judas and my daughter. Hanging from a redbud tree."

92

"I have a question for you."

"I imagine you have many. Go on..."

"Why did you hang her like that? From the tree? You must know the connection between her and the tarot cards. But I can't figure out why you did it."

Petrov smiled. Let out a satisfied sigh.

"I knew you would puzzle over that one, Mr Brady. And there – of course – is your answer."

Brady furrowed his brow. Didn't understand.

"I thought it would be funny," Petrov shrugged. "There was a certain irony behind it. She'd taught chemistry at school. Believed in facts. In science. And then she let herself get controlled by silly playing cards and whimsical beliefs.

"I decided if that was the world she wanted to live in, then it was the world she could die in too. Plus, I knew it would send you on a wild goose chase. But just because there are crumbs on the ground doesn't mean the trail leads somewhere. That's a lesson you'll do well to remember, Mr Brady."

Brady opened his mouth to respond. Decided against it.

Petrov was like no man he had ever dealt with before. He was unpredictable. He was ruthless. And Brady knew exactly what he needed to do.

He glanced out of the window. It was almost completely dark outside. Not much longer and Anya would be signalling the end of her twenty minutes.

Just keep him talking. Keep him distracted. Then you can make your move...

"I have to admit, I have some sympathy for you. God knows how I'd react if anything happened to my daughter. *Some* sympathy. But I wouldn't start murdering people. I wouldn't try to hide the truth about what happened. That would dishonour her memory. And I would never do that."

"You speak like a good man, Mr Brady, but tell me – if I held your daughter here in my hands, would you say the same thing?"

Definitely not.

"I would."

Petrov tutted. Shook his head.

"You disappoint me, Mr Brady. Maybe we're not as alike as I first thought. I would never lie."

Now it was Brady's turn to laugh.

"You lie about everything. The whole reason we're here is because you lied about how your daughter died. And now you're doing whatever it takes to cover up the truth."

Brady watched Petrov clench his jaw at the mention of his daughter. That was his weak point. Brady needed to focus on it.

"But what are you going to do about me? I know that your daughter hung herself. You've just told me the story yourself. Are you going to kill me for knowing the truth? Hunt me down and hang me from a tree like you did Sarah Trueman?"

Petrov grinned. "I'm not going to kill you, Mr Brady. But you're going to wish I had."

He took a step closer to Brady. His pale eyes glinted with anger. With a thirst for revenge. For salvation.

"I'm going to cut your eyes out. And your tongue. Then I'm going to cut off your hands. You'll hear your daughter. But you'll never see her. You'll never speak to her again. You'll never hold her. And one day, she'll come to you with a grandchild. A grandchild you'll never see. Never hold. Never take for a walk. 'Why can't Grandpa come with us?' 'Because Vasili Petrov cut his eyes out for thinking he was clever.'"

Before Brady knew what was happening Petrov lunged for him. A sharp piece of metal glinted in his hand. Brady moved his arm up to block. Felt the slash of metal through skin. Cried out in pain.

He pushed back against Petrov. Managed to knock the blade from his hand. Blood poured freely from Brady's arm as he fought back. Grappling with Petrov on the worn linoleum floor.

But Petrov was fitter than Brady. Tougher than Brady. He found himself pinned underneath the Russian's bulky frame. Petrov's hands around his throat. He held him steady. Applying just enough pressure to stop Brady from moving, but not enough to cause any serious damage.

"I said I'm not going to kill you. But you're going to wish I had."

Brady squirmed in horror as Petrov reached into his inside pocket. Produced another blade. He kicked out with his legs, but Petrov held him firmly in place with his own. Brady was trapped. He'd finally met his match.

"Let's start with an eye, shall we? Then you can watch me do the rest."

Brady moved his head frantically from side to side. Tried

to pivot with his legs. Punch with his arms. He clipped Petrov on the side but the man barely flinched. His smile grew wider across his face. He was enjoying this. Thriving off it.

"I wouldn't struggle so much if I were you. You don't want this to leave a scar. That'll only make your grandchildren more frightened of you."

Brady snapped his eyes shut and continued to fight back. He felt like a baby gazelle trapped underneath lion's paw. He felt helpless. Frightened. Desperate.

He pictured Ash's face. Held onto the image of his daughter.

I'm sorry, Ash. I'm sorry for always trying to be the hero.

Brady felt the blade on his face. Felt the searing pain as it cut into his cheek. He couldn't help it anymore. He opened his mouth. Cried out in pain. Blocked out all other sensations until all he could hear was his own cry.

Then all the air was knocked out of him.

Petrov collapsed.

The force of it made Brady open his eyes. Both of his eyes. He could see. Blood obscured his vision. But he still had it.

He blinked. Felt Petrov on top of him. Felt the pressure on his limbs subside. Pushed. Strained. Forced the body off him. Shuffled backwards. Caught his breath.

Petrov was dead.

Brady looked at the body. Couldn't believe what he was seeing.

Petrov lay motionless. A bullet hole in his forehead. Blood slowly pooling round him.

How? Where? Who?

Brady repositioned himself onto his hands and knees. He was covered in blood. His own. Petrov's.

He put a hand to his face and felt a gash below his right eye. Saw the defensive cut on his arm. Felt himself go dizzy.

Crawling over toward the body, Brady put two fingers against Petrov's neck to confirm what he already knew.

He looked closer at the bullet hole. Whoever had shot him had known what they were doing.

Frankie didn't carry a gun. Whatever backup Anya had called couldn't have done this either.

Brady rolled back onto his heels. He had one murderer dead in front of him. But another case had just landed in his lap.

"Boss?"

Brady looked up and saw Frankie standing in the doorway. She stopped just before crossing the threshold into the room. Took in the scene.

"Jesus Christ. What happened. Are you okay?"

"He's dead. Petrov's dead."

"I can see that. Who shot him?"

Brady let out a deep breath. Felt another wave of dizziness crash over him. Wondered how much blood he'd lost.

"I have no idea."

93

The first thing he recognised was the sound of hospital machines beeping. Then the pain.

Brady opened his eyes. Panicked. Could only see through one of them. Brought his arms up in fear.

"Dad, it's okay. You've got an eye patch on. You're okay."

Relief washed over him as Brady heard his daughter's voice. He looked to the side. Saw her sitting in a hospital chair. A blanket draped over her.

"Hi sweetheart," he forced a smile onto his face. "Are you okay?"

Ash laughed.

"Yeah, I'm okay Dad. Are *you?* I can't decide whether you look more like a pirate or a *Bond* villain. The nurses seem to like it though."

Right on cue two women walked into the room. One doctor, one nurse.

"How are you feeling, DCI Brady?" The doctor spoke while the nurse checked the dressing on his arm. "Any pain?"

"A little." Brady lied. "When can I take the eyepatch off?"

"Two weeks. You've got a nasty cut there. Lucky not to lose the eye. But you'll recover to full health. Have you fighting fit again before the summer."

The summer... Fuck.

"Ash – what day is it?"

Brady looked at his daughter. Saw her smile. Tease down the blanket to reveal a 'Birthday Girl' badge pinned to her chest.

"I am the worst father ever," Brady groaned. "You can't be spending your birthday looking after me in a hospital ward. I'm sorry, darling. Happy birthday. We'll celebrate properly I promise. Extra cake and presents. Whatever you want."

"It's fine Dad, don't worry."

Ash smiled again. Brady felt his heart thump in his chest.

When he'd been on the floor of that farmhouse with Petrov, there was a real part of him that had believed he'd never see his daughter again. Now just seeing her smile – it meant everything to Brady.

"Come here."

"Are you sure? Doesn't your arm hurt?"

"My arm could be hanging off and I'd still want to give you a hug. Now come here, Ash. Let me hold you."

Brady held his daughter and thanked whoever was watching over him for granting him that moment. He closed his eyes and breathed in her familiar smell. Took comfort in the way her hair tickled his face.

You were right, you bastard. I'd do anything for this girl. Anything and more.

94

The incessant beeping of machines echoed round the ward. Brady glanced at the clock. *04:47.* He'd slept for longer than usual. The drugs must have taken an effect.

Carefully he pushed himself into an upright position. Using his one good arm that wasn't strapped up in a sling. His eye patch was still in place. For now. There was no chance he was keeping that on for two weeks. Brady didn't fancy walking around Whitby like a Halloween pirate.

I'm going to cut your eyes out. And your tongue. Then I'm going to cut off your hands. You'll hear your daughter. But you'll never see her. You'll never speak to her again.

Petrov's words haunted Brady.

One day, she'll come to you with a grandchild. A grandchild you'll never see. Never hold. Never take for a walk. 'Why can't Grandpa come with us?' 'Because Vasili Petrov cut his eyes out for thinking he was clever.'

Who had shot him?

Frankie and Dan Keillor had done a full sweep around the farmhouse after Brady had been taken away in an ambulance. They'd found nothing. No footprints. No tracks. No evidence of anyone being there. Nothing.

Except a bullet hole in a Russian man's head...

Now Whitby was dealing with an assassin. A murderer was bad enough. A professional marksman like that was something else.

Brady swung his legs out of bed. He needed to walk around. To get his blood pumping. Try to figure out what had happened.

He wrapped his hospital gown round himself. Shuffled his feet into a pair of paper slippers. Pushed back the curtain around his bed. There were three other people on the ward, all sleeping soundly. Brady made it to the door as quietly as possible. Surveyed the hallway. The nurses station sat to his right; an elderly nurse hunched over some paperwork. Brady turned left. Rounded a corner without being seen.

He was heading in the direction of the canteen when his pocket started buzzing. His phone. Brady pulled it out. Looked at the screen. Saw a number he didn't recognise.

"Michael Brady."

"Hello Mihailo."

The accent was immediately recognisable. Southern European mixed with 70s American TV. And there was only one person who called him Mihailo.

Marko Vrukić.

You've changed your number.

Brady pulled open a door. Stepped into an empty storage cupboard. Turned on the light. Took a deep breath.

Marko Vrukić was not a man to take lightly. The Serbian warlord had come into Brady's life a few years ago when he was working on another case. The stories Brady had read about him made for the most chilling of bedtime stories.

Born into a mountain village with a fierce, tribal culture. Vrukić's first killing was rumoured to be his own father, when he was aged just fifteen. By the time he turned twenty he was a fully-fledged armed robber, spending the 70s running around Europe, holding up banks, gambling away the proceeds and fathering children.

He then became the leader of the *Delije* and formed his own Volunteer Guard at the dawn of the Serb-Croat war. By the time the war ended he was a hero, with a hardcore following of hundreds of men willing to die for him. The blood of tens of thousands of others on his hands.

Through some bizarre twist of fate he winds up in the English countryside. Trades information for safety. Supports Aston Villa. Raises money for charity.

And calls Michael Brady in the early hours of the morning...

"Marko. This is an unexpected call. What can I do for you?"

"Unexpected perhaps, but never unplanned, Mihailo. Tell me, is the eye patch just for show or did he manage to take your eye after all?"

A chill ran down Brady's spine. He tugged on his hospital gown. Felt exposed. How did Vrukić know?

He chose his words carefully.

"He missed, thankfully. And I still have my tongue and my hands too. Though I get the feeling you already know that."

"I do, Mihailo. I do. You asked me what you could do for me – I will tell you; you have already done it. I am in your debt once again."

Brady paused again.

"Sorry, Marko. I'm not sure I understand."

"Vasili Petrov."

"He's dead."

"Yes. I shot him."

"You – "

Not for the first time when speaking to Vrukić, Brady was lost for words. He leant backwards against the door of the storage cupboard. Steadied himself.

"Why?"

"Well, not myself exactly. But I gave the order. Vasili Petrov had been a thorn in my side for many years. You brought him out of the shadows. You presented me with an opportunity that I could not ignore."

"You had business with Petrov?"

"Business is not exactly the term I would use, Mihailo. But we had a history, yes. Not a very pleasant one. His work over the last few years had become – how to best put it – *inconvenient* for me. Troublesome, if you will. To have him so close by and working with someone who is in my debt, well... Like I say the opportunity arose and I took it. For both of our benefits it would seem."

"I assume I'll never find any evidence of whoever you had shoot him?"

"You will not."

"So what am I supposed to do now? Close the case? Move on with my life?"

"Exactly that, Mihailo. Enjoy the quiet time with your daughter. Maybe take a holiday. Celebrate being alive."

Brady chewed on his bottom lip. Didn't know what to say. Vrukić had saved his life. But that didn't mean he liked the way it had happened. As a detective he only wanted to stamp *case closed* when he'd gathered all the evidence. When someone was locked up behind bars. This felt wrong. But there was nothing he could do about it.

"It puts me however, in a bit of a difficult situation."

Brady raised his eyebrows. "How?"

"I was in your debt before this and now – albeit inadvertently – but you have done something else which benefits me. I am in your debt twice over and..." Vrukić paused. Gave Brady some time to think. "You remember how I had planned to repay my debt to you."

"I do."

Grace...

"Last time we spoke, you said you didn't want the name. You said it could not sit quietly on your desk. What if I told you it did not have to sit quietly anymore? What if I told you that Vasili Petrov is not the only one who met an untimely end this last week?"

Brady felt his knees buckle beneath him. Steadied himself.

How long have I wanted to know this? To have revenge on the man who gave that order. The man who ended my Gracie's life. But...

Brady saw the glint in Petrov's pale eyes. The thirst for revenge. For salvation. He saw the smile on the man's face as he wielded the knife. The joy that the violence brought him.

Then he saw his daughter. Ash. Grace.

Brady saw his family together. Smiling. Laughing.

He pictured him and Ash walking Archie on the beach. Splitting a pizza on the balcony. Watching a movie.

That was what he wanted this future to look like. Light and happiness. Not shrouded in darkness and revenge.

"He's dead?"

"He's dead, Mihailo. I confirmed the reports myself."

There was another long pause.

"Then that's enough for me. Thank you, Marko."

"You don't want the name?"

"What good will a dead man's name do? My wife is dead.

She's not coming back. But my daughter is still alive. That is what I choose to focus on."

"A valiant motivation, Mihailo. Then I shall leave you. You know where I am if you ever change your mind."

I do. But if I play my cards right, then hopefully it will never come to that...

95

"Boss. I didn't expect to see you in today. How are you feeling?"

"Like I've been hit by a Russian semi-truck. But I'm alive. That's all that matters. How're things here?"

"We've done everything we can at the farmhouse. Closed off the Cleveland Way. Anya's scoured the whole area. Dan Keillor too. They've not found anything. But we'll keep looking."

You can look all you want Frankie, you'll never find anything.

"Good stuff. Is Martha doing okay?"

"As okay as you can be after being held by a murderer who your mother was in cahoots with. I think it'll be the latter bit that's harder to come to terms with."

Brady nodded. Fiddled with his tie.

"I hate wearing this thing."

"Here."

Frankie stepped in front of him. Put her hands up to his tie. Just like Brady she was dressed in all black. Her dress hugged her figure, accentuating her curves in just the right places. Brady's eyes moved fleetingly down and back up her body, resting on her lips. She chewed the bottom one faintly as she re-tied his tie. Brady watched closely.

"There."

Frankie looked up at him. Held his eye contact. Opened her mouth slightly. Didn't say anything else.

Brady copied her movement. Found – as was happening a lot to him recently – that he didn't know what to say. Didn't want her to leave.

"Ready?" Frankie asked eventually.

Brady nodded. Followed her out of the precinct. Walked slowly to the church.

JAKE'S FUNERAL was busier than Brady had expected.

He sat four rows back. A respectable, but acceptable distance. There were a lot of faces he couldn't place. Some that he could. Claire sat at the front. Flanked by parents on both sides. There were a few lads Brady recognised from the pub, Jake's friends from football. Maybe about twenty or thirty others.

The officiant spoke fondly of Jake. Gave the usual spiel about how he was loved by his friends and family. How he served the community. How he was taken from the world too soon.

Then Claire stood up to give the eulogy.

Brady watched her closely. Saw the lump in her throat. Her bottom lip quivering as she walked up to the lectern. Placed her piece of paper down. Looked up for the first time.

There was silence for a few moments as Claire gathered her emotions, then she spoke.

Brady didn't attempt to hide how he was feeling. He let the tears fall freely as Claire spoke. Let her see that she wasn't suffering through this alone.

I should go round. Not straight away. Give it a week or so. But I should definitely go round. Show her that she's not alone.

He couldn't help but feel guilty for not doing more. For not realising. For not speaking to Jake sooner.

The case always seemed to get in the way.

It had got in the way of Jake. In the way of his relationship with Siobhan. In the way of his daughter's birthday. In the way of his wife...

Brady listened to Claire speak and wondered how much more his job would take from him. If there would eventually come a day when he couldn't put up with it any longer. He'd thought that day had come when he'd first moved to Whitby. Then Patrick's death changed everything. Now he'd lost someone else.

How many more people would his job claim?

When would it be enough?

96

Brady waved goodbye to Frankie and the others. Declined the invitation to the Black Horse. Wanted to be with family.

He parked outside his sister's house. Knocked on the front door. Let himself in. Found her sat at the kitchen table.

"Mike? Is everything okay?"

Brady shook his head. Waited for Kate to stand up. Wrapped his arms around her. Cried.

"It's okay, Mike. I've got you."

Brady let his sister hold him. Felt the emotions rush through him. Of losing Jake. Of nearly losing everyone that night in the farmhouse. Of Grace…

Vrukić's words still echoed in his head.

He's dead, Mihailo. I confirmed the reports myself.

His wife's killer was dead. That chapter was closed. But then why did Brady feel like he had lost her all over again?

His body shook with sobs. Kate squeezed him. Supported his weight. Gave him all the time he needed.

"Sit down." She said after the tears had eventually dried up. "I'll make you a cup of tea."

He did as he was told.

"It's healthy to let it out, Mike. You need to have moments like this. Was it the funeral today?"

Brady nodded.

"Good. Then you're doing the right thing. It's healthy to show your emotions. Remember when Dad died? You went into auto-pilot. Made all the arrangements. Sorted Mum out. Wrote the eulogy. And never allowed yourself any time to grieve."

Kate placed a mug of tea in front of him. Slid the sugar over.

"It didn't do you any good then, and it won't do you any good now. You need to talk about how you're feeling."

"I feel stupid, Kate. I feel responsible. Why didn't I see it sooner? Why didn't I do something about it?"

"You can't blame yourself, Mike. Some people – there's just no saving them. That doesn't mean they don't deserve to be saved or anything like that. It just means that no matter what anyone does, their path is already laid for them. And you can't hold yourself responsible for that."

Brady sniffed. Sipped his tea.

"It's not just Jake," he admitted. "It's Grace too. It's like everything that's happened recently has brought all of that back up again."

That, and Vrukić telling me the man who killed her is finally dead.

"That's only natural, Mike. Grief doesn't work in a straightforward manner. I'm the same with Bill and before the old bugger got cancer, I didn't even want to be with him anymore. Then, next thing, I'm in the post office and the cashier mentions him and I burst into tears. There's no logic to it. It's shit. But we've just got to roll with the punches and believe that eventually we'll come out the other side stronger."

Brady exhaled. Looked up at his sister. Reached out for her hand across the table. Held onto it.

"Thank you, Kate. I know I haven't been round as much as I should have been recently. I haven't always been there. But thank you. Thank you for being there for me."

"That's what I'm here for you daft bugger." Kate smiled. Squeezed his hand again. "Besides, there's something I've been meaning to ask you."

"Oh?"

"Have you ever been to Carlisle?"

Brady looked at his sister with a confused expression. Raised his eyebrows.

"I found a nice-looking holiday house out there the other week. Four bedrooms. On the edge of the river Eden. Plenty of space for Archie to run around in. I thought maybe you and I could take the girls out there for a little family holiday? Take a week off work. Clear our heads for a little while."

Brady looked at his sister again. Saw the hopeful smile on her face.

"That sounds like a brilliant idea. Just brilliant, Kate. I'd love to. Ash would love to. Archie I know for sure would love to. When?"

"Soon? I was thinking over the second May Bank Holiday weekend."

"Perfect. Thank you, Kate. That is exactly what we need."

97

Brady walked out of his sister's house with a smile on his face. After everything that had happened over the last few weeks, it was nice to know that Kate was always on his side. That there was always someone in his corner.

There was just one more conversation Brady needed to have before he could go home.

HE PARKED where he usually did. Almost instinctively reached over to the passenger seat for a bottle of wine or a bunch of flowers. Had neither. Wondered if he should.

Or would that be offensive? I've come to officially break up with you. But I brought flowers...

Brady shook his head. Climbed out of the Tiguan. Walked toward the front door. Watched it open before he'd even had a chance to knock.

Siobhan stood there. Two plastic bags of clothes over-flowing in her hands. Her hair was a mess. She wore a white t-shirt under a pair of old dungarees. One side of them done up, the other hanging loose.

"Michael. Hey."

Brady found himself dumbstruck for a few moments. He'd wanted a minute to compose himself. To prepare what he was going to say. He'd had neither.

"Are you going somewhere?"

America you idiot...

"I was just going to put these in the car. Clothes for the charity shop. I'm having a bit of a clear out."

"Oh." Brady nodded. Continued to stand awkwardly in the way. "When do you leave?"

"Saturday."

Brady looked at Siobhan, bags in hand. Even with her hair tied up in a messy bun and her dungarees on, she still looked beautiful. Beautiful, but not like the woman he wanted.

"Do you want to come inside?"

Brady nodded. Followed her in.

Siobhan put the plastic bags down by the front door. Walked into the kitchen.

"Cup of tea?"

"Sure."

Brady waited until her back was turned before he spoke again.

"Siobhan, I'm sorry. I know I've not treated you properly these last few weeks. I could use the case as an excuse again but I'm not going to. You deserve a lot better than me. And I really, truly hope you find it in America."

Siobhan let out a deep sigh. Turned around. Looked at Brady. He couldn't read her expression.

"I do love you, Michael Brady. But even I have to admit I doubt whether we could ever properly work."

"And that's my fault. I can only apologise again, Siobhan. I'm really sorry."

"Don't be." Siobhan took a step toward him. Put a finger on his lips. "I've enjoyed the time we've had, Michael. Some romances are meant to be like ours. Fast. Hot. Exciting."

Brady laughed. "I can't remember the last time anyone described me as hot or exciting. As for fast, I hope that isn't referring to the bedroom..."

Siobhan rolled her eyes. Smiled. Turned back to making the tea. But just like that Brady felt the tension disappear between them.

There had been a time when he'd thought he could have a future with Siobhan. Then a time when he thought he couldn't have a future at all. Now he was just happy to see what happened next.

Siobhan would go to America. Maybe they'd keep in touch for a little while, exchange a few text messages here and there. But then she'd move on. Find someone new.

And Brady was fine with that. Happy even. Because if Siobhan moved on, then perhaps he could do the same too...

98

"**D**ad, there's someone at the door for you. That girl who came round the other week."

"That girl from the other week?"

"Claire, I think?"

"Oh, Christ. Ash – take Archie upstairs, will you? I should be the one visiting her not the other way around."

Brady ran a hand through his hair. Did his best to tame it.

"Sure," Ash took Archie by the collar. Led him upstairs. "But if she comes round a third time you know I'll start to get suspicious."

"Very funny, Ash. Why don't you go and research activities for Carlisle? Find some nice walks to take Archie on."

"Great, now you've said W-A-L-K, Dad. You've got him all excited."

Brady smiled as Ash disappeared upstairs. Wondered what Claire was doing on his doorstep. The funeral was only yesterday. He'd planned to go round later in the week. She must have something important to say.

. . .

"Claire, how are you doing?"

She looked different from yesterday. Less pale. More determined. He invited her inside.

"I'm good, Mr Brady. That is, I'm not good, but I'm getting there. I've found a new place. Moving in a couple of weeks. Fresh start. And, I'm twenty-two now. Time for a clean slate. A change. That's why I'm here."

"Sorry, Claire. I don't follow... You want to sit outside? The sun's going down but it's warm enough. You want a drink? There's some beer in the fridge."

She shook her head, the blonde hair slightly shorter.

"I want to ask your advice."

"No problem. Fire away."

"Jake. He loved being a copper. Maybe he wasn't a very good one – "

"He was – "

She held her hand up. "You don't have to say anything. I knew his faults. I think maybe... I was talking to someone at work. She was telling me about addictive personalities. I think maybe Jake was just unlucky. That's what I tell myself anyway."

Brady nodded. "There might be a grain of truth in that."

And it's something to hold onto...

"Anyway, he'd come home at night. And he'd tell me what he'd done. And..."

"It started to sound appealing? Didn't he ever mention the paperwork?"

She shook her head. "Not appealing. It started to sound important."

"Blimey, Claire, what do you do? Deliver babies. There can't be many things more important than that."

"Maybe. But I've been online. I've got the qualifications. I'd like to join the police."

Brady heard the conviction in her voice. Nodded. "What's it say online? You'll need the ability to stay calm in stressful situations? Midwife probably ticks that box. You're sure you're not doing this as a reaction to Jake?"

She shook her head. "I don't think so. I talked about it with my mum. There's the practical side as well. The NHS hasn't got any money. There's a good chance midwifery will be off to York or Middlesbrough."

"And you don't want that?"

"No."

"Come out here, Claire." Brady stood up. Opened the balcony doors. Stepped outside.

"Here," he said. "Being a copper's given me the best times of my life," Brady paused. "It's given me the worst as well. You see that hill?"

"The moon?"

Brady nodded. "It does look like the moon doesn't it? That's where I scattered my wife's ashes. If I wasn't a copper she'd still be alive. So being a copper can take you as far down as it's possible to go. You're going to neglect the people you love. Find there's things you can't talk to them about. Find there's things you *daren't* talk to them about. But I wouldn't do anything else. 'Cos you're doing the right thing, Claire. I'm old-fashioned. I believe in right and wrong. Crime and punishment. Crime and capturing the bastards that did it. So there's highs and lows, Claire. Real highs, bloody dark lows. But look at Whitby. The people walking past. They're worth keeping safe."

He looked at her. Saw she was listening. Really listening.

"That's a long speech, I'm sorry. If that's what you want to do, go home and fill in the forms. You're tough and you're brave, Claire. And you know what – Jake would be bloody proud of you."

99

B rady was up early. The sun was shining and he found he had a smile on his face. Dave's bacon and a walk on the beach lay ahead of him. There were few better ways to start the day.

"Sorry Arch. I know I'm always apologising. What if I bring you back a sausage? And then we do a long walk this afternoon? Deal?"

He reached down and scratched Archie behind the ears. Noticed something on the welcome mat.

An envelope.

It was far too early for the postman.

Brady reached down. Picked it up. Turned it over.

Mihailo.

He almost dropped the envelope. Vrukić knew where he lived.

Of course, he does. He knows whatever he wants to know. That shouldn't surprise you.

Faltering for a moment, Brady remained by the front door. His last conversation with Vrukić hung heavy in his head. He'd declined the finer details. Grace's killer was dead. But he still didn't know who that was...

Carefully – as if he was opening someone up for heart surgery – Brady teased open the envelope. Inside was another smaller envelope, and a letter.

Mihailo.

You said you did not want to know the details of your wife's murderer, and I honour that. However, you strike me as a man much like myself, and I know that many nights alone lead to nothing but questions.

In this envelope you will find all the details. Everything I know. Everything I have uncovered. It is yours to do with as you please.

Use it wisely. As I'm sure you will.

Your friend, Marko.

Brady turned the smaller envelope over in his hand. Ran his finger across the seal. Knew what he had to do.

'I need to know who killed her, Dad. Who took her from me. From both of us. Because... Out there. Somewhere out there. Is the person who killed her. And if I don't know... Well, I don't know if I can cope with that. And I don't know how you'll cope with that. Forever.'

HE MADE his way back upstairs as quietly as he could and placed the envelope in the bottom drawer of his bedside table.

One day it would be time for Ash to know the truth about her mother. Now Brady could give it to her. He truly didn't feel like he needed that information to move on anymore, but if his daughter did, then he would give it to her.

Whatever Ash wanted, he would do his best to provide.

100

"I've got you a bacon sandwich." Brady handed the brown paper bag to Frankie. "Unless you've changed your order? Feels like it's been a while."

"Too long. But no, I'll never turn Dave's bacon down." Frankie smiled and took the paper bag. "Bandstand?"

"I thought maybe we'd walk along the beach?"

"Sure. Nice day for it."

The two of them made their way down to the sand. Seaweed littered the beach. Evidence of a very high tide the night before. Brady and Frankie picked their way through it. Walked north toward Sandsend.

"There's still no word on the gunman, boss. Before you ask. No leads either."

"I think that might be one that we have to admit defeat on, Frankie. I'm thinking there could be any number of people who'd want to put a bullet in Petrov's head."

"But who knew exactly where he'd be? At exactly that time? That's got to narrow the list down a little."

"Sure. We'll keep Dan Keillor on it. See what he can find."

He'll find nothing. But I'll give it a week or so. Make it look like we're giving it a proper try...

The two of them walked in silence for a while. The early morning sun broke through the clouds. Provided a bit of respite from the ever-present wind off the sea.

Brady thought about everything they'd been through with Petrov. About everything he'd said.

"He made me realise something Frankie."

"Who's that?"

"Petrov. There was a point when he was on top of me, when he was pinning me down. I truly believed that was it for me. I thought that was the end. And you know what – it's taught me a hard lesson."

"What?"

"All my life I've played by the rules. Sure, I've twisted them at times, but I've never crossed that line. Then the other week when I had that tarot reading. He said to me: *you'll get all the answers you want, but you'll pay a heavy price.*

"At the time I didn't understand it. I thought I'd have to lose something. Give something up. But I understand what the price is now. I'm just like him. Petrov. I play by the rules until they don't suit me. Then I bend them. Twist them. Find the corners I can cut to get what I want. I always tell myself it'll only go so far. That I'll never cross that line. But when he was there, when he was in front of me, talking about my daughter. I wanted to cross it. I wanted to hurt him. And it made me realise I'm just like him. I just haven't had that moment yet which sends me over the edge."

"I think that's a slight over exaggeration, boss. Just because you'd do anything for Ash doesn't mean there's a murderer lying in wait within you."

"There could be. I guess we'll never know. And I'll have to live with that. Console myself that I'm on the side of the angels. And if I'm not at least I'm stopping the demons. Until something changes. Until I have that moment."

"So what do you want us to do? Lock you up like Frankenstein's monster? Keep you prisoner in case you suddenly snap and go on a killing spree?"

"It just made me realise that things aren't always as they seem, that's all. That maybe there is no good and bad. No right or wrong. No cold, hard evidence."

"Michael Brady giving up on cold, hard evidence. I never thought I'd see the day."

"Neither did I, Frankie. But I guess there's going to be a lot of changes around here in the coming months. Me opening up my horizons to other methods of policework likely won't be the most dramatic. In fact..."

Brady paused and looked at Frankie. Knew it was time.

"I think you have something to tell me. Don't you, DS Thomson?"

Frankie looked at him. Looked down at the sand. Looked back up.

"How long have you known?"

"Kershaw told me just after we found Jake. That man really knows how to twist the knife."

Frankie dropped her head. Talked into the collar of her leather jacket.

"I'm sorry, Mike. I wanted to tell you. I just didn't know how to find the words."

"It's okay. I've come to terms with it now. Besides – I had a visitor last night. I might already have your replacement lined up."

"That fast, huh?"

"Claire Gardner. Jake's girlfriend. Said all that time with Jake had made policework feel important to her. Said she wanted to sign up."

"She'll make a good copper."

"I don't doubt it. Though not many come as good as you. Where is it you're going?"

"Leeds."

"Bloody Leeds. What's Lochie got to say about that? I thought you were enjoying the countryside life in Hutton-le-Hole with him?"

"We broke up."

"What? When? Christ, I'm sorry Frankie. This case... I've lost track of everything."

"Don't worry about it, Mike. I wasn't exactly broadcasting it. Too many trips up to Scotland. Too many evenings coming second best to his mother..."

"Ah, say no more. It can't be easy coming between a Scotsman and his mother."

"Or enjoyable."

"So when do you leave?"

"June. They want me over there for the Headingley Test. Just my luck."

"And I bet you thought leaving me behind would mean you heard less about cricket. Hard luck Frankie..."

Frankie laughed. The two of them turned around. Started walking back toward Whitby.

Brady looked across at Frankie as they walked. Watched her hair blowing in the breeze. Saw the blush that had formed on her cheeks from their walk.

Things with Grace felt like they had finally turned a corner. Like he could finally move on. Siobhan was on the other side of the world. Frankie wasn't his colleague anymore.

Whitby to Leeds was only seventy miles.

And I've always wanted to see England bat at Headingley...

SALT IN THE WOUNDS (MICHAEL BRADY: BOOK 1)

His best friend has been murdered, his daughter's in danger.

There's only one answer. Going back to his old life.

The one that cost him his wife...

Michael Brady was a high-flying detective, working on a high-profile case.

And much too close to the truth.

Someone arranged a hit-and-run.

But they missed Brady. And hit his wife.

And after six months sitting by her bed, he took the only decision he could take. He turned the machine off.

Now he's back home in Whitby. Trying to rebuild his life. And be a good dad to his teenage daughter.

But when his best friend is murdered Brady – unwillingly at first – is drawn into the investigation.

And when the only people he has left are threatened, he finds there's only one answer.

Going back to his old life...

THE RIVER RUNS DEEP (MICHAEL BRADY: BOOK 2)

Good people do bad things

Bad people do good things

Sometimes it's hard to tell the difference...

Gina's body has floated down the River Esk. She was a farmer's wife. And it looks like an accident.

But Michael Brady has his doubts.

Brady's back in the police – and he needs to prove himself.

Is it murder? Or does Brady *need* it to be murder?

It's a year since his wife died. He's feeling lonely. And he's still trying to balance being a single dad and being a Detective Chief Inspector.

"Would this be a good place to kill her?"

The pathologist put his reading glasses on. Looked at Brady's phone. "Looks perfect. Looks better than perfect. If I had to drown someone that'd be as good a place as any. No paths near it?"

"None that I could see."

"So he's met her there. Something's happened. He's dragged her down to the edge..."

Brady's convinced the answer lies in Gina's past. But his boss is doing everything he can to stop Brady discovering what that past was.

Then DS Frankie Thomson uncovers the truth. And suddenly there's not one person who might have wanted to kill Gina. There's a hundred and one...

Brady stood up and walked over to the window. Tried to process what Frankie had told him. Tried to work out the implications. He turned round. Frankie was bending forward, reaching for her laptop. "You need to prove this to me," he said. "And you need to do it now. Because there's no way I'm going to sleep. Not knowing I've wasted two weeks. And that Kershaw has known all the time. And that..."

"That someone has to tell Ian Foster."

"What did I say in the car? His life was unravelling. This is going to tear it apart."

THE ECHO OF BONES (MICHAEL BRADY: BOOK 3)

"Find her for me, Mr Brady. I know she's dead. I know I'll never see her again. But find her. Give me a place to go on her birthday. Christmas Day. Somewhere I can take her teddy bear. Lay flowers. Find Alice for me, Mr Brady. Please..."

It's 20 years since Alice went missing.

There's never been any trace.

Until now.

Until some bones are found in a shallow grave on the cold, bleak North York Moors.

But is it Alice?

Or Becky? The other girl – who disappeared a month earlier...

Two local girls: two families that have finally learned to live with their grief.

But now Michael Brady must tell one family their daughter has been found.

And break the bad news to the other family.

No-one was ever convicted. Everyone's convinced the killer is in jail.

Everyone except Brady.

He thinks the real killer is still out there.

Brady has to re-open the old wounds. He has to find the real killer. And he has to stop seeing the similarities between his daughter and one of the murdered girls.

With the local families waiting for the 'killer' to come out of jail, with a boss determined to stop him discovering the truth – and without Frankie Thomson to help him – this is a case that affects Michael Brady like no other.

CHOKE BACK THE TEARS (MICHAEL BRADY: BOOK 4)

Michael Brady looked at Sandra Garrity's face. Grey skin. Bloodshot eyes open. Blue lips, her tongue protruding.

"Did you watch your husband die, Sandra? Or did he watch you die?"

"Brilliant. Brady is fast becoming the Yorkshire Rebus."

Billy and Sandra were childhood sweethearts.

Writing their names on a lovelock. Fastening it to the end of Whitby pier. Throwing the key into the sea.

A lifetime together. A happy retirement in a peaceful hamlet on the North Yorkshire Moors.

Until the day they were brutally murdered.

"Whoever did this – he didn't do it quickly. And he enjoyed it..."

Billy was a fisherman, making a living in the cold, cruel North Sea. One night his boat went down. Two crewmen drowned. Billy survived.

Are the families looking for revenge? It's the obvious conclusion.

But why have they waited so long?

Why have they killed Billy *and* Sandra?

And why kill them in such a barbaric way?

"This isn't a murder, Mike. It's an execution. A medieval execution."

THE EDGE OF TRUTH (MICHAEL BRADY: BOOK 5)

There are three sides to every story

Yours. Theirs.

And the Truth.

Michael Brady is back. *The Edge of Truth* is the fifth book in the series. And there's a ghost from Brady's past...

'This series gets better and better and better.'

'Brilliant. Brady is fast becoming the Yorkshire Rebus.'

The push that sent Diane Macdonald over the cliff edge was surprisingly gentle.

She was walking her dog on the cliff top. Runswick Bay, a few miles north of Whitby.

Thirty-six hours later her body is found at the bottom of the cliff.

Brady's convinced it's murder.

But there's no evidence.

And only one witness.

Gerry Donoghue, a homeless ex-veteran. A man with a deep, dark secret.

And now he's disappeared.

Leaving Brady with Diane's husband, Graham Macdonald – the ghost from Brady's past.

"It was Christmas Eve. We were eighteen or nineteen. Just back from our first term at university. Four of us went to Robin Hood's Bay. Why we didn't just get pissed in Whitby I'll never know. Lizzie gets into a car

driven by a boy called Graham Macdonald. His dad's the Chief Constable."

"This isn't going to end well."

"There was a crash. Lizzie died at the scene. Macdonald wasn't there. A crash that killed Lizzie, he escaped with a few bruises. The son of the Chief Constable was running away. Scampering across the fields, hand-in-hand with his guardian angel."

Twenty-five years later and Macdonald is an MP.

And a good friend of Brady's boss, Kershaw.

So there's pressure. Plenty of pressure.

And Michael Brady's not dealing with it very well.

He starts to make increasingly rash decisions – putting his personal and his professional relationships at risk.

But you know Brady by now.

He won't let it go.

He *can't* let it go...

REVIEWS & FUTURE WRITING PLANS

Thank you for reading *The Hanged Woman,* I really hope you enjoyed it.

If you did, could I ask you to leave a review on Amazon?

Reviews are really important for several reasons. Firstly, good reviews help to sell the book. Secondly, there are some review and book promotion sites that will only look at a book if it has a certain number of reviews and/or a certain number of 5* reviews. And lastly, reviews are feedback.

Feedback was so important to my Dad and he honestly took every comment, good or bad, on board. He always taught me that this was the only way to improve. And while he won't be able to read the reviews this time, I will. And I want to make sure I've done him justice.

As for future writing plans – this will most likely be the final book in the Brady series. Whilst Dad had made some plans for Brady 7 & 8, I feel for now, starting another Brady book without Dad around would be too difficult.

I will however continue my own writing, under my pen name, E S Richards.

My background is in dystopian and post-apocalyptic fiction and I have some plans for a new book which has come to me since my Dad's passing. If you'd like to stay up to date with my work, you can subscribe on my website:

www.esrichards.com

ACKNOWLEDGMENTS

There are so many people that need to be thanked for making this book happen.

Everyone on the Mark Richards: Writer group who replied to my questions and queries about the storyline. Francessca Wingfield, who supported me with cover design changes. Katherine Taylor, Stephanie Cooke and Carolyn Towse, who each went that extra mile to help me with edits and plot holes, without whom the book would no doubt be less developed.

My fiancé, Jonny, who encouraged me every step of the way and helped me conduct research into areas of Brady's world I didn't fully understand – particularly the cricket references.

My mum, Beverley, who gave up so many hours of her time discussing the plot with me, reading and re-reading sections of the book and helping me close the Brady story in the best way possible. I know it can't have been easy for you, but I wouldn't have been able to do it without you and I love and appreciate you so much for that.

And lastly, I have to thank my dad.

Mark Richards was the one who made Brady's world possible. But not only that, he was the one who made me believe I could finish it. Without the years of hard work he put in as a parent, Brady 6 would have remained unfinished and eventually forgotten.

Dad was the best father anyone could ever ask for. I

know how fiercely he loved me and how important his family was to him. I'll miss him every day for the rest of my life, but I'm so proud and so grateful I had the opportunity to finish this for him.

I love you, Dad. And wherever you are, I hope you read this and know that.